The Further Adventures of Jimmie Dale

Frank L. Packard

Contents

THE FURTHER ADVENTURES OF JIMMIE DALE

BY

Frank L. Packard

CHAPTER I
SMARLINGHUE

A diminutive gas-jet's sickly, yellow flame illuminated the room with poverty-stricken inadequacy; high up on the wall, bordering the ceiling, the moonlight, as though contemptuous of its artificial competitor, streamed in through a small, square window, and laid a white, flickering path to the door across a filthy and disreputable rag of carpet; also, through a rent in the roller shade, which was drawn over a sort of antiquated French window that opened on a level with the floor and in line with the top-light, the moonlight disclosed a narrow and squalid courtyard without.

In one corner of the room stood a battered easel, while against the wall near it, and upon the floor, were a number of canvases of different sizes. A cot bed, unmade, its covers dirty and in disorder, occupied the wall space opposite the door. In the centre of the mean and uninviting apartment stood a table, its top littered with odds and ends, amongst which the remains of a meal, dishes and food, fraternised gregariously with a painter's palette, brushes and paint tubes. A chair or two, long since disabled, and a rickety washstand completed the appointments.

The moonlight's path across the floor wavered suddenly, the door opened, was locked again, and with a quick, catlike step a man moved along the side of the wall where the shadows lay thickest near the door, dropped on his knees, and began to fumble hurriedly with the base-board of the wall, pausing at every alternate second to listen intently.

A minute passed. A section of the base-board was lifted out, the man's hand was thrust inside--and emerged again with a large roll of banknotes. He turned his head for a quick glance around the room, his eyes, burning out of a gaunt, hollow-cheeked, pallid face, held on the torn window shade--and then, in almost frantic haste, he thrust the banknotes back inside the wall, and began to replace the base-board. But it was not the window shade, nor yet the courtyard without with which he was concerned--it was the sound of a heavy footstep outside the door.

And now the door was tried. The man on the floor, working with desperate energy to replace the base-board, coughed in an asthmatic, wheezing way, as there came the imperative smashing of a fist upon the door panels, coupled with a gruff, curt demand for admittance. Again the man coughed--to drown perhaps the slight rasping sound as the base-board slid back into place--and, rising to his feet, shuffled hastily to the door and unlocked it.

The door was flung violently open from without, a heavy-built, clean-shaven, sharp-featured man stepped into the room, slammed the door shut behind him, re-locked it, and swept a shrewd, inquisitive, suspicious glance about the place.

"It took you a damned long time to open that door, **Mister** Smarlinghue!" he said sharply.

The man addressed touched his lips with the tip of his tongue nervously, shrank back, and made no reply.

The lapel of the visitor's coat thrown carelessly back displayed a police shield on the vest beneath; and now, completing a preliminary survey of the surroundings, the man's eyes narrowed on Smarlinghue.

"I guess you know who I am, don't you? Heard of me perhaps, too--eh? Clancy of headquarters is my name!" He laughed menacingly, unpleasantly.

Smarlinghue's clothes were threadbare and ill-fitting; his coat was a size too small for him, and from the short sleeves protruded blatantly the frayed and soiled wristbands of his shirt. He twined his hands together anxiously, and retreated further back into the room.

"I haven't done anything, honest to God, I haven't!" he whined.

"Ain't, eh?" The other laughed again. "No, of course not! Nobody ever did! But now I'm here--just dropped in socially, you know--I'll have a look around."

He began to move about the room. Smarlinghue, still twining his hands in a helpless, frightened way, still circling his lips nervously with the tip of his tongue, followed the other's movements in miserable apprehension with his eyes.

Clancy, as he had introduced himself, shot up the roller shade, peered out into the courtyard, yanked the shade down again with a callous jerk that almost tore it from its fastenings, and strode over toward the easel, contemptuously kicking a chair that happened to be in his way over onto the floor. Reaching the easel he picked up the canvas that rested upon it, stared at it for a moment--and with a grunt of disdain flung it away from him to the ground.

There was a crash as it struck the floor, a ripping sound as the canvas split, and with a pitiful cry Smarlinghue rushed forward and snatched it up.

"It--it was sold," he choked. "I--I was to get the money to-morrow. I have had bad luck for a month--nothing sold but this--and now--and now--" He drew himself up suddenly, and, with the ruined painting clutched to his breast, shook his other fist wildly. "You have no right here!" he screamed in fury. "Do you hear! I have not done anything! I tell you, I have not done anything! You have no right here! I will make you pay for this! I will! I will!" His voice was rising in a shrill falsetto. "I will make you--"

"You hold your tongue," growled Clancy savagely, "or I'll give you something more than an old chromo to make a row about! I don't want any mass meeting of your kind of citizens. Get that?" He caught Smarlinghue roughly by the shoulder, and pushed him into a chair near the table. "Sit down there, and close your jaw!"

Cowed, Smarlinghue's voice dropped to a mumble, and he let the torn canvas slip from his fingers to the floor.

Clancy laughed gruffly, pulled another chair to the opposite side of the table, sat down himself, and eyed Smarlinghue coldly for a moment.

"Sold it, eh?" he observed grimly. "How much were you going to get for it?"

A cunning gleam flashed in Smarlinghue's eyes--and vanished instantly. He wet his lips with his tongue again.

"Ten dollars," he said hoarsely.

Clancy brushed aside the litter on the table, and nonchalantly laid down a ten-dollar bill.

With a sharp little cry that brought on a fit of coughing, Smarlinghue stretched out his hand for the money eagerly.

Clancy drew the money back out of reach.

"Oh, no, nothing like that!" he drawled unpleasantly. "Don't make the mistake of taking me for a fool. I'm not buying any ten-cent art treasures at ten dollars a throw!"

Smarlinghue's eyes remained greedily riveted on the ten-dollar note. He began to twine his hands together once more.

"I don't know what you mean," he muttered tremulously.

"Don't you!" retorted the other shortly. "Well, I mean exactly what I say. I'm not buying any pictures, I'm buying-- *you*. I have been keeping an eye on you for the last three or four months. You're just the guy I've been looking for. As far as I can make out, there ain't a dive or a roost in the Bad Lands where you don't get the glad hand--eh?"

"I--I haven't done anything! Not a thing! I--I swear I haven't!" Smarlinghue burst out frantically.

"Aw, forget it!" Clancy permitted a thin smile to flicker contemptuously across his lips. "You've got a whole lot of friends that I'm interested in. Get the idea? There ain't a crook in New York that's shy of you. You got a 'stand-in' everywhere." He held up the ten-dollar bill. "There's more of these--plenty of 'em."

Smarlinghue pushed back his chair now in a frightened sort of way.

"You--you mean you want me for--for a stool pigeon?" he faltered.

"You got it!" said Clancy bluntly.

Smarlinghue's eyes roved about the room in a furtive, terror-stricken glance, his hand passed aimlessly over his eyes, and he crouched low down in his chair.

"No, no!" he whispered. "No, no--for God's sake, Mr. Clancy, don't ask me to do that! I can't--I can't! I--I wouldn't be any good, I--I can't! I--I won't!"

Clancy thrust head and shoulders aggressively across the table.

"You will--if you know what's good for you!" he said evenly. "And, what's more, there's a little job you're going to break your hand in on to-night."

"No! No, no! I can't! I can't!" Smarlinghue flung out his arms imploringly.

Clancy lowered his voice.

"Cut that out!" he snapped viciously. "What's the matter with you! You'll be well paid for it-- *and have police protection*. You ought to know what that'll mean to you--eh? You live like a gutter-snipe here--half starved most of the time, for all you can get out of those ungodly daubs!"

A curious dignity came to Smarlinghue. He sat upright.

"It is my art," he said. "I have starved for it many years. Some day I will get recognition. Some day I--"

"Art--hell!" sneered Clancy; and then he laughed coarsely, as, his fingers prodding under the miscellany of articles on the table, he suddenly held up a hypodermic syringe. "This is *your* art, my bucko! Why, you poor boob, don't you think I know you! Cocaine's the one thing on earth you live for. You're stewed to the eyes with it now. Here, just watch me! Suppose"--he caught the syringe in a quick grip between the fingers of both hands--"suppose I just put this little toy out of commission now, and--"

With a shrill screech, Smarlinghue sprang from his chair, and clawed like a demented man at the other's hands for possession of the hypodermic.

Clancy surrendered the syringe with a mocking grin, and shoved Smarlinghue backward into his chair again.

"Oh, yes; you're an artist all right--a coke artist!" he remarked coolly. "But that's what makes you solid in every den in New York, and that's how you come in useful--to me. Well, what do you say?"

There was a hunted look in Smarlinghue's eyes.

"They'd--they'd kill me," he said huskily.

"Sure, they would!" agreed Clancy easily. "If they found you out it would be good-night, all right--that's what you're getting paid for. But"--his voice hardened--"if you don't come across, I'll tell you what *I'll* do to you. I'll--"

"You can't do anything! Not a thing!" Smarlinghue cried wildly. "You haven't anything on me at all. I've never done a thing, not a single--"

"Oh, I guess there's enough to make you sweat," Clancy cut in brutally. "You give me the icy paw, and I'll see that the tip leaks out from the right quarters that you *are* a stool pigeon. That'll take care of your finish, too, won't it--good and plenty!"

Smarlinghue stared miserably. Again and again his tongue circled his lips. Twice he tried to speak--and only succeeded in mumbling inarticulately.

Clancy got up from the table, walked around it, and, standing over the crouched figure in the chair, tapped with his finger on the hypodermic in Smarlinghue's hands.

"And that ain't all," he announced with a malicious grin. "You come in and play the game with me, or I'll fix it so that you'll never get another squirt of dope if you had a million bucks to buy it with--ah, I thought that would get you!"

Smarlinghue was on his feet. The terror of the damned was in his face.

"No! No! My God--no--not that! You--you wouldn't do that!" He reached out his arms to the other.

"You know--I've gone too far to do without it. If I didn't have it, I--"

"I've seen a few of them in that sort of jim-jams," said Clancy malevolently. "You can't tell me anything about it. If you appreciate it, that's enough--it's up to you. You heard what I said. If you're looking for that particular kind of hell, go to it. Only don't kid yourself. When I pass the word to put the screws on, the lid's down for keeps. Well, what's the answer? Coming across? Quick now! I haven't got all night to spend here!"

Smarlinghue's hands were trembling violently; he sat down in his chair in a pitiful, uncertain way.

"Yes, yes!" he whispered. " *Yes!* I got to do it. I'll do it, Mr. Clancy, I'll do it! I'll--I'll do anything!"

A half leer, half scowl was on Clancy's face, as he stood regarding the other.

"I thought you would!" he grunted roughly. "Well then, we'll get down to business--and *to-night's* business. You know the back entrance to Malay John's hang-out?"

Smarlinghue's eyes widened a little in a startled way. He nodded his head.

"Very good," said Clancy gruffly. " *You'll* have no trouble in getting in there. And once in there you'll have no trouble in getting up to Malay's private den. I've been wised up that Malay and a few of his pals are getting ready to pull off a little game uptown. I want the dope on it-- *all* of it. They've been meeting in Malay's den for the last few nights--understand? They drift in between half past eleven and twelve--you get there a little *before* halfpast eleven. You haven't anything to be afraid of, so don't lose your nerve. Malay himself is away this evening and won't be back before midnight; and the door won't be locked, as otherwise the others couldn't get in. Everything's clear for you. Savvy? Once you're in the room, there's plenty of places to hide--and that's all you've got to do, except keep your ears and eyes open. Get the lay?"

Again Smarlinghue nodded--unhappily this time.

"All right!" said Clancy crisply. "I'm not coming around here any more-- *unless I have to* . It might put you in bad. You can make your reports and get your orders through Whitie Karn at his dance hall."

"Whitie Karn!" The exclamation seemed to come involuntarily, in a quick, frightened way from Smarlinghue.

Clancy's lips twisted in a smile.

"Kind of a jolt--eh--Smarlinghue? You didn't suspect he was one of *us*, did you?--and there's more than Whitie Karn. Well, it will teach you to be careful. Suppose Whitie, for instance, passed the word that you were a snitch--eh? It won't do you any harm to keep that in mind once in a while." He moved over to the door. "Well, good-night, Smarlinghue! I guess you understand, don't you? You ought to be a pretty valuable man, and I expect a lot from you. If I don't get it--" He shrugged his shoulders, held Smarlinghue for an instant with half-closed, threatening eyes-- and then the door closed behind him.

Smarlinghue did not move. The steps receded from the door, and died away along the passage. A minute, two minutes went by. Suddenly Smarlinghue pushed back the wristband of his shirt, and pricked the skin with the needle of the hypodermic. The door, without a sound, swung wide open. Clancy stood in the doorway.

"Good-night again, Smarlinghue," he said coolly.

The hypodermic fell clattering to the floor; Smarlinghue jumped nervously in his chair.

Clancy laughed--significantly; and, without closing the door this time, strode away again. His steps echoed back from the passageway, the front door opened and shut, his boot heel rang on the pavement without--and all was silence.

Smarlinghue rose from his chair, shuffled across the room, closed the door and locked it, then shuffled back again to the roller shade over the little French window, and, taking a pin from the lapel of his coat, fastened the rent together.

A passing cloud for a moment obscured the moonrays from the top-light; the gas-jet choked with air, spluttered, burning with a tiny, blue, hissing flame; then the white path lay across the floor again, and the yellow flare of gas spurted up into its pitiful fulness--and in Smarlinghue's stead stood another man. Gone were the stooping shoulders, gone the hollow cheeks, the thin, extended lips, the widened nostrils, as the little distorting pieces of wax were removed; and out of the metamorphosis, hard and grim, set like chiselled marble, was revealed the face of--Jimmie Dale.

CHAPTER II
THE WARNING

For a moment Jimmie Dale stood there hesitant, the long, slim, tapering fingers curled into the palms of his hands, his fists clenched tightly, a dull red suffusing his cheeks and burning through the masterly created pallor of his make-up; and then slowly as though his mind were in dismay, he walked across the room, turned off the gas, and going to the cot flung himself down upon it.

What was he to do? What ghastly irony had prompted Clancy to sort *him* out for a police spy? If he refused, if he attempted to stall on Clancy, Clancy's threat to stamp him in the eyes of the underworld as a snitch meant ruin and disaster, absolute and final, for "Smarlinghue" would then have to disappear; on the other hand, to be allied with the police increased his present risks a thousandfold--and they were already hazardous enough! It meant constant surveillance by the police that would hamper him, rob him of his freedom of movement, adding difficulties and perils innumerable to the enacting of this new dual personality of his.

Jimmie Dale's hands clenched more fiercely. It was an impossible situation--it was untenable. That he could play his role in the underworld with only the underworld to reckon with--*yes*; but with the police as well, watching him in his character of a poor, drug-wrecked artist, constantly in touch with him, likely at any moment to make the discovery that Smarlinghue and Jimmie Dale, the millionaire clubman, a leader in New York's most exclusive set, were one and the same-- *no*! And yet what was he to do? With the Gray Seal it had been different. Then, police and underworld alike were openly allied as common enemies against him--but none had known who the Gray Seal was until that night when the Magpie had roused the Bad Lands like a hive of swarming hornets with the news that the Gray

Seal was Larry the Bat; none had known until that night when it was accepted as a fact that Larry the Bat, and therefore the Gray Seal, had perished miserably in the tenement fire.

Around the squalid room, lighted now only by the moonrays, Jimmie Dale's eyes travelled slowly, abstractedly. Yes, in that one particular it was different; but here was the New Sanctuary, and again he was living the old life in close, intimate companionship with the underworld--the old life that only six months ago he had thought to have done with forever!

He turned his face suddenly to the wall, and lay very still--only his hands still remained tightly clenched, and the hard, set look on his face grew harder still.

Six months ago, like some mocking illusion, like some phantom of unreality that jeered at him, it seemed now, he had lived for a few short weeks in a dream-land of wondrous happiness, a happiness that all his own great wealth had never been able to bring him, a happiness that no wealth could ever buy--the joy of her--the glad promise that for always their lives would be lived together--and then, as though she had vanished utterly from the face of the earth, she was gone.

The Tocsin! Marie LaSalle to the world, she was always, and always would be, the Tocsin to him. *Gone*! A hand unclenched and passed heavily across his eyes and flirted the hair back from his forehead. She had taken her place in her own world again; her fortune had been restored to her, its management placed in the hands of a trust company; the interior of the mansion on Fifth Avenue, with its sliding walls and secret passages, that had served as headquarters for the Crime Club, was in the process of reconstruction--and she had disappeared.

It had come suddenly, and yet--as he understood now, though then he had only attributed it to an exaggerated prudence on her part--not without warning. In the three weeks that had intervened between the night of the fire in the old Sanctuary and her disappearance, she had permitted him to see her only at such times and at such intervals as would be consistent with the most casual of acquaintanceships. He remembered well enough now her answer to his constant protests, an answer that was always the same. "Jimmie," she had said, "a sudden intimacy between us would undo all that you have done--you know that. It would not only renew, but would be almost proof positive to those who are left of the Crime Club that their suspicions of Jimmie Dale were justified, and from that as a starting point it would not take a very clever brain to identify Jimmie Dale as Larry the Bat--and the Gray Seal. Don't you see! You never knew me before all the misery and trouble came--there was nothing between us then. To see too much of each other now, to have too much in common now would only be to court disaster. Our intimacy must appear to come gradually, to come naturally. We must wait--a year at least--Jimmie."

A year! And within a few hours following the last occasion on which she had said that, Jason, his butler, had laid the morning mail upon the breakfast table, and he had found her note.

It seemed as though he were living that moment over again now, as he lay here on the cot in the darkness--his eagerness as he had recognised the well-known hand amongst the pile of correspondence, the thrill akin to tenderness with which he had opened the note; and then the utter misery of it all, the room swirling about him, the blind agony in which he had risen from his chair, and, as he had groped his way from the room, the sudden, pitiful anxiety on the faithful old Jason's face, which, even in his own distress, he had not failed to note and understand and be grateful for.

There had been only a few words in the note, and those few carefully chosen, guarded, like the notes of old, lest they should fall into a stranger's hand; but he had read only too clearly between the lines. She had had only far too much more reason for fear than she had admitted to him; and those fears had crystallised into realities. One sentence in the note stood out above all others, a sentence that had lived with him since that morning months ago, the words seeming to visualise her, high in her courage, brave in the unselfishness of her love: "Jimmie, I must not, I cannot, I will not bring you into the shadows again; I must fight this out alone."

He recalled the feverish haste in which he had acted that morning--the one thought that had possessed him being to reach her if possible before she could put her designs into execution. Benson, his chauffeur, reckless of speed laws, had rushed him to the hotel where, pending the remodelling of the Fifth Avenue mansion, she had taken rooms. Here, he learned that she had given up her apartments on the previous afternoon, and that it was understood she had left for an extended travel tour, and that her baggage had been taken to the Pennsylvania Station. From the hotel he had gone to the trust company in whose hands she had placed the management of her estate. With a few additional details, disquieting rather than otherwise, it was the story of the hotel over again. They did not know where she was, except that she had told them she was going away for a long trip, had given them the fullest powers to handle her affairs, and, on the previous afternoon, had drawn a very large sum of money before leaving the institution.

He had returned then, like a man dazed, to his home on Riverside Drive, and had locked himself in his den to think it out. She had covered her tracks well--and had done it in a masterly way because she had done it simply. It was possible that she had actually gone away for a trip; but it was more probable that she had not. He had had, of course, no means of knowing; but the sort of peril that threatened her, his intuition told him, was not such as to be diverted by the mere expedient of absenting herself from New York temporarily; and, besides, she had said that she would *fight* it out. She could hardly do that in the *person* of Marie LaSalle, or away from New York. She was clever, resourceful, resolute and fearless--and those very traits opened a vista of possibilities that left his mind staggering blindly as in a maze. She was gone--and alone in the face of deadly menace. He remembered then the curious, unnatural calmness underlying the mad whirling of his brain at the thought that that was not literally true, that she was not, nor would she ever be alone--while he lived. It was only a question of *how* he could help her. It had seemed almost certain that the danger threatening her came from one of two sources--either from those who were left of the Crime Club, relentless, savage for vengeance on account of the ruin and disaster that had overtaken them; or else from the Magpie, and behind the Magpie, massed like some Satanic phalanx, every denizen of the underworld, for Silver Mag had disappeared coincidently with Larry the Bat, coincidently with the Magpie's attempted robbery of the supposed Henry LaSalle's safe, to which plot she was held by the underworld to be a party, coincidently with the dispersion of the Crime Club, ***and coincidently with the reappearance of the heiress Marie LaSalle***--and, further, Silver Mag stood condemned to death in the Bad Lands as the accomplice of the Gray Seal. But Silver Mag had disappeared. Had the underworld, prompted by the Magpie, solved the riddle--did it know, or guess, or suspect that Silver Mag was Marie LaSalle?

Which was it? The Crime Club, or the Magpie? Here again he could not know, though he inclined to the belief that it was the latter; but here, in either case, the means of knowing, of helping her, the way, the road, was clearly defined--and the road was the road to the underworld. But Larry the Bat was dead and the road was barred. And then a half finished painting standing on an easel at the rear of his den had brought him inspiration. It was one of his hobbies--and it swung wide again for him the door of the underworld. None, in a broken-down, disappointed, drug-shattered artist, would recognise Larry the Bat! The only similarity between the two--the one thing that must of necessity be the same in order to explain plausibly his intimacy with the dens and lairs of Crimeland, the one thing that would, if nothing more, assure an unsuspicious, tolerant acceptance of his presence there, was that, like Larry the Bat, he would assume the role of a confirmed dope fiend; but as there were many dope fiends, thousands of them in the Bad Lands, that point of similarity, even if Larry the Bat were not believed to be dead, held little, if any, risk. For the rest, it was easy enough; and so there had come into being these wretched quarters here, the New Sanctuary--and Smarlinghue.

But the mere assumption of a new role was not all--it was not there that the difficulty lay; it was in gaining for Smarlinghue the **confidence** of the underworld that Larry the Bat had once held. And that had taken time--was not even yet an accomplished fact. The intimate, personal acquaintance of Larry the Bat with every crook and dive in Gangland had aided him, as Smarlinghue, to gain an initial foothold, but his complete establishment there had necessarily had to be of Smarlinghue's own making. And it had taken time. Six months had gone now, six months that, as far as the Tocsin was concerned, had been barren of results mainly, he encouraged himself to believe, because his efforts had been always limited and held in check; six months of anxious, careful building, and now, just as he was regaining the old-time confidence that Larry the Bat had enjoyed, just as he was reaching that point where the whispered secrets of the underworld once more reached his ears and there was a promise of success if, indeed, she were still alive, had come this thing to-night that spelt ruin to his hopes and ultimate disaster to himself.

If she were still alive! The thought came flashing back; and with a low, involuntary moan, mingling anguish of mind with a bitter, merciless fury, he turned restlessly upon the cot. If she were still alive! No sign, no word had come from her; he had found no clue, no trace of her as yet through the channels of the underworld; his surveillance of the Magpie, whose friendship he had begun to cultivate, had, so far, proved fruitless.

It came upon him now again, the fear, the dread, which he had known so often in the past few months, that seemed to try to undermine his resolution to go forward, that whispered speciously that it was useless--that she was dead. And misery came. And he lay there staring unseeingly into the moonrays as they streamed in through the top-light.

Time passed. Then a smile played over Jimmie Dale's lips, half grim, half wistful; and the strong, square jaw was suddenly out-flung. If she was alive, he would find her; if she was dead--his clenched hand lifted above his head as though to register a vow--the man or men, her murderer or murderers, whether to-morrow or in the years to come, would know a day of reckoning when they should pay the debt!

But that was for the future. To-night there was this vital, imminent danger that he had to face, this decision to make whose pros and cons seemed each to hold an equal measure of dismay. What was he to do?

He laughed shortly, ironically after a moment. It was as though some malignant ingenuity had conspired to trap him. He was caught either way. What was he to do? The question kept pounding at his brain, growing more sinister with each repetition. What was he to do? Defy the police--and be branded as a stool-pigeon, a snitch, an informer in every nook and cranny of the underworld! He could not do that. Everything, all that meant anything in life to him now would be swept from his reach at even the first breath of suspicion. Nor was it an idle threat that his unwelcome visitor had made. He was not fool enough to blind himself on that score--it could be only too easily accomplished. And on the other hand--but what was the use of torturing his brain with a never-ending rehearsal of details? Was there a middle course? That was his only chance. Was there a way to safeguard Smarlinghue and, yes, this miserable hovel of a place, priceless now as his new Sanctuary.

He followed the moonpath's slant with his eyes to where it touched the floor and disclosed the greasy, threadbare, pitiful carpet. A grim whimsicality fell upon him. It would be too bad to lose it! It was luxury to what Larry the Bat had known! There had not even been a carpet in the old Sanctuary, and--he sat suddenly bolt upright on the cot, his eyes, that had mechanically travelled on along the moon-path, strained now upon where the light fell upon the threshold of the door. There was a little white patch there, a most curious little white patch--that had not been there when he had thrown himself on the cot. Came a sudden, incredulous thought that sent the blood whipping fiercely through his veins; and with a low cry, in mad, feverish haste now, he leaped from the cot and across the room.

It was an envelope that had been thrust in under the door. In an instant he had snatched it up from the floor, and in another, acting instinctively, even while he realised the futility of what he did, he wrenched the door open, stared out into a dark and empty passageway--and, with a strange, almost hysterical laugh, closed and locked the door again.

There was no writing on the envelope; there was not light enough to have deciphered it if there had been--but he had need for neither writing nor light. Those long, slim, tapering fingers, those wonderful fingers of Jimmie Dale, that seemed to combine all human faculties in their sensitive tips, had already telegraphed their message to his brain--it was the same texture of paper that she always used--it was from *her*--it was from the Tocsin.

Joy, gladness, a relief so terrific as it surged upon him as to leave him for the moment physically weak, held him in thrall, and he stumbled back across the room, and slipped down into a chair before the table, and dropped his head forward into his arms, the note tightly clasped in his hand. She was *alive*. The Tocsin was alive--and well--and here in New York--and free--and they had not caught her. It meant all those things, the coming and the manner of the coming of this note. A deep thankfulness filled his heart; it seemed that it was only now he realised the full measure of the fear and anxiety, the strain under which he had been labouring for so many months. She was alive--the Tocsin was alive. It was like some wonderful song that filled his soul, excluding all else. How little the contents of the note itself mattered--the one great, glorious fact for the moment was that she was alive!

It was a long time before Jimmie Dale raised his head, and then he got up suddenly from his chair, and lit the gas. But even then he hesitated as he turned the note over, speculatively now, in his fingers. So she knew him as Smarlinghue! In some way she had found that out! His brows gathered abstractedly, then cleared again. Well, at any rate, it was added proof that so far her cleverness had completely outwitted those who had pitted themselves against her--so much so that even her freedom of action, in whatever role she had assumed, was still left open to her.

He tore the envelope open. There was no preface to the note, no "Dear Philanthropic Crook" as there had always been in the old days--instead, the single, closely-written sheet began abruptly, the writing itself indicating that it had been composed in desperate haste. He glanced quickly over the first few lines.

"You should not have done this. You should never have come into the underworld again. I begged, I implored you not to do so. And now you are in danger to-night. I can only hope and pray that this will reach you in time, and--" He read on, in a startled way now, to the end; then read the note over again more slowly, this time muttering snatches of it aloud: "... Chicago ... Slimmy Jack and Malay ... Birdie Lee ... released from Sing Sing to-day ... triangular scar on forehead over right eye...."

And then, for a little while, Jimmie Dale stood there staring about the room, motionless, rigid as stone, save that his fingers moved in an automatic, mechanical way as they began to tear the note into little shreds. But presently into his face there crept a menacing look, and an angry red began to tinge his cheeks, and his jaws clamped ominously.

So that was the game at Malay John's, was it? Birdie Lee was out again! She had not needed to mention any scar to enable him to identify Birdie Lee. He knew the man of old. The slickest of them all, the cleverest of them all, before he had been caught and sent to Sing Sing for a five-years' term, was Birdie Lee--the one man of them all that he, Jimmie Dale, might regard as a rival, so to speak, where the mastery of the intricate mechanism of a vaunted and much advertised "guaranteed burglar-proof safe" was concerned! And Birdie Lee was out again!

There was danger if he went to Malay John's, she had said--and it was true. But what if he did *not* go! What, for instance, if Birdie Lee went through with this night's work!

Jimmie Dale walked slowly across the room, halted before the wall near the door, stood for an instant hesitant there--and then, as though in a sudden, final decision, dropped down on his knees, and, working swiftly, removed the section of the base-board from the wall for the second time that night.

Out came the neatly folded clothes of Jimmie Dale; and with them, serving him so well in the days gone by, the leather girdle, or undervest, with its stout-sewn, upright pockets in which nestled, in an array of fine, blue-steel, highly tempered instruments, a compact powerful burglar's kit. It was the one thing that he had saved from the fire in the old Sanctuary--and that more by accident than design. He had been wearing the girdle that night when he had stolen into the Crime Club, and afterwards had returned to the Sanctuary with the intention of destroying forever all traces of Larry the Bat; and then, only half dressed, as he was changing into the clothes of Jimmie Dale, the alarm had come before he had taken off the girdle, and, without thought of it again at the time, he had still been wearing it when he had made his escape. He looked at it now for a moment grimly--and smiled in a mirthless way. He had not used it since that night, and that night he had never meant or thought to use it again--only to destroy it!

He reached into the aperture in the wall once more, drew out a pocket flashlight and an automatic pistol, and laid them down beside the clothes and the leather girdle; then, pulling off his coat and shirt, he ran noiselessly across the room to the washstand. A few drops from a tiny phial poured into the water, and the pallor, the sickly hue from his face was gone. It was to be Jimmie Dale--not Smarlinghue--who would keep the rendezvous at Malay John's!

And now he was back across the room once more, turning out the light as he passed the gas-jet. The leather girdle, that went on much after the fashion of a life-preserver, was fastened over his shoulders and secured around his waist. The remainder of his clothes were stripped off with lightning speed, and in their place were donned the fashionably tailored, immaculate tweeds of Jimmie Dale. It was like some quick-moving, shadowy pantomime in the moonlight. He gathered up the discarded garments, tucked them into the opening in the wall, replaced the baseboard, slipped the automatic and flashlight into the side pockets of his coat--and stood up, his fingers feeling swiftly over his vest and under the back of his coat to guard against the possibility of any tell-tale bulge from the leather girdle underneath.

An instant he stood glancing critically about him; then the roller shade over the window was lifted aside, the window itself, on carefully oiled hinges, was opened noiselessly, closed again--and, hugged close against the wall of the building, hidden in the black shadows, Jimmie Dale, so silent as to be almost uncanny in his movements, crept along the few intervening feet to the fence that enclosed the courtyard. Here, next to the wall, a loosened plank swung outward at a touch, and he was standing in a narrow, black areaway beyond. There was only the depth of the house between himself and the street, and he paused now, crouched motionless against the wall, listening. He heard no footfalls from the pavement--only, like a distant murmur, the night sounds from the Bowery, a block away--only the muffled roar of an elevated train. The way was presumably clear, and he moved forward again--cautiously. He reached the front of the building, which, like the old Sanctuary, was a tenement of the poorer class, paused once more, this time to peer quickly up and down the dark, ill-lighted cross street--and, satisfied that he was safe from observation, stepped out on the sidewalk, and began to walk nonchalantly along to the Bowery.

And here, at the corner, under a street lamp he consulted his watch. It was ten o'clock! He smiled a little ironically. Certainly, they would hardly expect him as early as that! Well, he would be a little ahead of time, that was all!

CHAPTER III
THE MAN WITH THE SCAR

Jimmie Dale walked on again, rapidly now, heading down the Bowery. At the expiration of perhaps ten minutes, he turned east; and still a few minutes later, in the neighbourhood of Chatham Square, plunged suddenly into a dark alleyway--there was, of course, as there was to all such places, an unobtrusive entrance to Malay John's.

His lips tightened a little as he moved quietly forward. To venture here in an unknown character was not far from being tantamount, if he were discovered, to taking his life in his hands. Malay John was a queer customer and a bad enemy, though counted "straight" by the underworld, and trusted by the crooks and near-crooks as few other men were in the Bad Lands. And, if Malay John was queer, the place he ran was queerer still. Ostensibly he conducted a dance hall, and a profitable one at that; but below the dance hall, known only to the initiated, deep down in a sub-cellar, was perhaps the most remunerative gambling joint and pipe lay-out in Crimeland.

Jimmie Dale halted before a doorway in the alley. The rear of a low building rose black and unlighted above him. A confused jangle from a tinny piano, accompanying a blatant cornet and a squeaky violin, mingled with the dull scrape of many feet, laughter, voices, singing--the dance hall at the front of the building was in full swing. He glanced sharply up and down the dark alleyway, then, leaning forward, placed his ear to the panel of the door--and the next instant opened the door softly and stepped inside.

It was pitch black here, but it was familiar ground to Larry the Bat in the old days, and therefore to Smarlinghue in the new. The short passageway in which he was standing terminated, he knew, in a rear entrance to the dance hall, which was always kept locked and used only by Malay John himself, and which was just at the foot of the stairs that led upward to Malay John's combination of private den, office, and sleeping apartment; while at the side of the passage, half way along, was that other door, always guarded on the inside, that required an "open sesame" to gain admittance to the dive below.

And now he crept stealthily past this latter door, reached the staircase, and went swiftly up to the landing above. Here another door barred his way, and here again he placed his ear to the panel--but this time to listen, it seemed, interminably. Every faculty was strained and alert now. He could take no chances here, and the uproar from the dance hall below, while it had safeguarded his ascent of the stairs, was confusing now and by no means an unmixed blessing.

Still he crouched there, his ear to the panel--and then, satisfied at last, he tried the door. It was locked.

"The penalty of being early!" murmured Jimmie Dale softly to himself.

His hand reached in under his vest to one of the pockets in the leather girdle, and a tiny steel instrument was inserted in the lock. There was a curious snipping sound, the doorknob turned slowly under his hand; then cautiously, inch by inch, he pushed the door open, slipped through--and stood motionless on the other side of the threshold. Save only from the dance hall below, there was not a sound. The door closed again; again that snipping sound as it was relocked--and then the round, white ray of Jimmie Dale's flashlight circled his surroundings.

There was a sort of barbaric splendour to the place. Malay John was something of a sybarite! It was a single room, whose floor was covered with rich Turkish rugs, whose walls were covered with Oriental hangings, and in one corner was a great, wide divan, canopied, also with Oriental hangings at head and foot, serving presumably for a bed; but, striking a somewhat incongruous note, others of the appointments were modern enough--the flat-topped desk in the centre of the room with its revolving chair, for instance, and a large, ponderous safe that stood back against the rear wall.

Jimmie Dale crossed the room for a closer inspection of the safe, and, as his flashlight played over the single dial, he shook his head whimsically. No, it would be hardly true to call *that* modern; it was only an ancient monstrosity, a helpless thing at the mercy of any cracksman who--

The flashlight in his hand went out. Like lightning, Jimmie Dale, his tread silent on the heavy rugs, leaped back across the room, and in an instant slipped in behind the end hangings of the divan and stood, pressed closely, against the wall.

A key turned stealthily in the lock, the door opened as stealthily--then silence--then a flashlight swept suddenly around the room--darkness again--and then a hoarse whisper:

"All clear, Birdie. Lock the door."

The door closed. The flashlight played down the room again--and upon Jimmie Dale's lips came a twisted smile, as, his fingers edging the hanging slightly to one side, he peered out.

The light ray moving before them, two dark forms stole across the room to the safe.

"There you are, Birdie!" said one of them. "Ain't she a beaut! Say, a kid could open it! Didn't I tell you I was handing you one on a gold platter!"

The light ray now flooded the front of the safe, and outlined the forms of the two men. One of them, holding the flashlight, dropped on his knees, and began to twirl the dial tentatively; the other leaned negligently against the corner of the safe.

"I ain't so sure it's easy, Slimmy," replied the man on his knees, after a moment. He stopped twirling the dial, and looked up. "Mabbe it'll take longer than we figured on. Are you sure there ain't no chance of Malay gettin' back? I'd rather stack up against every bull in New York than him."

The twisted smile on Jimmie Dale's lips still lingered. So that was Slimmy Jack there, leaning against the safe! Slimmy Jack--and Birdie Lee! His fingers drew the hangings a little further apart. The room was in complete darkness except for the circle of light around the safe, and it was as though what was being enacted before him were some strange, realistic film thrown upon a screen--just two forms in the white light, their faces masked, against the background of the safe, with its glittering nickel dial. And now Slimmy Jack, from his negligent pose, straightened sharply and leaned toward Birdie Lee.

"Say, what's the matter with you, Birdie!" he exclaimed roughly. "You didn't let 'em get your nerve up the river, did you? You've been acting kind of queer all day. I told you before, Malay wouldn't be back in time to monkey with *us*. We don't have to stand for this--I told you that, too. You don't think I'm a fool, do you, to steer you into a lay that's got a come-back on myself unless the thing was planted right? Why, damn it, Malay knows I saw the coin put in there. D'ye think I'd give him a chance of suspecting *me*! It's all fixed--you know that. Now, go to it--there's a nice little piece of money in there that'll keep us going till we pull that Chicago deal."

"All right!" Birdie Lee answered tersely. "Keep quiet, then, and I'll see what I can do."

He laid his ear against the safe, listening for the tumblers' fall, as, holding the flashlight in his left hand, its rays upon the dial, the fingers of his right began to work swiftly again with the glistening knob.

From below, the confused, dull medley of sound from the dance hall seemed only to intensify the silence in the room. Slimmy Jack stood motionless at the side of the safe, his elbow resting against the old-fashioned, protruding upper hinge. A minute, two, another, and still another dragged by. Came then a short ejaculation from Birdie Lee.

Slimmy Jack bent forward instantly.

"Got it?" he demanded eagerly.

"No--curse it!" gritted Birdie Lee. "My fingers seem to have lost their touch--I ain't had much practice for the last five years up there in Sing Sing!"

"Well, then, 'soup' it!" grunted Slimmy Jack. "You could blow the roof off, and no one would be the wiser with that racket downstairs. We can't waste all night over it."

"What are you going to 'soup' it with?" Birdie Lee flung back gruffly. "We didn't bring nothing. You said--"

"I know I did!" A sullen menace had crept suddenly into Slimmy Jack's voice. "I said you could open an old tin can like that with your hands tied--and so you can. Try it again!"

Jimmie Dale's fingers stole inside his shirt, and into a pocket of the leather girdle, and brought forth a black silk mask. He slipped it quickly over his face. Birdie Lee was at work once more. It was about time to play his own hand in the game. The Tocsin had made no mistake, he was sure of that now, and--

Birdie Lee spoke again.

"It's no use, Slimmy!" he muttered. "I guess I ain't any good any more. I can't open the damned thing!"

"Try it again!" ordered Slimmy Jack shortly.

"But it's no use, I tell you!" retorted Birdie Lee. "I ain't got the feel in my fingers."

"You--try--it--again!" There was a cold, ominous ring in Slimmy Jack's voice.

Birdie Lee drew back a little on his knees, glancing quickly up at the other.

"What--what d'ye mean by that, Slimmy!" he exclaimed in a startled way.

"I'll show you what I mean, and I'll show you blamed quick if you don't open that safe!" Slimmy Jack threatened hoarsely. "Blast you, you're stalling on me--that's what you're doing! I've seen you work before. You could open that thing with your finger nails, if you wanted to! Now, open it!"

"But, I can't!" protested Birdie Lee. "I wouldn't hand you anything like that, Slimmy--you know that, Slimmy. I--"

"*Open it!* And open it-- *quick*!" Slimmy Jack's hand was wrenching at his side pocket.

"But, I tell you, I can't, Slimmy!" cried Birdie Lee, almost piteously. "It's queered me up there in the pen. I"--he was rising to his feet--"Slimmy--for God's, sake--what are you doing--you--"

There was a flash, the roar of the report, a swaying form, a revolver clattering to the floor--and with a crash Slimmy Jack pitched forward and lay motionless.

Then silence.

It had come without warning, in the winking of an eye, and for a moment it seemed to Jimmie Dale that he could not grasp the full significance of what had happened--that Slimmy Jack, his sleeve catching on the hinge of the safe as he had finally succeeded in jerking his revolver from his pocket, had, a grim, ironical trick of fate, accidentally shot himself! Mechanically, automatically, Jimmie Dale's hands went to his pockets and produced his own flashlight and revolver--but he did not move. His eyes now were on Birdie Lee, who, like a man dazed and terror-stricken, had lurched back against the safe, the flashlight that dangled in his hand sweeping queer, aimless patches of light about the floor.

Still silence--only the uproar from the dance hall that would have drowned out to those below the sound of the revolver shot. Then Birdie Lee staggered forward, and knelt beside the prostrate form on the floor. He stood up again presently, swaying unsteadily on his feet, turning his head wildly about, now this way, now that. And then his whisper, broken, hoarse, quavered through the room:

"He's dead. My God--he's--he's dead."

"Drop that flashlight!" Jimmie Dale's voice rang cold, imperative. "*Drop it!*" And, sweeping the hangings aside, the ray of his own light suddenly full upon Birdie Lee, he leaped forward.

With a low, terrified cry, the other let the flashlight fall as though from nerveless fingers, and shrank back against the safe.

"Now put your hands above your head!" directed Jimmie Dale curtly.

The man obeyed.

Dark, frightened eyes stared out at Jimmie Dale from behind the mask that covered Birdie Lee's face. Swiftly, deftly, Jimmie Dale felt over the other's clothing for a weapon. There was none. Then, himself in darkness, the blinding light in Birdie Lee's face, he pulled off the other's mask, and with a grim, quick touch of his revolver muzzle traced out the white, pulsing, triangular scar on the man's forehead.

"So you're up to your old tricks again, are you, Birdie?" he inquired coldly. "Five years up the river wasn't enough for you--eh?"

The man drew himself up suddenly, and, squaring his shoulders, made as though to speak--and then, with a swift, hopeless gesture, turned his back, and, leaning over the top of the safe, buried his head in his arms.

A strange smile touched Jimmie Dale's lips. He stooped down, picked up the revolver from the floor, slipped it into his pocket, bent over Slimmy Jack for an instant to assure himself that the man was dead--then stepping back to the safe, he laid his hand on the ex-convict's shoulder.

"Birdie," he said quietly, "could you open this safe if you wanted to?"

The man swung sharply around, the prison pallor of his face a pitiful, deathlike colour in the flashlight's rays.

"Who are you?" he asked thickly.

"A friend perhaps--if you can open that safe," Jimmie Dale answered.

A puzzled look crept into Birdie's eyes.

"W-what do you mean?" he stammered.

"I mean that I want the *proof* that you are straight," Jimmie Dale said softly. "I've been here in the room all the time. I want to know whether you were stalling on Slimmy Jack, or not. And I want to know, if you *were* stalling, how you came to be here with him."

"That's a queer spiel," said Birdie Lee, in a troubled way. "I thought at first you were a bull--but you don't talk like one. Mabbe you're playin' with me; but, whether you are or not, I guess it won't make much difference what I say. You couldn't help me if you wanted to now--with him dead there"--he jerked his head toward the form on the floor.

"Tell me, anyhow," insisted Jimmie Dale quietly.

Birdie's hand lifted and swept across his eyes.

"Well, all right," he said, after a moment; "I'll tell you. Me and Slimmy used to work together all the time in Chicago and out West after I left New York, and until I came back here one day and pulled one alone and got sent up for it. Well, to-day, when they let me out of Sing Sing, Slimmy had come on from Chicago and was waitin' for me. He had a deal all fixed in Chicago that we was to pull together, a big one, and this little one here was to keep us goin' until the big one came off. He was with Malay John in this room to-day when a gambler from up the State somewhere blew in with a roll of about three thousand dollars, and handed it over to Malay to keep while he knocked around town for a day or two. Malay put the money in this safe here, and that's what Slimmy was after for a starter. I told Slimmy I was all through--that I was goin' straight. He wouldn't believe me. I guess you don't. I guess nobody will. I got a record that's mabbe too black to live down, and--oh, well, what's the use! I meant to live decent, but I guess any chance I had is gone now." His voice choked. "That's the way I had doped it out up there in the pen--that I was goin' straight. That's all, isn't it? I told Slimmy I was through--but Slimmy held something over me that was good for twenty years. What could I do? I said I'd come in on this, figurin' that I could queer the game by stallin'. I--I tried it. If you were here, you saw me. I pretended that I couldn't open the safe, and--"

" *Can* you?" inquired Jimmie Dale gently.

"That thing!" Birdie Lee smiled mirthlessly. "Why it's only a double combin--"

"Open it, then," prompted Jimmie Dale.

Birdie Lee stooped impulsively to the dial of the safe; hesitated, then straightened up again, and shook his head.

"No," he said. "I guess I'll take my medicine. I don't know who you are. I might just as well have opened it for Slimmy as for you. It looks as though you were after the same thing he was."

Jimmie Dale smiled.

"Stand a little away from the safe, Birdie--there," he instructed. And, as the other obeyed wonderingly, Jimmie Dale knelt to the dial. "You see, I trust you not to move," he said. The dial was whirling under the sensitive fingers, and, like Birdie before him, his ear was pressed against the face of the safe.

The moments went by. Birdie Lee was watching in an eager, fascinated, startled way. Came at last a sharp, metallic click, as Jimmie Dale flung the handle over--and the door swung wide. He shut it again instantly--and locked it.

"It's your turn, Birdie," he said calmly. "You see that, as far as I or my intentions are concerned, it doesn't matter whether you open it or not."

"Who are you?" There was awed admiration in Birdie's voice. "You're slicker than ever I was, even in the old days. For God's sake, who are you?"

"Never mind," said Jimmie Dale. "Open the safe, if you can."

"I can open it all right," said Birdie, moving slowly forward; "and quicker than you did, because I got the combination when I was workin' on it with Slimmy watchin'. Throw the light on the knob, will you?"

It was barely an instant before Birdie Lee swung back the door.

"Now lock it again," directed Jimmie Dale. And then, as the other obeyed, he held out his hand to Birdie Lee. "You're clear, Birdie."

A tremor came to the other's face.

"Clear?" repeated Birdie unsteadily.

"Yes--you get your chance. That's one reason why I came here to-night--to spoil Slimmy Jack's play, to see that you got your chance if you really wanted it, as"--he added whimsically--"I was informed you did. Go ahead, Birdie--make your get-away--you're free."

But Birdie Lee shook his head.

"No," he said, and his voice caught again. "It's no good." He pointed to the still form on the floor. "I guess I go up for more than safe-crackin' this time. I--I guess it'll be the *chair*. When they find him here--dead--shot--they'll call it murder--and they'll put it onto me. The police know we have been together for years. They know he came here to-day when I got out. We've been seen together to-day. We--we were seen *quarrelling* this afternoon in a saloon over on the Bowery. That was when I was refusin' to start the old play again. They'd have what looked like an open and shut game against me. I wouldn't have a hope."

It was a moment before Jimmie Dale answered. What the man said was true--he would not have a hope--for an honest life--after five years in the penitentiary. He lifted his flashlight again and played it over Birdie Lee. They showed, those years, in the pallor, the drawn lines, the wan misery in the other's face.

And then Jimmie Dale's lips set firmly under his mask. There was a way to save the man. It was something he had never intended to do again--but it was worth the price--to save this man. It would be like a bombshell exploded in the underworld; it would arouse the police to infuriated activity; it would stir New York to its depths--but, after all, it could not touch Smarlinghue. It would only instill the belief that somehow Larry the Bat had escaped from the tenement fire; it would only mean a hunt for Larry the Bat day and night--but Larry the Bat no longer existed--and it would save this man.

He clamped the flashlight between his knees, leaving his hands free, and from the leather girdle drew the old-time metal case, thin, like a cigarette case, and from the case, with a pair of little tweezers that precluded the possibility of telltale finger prints, lifted out a small, diamond-shaped, gray-coloured paper seal, adhesive on one side, which he moistened now with his tongue--and, stooping quickly, attached it to the dead man's sleeve.

There was a sharp, startled cry from Birdie Lee.

"*The Gray Seal*! You're--you're Larry the Bat! They passed the word around in Sing Sing that you were dead, and--"

"And it will be the Gray Seal who is wanted for this--not you," said Jimmie Dale quietly. Then, almost sharply: "Now make your get-away, Birdie. Hurry! You and I part here. And the greater distance you put between yourself and this place to-night the better."

But the man seemed as though robbed of the power of movement--and then his lips quivered, and his eyes filled.

"But you," he faltered, "you--you're doing this for me, and I--I--"

Jimmie Dale caught the other's arm in a kindly grip.

"Good-night, Birdie," he said significantly. "I'm the last man now that you could afford to be seen with. You understand that. And I guess you can understand that I've reasons for not wanting to be seen myself. You've got your chance; give me mine to get away--alone." He pushed the man abruptly toward the door.

Still Birdie Lee hesitated; then catching Jimmie Dale's hand, he wrung it hard--and, with a half choked sob, turned and made his way from the room.

For an instant Jimmie Dale stood looking after the other through the darkness, listening as the stealthy steps descended the stairs--then suddenly he knelt again beside the dead man on the floor.

"You were clever, Slimmy!" he murmured. "Smarlinghue wouldn't have had a chance of getting out from under this break--if your plans had worked out! And I didn't know you, of course, because you were a Chicago crook."

He took off the dead man's mask, and played his flashlight for a moment over the cold, set features.

A queer smile twisted Jimmie Dale's lips.

It was "Clancy of Headquarters"!

CHAPTER IV
THE DIAMOND PENDANT

The "murder" of Slimmy Jack had evidently been discovered too late for the make-up of the early morning papers; but from the noon editions onward it had been flung across the front pages in glaring type--even the most stately journals, for the nonce aroused out of their dignified calm, indulging in "display" headlines that, quite apart from the mere text, could not but have startled their equally stately and dignified readers. The Gray Seal, the leech that fed upon society, the murderer, the thief, the menace to the lives and property of law-abiding citizens, the scourge that for years New York had combated in the no more effective fashion than that of gnashing its teeth in impotent fury, had suddenly reappeared with a fresh murder to his credit. And New York had thought him dead!

Jimmie Dale, leaning back on the seat of his limousine as the car, now halting at a corner, now racing with a hundred others to snatch a block or two of distance before the next monarchial traffic officer of Fifth Avenue should hold it up again a victim to the evening rush, turned from first one to another of the pile of papers beside him. His strong, clean-shaven face was grave; and there was a sober light in the dark, steady eyes. In the St. James Club, which he had just left, perhaps the most sedate, certainly the most exclusive club in New York, it had been the one topic of conversation. Elderly gentlemen, not usually given to excitability, had joined with the younger members in a hectic denunciation of the police as criminally inefficient, and had made dire and absurdly vain threats as to what they, electing themselves for the moment a supreme court of last resort, proposed to do under the circumstances. The irony was exquisite, if they had but known! Also there was the element of humour, only there was a grim tinge to the humour that robbed it of its mirth--some day they *might* know!

He glanced out of the window, as the car was held up again. Everybody in the crowd, that waited on the corners for the stream of traffic to pass, seemed to have their eyes glued to their newspapers--even Benson, his chauffeur, during the moment of inaction, was surreptitiously reading a paper which he had flattened out on the seat beside him!

Jimmie Dale's eyes reverted to the newspaper in his hand, one of the most conservative. There was no mistaking the tenor of the leading article on the editorial page:

"It is not so much that a thug and criminal known as Slimmy Jack should have been murdered by another wretch of his own breed; indeed, that such should prey upon one another is far from being a matter of regret, for we might hope in time for the extermination of them all by the simple process of mutual attrition and at correspondingly little expense to ourselves--but that this so-called Gray Seal should still prove to be alive and at large is a matter that concerns every citizen personally. He does not confine his attentions to the Slimmy Jacks. The criminal records of the past few years reek with his acts, that run the gamut of every crime in the decalogue, crimes for the most part actuated apparently by no other motive than a monstrously innate thirst for notoriety--and the victims, for the most part, too, have been the innocent and the defenceless. What is the end of this to be? If the police cannot cope with this blood-mad ruffian, is New York to sit idly by and submit to another reign of terror instituted and carried on under the nose of authority by this inhuman jackal? If so, we are committing a crime against ourselves, we are insulting our intelligence, and--"

The man who had written that was a personal friend! Jimmie Dale threw the paper down, and picked up another, and after that another. They were pretty well all alike. They rehearsed the discovery of Larry the Bat as the Gray Seal; they rehearsed the story of the fire in the tenement of six months ago in which it was supposed that Larry the Bat had perished--they differed only in the virulence, a mere choice of words, with which they now demanded that this Larry the Bat, alias the Gray Seal, should be dug out like a rat from his hole, and the city be freed once and for all, and with no loophole for misadventure this time, of this "ogre of hell," as one paper put it, that was gorging itself upon New York.

The furrows gathered on Jimmie Dale's forehead, as he folded up the papers, and stared at his chauffeur's back through the plate-glass front of the car. He had known that the reappearance of the Gray Seal would arouse the community to a wild pitch of excitement, but he had far underestimated the effect. He could gauge it better now, though--he had only to look out of the windows at the passers-by. And this was only the respectable element of the city whose head and front was the police, and dangerous enough for all the bitter taunts, gibes and recriminations with which the police was maligned! There was still the far more dangerous element of the underworld! He had not been in that quarter since he had left Malay John's the night before, but he could picture it now well enough. God help him if he ever fell into those hands! In dens and dives, in the dark corners of that sordid world, they would be whispering blasphemous vows of vengeance against him one to another--and, relative to the hate and fear that welded them into a single unit, the police sank into insignificance. More than one of their elite had gone to the electric chair through the instrumentality of the Gray Seal; more than one was serving at that moment a long term behind penitentiary walls. Whose turn was it to be next? They needed no editorial prod in the underworld to run Larry the Bat to earth--there was the deeper spur of self-preservation! They knew who the Gray Seal was now, and the first blow that he had aimed upon his reappearance had apparently been at one of themselves. Their search for Larry the Bat would not be an indifferent one!

It was true that Larry the Bat no longer existed, that in that respect he was encompassed by a certain security he had not enjoyed before, but how long would that last? One slip, one moment off his guard, would wreck all that in the twinkling of an eye. Between the police and the underworld New York would be scoured from end to end for Larry the Bat; and, failing to find trace or sign of their quarry, how long would it be before they would put more faith in the evidence of the tenement fire than in the evidence of the Magpie, upon whose testimony alone Larry the Bat had been accepted as the Gray Seal, and believe again that Larry the Bat was dead, and that therefore they had not yet solved the identity of the Gray Seal!

He had never intended that the Gray Seal should ever have been heard of again. He shrugged his shoulders philosophically. One's intentions in this world did not always count for much! His hand had been forced, and he had paid the price to save Birdie Lee. He could not regret that! Whatever the consequences, the price had not been too high, and yet--his eyes roved again over the crowded thoroughfare. A car edged by his own. Two men were in the tonneau. One held a newspaper which he thumped with a menacing fist as he talked. The door windows of Jimmie Dale's limousine were down, and he caught two bitter, angry words:

"... *Gray Seal*--"

The sober expression on Jimmie Dale's face deepened. Only a fool would attempt to minimise or underestimate the meaning of what he saw around him. A hint, for instance, that he, Jimmie Dale, millionaire clubman, riding here in his limousine, was the Gray Seal, and this great, teeming, though orderly, Fifth Avenue would be transformed like magic into a seething, screaming whirl of madmen, and--he did not care to follow that trend of thought. He was quite well aware what would happen!

The car, close up against the curb, stopped once more in a traffic blockade. Smarlinghue was the most vital factor to be considered now, for--he caught his breath quickly. Through the open window of the limousine a white envelope fluttered and fell at his feet. The car was moving forward again. For the fraction of a second Jimmie Dale did not move, save to straighten rigidly as though from some sharply administered galvanic shock; and then, with a low cry--"the Tocsin!"--he was at the door, his head thrust out through the window, his fingers mechanically wrenching at the door handle. A mass of people were surging across the street toward the opposite corner. Eagerly his eyes swept over them; he pushed the door open a little as though to step out--and shut it again quickly, as, with a yell of warning, another car, jockeying for position as his own moved out into the stream of traffic, swept by from behind.

It had been quite useless--he knew that, he had known it subconsciously even at the moment when he had sprung to his feet. Apart entirely from the crowd, she would undoubtedly be in some clever disguise, and he could not have recognised her in any event.

He stooped, picked up the envelope, and sat down again quietly, his eyes travelling swiftly in the direction of his chauffeur. Benson's back was still imperturbably turned toward him. In the roar of dozens of motors all starting forward at once, Benson evidently had not heard the yell of warning, or, if he had, had been too much occupied with his own immediate duties to pay any attention to it.

Jimmie Dale tore the envelope open; and, in a sort of grim, feverish haste, unfolded the sheets which it had contained.

"Dear Philanthropic Crook--since you *will* be called that," he read. A quick, eager flush came to his cheeks. She knew how, since she had shown last night that she knew him as Smarlinghue, that, despite all her own brave, resolute protests, he was determined to fight this thing out to the end--separately, if she would not let him join forces with her--but, in any case, to the end. It was the old name again-- Dear Philanthropic Crook! Did it mean that she had surrendered, then, at last, that she had finally accepted the situation, and that he was to enter this shadowland of hers beside her! The flush died away. It was only his own wish that had been father to the thought. This was another "call to arms" of quite a different nature, and born, not out of her own peril, but born, as in the old days again, out of the maze of her strange environment. "You have set New York ablaze, you have made me far more afraid for you than I am for myself; but I cannot see where there is any danger here, or else I would not have written this. You--" He was reading impetuously now, his brain, alert and keen, sorting and sifting out, as it were, the salient, vital points, "... old Colonel Milford and his wife... Louisiana... letter... family heirloom... French descent... old setting, three large diamonds pendant from necklet of smaller ones... ten to twelve thousand dollars... steel bond box... lower right-hand drawer of desk... plan of second floor... West 88th Street..."

He turned the page, studied for a moment the carefully drawn plan that covered the next sheet, then turned to the third and last page--and suddenly his face hardened. He had been called a jackal by the papers--but here were two who bore a clearer title to the name! He knew them both--Jake Kisnieff, better known as Old Attic in the underworld, as crooked as his own bent and twisted form, a miserly, cunning "fence," crafty enough, if report were true, to have garnered a huge, ill-gotten harvest under the nose of the police; and the other, one self-styled Henry Thorold, alias whatever occasion might require, smooth, polished, educated, the most dangerous of all types of crook, was the brains of a certain clique whose versatile operations were restricted only between the limits of porch-climbing and the callous removal, via the murder route, of any one when deemed expedient for either personal or financial reasons!

Jimmie Dale read on to the end of the page. His jaws were clamped together now, the square, determined chin out-thrust; and while one hand held the letter, the other curled into a clenched fist. It was dirty work--vile, miserable work--a coward's work! And then Jimmie Dale smiled grimly, as his eyes fell upon the glaring headline of the paper on the top of the pile beside him. Perhaps the **morning** papers would carry other headlines that would be still more startling!

He began to study the several sheets again, critically, carefully this time. There should be no danger here, she said. He knew what she meant--that she counted on his being able to nip the whole scheme in the bud. He shook his head thoughtfully. That might be true; he might be able to do that, probably would, for it was still very early; but if not--what then? He glanced out of the window--they were just turning into Riverside Drive. He looked at his watch. It wanted but a few minutes of seven--progress up the Avenue had been unusually slow. He tore the letter into small fragments, and reaching out through the window, let the pieces flutter away in the wind. It was none too early at that, and it was unfortunate that he must first of all go home--there were certain things there indispensable to the night's work. On the other hand, it was fortunate that he did not have to lose even more time by being obliged instead to go to the new Sanctuary for what he needed, fortunate that he had been "Jimmie Dale" last night when he had left Malay John's, and that he had gone directly home from there.

The car stopped. Benson sprang from his seat, and opened the door.

"Don't put up the car yet, Benson; I am going a little further uptown," said Jimmie Dale, with a pleasant nod--and ran up the steps of his house.

Jason, his butler, opened the door for him.

"I shall not be dining at home to-night, Jason." Jimmie Dale handed over his hat--not a suitable one for the evening's special requirements.

The old man's face wrinkled up in disappointment.

"That's too bad, sir, Master Jim." Jason took liberties; but they were the genuine heart liberties of a lifetime's service--and why not, since, as he was fond of saying, he had dandled his Master Jim as a baby on his knee! "There was to be just what you are especially fond of to-night, Master Jim; the cook made a particular point of--"

"Yes; I know." Jimmie Dale's hand squeezed the old man's shoulder in friendly fashion. It was not the cook, but Jason, who would have originated the menu with the painstaking care and thoughtfulness of one dealing with a life-and-death matter. "But it can't be helped. I didn't know until just a little while ago, or I would have telephoned. I am going right out again."

"Very good, sir," Jason bowed. "Your clothes, Master Jim, are--"

"I shan't dress, Jason," said Jimmie Dale--and, crossing the reception hall, with its rich, oriental rugs, he ran up the wide staircase, opened the door of his "den," locked it behind him, and, switching on the lights, began to strip off his coat and vest, as he hurried toward the further end of the great, spacious, luxuriously appointed room that ran the entire depth of the house.

He threw coat and vest on a nearby chair; and, sweeping the portieres away from in front of a little alcove, knelt down before the barrel-shaped safe with its multitudinous glistening knobs, that, in the days gone by when he had been with his father in the business of manufacturing safes, the business that had amassed the fortune he had inherited, he had designed himself. His fingers flew over the dials. He swung the outer and the inner doors open, reached inside, took out the leather girdle with its burglar kit, and fastened it around his waist. Then, slipping an automatic and a flashlight into his pocket, he closed the safe, drew the portieres together, and put on his coat and vest again.

An instant later he was downstairs, and, selecting a soft slouch hat--Jason for the moment not being in evidence--went down the steps to his waiting limousine.

"The Marleton, Benson," he directed, as he stepped into the car. "And hurry, please."

The car started forward. It was not far to 88th Street, but the car would save time--and time was counting now, every minute of it priceless, if, as the Tocsin had intimated, he was to forestall the game that was in hand. The Marleton was for Benson's benefit--but the Marleton, unless he had miscalculated the numbers, was barely more than a block away from the house he sought.

And then, besides, there was another reason for haste--Colonel Milford and his wife would probably be at dinner now, and that left the upstairs part of the house at his disposal, since, apart from the elderly couple, the household consisted, according to the Tocsin, of only a single maid. He went over in his mind again the plan the Tocsin had drawn. Yes, she was quite right, there should be no danger, the whole matter as far as he was concerned was almost childishly simple and easy--if he were only in time! He shook his head a little impatiently at that; and, as he saw that they were approaching his destination, consulted his watch. It was exactly twenty minutes after seven.

The car rolled up to the curb in front of the fashionable family hotel. Jimmie Dale alighted.

"I shall not need you any more to-night, Benson," he said.

He walked quietly into the hotel, through the lobby, down a corridor, and out of the entrance that gave on the cross street--then his pace quickened. He traversed the block, crossed the road, turned the corner, and a minute later was approaching the house she had designated. It was one of a row. His pace slowed to a nonchalant stroll again. It was still quite light, and he was by no means the only pedestrian on the street; a moment's preliminary, even if cursory, examination of the exterior would not be amiss! Counting the numbers ahead of him, he had already located the house. He frowned a little. A light burned in the upstairs front room. There was a light in the lower hallway as well, but that was to be expected. Why the one upstairs? Had the Colonel and Mrs. Milford already finished their dinner?

Jimmie Dale reached the house--and casually, without hesitation, mounted the steps--and quite as casually, making a pretence of ringing the electric bell, opened the unlocked outer door, stepped into the vestibule, and, without a sound now, closed the door behind him.

He tried the inner door tentatively. It was locked, of course--but it was locked only for an instant. From the girdle under his vest came a little steel instrument; there was a faint, almost inaudible, protesting *snip* from the interior of the lock; and, his fingers turning the knob with a steady, silent pressure, he opened the door slightly.

Crouched there, he listened. And then, a smile of relief flickering on his lips, he pushed the door open, and slipped into the hallway. The explanation of the light upstairs was that it had probably been left burning inadvertently. They were still at dinner, for he could hear voices from the dining room at the rear of the hall.

As silent as a shadow now, Jimmie Dale, closing the inside door, moved across the hall, and went up the stairs. On the landing he paused; and then advanced cautiously. The light streamed out from the open door of the front room, and there was always the possibility that--no, a glance from where he stood close against the wall at the edge of the door jamb, showed him that the room was unoccupied.

He entered the room quickly, crossed quickly to a quaint old escritoire against the opposite wall, and stooped beside it. The lower right-hand drawer, she had said. The little steel instrument with which he had opened the vestibule door was still in his hand, but he did not use it now! Instead, with a low, dismayed ejaculation, as his fingers ran along the drawer edge, he dropped on his knees for a closer examination--and his lips closed tightly together.

He was too late! The first finger touch had told him that, and now his eyes corroborated it. The drawer had been forced by a jimmy of some sort, judging from the indentations in the wood. The lock was broken, and he pulled the drawer open. Inside lay the steel bond-box, its lid bent back, and wrenched and twisted out of shape. The box was empty.

Without disturbing the box, Jimmie Dale mechanically closed the drawer again and stood up, looking around him. In a subconscious way, when he had entered the room, he had been cognisant of a certain strangeness in its appointments, but then his mind had been centred only on the work in hand; now there seemed a sort of pitiful congruity in the surroundings themselves and in the old heirloom that had been stolen. It seemed as though the room spoke to him of past glories. The furniture was out-of-date, and, too, a little in disrepair. It seemed as though there clung about it the pride and station of other days, a station that it was finding it hard to maintain in these. And he thought he understood. It was a fine old family, that of the Milfords of Louisiana, a very proud old family in the way that it was fine to be proud--proud of its name, proud that its sons were gentlemen, proud of its loyalty to its own traditions and standards, a pride that neither condition nor adversity could mar. And now the diamond pendant was gone! He could well understand how they had clung to that, and--

He started suddenly. Was he a fool, that he had wasted even a moment in giving play to his thoughts! Voices were reaching him now from below, footsteps were sounding from the lower hall, there was a creak upon the stairs. They were coming!

He had hardly any need for the quick, searching glance he flung around him-- the plan that the Tocsin, had drawn was mapped out vividly in his mind. He stepped backward softly through half-opened folding doors into the room in the rear. From this room a door, he knew, opened into the hallway. His escape, after all, need give him little concern. He had only to step out into the hall after they passed, and make his way downstairs. A woman's voice from the stairway came to him:

"My dear, you must have left the light burning."

"Unless, it was you," a man's voice answered in good-humoured banter. "You were the last one in the room."

"But I am sure I didn't!" the feminine tones asserted positively.

The steps passed along the hall, and from behind the folding doors Jimmie Dale saw an elderly couple enter the front room. Both were in evening dress--and somehow, suddenly, at sight of them Jimmie Dale swallowed hard. The old gentleman, kindly, blue-eyed, white-haired, was very erect, very straight in spite of the fact that he must have been close to seventy years of age, and with the sweet-faced, old-fashioned little lady, with the gray hair, who stood beside him, they made a stately pair--for all that their clothes, past glories like the furniture, were grown a little shabby, a little threadbare. But with what a courtly air they wore them! And with what a courtly air now he led her to a chair, and bent over her, and lifted up her face, and held it tenderly between both his hands!

"How well you look to-night in your dress," he said, and his blue eyes shone. "I am very proud of you."

She stroked the hand against her cheek.

"Do you remember the first time I ever wore it?" She was smiling up at him.

"Oh, yes!" he nodded his head slowly. "It is strange, isn't it? That was a long time ago when our friends were married back there in the old State, and to-night again, way up here in New York, they have not forgotten us on this their anniversary."

Silence fell for a moment between them.

Then he spoke again, a little sadly:

"Would you wish those days back again, if you could?"

She hesitated thoughtfully.

"I do not know," she said at last. "Sometimes I think so. We had John then."

"Yes," he said, and turned away his head.

Her hand, as Jimmie Dale watched, seemed to tighten over her husband's; and now, though her lips quivered, there came a little smile.

"But we have his memory now, dear," she whispered.

Agitated, the old gentleman moved abruptly away from the chair, and Jimmie

Dale could see that the blue eyes were moist.

"That is true--we have his memory." The old colonel's voice trembled. And then his shoulders squared like a soldier on parade. "Tut, tut!" he chided. "Why, we are to be gay to-night! And it is almost time for us to be going. We, too, shall celebrate. You shall wear the pendant, just as you did that other night."

"Oh, colonel!" There was mingled delight and hesitation in her ejaculation. "Do you really think I ought to--that it wouldn't be out of keeping with our present circumstances?"

"Of course, I think you ought to!" he declared. "And see"--he started across the room--"I will get it for you, and fasten it around your throat myself."

He reached the escritoire, opened a little drawer at the top, took out a key, stooped to the lower drawer, inserted the key, turned it once or twice in a puzzled way, then tried the drawer, pulled it open--and with a sharp, sudden cry, reached inside for the steel bond-box.

The little old lady rose hurriedly, in a startled way, from her chair.

"What is it? What is the matter?" she cried anxiously.

The box clattered from the colonel's hands to the floor.

"It is gone!" he said hoarsely. "It has been stolen!"

"*Gone!*" She ran wildly forward. "Stolen! No, no--it cannot be gone!"

They stared for a moment into each other's faces, and from each other's faces stared at the rifled box upon the floor--and then a look of wan misery crept gray upon the little old lady, and she swayed backward.

With a cry, that to Jimmie Dale seemed one of more poignant anguish than he had ever heard before, the old gentleman caught her in his arms and supported her to a chair; then running quickly to the hall, called loudly for the maid below.

There was a merciless smile on Jimmie Dale's lips. He was retreating now further back into the room toward the door that gave on the hall.

"I wonder," said Jimmie Dale to himself through set teeth, "I wonder if a man wouldn't be justified in putting an end *for keeps* to that devil Thorold for this!"

He heard the maid come rushing up the stairs. He could no longer see into the other room now, but a confused mingling of voices reached him:

"... The police ... next door and telephone ... the light ... while we were at dinner...."

Jimmie Dale opened the door, slipped across the hall, made his way silently and swiftly down the stairs, and with the single precaution of pulling his slouch hat far down over his eyes, stepped boldly out of the front door, walked quietly down the steps, walked briskly, but without apparent haste, along the street--and turned the first corner.

CHAPTER V
"DEATH TO THE GRAY SEAL!"

Jimmie Dale hurried now, making his way to the nearest subway station, and took a downtown train. "There should be no danger," the Tocsin had written. His eyes darkened with a flash of passion. Danger! Danger was a small, pitiful factor now! He had been too late through no fault either of his or the Tocsin's--but he still knew where the pendant was, or would be! Time was counting again; he was afraid now only that he might be too late a second time. Old Attic would not let any grass grow under his feet in disposing of the diamonds through one of the many channels at his command, and once they had passed out of that scoundrel's hands they were as good as hopelessly lost. Also there was Thorold to reckon with. Thorold would naturally get the pendant first, then turn it over to Jake Kisnieff. Had Thorold already done so? It depended, of course, on when the theft had been committed. That snatch of conversation--"the light ... when we were at dinner"--came back to him. His brows gathered. He crouched a little in his seat, staring abstractedly at the black tunnel walls without. Station after station was passed. Jimmie Dale's hand, resting on the window sill, was so tightly clenched that it seemed the skin must crack across the knuckles.

But he was smiling when he left the subway--only it was that same merciless smile once more. It was not alone the mere act of robbery that fanned his anger to a white heat. Again and again, he was picturing in his mind that fine old gray-haired couple; again and again he saw the old colonel bend and lift that sweet face to his, and saw them look into each other's eyes. There was something holy, something reverent in that love which the years had ripened and mellowed with tenderness; something that was profound, that made of this night's work a sacrilege in touching them--and that poor jewel, clung to all too obviously through adversity for its past associations, was probably the last real thing of intrinsic value they possessed!

"I am not sure," muttered Jimmie Dale--he was fingering the automatic in his pocket, "I am not sure that I can trust myself to-night!"

Ten minutes' walk from the subway brought him before a dingy and dilapidated three-story tenement on the East Side. The Nest, they called it in the underworld; and worthily so, for its roof sheltered more of the cheaper and petty class of criminals probably than any other single dwelling in New York--the steerers, the hangers-on, the stalls, those of the lesser breed of vultures, and the more vicious therefore, who at best made but a precarious livelihood from their iniquitous pursuits.

One of Jimmie Dale's shoulders was hunched forward, giving a crude and ill-fitting set to his fashionably tailored, Fifth Avenue coat; he staggered slightly, and the flap of his collar protruded, while his tie, pulled out, sprawled over his vest; also his slouch hat, badly crushed and looking as though it had rolled in the mire of the street, was tilted forward at an unhappy angle until it was balanced on the bridge of his nose. Men, women, and children passed him by--for the street was crowded--paying him not the slightest attention. He lurched in through the front door of the tenement, swayed up against the hallway inside--and stood there, still swaying a little.

It was dark here, and the atmosphere was musty and fetid; a murmur pervaded the place as of voices behind many closed doors, but apart from that the tenement might have been empty and deserted for all the signs of life it evidenced. And then the spot where Jimmie Dale had stood was vacant, and he was along the narrow hallway without a sound, and, opening a door at the rear, stood peering out. After a moment, he closed the door again without fastening it; and, back once more toward the front of the hallway, began to creep silently up the stairs.

He reached the top landing. Old Attic had two miserable rooms here, where he conducted his even more miserable business! Jimmie Dale dropped on his knees before the door that faced the head of the stairs, and placed his ear to the panel. Noiselessly he tried the door. It was locked. He was smiling that merciless smile again in the darkness, as his deft, slim fingers worked at the keyhole. He was not too late this time! Old Jake was there, and--yes, Thorold, too. They were even now haggling over the pendant--he could hear them quite distinctly now with the door open a crack.

He pushed the door open a little wider, but very slowly, scarcely an inch at a time. He was in luck again! They were in the inner room. He opened the door still a little wider, stepped softly over the threshold, and closed the door behind him.

Save for a dim light that filtered out through the half open door of the inner room, it was dark here. Slowly, with that almost uncanny, silent tread that he had acquired on the creaky, rickety stairs of the old Sanctuary, Jimmie Dale began to move forward, the weight of his body wholly and firmly on one foot before the other was lifted from the floor; and, as he advanced, the black silk mask, from a pocket in the leather girdle, was drawn over his face.

He could see them now quite plainly--the twisted, crunched-up form of old Jake, with his tawny-bearded face, and narrow, shifting little black eyes; the smooth-shaven, suave, oily, cunning countenance of Thorold, the super-crook. Both were sitting at a table in the miserly appointed room, whose only other articles of furniture were a cheap iron bed and a few chairs. Old Jake was whining; Thorold's voice held an angry rasp.

"Four thousand, you cursed miser, and not a cent less," Thorold was saying.

"Three," whined the other. "You ain't splitting fair. I got to take the stones out of their setting, and sell 'em for what I can get. Stolen stuff's got to go cheap. You know that."

"It's worth ten or twelve, and you'll get at least eight for it," growled Thorold. "That's four apiece--and I've got to split mine again with the guy that pinched it. Hurry up, d'yer hear--I've got a date with him in half an hour over in my office."

"Ha, ha!" cackled old Jake. "Are you trying to be funny? All the thief gets out of it from you won't make much of a hole in your share!"

"That's my business!" snapped Thorold. "You come across!"

"Three!" whined old Jake again.

"Four!" Thorold flung back angrily.

"Well, let's have a look at it then; I ain't seen it for years," grumbled old Jake. "I ain't trying to do you. We went into this thing so's we'd each get the same out of it; but I tell you it ain't easy to shove big stones when there'll be a police description out against them, and there ain't no big prices for 'em, either."

Thorold reached into his pocket--and even in the dull light of the single gas-jet that alone illuminated the room, Jimmie Dale caught the fire and flash of the magnificent stones in the pendant that swung to and fro now, as the man held it up.

Old Jake, his hand trembling with eagerness, snatched at it, and, as Thorold laughed shortly, dove his fingers into a greasy vest pocket, and produced a jeweller's magnifying glass, which he screwed into his eye.

"One of these has got a flaw, and it's cloudy," he mumbled.

"Never mind about the flaw! Flash your wad!" invited Thorold, with a thin smile.

Jimmie Dale's hand slipped under his vest to a pocket in the leather girdle, and from the thin metal case, with the aid of the tiny tweezers, lifted out a gray seal, and laid it lightly on the inside edge of his left-hand sleeve. He replaced the metal case with his right hand, and with his right hand drew his automatic from his pocket. He crept forward again, inch by inch toward the door of the inner room.

Old Jake laid the pendant on the table, and from some mysterious recess in his clothing pulled out a huge roll of banknotes.

"I'll make it three and a half until I see what I can get for it. That's all I've got here, anyway." He began to count the money, laying it bill by bill on the table. "If I get more than seven, I'll split the difference even. That's fair. That's the way it's been ever since we started this. I don't know exactly what I can get for this, and--"

And then Jimmie Dale was in the room, his automatic covering the two men.

"Don't move please, gentlemen!" he said quietly, as he stepped to the table. His eyes behind the mask travelled from the diamond pendant to the pile of banknotes, and from the banknotes to the two men, whose faces had gone suddenly white, and who now sat rigidly in their chairs, as though turned to stone. "I appear to be in luck to-night!" His lips, just showing beneath the mask, parted in a hard smile. "I was passing by, and--" His left hand reached out, swept up the money and the diamond pendant--and in their place, fluttering from his sleeve, a gray seal fell upon the table.

There was a sharp, quick cry from Thorold--and the muzzle of Jimmie Dale's automatic swung like a flash to a level with the man's eyes. Old Jake had crumpled up now in his chair, and was glaring wildly at the little diamond-shaped piece of paper; he licked his lips with his tongue, there was fear in his eyes.

"The Gray Seal! The Gray Seal!" he muttered hoarsely.

"I appear to be in luck to-night!" said Jimmie Dale again. "And"--he put the money and the diamond pendant coolly in his pocket--"it would be too bad if I didn't play it up, wouldn't it? It doesn't often come as easy as this. Amazing carelessness to leave that outside door unlocked! But, as I was saying, with such a lavish display of opulence on the table, one is almost led to hope that there might be more where that came from. Now--"

"I haven't got any more--not another cent! Honest, I haven't!" old Jake cried hysterically. "I swear to God, I haven't, and--"

"You hold your tongue!" There was a sudden snarl in Jimmie Dale's low tones. The man's voice was rising dangerously loud. "I'll attend to you in a moment!" He swung on Thorold again; and, with his pistol pressed close against the man, felt deftly and swiftly over the other in search of weapons. He laughed tersely, finding none. "Empty your pockets out on the table!" he ordered curtly.

The man hesitated.

Jimmie Dale smiled--unpleasantly.

Thorold swept a bead of sweat from his forehead. His lips were working nervously. All suavity and polish were gone now; there were only viciousness and fear, each struggling with the other for the mastery in the man's smug face.

"Damn you, you blasted snitch!" he burst out furiously. "We'll get you down here some day, and--"

"Some day, perhaps," said Jimmie Dale softly. "But to-night--did I explain that I was in a hurry-- *Thorold!* Every pocket inside out, please!"

Thorold's hand went reluctantly to his pockets. He began with the inside pocket of his coat, laying a pile of letters and papers on the table.

"Anything there you want?" he sneered.

"Go on!" prompted Jimmie Dale.

From vest pockets came a varied assortment of articles--watch, cigars, a cigar-cutter, a silver-mounted pencil, and a fountain pen. The man's hands travelled to his outside coat pockets.

"The *inside* pocket of the vest, Thorold," suggested Jimmie Dale coldly.

With a malicious snort, Thorold unbuttoned his vest, and turned the pocket out. There was nothing in it.

Jimmie Dale nodded complacently.

"My mistake, Thorold," he murmured apologetically. "Go on!"

The man continued to denude himself of his effects, but with increasing savagery and reluctance. There was silence in the room--and then suddenly, so faint as to be almost inaudible, there was a soft *pat* upon the floor. Jimmie Dale did not turn his head.

"I think you dropped something, Jake," he observed pleasantly. "Now take your foot off it, and put it on the table!"

A miserable smile twisting his lips, old Jake stooped, picked up a roll of bills, and, mumbling and crooning to himself, laid it on the table. Jimmie Dale immediately transferred it to his pocket.

"Yes," he said, "I certainly seem to be in luck tonight! That all you got, Thorold?" He reached forward, and possessed himself of a well-filled wallet that Thorold had added to the heterogeneous collection in front of him.

Thorold's face was black with fury.

"There's the watch, you cheap poke-getter!" he choked. "Don't forget to frisk that while you're at it!"

Jimmie Dale examined the collection with a sort of imperturbable appraisement.

"No," he said judicially. "You can keep your watch, Thorold; I haven't got the same lay as our friend Jake here, and that sort of thing is too hard to get rid of to make it worth while. I'll take these, and that's all." He whipped the pile of letters and papers into his pocket. "You see, with a man of your profession, there is always the chance of there being something valuable amongst--"

Jimmie Dale never finished the sentence. With a sudden, low, tigerish cry, Thorold heaved the end of the table upward between himself and Jimmie Dale--and, quick as a cat, as Jimmie Dale staggered backward, leaped from behind it.

"Get him, Jake! Get him, Jake!" he cried. "He won't *dare* to fire in here for the noise. Get him, you fool, he--"

But Jimmie Dale was the quicker of the two. A vicious left full on the point of Thorold's jaw stopped the man's rush--but only for the fraction of a second. Thorold, recovering instantly, flung his body forward, and his arms wrapped themselves around Jimmie Dale's neck. And now, old Jake, screeching like a madman, was circling around them, snatching, clawing, striking at Jimmie Dale's face and head.

Thorold was a powerful man; and at the first tight-locked grip, as they swayed together, trained athlete though he was himself, Jimmie Dale realised that he had met his match. Again and again, with all his strength he tried to throw the other from him. Around and around the room they staggered and lurched--and around and around them followed the wizened, twisted form of old Jake, like a hovering hawk, darting in at every opportunity for a blow, shrieking, yelling, cursing with infuriated abandon. And then from below, a greater peril still, came the opening and shutting of doors, voices calling--the tenement, at the racket, like a hive of hornets disturbed, was beginning to stir into life. If they caught him there! If they caught the Gray Seal there! It brought a desperate strength to Jimmie Dale. He had heard too often that slogan of the underworld-- ***death to the Gray Seal***!

He tore one of Thorold's arms free from his neck--they were cheek to cheek-- Thorold was snarling out a torrent of blasphemy with gasping breath--he wrenched himself free still--and then, their two hands outstretched and clasped together as though in some grim devil's waltz, they reeled toward the bed at the far end of the room, and smashed into a chair. And, as they lost their balance, Jimmie Dale, gathering all his strength for the one supreme effort, hurled the other from him. There was a crash that shook the floor, as Thorold, hurtling backwards, struck his head with terrific force against the iron bedstead, and dropped like a log.

Jimmie Dale was on his feet again in an instant--but not before old Jake had run, yelling madly, from the room. A glance Jimmie Dale gave at Thorold, who lay limp and motionless, a crimson stream beginning to trickle over temple and cheek; then, with a bound, he reached the gas-jet, and turned out the light.

Old Jake's voice screamed from the hallway without:

"Help! The Gray Seal! The Gray Seal! Help! Help! Quick! The Gray Seal!"

The staircase creaked under the rush of feet; yells began to well up from below. Jimmie Dale darted into the outer room, and crouched down beside the doorway.

"Death to the Gray Seal!" The whole building, in a pandemonium of hellish glee, seemed to echo and reecho the shout.

Jimmie Dale was deadly calm now, as his fingers closed around his automatic- -and, deadly cool, the keen, alert, active brain was at work. It was black about him, pitch black, there were no lights in the hallway--yes, a dull glimmer now--a door farther along had opened--but dark enough in here where he waited. There was a chance--with the odds heavily against him--but it was the only way.

They were on the landing outside now; and now, old Jake shouting excitedly amongst them, a dozen forms swept through the doorway, and scuffing, stamping, yelling, made for the inner room--and Jimmie Dale slipped out into the hall. His lips pressed tightly together. That had been as he had expected, but the danger still lay before him--in the three flights of stairs. Some one was coming up now, more than one, the stragglers--but there would be stragglers until the last occupant of the tenement was aroused. He dared not wait. In a minute more, in less than a minute, they would have lighted the gas again in there and found him gone.

He jumped for the head of the stairs--a dark form loomed up before him. Jimmie Dale launched himself full at the other. There was a cry of surprise, an oath, the man pitched sideways, and Jimmie Dale sprang by. A yell went up from the man behind him; it was echoed by a wild chorus from above, as of wolves robbed of their prey; it was re-echoed by shouts from the stairways and halls below--and with his left hand on the banisters to guide him, taking the stairs four and five at a time, Jimmie Dale went down--and now, aiming at the ground, his revolver spat and barked a vicious warning, cutting lurid flashes through the murk ahead of him.

Doors that were open along the hallways shut with a hurried bang; dark forms, like rats running for their holes, scuttled to safety; women screamed and shrieked; children whimpered. On Jimmie Dale ran. For the second time he crashed into a form, and won by. They were firing at him from above now--but by guesswork--firing down the stair well. The pound of feet racing down the stairs came from behind him--two flights behind him--he calculated he had that much start. He gained the entrance hallway where all was dark, leaped for the front door, opened it, pulled it shut with a violent slam--and, whirling instantly, running swiftly and silently back along the hall, he reached the rear door that he had left unfastened, darted out, and a moment later, swinging himself over a high, backyard fence, dropped down into the lane beyond. Whipping off his mask, he ran on like a hare until he approached the lane's intersection with a cross street. And here, well back from the street, he paused to regain his breath and rearrange his dishevelled attire; then, edging forward, he peered cautiously up and down--and smiled grimly--and stepped out on the street. He was a good block away from the tenement.

From the direction of the Nest came sounds of disorder and riot. A patrolman's whistle rang out shrilly. It had been as close a call perhaps as the Gray Seal had ever known--but, at that, the night's work was not ended! There was still the actual thief. Thorold had said he was to meet the man in his, Thorold's, office in half an hour to split their ill-gotten gains. Jimmie Dale's jaw squared. The thief! His hand at his side clenched suddenly. Would it be *only* the thief, or would he have to reckon with Thorold again as well? Could Thorold keep the appointment? It was a question of how badly Thorold was hurt, and that he did not know.

Jimmie Dale walked on another block, still another, then turned so as to bring him into, but well up, the street on which the tenement was situated. From here, far down the ill-lighted street, he could see a mob gathered outside the Nest. And then, as he stood hesitant, there came the strident clang of a bell, the beat of hoofs, and he caught the name of the hospital on the side of an ambulance as it tore by--and, at that, he swung suddenly about, and, making his way across to Broadway, boarded an uptown car.

Twenty minutes later, he closed the door of a telephone booth in a saloon on lower Sixth Avenue behind him, and consulting the directory for the number, called the hospital.

"This is police headquarters speaking," said Jimmie Dale coolly. "What's the condition of that tenement case with the broken head?"

"Hold the wire a minute," came the answer; and then, presently: "Not serious; but still unconscious."

"Thank you," said Jimmie Dale.

He hung up the receiver, and made his way out to the street. The coast was clear then, as far as Thorold was concerned. Jimmie Dale walked on halfway up the block, and turned into the lighted hallway of a small building whose second floor, above a millinery establishment, was rented out for offices. It was here that Thorold maintained what he called his "office." Mounting the stairs and emerging upon a narrow corridor, that was lighted at one end by a single incandescent, Jimmie Dale halted before a door that bore the legend: HENRY THOROLD--AGENT. Jimmie Dale's lips twisted into grim lines. Agent--of what? He glanced quickly up and down the corridor, slipped his little steel instrument into the lock, and opened the door.

He stepped inside, closing the door without re-locking it; and, using his flashlight now, moved forward, and entered a sort of inner office that was partitioned off from the rest of the room. There was a flat-topped desk here, a swivel chair, an armchair, a rather good drawing or two on the walls, and a soft yielding carpet underfoot. Thorold was far too clever to overdo anything--it was simply businesslike, with an air of modest success about it.

Jimmie Dale appropriated the swivel chair behind the desk. Half an hour from the time he had left the tenement! He should not have long to wait, for he had used up nearly, if not quite, all of that time already, and the thief would certainly have every incentive to be punctual. He laid his flashlight, turned on, upon the desk, and, taking his automatic from his pocket, examined it. There were still two cartridges remaining in the magazine. He slipped the weapon into the side pocket of his coat, and began to sort over the papers and letters he had taken from Thorold. He opened one--a letter--glanced at its contents--and nodded. It was the one to which the Tocsin had referred. He returned the others to his pocket, began to read the one in his hand and suddenly, leaning forward, snapped out his light. **Was that a step coming up the stairs?**

He listened now intently. Yes, it was coming nearer. He laid down the letter on the desk, and put on his mask. Still nearer came the step. It had halted now before the door. And now the hall door opened and closed. Jimmie Dale sat motionless, except that his hand crept to his coat pocket, and from his coat pocket to the desk again. The door closed softly--a man had entered the outer room--and certainly a man who was no stranger to the place, for he was moving unerringly in the darkness toward the partition door. The man was in the inner office now, passing the desk, so close that Jimmie Dale could have reached out and touched him. There was a soft, rubbing sound as the man's hand felt along the wall for the electric light switch, a click, the room was suddenly flooded with light; and, with a low cry, blinking there in the glare, staring at Jimmie Dale's masked face--stood Colonel Milford.

And then the old gentleman swayed, and caught at the back of the armchair for support--upon the desk lay the diamond pendant, glittering under the light.

"My God!" he whispered. "What does this mean?"

"It means, colonel," said Jimmie Dale softly, "that Thorold couldn't come, that old Jake found one of the diamonds cloudy and with a flaw, and that the deal fell through--and it means, colonel, that you will never be called upon to steal Mrs.

Milford's diamonds again; there is a letter here that--"

"The letter!" The old gentleman was staggering toward the desk. He reached out his hand for the letter, hesitated as though he were afraid that Jimmie Dale was only tantalising him, would never let him have it--and then with a little cry of wondrous gladness, he snatched it to him.

"I'd destroy that if I were you," suggested Jimmie Dale quietly. "I don't imagine that Thorold or old Jake will ever bother you again, but there are lots of 'Thorolds' in New York." He motioned toward the pendant. "That is yours, too, colonel."

The old gentleman was fingering the letter over and over, as though to assure himself that it was actually in his possession; and into his blue eyes, as they travelled back and forth from the pendant to Jimmie Dale, there crept a half wondering, half wistful light.

"I do not know why you have done this for me, or who you are, sir," he said brokenly. "But at least I understand that in some strange way you have stepped in between me and--and those men. You--you know the story, then?"

"Only partially," said Jimmie Dale with a smile, as he shook his head. "But you need not--"

"I would wish to thank you, sir." The old Southerner was stately now in his emotion. "I can never do so adequately. You are at least entitled to my confidence." His face grew a little whiter; he drew himself up as though to meet a blow. "My boy, my son, sir, stole a large sum of money from the bank where he was employed in New Orleans. He was not suspected; and indeed, as far as the bank is concerned, the matter remains a mystery to this day. Shortly afterwards the Spanish war broke out. My son was an officer in a local regiment. He obtained an appointment for the front." The old gentleman paused; then he stood erect, head back, at salute, like the gallant old soldier that he was. "My son, sir, was a thief; but he redeemed himself, and he redeemed his name--he fell at the head of his company, leading his men."

Jimmie Dale's eyes had grown suddenly moist.

"I understand," he said simply.

"He wrote this letter to me, making a full confession of his guilt; and gave it to me, telling me not to open it unless he should not come back." The colonel's voice broke; then, with an effort, steadied again. "It would have killed his mother, sir. It strained our resources most severely to pay back the money to the bank, and I lied to her, sir--I told her that our investments were proving unfortunate. Two years ago I completed the final payment without the bank ever having found out where the money came from; and then we moved up here to New York. You see, sir, it was a little difficult to maintain our former position in Louisiana, and amongst strangers less would be expected of us. And then, sir, shortly after that, I do not know how, this letter was stolen, and for two years Thorold has held it over my head, threatening to make it public if I refused his demands; I gave him all the money I could get. I have thought sometimes, sir, that I should put a revolver in my pocket and come down here and shoot him like a dog--but then, sir, the story, I was afraid, would come out. Yesterday he made a final demand for five thousand dollars. I did not have the money. He suggested Mrs. Milford's pendant there. He promised to return the letter, and any sum above the five thousand that he could get for the diamonds. I knew he was lying about the money; but I believed he would return the letter, knowing that I now had nothing left. That is why I am here to-night."

Again the old gentleman paused. It was very still in the room. Jimmie Dale had taken the thin metal case from his leather girdle and was fingering it abstractedly. And then the colonel spoke again:

"And so," he said slowly, "I stole the pendant this afternoon, and pretended to-night that it was done at dinner-time, and--and pretended, too, to make the discovery of the theft myself. You see, sir, it was not only the old name that would be smirched--there was the boy to think of, and he had redeemed himself. And Mrs. Milford would have wanted me to do that, to take a thousand of her jewels, if she had had them, if she had known--but, you see, sir, she could not know without it breaking her heart--I think the dearest thing in life to her is the boy's memory."

Outside on Sixth Avenue an elevated train roared and thundered by--it seemed strangely extraneous and incongruous.

"And now, sir"--the old gentleman's voice seemed tired, a little weary--"though you give me back the pendant, I do not see how I can return it to my wife. It was part of the agreement that I should notify the police--it made it impossible for me to inform against Thorold, for--for I was the thief."

Jimmie Dale nodded. "I was thinking of that," he said.

He opened the metal case; and, while the old gentleman watched in amazement and growing consternation, he lifted out a gray paper seal with his tweezers, moistened the adhesive side with the tip of his tongue, and pressed the seal firmly with his coat sleeve over the central cluster of the pendant.

The old gentleman tried twice to speak before a word would come.

"You! You--the Gray Seal!" he stammered at last. "But only to-night I was reading in the papers, and they said you were a murderer, an ogre of hell, and--"

"And now, possibly," interrupted Jimmie Dale whimsically, "though circumstances will force you to keep your opinion to yourself, you may have an idea that, as between you and the papers, you are the better informed. Well, at least, the Gray Seal's shoulders are broad! You need not worry about Thorold or old Jake; I took pains to make them aware that the Gray Seal--quite inadvertently, of course--had taken a passing fancy to the pendant. You have only to wrap it up, and send it by mail to *yourself*; and when it arrives"--he laughed softly, as he stood up--"notify the police again. Let them do the theorising--it is one of their cherished amusements! And, oh, by the way, colonel, have you any idea how much Thorold and his precious friend Kisnieff have blackmailed you out of in the last two years?"

"I did not have very much left when I came to New York," said the colonel, in a stunned way, still staring at the gray paper seal. "Between four and five thousand dollars."

"That's too bad," murmured Jimmie Dale. He took the banknotes from his pocket, and laid them on the desk. "I am afraid it is not quite all here--but I can assure you it is all they had."

He held out his hand.

"But you're not going! You're not going that way!" cried the colonel, and his eyes filled suddenly. "How am I to repay you, how am I to--"

"Very easily," smiled Jimmie Dale; "and, to use your own expression, very adequately--by remaining here, say, three minutes after I have left." He caught the colonel's hand in his and wrung it hard--and then, with a "Goodnight!" flung over his shoulder, Jimmie Dale was gone.

CHAPTER VI
THE REHABILITATION OF LARRY THE BAT

The small French window of the new Sanctuary, that gave on the dirty little courtyard which, in turn, paralleled a black and narrow lane, with its high, board fence, opened cautiously, noiselessly. A dark form slipped silently into the room. The window was closed again. The dilapidated roller shade was drawn down, and, guided by the sense of touch, the rent that gaped across it was carefully pinned together. There was no moon to shine in through the top-light and uncharitably disclose the greasy, ragged carpet, or the squalor of the room.

The dark form, like a shadow, moved across the room to the door, tried the lock, slipped an inner bolt into place, then returned halfway back to the windows, and paused by the wall. A match flame spurted through the blackness; and then, hissing as though in protest, the miserable, clogged gas-jet, blue with air, still leaving the corners of the room dim and murky, grudgingly lighted up its immediate surroundings--and Jimmie Dale, immaculate in evening clothes, stood looking sharply about him.

Here and there about the room, upon this article and that, as though fixing its exact and precise location, his glance fell critically; then he stepped back quickly to the door, and knelt by the threshold. The tiny, unobtrusive piece of thread, that must break if the door were opened by but that fraction of an inch, was still intact. No one, then, had been here since last, as Smarlinghue, the seedy, drug-wrecked artist, he had left the place the day before; for, on entering, he had already satisfied himself that the French window had not been tampered with.

A hard smile flickered across his lips. It was a grim transition, this, from the luxury, the wealth and refinement of New York's most exclusive club, which he had left but half an hour ago! The smile faded, and he passed his hand a little wearily across his eyes. The strain seemed to grow heavier every day--the underworld more prone to suspicion; the police more vigilant; that ominous slogan, in which Crime and the Law for once were one, "Death to the Gray Seal!" to ring more constantly in his ears. It was becoming more fraught with peril, danger and difficulty than ever before, this dual life he led. And he had thought it all ended--once. That was only a few months ago, when the way had seemed clear for them both, for the Tocsin and himself. Well, he was here to-night to end it again if he could--by playing perhaps the most desperate game he had ever attempted.

He shook his head. It was more than the hazard, the danger and the peril of his dual life that brought the strain--it was the Tocsin, his love for her, *her* peril and *her* danger, the unbearable anxiety and suspense on her account that was never absent from him. And it was that that kept him in the underworld, that had forced him to create again a role in gangland, the role of Smarlinghue, in the hope that he might track her enemies down. She would not help him. If she knew, and she must know, the authors of this new danger that had driven her once more into hiding, she would not tell him. She was afraid--for *him*. She had said that. She had said that she would fight this out alone, that she would not, could not, whatever the end might be, bring him again into the shadows, throw his life again into the balance. It was her love, pure, unselfish, a wondrous love, that had prompted her to this course, he knew that--and yet--But why all this again! His brain was numbed with its incessant dwelling upon it day after day.

Jimmie Dale's hands clenched suddenly. That night, a week ago, when he had been so nearly caught in the Nest, had brought very forcibly upon him the realisation that he could not risk any longer a haphazard course of action, if he was to be of help to her, for next time his own luck might go out. And so the idea had come-- the one, single, definite mode of attack that lay within his power--and he had used the week to advantage, and he was ready now. From the first it had seemed almost certain that the danger which threatened her must come from one of two sources-- and there was a way to probe one of these to the bottom. He did not know who they were, those who remained of the Crime Club, or where they were; but he knew the Magpie, and he knew where the Magpie was to be found--and to-night he would know, settling the question once for all, *all* that the Magpie knew!

He turned, walked back across the room, and, a few feet along from the door, knelt down close to the wall. An instant later, with the loose section of the base-board removed, he reached inside, and took out a curious assortment of garments, which he laid on the floor beside him. They were not Smarlinghue's clothes--they were even more shoddy and disreputable. His brows gathered critically as he surveyed the wretched boots, the mismated socks, the frayed, patched trousers, the greasy flannel shirt, the ragged coat, and the battered, shapeless slouch hat. Matched closely enough to the originals to pass without question, gathered from here and there, painstakingly, with infinite trouble during the week that had passed, were the clothes of--Larry the Bat.

It was a dangerous, almost desperate chance; but he, too, was desperate now. To be caught, even to be seen as Larry the Bat meant flinging every stake he had in life into the game. More rabid than ever was the cry of the populace for vengeance upon the Gray Seal; more active than ever, combing den and dive, their dragnet spreading from end to end of the city, were the efforts of the police to effect the Gray Seal's capture; more like snarling wolves than ever, the blood lust upon them, mad to sink their fangs into the Gray Seal, were the denizens of the underworld--and populace and police and underworld alike knew Larry the Bat as the Gray Seal! If he were seen--if he were caught! They had thought that Larry the Bat had perished in the Sanctuary fire that night, and that in Larry the Bat had perished the Gray Seal. But the Gray Seal had been at work again since then; and, logically enough, there had followed the deduction that, after all, Larry the Bat had in some way escaped.

Jimmie Dale began to remove his expensively tailored dress suit. It had made it much easier for him, easier to play the role of Smarlinghue, easier for the Gray Seal to work, that they, the populace, police and underworld, had of late searched only for a **character**, a character that, in truth, until to-night had literally vanished from the face of the earth--a character known as Larry the Bat. But now Larry the Bat was to assume tangible form again, to accept the risk of recognition, to go out amongst those whose one ambition was his destruction, to court his own death, his ruin, the disclosure that Larry the Bat was Jimmie Dale, that Jimmie Dale, the millionaire clubman, a leader in New York's society, was therefore the Gray Seal, and with this disclosure drag an honoured name in the mire, be execrated as a felon. It seemed almost the act of a fool--worse than that, indeed! Even a fool would not invite the blow of a blackjack, the thrust of a knife, or a revolver bullet from the first crook in gangland who recognised him; even a fool would not voluntarily take the chance of thrusting his head through the door of one of Sing Sing's death cells!

And for an instant, fought out with himself times without number though this had been since he had first conceived the plan, Jimmie Dale hesitated. It was very still in the room. In his hands now he held a bundle of neatly folded clothing ready to be tucked away in the aperture in the wall. He looked around him unseeingly. Then suddenly the square jaw clamped hard, and he stooped, thrust the bundle into the opening, and began rapidly to dress again--as Larry the Bat.

If it was the act of a fool, it was even more the act of a *coward* to shrink from it! It was the one way to force the Magpie to lay his cards face up upon the table. It was the Magpie who had discovered that Larry the Bat was the Gray Seal; it was the Magpie who had led gangland to batter down the Sanctuary doors; it was the Magpie who had clamoured the loudest of them all for the Gray Seal's death--and it was the Magpie, therefore, who had reason to fear Larry the Bat as he would fear no other living thing on earth. And it was upon that which he, Jimmie Dale, counted--the psychological effect upon the Magpie on finding himself suddenly face to face and in the power of Larry the Bat, with the unhallowed reputation of the Gray Seal, that did not stop at murder, to discount any thought in the Magpie's mind that the choice between a full confession and death was an idle threat which would not be put into instant execution.

Yes; it was simple enough, and *sure* enough--that part of it. The Magpie would tell what he knew under those circumstances--and tell eagerly. But if, after all, the Magpie knew nothing! Jimmie Dale snarled contemptuously at himself. Childish! That, of course, was possible--but in that case he would at least have run a false lead to earth, and have eliminated the Magpie from any further consideration.

Jimmie Dale took out a make-up box from the opening in the wall, and, carrying it with him to the table, propped up a small mirror against a collection of Smarlinghue's paint tubes. His fingers were working swiftly now with sure, deft touches, supplying to his face, his neck, his hands and wrists, not the unhealthy pallor of Smarlinghue, but the grimy, unwashed, dirty appearance of Larry the Bat. It was the toss of a coin, heads or tails, whether the Magpie was at the bottom of this or not. The Magpie knew that Silver Mag had been in the affair that night when Larry the Bat was discovered to be the Gray Seal; the Magpie knew that Silver Mag was a pal of Larry the Bat, and, therefore, equally with the Gray Seal, the underworld had passed sentence of death upon her--but did the Magpie know that Silver Mag was Marie LaSalle, any more than he knew that Larry the Bat was Jimmie Dale? That was the question--and its answer would be wrung from the Magpie's lips to-night!

A piece of wax was inserted in each nostril, and behind the lobes of his ears, and under his lip. Jimmie Dale stared into the mirror--the vicious, dissolute face of Larry the Bat leered back at him. And then, returning abruptly to the loosened section of the base-board, he restored the make-up box to its hiding place. He reached inside again, and procured a pistol and flashlight, which he stowed away in his pockets; there would be no need to-night for that belt with its compact little kit of burglar's tools; no need for that thin metal box with the gray-coloured, adhesive paper seals, the insignia of the Gray Seal, for to-night the Gray Seal would appear in *person*. No--wait! That collection of little steel picklocks--and a jimmy! He would need those. He felt for them in one of the pockets of the leather girdle, transferred them to the pocket of his ragged trousers, and slipped the base-board back into place.

And now he stepped to the gas-jet, and turned out the light. Then the roller shade was raised, the French window silently opened, silently closed--and Larry the Bat, hugging close against the wall of the building, crept to the fence, and, lifting aside a loose board, passed out into the lane, and from the lane to an empty and drearily-lighted cross street.

There was no "sanctuary" now. Who in the underworld would fail to recognise Larry the Bat! He was out in the open, on the fringes of the Bad Lands, where recognition was to be feared from every passer-by, and where, if caught, he would do well and wisely to use his own automatic upon himself! And he must go deeper still, into the heart of gangland, to reach that room in the basement beneath Poker Joe's gambling hell where the Magpie lived--or, rather, burrowed himself away in those hours that were miserly devoted to sleep.

But Jimmie Dale knew his East Side as no other man in New York knew it; knew it as a man whose life again and again had depended solely upon that knowledge. By lane and alley, by unfrequented streets, now running, now crouched motionless in some dark corner waiting for footsteps to die away along the pavement before he darted across the street in front of him, Jimmie Dale threaded his way through the East Side, as through the twistings and turning of some maze, puzzling, grotesque and intricate, but with whose secrets notwithstanding he was intimately familiar.

When he paused at last, it was in a backyard, which he had entered by the simple expedient of climbing the fence from the lane behind. A low building loomed up before him, whose windows at first glance were dark, but through whose carefully closed blinds and tightly drawn shutters might still be remarked, if one were sufficiently inquisitive, the faint, suffused glow of lights from within.

Jimmie Dale scarcely glanced at the windows. Poker Joe's at this hour--it must be close to eleven o'clock, he calculated--would be just about settling into its night's swing. He was quite well aware both that the place was lighted and that there were by now perhaps a score of gangland's elite already at the tables; and that the blinds and shades were closed and drawn interested him only in that it safeguarded him *without* from being seen by any one from *within*!

But there was another window upon which Jimmie Dale now centred his entire attention--a narrow, oblong window, cellar-like, just on a level with the ground--and here there was neither a light nor a drawn shade. He stole across the yard, and, five yards from the wall of the house, dropped down on his hands and knees, and crawled silently forward. Keeping a little to one side, he reached the window, and lay there listening intently. There was no sound, save a low, almost inaudible murmur of voices from the windows above him--nothing from the direction of that dark, oblong window that he could reach out and touch now. The Magpie was presumably not at home!

The long, slim, tapering fingers, whose nerves, tingling sensitively at the tips, were as eyes to Jimmie Dale, those fingers that, to the Gray Seal, were like some magical "open sesame" to the most intricate safes and vaults, felt along the window sill, and, from the sill, made a circuit of the sash. The window, he found, was hinged at one side and opened inward; and now, under the pressure of his steel jimmy, inserted between the ledge and the lower portion of the frame, it began to yield.

Lying there on the ground, Jimmie Dale, his head close to the opening, listened with strained attention again. He had not made much noise, scarcely any--not enough even to have aroused the Magpie if, say, by any chance, the Magpie were within asleep. The sounds from the floor above seemed to be louder now, to reach him more distinctly, but from the basement room itself there was nothing, no sound even of breathing.

Satisfied that the room was unoccupied, Jimmie Dale pushed the window wide open, and peered in. It was like looking into some dark cavernous hole, and he could not distinguish a single object. Then his hand slipped into his pocket for his flashlight, and the round, white ray shot downward and around the place. The floor of the room was perhaps five feet below the level of the window sill; to the left, against the wall, was a bed; there was a chair, a table sadly in need of repair, a few garments hanging from nails driven haphazardly into the plaster, and, save for a dirty piece of carpet on the floor, nothing else. The flashlight played slowly around the room. Opposite the window was the door, and suspended from the centre of the ceiling was a single incandescent lamp.

With a sort of grim nod of approval, Jimmie Dale snapped off his flashlight, and, turning around, worked himself in through the window feet first, and dropped silently to the floor. He had only to wait now until the Magpie returned--whether it was a question of hours or minutes.

Jimmie Dale made his way to the chair, and sat down--and again he nodded his head grimly. It was very simple; he had only to wait, and this place, this burrow of the Magpie's, could not have been improved upon for his purpose. It was eminently suitable, so suitable that there seemed something ironical in the fact that it should have been the Magpie who had chosen it. One could commit **murder** here, and none would be the wiser--and none would be more keenly alive to that than the Magpie himself! A threat from the Gray Seal in these surroundings left nothing to be desired. They were making too much noise above to hear anything in this room below the ground, and the little window afforded an instant means of escape without the slightest danger of discovery. Yes; the Magpie, not being a fool, would very thoroughly appreciate all this.

Time passed. It was a nerve racking vigil that Jimmie Dale kept, sitting there in the chair--waiting. It was so dark he could not have seen his hand before his face. And it was silent, in spite of that queer composite sound of voices, and shuffling feet, and the occasional squeak of chair legs from above--a silence that seemed to belong to this miserable hole alone, that seemed immune from all extraneous noises. And after a time, in a curious way, the silence seemed to palpitate, to beat upon the ear-drums, to grow almost uncanny.

His lips tightened a little, and he smiled commiseratingly at himself. His nerves were getting a little too tautly strung, that was all; he was listening too intently for that expected step upon the stair, for the opening of that door he faced. And it was not like him to have an attack of nerves--and especially in view of the fact that his plan, in the simplicity of its execution did not even warrant anxiety for its success. He had only to remain quiet until the Magpie entered and turned on the light, then clap his automatic to the Magpie's head--the psychology of fear would do the rest. And yet--what was it? As the minutes dragged along, fight it as he would, a distinct depression, a panicky sort of uneasiness, was settling down upon him. The darkness, in a most unpleasant and disconcerting way, seemed to be full of eeriness, of warnings.

For perhaps ten minutes he sat there in the chair, silent and motionless, angry, struggling with himself--but his disquietude would not down; rather, it but grew the stronger, until it took the form of imagining that he was not *alone* in the room. He scowled contemptuously at himself. There was another psychology than that of fear--the psychology of suggestion. That silence, palpitating in his ear-drums, began to whisper: "You are not alone here--you are not alone--you are not alone."

Was that a sound there outside the door? A step cautiously approaching? He leaned forward tensely. No--his laugh was low, short, furious-- *no!* It was only from above, that sound.

Jimmie Dale's face hardened. It was childish, this sensation of *presence* in the room; but it was also unnerving. Why should so unusual a thing happen to him to-night? Was it purely over-wrought nerves, due to the strain of the peril he ran as Larry the Bat--or was it intuition? Intuition had never failed him yet. Well, whatever it was, he would put a stop to it. He was here to-night to get the Magpie, and nothing should interfere with that. Nothing! He and the Magpie would square accounts to-night--and square them once for all!

Not alone here in the Magpie's den--eh? His flashlight streamed out, and began slowly and deliberately to circle the room. If his brain was so restless and active that it must indulge in fantasies, it could at least be diverted into another channel than--Jimmie Dale strained forward suddenly in his chair. That was a pair of boots there at the foot of the bed. There was nothing strange in a pair of boots, but these boots were poised most curiously on their heels, with the toes pointing upward. They just barely protruded from the foot of the bed, which accounted for his not having been able to see them from the window when he had flashed his light around--he could not see the upper portions of them even now. And then, under his breath, Jimmie Dale jeered at himself again. True, the boots were in a most peculiar position, but had his nerves reached the state where a pair of boots would throw him into a panic! How logical for some one to be hiding there under the bed--with his feet in plain view! And yet what held the boots upright like that? The foot of the bed itself? Jammed there, perhaps? Or--

"Damn it!" gritted Jimmie Dale. "I'm worse than a child to-night!"

He rose from his chair, stepped across the room to the foot of the bed--and like a man dazed, his flashlight playing on the boots, his automatic flung forward in his hand, he stood staring downward, following his flashlight's ray with his eyes. Was he mad! Was his brain now playing him some hideous trick! The boots were not empty, he could see a man's ankles, the bottoms of a town's trousers; but the ankles and the trousers seemed utterly insignificant-- *on the sole of the right boot was a diamond-shaped, gray-coloured, paper seal!* His own insignia--the insignia of the Gray Seal!

For an instant it might have been, he stood there rigidly, realising in a sort of ghastly, subconscious way that the man under the bed made no movement, made no attempt to evade discovery, made no sound; and then Jimmie Dale stooped quickly, and raised one of the other's feet a few inches from the floor. It fell back--a dead weight.

Jimmie Dale's jaws were hard clamped. There was devil's work here--some of the Magpie's, possibly. Every faculty alert now, Jimmie Dale was quietly lifting aside the small iron bed. The Magpie was no fool! By underworld and police alike it would be accepted without questions that the Gray Seal had held a day of reckoning in store for the Magpie. Had the Magpie traded on that--to get rid of some one who was in his way, this out-stretched, inert thing on the floor, and lay it to the door of the Gray Seal? It was clever, hellish in its cunning. And it would appear plausible enough. The Gray Seal had come here, say, searching for the Magpie, and in the darkness had struck another down! Yes, the Magpie could get away with that. It would stand to reason that the Magpie would not lure a victim to his own den, and--

A low cry was on Jimmie Dale's lips. The bed was moved out now, and he was stooping over a man whose head was gruesomely battered above the right temple and back across the skull. The flashlight wavered in his hand, as he held it focussed on the other's face. It was the Magpie--dead.

CHAPTER VII
THE BOND ROBBERY

It seemed to Jimmie Dale that, in the darkness, the room was full of unseen devils laughing and jeering derisively at him. It seemed that reality did not exist; that only unreality prevailed. The Magpie--dead! It seemed for the moment that he had utterly lost his grip upon himself; that mentally he was being tossed helplessly about, the sport of fate. The Magpie-- *dead*! It meant--what did it mean? He must think now, and think quickly. It meant, first of all, that any hope for the Tocsin which he had built upon the Magpie was shattered, gone forever. And it meant, that gray seal on the sole of the dead man's boot, that the murder had been committed with even greater cunning and finesse, and an even greater security for the murderer, than he had attributed to the Magpie a moment since, when he had thought the Magpie the instigator, and not the victim, of the crime.

He was examining the wound, searching for the weapon--it must have been a blunt instrument of some sort--with which the blow, or blows, had been struck. There was nothing. The Magpie lay there--dead. That was all.

Mechanically Jimmie Dale replaced the bed in its original position over the murdered man, and stood staring down again at the gray seal on the Magpie's boot. It was not *why* the Magpie had been murdered, it was *who* had murdered him! Once, long, long ago, almost at the outset of the Gray Seal's career, a spurious gray seal had been used before. But this was a vastly different, and far more significant matter. Then it had been an attempt to foist the identity of the Gray Seal upon a poor, miserable devil in order to secure a reward--here it was a crime, *murder*, coolly, callously laid to the Gray Seal, that the guilty man might escape without a breath of suspicion. Just another crime credited to the Gray Seal! No one would dispute it; no one would question it; no one would dream that it had been done by any one other than the Gray Seal. There was a brutal possibility about the ingenuity of the man who had struck the blow. It was the Magpie who had put his finger upon Larry the Bat as the Gray Seal; it was the Magpie who had tried to accomplish the Gray Seal's death. Would it, then, occasion even surprise that the Magpie should be found murdered in his own den at the hands of the Gray Seal? It was even his own argument, the very reason that had led him to assume the role of Larry the Bat, and had brought him here to the Magpie's to-night!

Jimmie Dale bent down for a closer inspection of the diamond-shaped gray seal on the boot's sole. It was not one of his own; but it was so similar that it would unquestionably pass muster. The red crept to Jimmie Dale's cheeks and burned there, as a sudden, merciless anger swept upon him. **Who** was the man who had done this, who sheltered himself from murder behind the Gray Seal!

He laughed low and bitterly. Only another crime attributed to the Gray Seal! It would not smirch the Gray Seal any--the Gray Seal had been accused of worse than this! But the man who had dared to place that gray seal there would answer for it!

He was still laughing in that low, bitter way, as he knelt now, and took out his pocketknife. The gray seal, at least, would not be found--he was lucky there--he had only to scrape it off, and--No--wait! Would it not be better to leave it there? It would throw the murderer off his guard if he believed that his plan had worked; and it could make little difference to the Gray Seal's record to be held guilty of another murder--temporarily. Temporarily! Yes, that was it! Here was one crime of which the Gray Seal would be vindicated, and the guilty man be--

"*Jimmie!*"

It seemed to quiver, low-breathed, through the darkness--his name. His name! Was he bereft of all his senses! His name! Here in this horrible murder hole! Was he indeed mad with his imaginings, with these voices that had been whispering, and laughing, and jeering at him out of the blackness! And, absurdly, it had seemed this time that it was the Tocsin's voice!

"Jimmie--quick! On the floor under the window!"

He whirled like a flash. Mistake! Imaginings! No! It *was* the Tocsin! It was her voice! The gleam of his flashlight cut the black, and, leaping across the room, played upon the small, narrow, oblong window--it was from there the voice had come. But it was only black and empty there. And around the room his flashlight swept, and it was black and empty there, too--except for a square, white object upon the floor below the window. She was gone.

And it was like a half sob that came from Jimmie Dale's lips.

"Gone!" he whispered miserably. "Gone!"

Why had she gone like that? Why had she not waited--just for a moment, just for the single instant, if he could have had no more, that he would have given his life to have? And the answer was in his soul. He knew, and he, knew that she, too, knew, that it would not have been moment or an instant--that he would never have let her go again. And to follow her? He shook his head. By the time he had climbed out of the window, what trace, any more than there was now, would there of her! She was gone--a sort of finality in her act, as there always was, that left nothing to be done, or said.

But the note! That white thing there upon the floor! He crossed the room, picked it up, tore it open, and, with his flashlight upon it, began to read.

"Jimmie--Jimmie--" It was scrawled in haste, only a few lines. His eyes travelled rapidly over the words, and suddenly his breath came fast.

"My God!" he cried out sharply.

As though he could not have read aright, he read again; disjointed words and phrases muttered audibly: "... Afraid not in time ... hurry ... this afternoon ... the Magpie and Virat ... Kenleigh, insurance broker ... safe in Kenleigh's house ... ground floor--left ... one hundred thousand dollars ... bonds ... will try it ... Meighan of headquarters ... half-past one at Virat's ... Gray Seal ... Larry the Bat ... if dangerous, keep away ..."

One glance around the room Jimmie Dale gave instinctively; and then he was crawling through the window, and, outside, regaining his feet, he darted across the yard, and out into the lane. Kenleigh, the insurance broker--he repeated the address she had given in the note over to himself. It was an apartment house on Avenue near Washington Square.

He ran on, as he had come, through lane and alley, working his way out of the Bad Lands. It was dangerous, of coarse, in any case, but once clear of that section of the city which houses the underworld, his risk of discovery was greatly minimised, since, though familiar to every denizen of gangland, Larry the Bat was naturally not the same intimate figure in the more law-abiding and respectable districts; and he should, except for an extraordinary piece of bad luck, pass in the quarters he was now heading for as no more than exactly what his appearance proclaimed him to be--a disreputable and seedy vagrant.

It was slow work, hurry as he would, doubling and zigzagging his way up through the East Side; discouraging, when time was so great a factor, to cover three and four times the actual distance in order to keep to the lanes and alleys whose shelter he dared not leave; but he was spurred on now by a sort of grim, unholy joy. He knew now who had murdered the Magpie, and why; he knew now who was making a tool, a cat's-paw of the Gray Seal; he knew now who had so cynically elected him, if caught, as a substitute for the other to the electric chair. It was Virat! Frenchy Virat, the suave, sleek gambler, confidence man and crook! Well, the game was of Virat's choosing--and they would play it out now to the end, Virat and the Gray Seal, if it was the last act of his, Jimmie Dale's, life! It was only a question now of whether or not Virat had completed all his work, of whether there was yet time to get to Kenleigh's.

It was close to midnight, as Jimmie Dale came out on Washington Square. He crossed to Waverly Place, and, on the point of starting along Fifth Avenue, drew suddenly back around the corner. A man, walking rapidly, was just turning into Fifth Avenue from the opposite corner. Jimmie Dale drew in his breath sharply. He had got out of sight just in time. He recognised the quick, springy walk of the other. It was Meighan, of Headquarters. And then Jimmie Dale smiled a little whimsically. They were both bound for the same place, he and Meighan, of Headquarters--Kenleigh's apartment, that was a little way further on there along the Avenue.

A short distance behind the other, but on the opposite side of the street, Jimmie Dale followed the detective. There was hardly any use now in going to Kenleigh's, for, if the detective was really bound for there, it made his, Jimmie Dale's, errand useless--the summoning of the Headquarters' man was *prima facie* evidence that the robbery had already been committed. And yet a certain grim curiosity remained. Just how had it been done? And besides, she had said, "half-past one at Virat's," so there was time to spare. The distorted lips of Larry the Bat thinned ominously. No; it was not useless even now. He had a very strong personal interest in all that had taken place--Virat would be the less likely to slip through his fingers, or through the fingers of the law, for the information that the scene of the robbery might supply!

Meighan disappeared suddenly inside an apartment house, which Jimmie Dale recognised as a rather fashionable one, devoted exclusively to bachelors' quarters, Jimmie Dale quickened his step, walked on to the next corner, crossed the street, and came back along the block. As he approached the apartment-house entrance, voices reached him from the vestibule, and then he heard the closing of a door.

"Ground floor--left," murmured Larry the Bat to himself. He smiled facetiously. "Saves an interview with the janitor!"

He glanced sharply around him in all directions--and the next instant was inside the vestibule--and in another, without a sound, was crouched close against the apartment door. A delicate little steel picklock was working now, the deft fingers manipulating it silently, and then stealthily he pushed the door open a crack. A man's voice, agitated, came to him from within: "... Perhaps twenty minutes, I don't know--the length of time it took you to get here. I was dining out. I 'phoned Headquarters the instant I came in."

Jimmie Dale pushed the door further open, slipped through, and left the door just ajar behind him. He was in the hallway of a very small apartment, of not more than two or three rooms, he judged. Diagonally ahead of him a light streamed out from an open door. He stole toward this, and, pressed close against the jamb of the door, peered in.

It was a sort of sitting-room, or den, cosily furnished with deep, comfortable lounging chairs. There was a flat-topped desk in the centre, a telephone on the desk; and at the rear of the room a connecting door, leading presumably to the bedroom, was open. A clean-shaven, dark-eyed man of perhaps thirty-five, Kenleigh obviously, was pacing nervously up and down. His face was pale, his hair ruffled; and, in his distraction, apparently, he had forgotten to remove the cloak which he was wearing over his evening clothes. In the far corner of the room, Meighan, the detective, knelt upon the floor amidst a scene of grotesque disorder. The door of a very small safe had been "souped," and now sagged open. Books and papers littered the floor, and were strewn over a mattress that, evidently dragged from the inner room, had been swaddled around the safe to deaden the sound of the explosion.

"You don't understand!" Kenleigh burst out, with a groan. "This means absolute ruin to me! A hundred thousand dollars in bonds--payable to bearer--and--

and, God help me, they weren't mine!"

"Say"--Meighan, still busily occupied with the fractured safe, spoke gruffly, though not unkindly, over his shoulder--"I understand all right, but don't lose your nerve, Mr. Kenleigh. It won't get you anywhere, and it doesn't follow because the swag is gone that we can't get it back. I know the guy that pulled this job."

"You-- *what!*" Kenleigh, his face lighting up as though with a sudden hope, stepped quickly toward the detective. "What did you say? You know who did it!"

"Don't get excited!" advised Meighan coolly. "Sure, I know! That is, it's a toss-up between one of two, and that's easy. We'll round 'em both up before morning, and then I guess it won't be much of a trick to pick the winner. They won't be looking for trouble as quick as this. We'll get 'em, all right. It's a toss-up between Mug Garretty and the Magpie."

Kenleigh was staring incredulously at the detective.

"How do you know?" he gasped out. "I--I don't--"

"I daresay you don't." Meighan was chuckling now. "It's like this, Mr. Kenleigh. A crook's like any one else, like an artist, say--you get to know 'em, get to spot 'em, especially safe workers, from certain peculiarities about their work. They can't any more help it than stop breathing. Here, for instance, the way he--" Meighan stopped suddenly. He had been pulling the mattress away from the front of the safe, and now, with a sharp, exultant exclamation, he stooped quickly and picked up a small object from the floor. He held it out, twirling It between thumb and forefinger, for Kenleigh's inspection--a flashy scarf pin, horseshoe-shaped, of blatantly imitation diamonds.

Kenleigh shook his head bewilderingly.

"I suppose you mean that you recognise it?" he ventured.

"Recognize it!" Meighan laughed low, and, stepping past Kenleigh to the desk, picked up the telephone, and called Headquarters. "Recognise it!" With the receiver to his ear, waiting for his connection, he turned toward Kenleigh. "Why, say, walk over to the Bowery and show it to the first person you meet, and he'd call the turn. Pretty, isn't it? When he's dolled up, he's some--hello!" He swung around to the telephone. "Headquarters?... Meighan speaking from Kenleigh's apartment... Get a drag out for the Magpie on the jump.... Eh?... Yes!... Left his visiting card.... What?... Yes, wound a mattress around the box and souped it; his scarf pin must have caught in the ticking and pulled out.... Sure, that's the one--the horseshoe--found it on the floor.... What?... Yes, the chances are ten to one he will, it's his only play.... All right, I'll get Mr. Kenleigh's story meanwhile.... I'll be here till you 'phone.... Yes.... All right!"

Meighan hung up the receiver, sat down in a chair, and motioned toward another that was close alongside the desk.

"Turn out the light, Mr. Kenleigh," he said abruptly; "and sit down here."

Kenleigh looked his amazement.

"Turn out the light?" he repeated perplexedly.

"Yes," Meighan nodded. "And at once, please."

Obeying mechanically, Kenleigh moved toward the electric-light switch. There was a faint click, and the apartment was in darkness. Came then the sound of Kenleigh making his way back across the room, and settling himself in the chair beside the detective.

"I--I don't quite see," said Kenleigh, a little nervously. "I--"

"You will in a minute," interrupted Meighan, in a low voice. "Don't make any noise now, and don't speak much above a whisper. That little glass stick pin is worth twenty years to the Magpie. See? When he finds that he has lost it, he'll take any risk to make sure that he didn't lose it *here*. Get the idea? It would plant him for keeps, and nobody knows it any better than he does."

"You mean he'll come back here?" whispered Kenleigh eagerly.

Meighan chuckled.

"Sure, he'll come back here--if he isn't nabbed beforehand! It's the only chance he's got. Don't you worry, Mr. Kenleigh. He's a shy bird, is the Magpie, or he'd have been up the river long before now, but we've got him coming and going this deal. Now then, I haven't got the details from you yet. What time this evening did you get back here before you went out to dine?"

It was quite dark now, and Jimmie Dale leaned forward a little to catch the words. Both men were speaking in guarded undertones.

"About six o'clock," Kenleigh answered. "I came straight from the office. I put the bonds in that safe there, and I should say it was a quarter to seven by the time I had dressed and gone out again."

"And, say, halfpast eleven when you got back. So some time between seven o'clock and halfpast eleven, Mr. Magpie got into the courtyard, put a jimmy at work on the bathroom window beyond the bedroom there, got busy--more likely to be nearer eleven than seven--he would have been back before now, otherwise, eh?" Meighan seemed to be communing with himself, rather than talking to Kenleigh. "Wouldn't make such an awful noise--didn't need much juice on that safe--pretty slick with the smother game--didn't raise an item, anyway."

There was silence for a moment. Then Meighan spoke again:

"Let's have your story, Mr. Kenleigh. How did you come to bring a hundred thousand dollars' worth of bonds home with you? And how did the Magpie get onto the lay?"

"I don't know, unless he stood in with the bond firm's messenger; that's the only way in which I could account for it," said Kenleigh huskily. "And I've no right to say that God knows I've no wish to get an innocent man into trouble. I've no proof--but I can't see any other solution." Kenleigh's voice broke. He seemed to steady himself with an effort. "I'm an insurance broker with an office on Wall Street, as I daresay you know. A client of mine, a well-known millionaire here in the city, wanted a hundred thousand dollars' worth of the Canadian War Loan bonds, but for business reasons, he has a large German connection, he did not want his name to appear in the transaction." Kenleigh hesitated.

"Sure!" said Meighan. "I see. Wise guy! Go on!"

"He commissioned me to get them for him." Kenleigh's voice was agitated as he continued. "I telephoned Thorpe, LeLand and Company, the brokers, where I was personally known, explained the circumstances, and placed the order. My client was to give me a check for the amount on the delivery of the bonds to him. I was to place this to my own credit in the bank, and check against it in favour of Thorpe, LeLand and Company. They sent the bonds over to my office by a messenger about five o'clock this afternoon. It was too late to put them in a safe-deposit vault. I locked them first in my office safe, and then I grew nervous about them, and took them out again."

"Anybody see you do that?" queried Meighan quickly.

"No; I don't see how they could. I've only a small one-room office, and there was nobody there but myself."

"And so they kind of got your goat, and you figured the safest thing to do was to bring them home with you?" suggested Meighan.

"Yes." There was a miserable note of dejection in Kenleigh's voice. "Yes; that's what I did. And I put them in that safe. You know the rest, and--and, oh, my God, what am I to do! My client, naturally, won't pay for what he does not receive, and I owe Thorpe, LeLand and Company a hundred thousand dollars." He laughed out a little hysterically. "A hundred thousand dollars! It sounds like a joke, doesn't it? I've got a little money, all I've been able to save in ten years' work, a few thousand. I'm ruined."

"Don't talk so loud!" cautioned Meighan. He whistled low under his breath. "You're certainly up against it, Mr. Kenleigh, but you buck up! We'll get 'em. And, anyway, bonds can be traced."

"These are payable to bearer," said Kenleigh numbly. "There were three classes of bonds in this issue--those payable to bearer; those registered as to principal; and those fully registered, that is where the interest is paid by government check instead of the bonds having coupons. Naturally, under the circumstances, it was the 'payable-to-bearer' bonds that my client wanted."

"Well, they're numbered, aren't they?" Meighan returned encouragingly.

"That's poor consolation for me," said Kenleigh bitterly. "Suppose some of them, or even all of them, were recovered that way in time--where do I stand tomorrow morning?"

"I guess that's right--if the Magpie ever got a chance to hand them over to some fence," admitted Meighan. "The fence could dispose of them by the underground route all over the country where the numbers weren't staring everybody in the face. Yes, I guess they could cash in, all right. Or it wouldn't be much of a trick for a good plate-worker to alter a number or two, either--the game's big enough. But"--Meighan chuckled again--"he hasn't got away with it yet!"

Kenleigh made no answer.

It was still again in the apartment. Through the darkness only a few feet away from Jimmie Dale, the two men sat there silently, waiting, as he had waited, in the darkness, and the silence--for the Magpie. There seemed an abhorrent, gruesome analogy in the situation--this waiting for a *murdered* man to come!

The minutes dragged by, ten, fifteen of them. And now Jimmie Dale, cramped though he was, dared not shift his position; the movement of a foot, the slightest stir would be heard. It would have been better if he had gone before they had ceased talking. He had heard enough long before then, and yet--

Suddenly, startling, like the clash of an alarm bell through the silence, the telephone rang. Jimmie Dale heard Meighan fumble for the receiver; and then, as the other spoke, seizing the opportunity, he began to retreat stealthily back across the hallway toward the vestibule door.

"Hello!" Meighan's voice was still guarded. "Yes--yes ... What!" His voice rose suddenly in a rasping cry. "What's that! Dead! *Murdered*! Wait a minute! Kenleigh, they've found the Magpie murdered in his room!"

"Murdered!" cried Kenleigh; then, frantically: "But the bonds, the bonds! Did they find the bonds? Ask them! Tell them to look! The bonds! Are the bonds there?"

"Hello!" Meighan was evidently speaking into the 'phone again. "Any trace of the bonds? ... What? ... Yes, yes; go on, I'm listening! ... *Who*? ... *What*?... Good Lord!" The receiver clicked back on its hook.

"What is it? What do they say?" demanded Kenleigh feverishly.

"Mr. Kenleigh," said Meighan soberly, "there's been a little feud on in the underworld for the last few months. It came to a showdown to-night, and the man that won played in luck--he's killed two birds with one stone, I guess. It looks damned black for your bonds, I'm afraid."

"They're--they're gone?" faltered Kenleigh.

"Yes--and for keeps, I guess," said Meighan gruffly. He laughed shortly, mirthlessly. "You can turn the light on now; we'd wait a long time here--for the Gray Seal!"

CHAPTER VIII
AT HALFPAST ONE

L arry the Bat closed the outer door noiselessly behind him, slipped through the vestibule--and, an instant later, was slouching along Fifth Avenue, heading back toward Washington Square. His hands in his ragged pockets clenched. It had been well worked out--with a devil's ingenuity. The police had swallowed the bait, jumped to the inevitable conclusion desired, and credited the Gray Seal with the double crime of theft and murder without an instant's hesitation. Well, why shouldn't they! It had been well planned; it was natural enough! Larry the Bat, in his turn, laughed, mirthlessly. But the game was not yet played out!

Through the by-ways, lanes and alleys of the underworld, Jimmie Dale once more threaded his way, and finally, mounting the dark stairway leading upward from the side entrance of a small house just off Chatham Square, he let himself stealthily into a room on the first landing. It was Virat now, and this was where Vi rat lived--a locality where a stranger took his life in his hand any time! Below stairs was a pseudo tea-merchant's store--kept by a Chinese "hatchet" man. But Lang Chang had not been in evidence when he, Jimmie Dale, had crept up the stairs, for there had been no light in the store windows.

And now Jimmie Dale's flashlight was playing around the room. Halfpast one, she had said. It could not be more than one o'clock as yet There was ample time to search for the bonds.

He began to move noiselessly around the room--a rather ornately furnished combination sitting and bedroom. "Keep away, if dangerous," had been the Tocsin's caution. He smiled grimly. What danger could there be? He had only to face one at a time; the Tocsin could absolutely be depended upon to see to that, and the advantage of surprise was with him. He was pulling out the drawer of a bureau now--and now his hands were searching swiftly under the mattress of the bed. It was necessary to secure the bonds. Barring that little matter of the numbers, they were as good as cash--and the matter of numbers would not trouble Virat. He knew Virat, and he had known Virat very well--but not so well by far as he knew him now! Virat was as suave and polished a gentleman crook as the country possessed. Viral was the sort of man who, after the uproar had died down, would have the nerve and address to take up his residence in some little out-of-the-way place, and either dispose of as many of the bonds at a time as he dared to those he would cultivate as friends, or even have the audacity to secure a loan on a modest number of them from the local bank itself, whose conversance with the missing numbers might be expected to be of the haziest description. Also Virat would be careful to see that his offerings were not made at such dates as to have the interest coupons cause him any inconvenience by falling due within twenty-four hours! It would be quite simple--for Virate! In six months, in as many places, with the length and breadth of the country to choose from, Virat could quite readily dispose of the lot; not quite at the issue price perhaps if he secured loans, but still at a figure that would be very profitable--for Virat! Or, as Meighan had suggested, with the aid of a confederate of the right sort, the change of a figure--ah! Jimmie Dale; flat upon the floor, his hand stretched in under the washstand, drew out a short, round, heavy object. He examined this attentively for a second; and then, his face hardening, he slipped it into his coat pocket.

He resumed his musings, and resumed his search through the room. Virat was clever enough to find means of disposing of the bonds in some fashion or other, and too clever to have ever committed murder for them otherwise--there was no doubt of that. And, after all, what difference did it make whatever Virat's method might be! It was extraneous, immaterial. Jimmie Dale shrugged his shoulders. The vital question was--where were the bonds?

It was a strange search there in the murderer's room, the flashlight winking and flinging its little gleams of light through the blackness; a strange search, thorough as only Jimmie Dale could make it--and still leave no tell-tale sign behind to witness that a single object in the room had been disturbed. But the search was futile; and at the end Jimmie Dale smiled whimsically.

"The process of elimination again!" he muttered. "I seem to be obsessed with that to-night. Well, not being here, there's only one place the bonds *can* be. The process of elimination has its advantages." The flashlight circled around the room, and held for a moment on the electric-light switch near the door. "It must be after halfpast one," said Jimmie Dale--and suddenly snapped off his light.

There came a faint creaking noise--some one was cautiously mounting the stairs. Jimmie Dale snatched his automatic from his pocket, and without a sound stole forward across the room to a position by the door. The footsteps were on the landing now. The doorknob was tried; the door began to open slowly, inch by inch, wider; a dark form slipped through into the room; the floor was closed again--and Jimmie Dale, reaching forward, clapped the muzzle of his automatic against the other's head. But it was Larry the Bat who spoke--in a hoarse, guttural whisper.

"Youse let a peep outer youse, an' youse goes bye-bye for keeps! See? Put yer hands over yer head, an' do it-- *quick*!"

Jimmie Dale's left hand reached out and switched on the light. It was Meighan, hands elevated, startled, angry, who stood blinking in the glare--and then a low cry came from the man.

"Larry the Bat--the Gray Seal! So it's a plant, is it! That damned she-pal of yours handed it to me good over the 'phone!" Meighan's lips tightened. "And where's Virat--did you kill him, too?"

Jimmie Dale's hand was searching swiftly through the detective's clothes. He transferred a revolver and a pair of handcuffs to his own pockets.

"I had ter take a chance on de light," said Larry the Bat plaintively; "'cause I had ter frisk youse." He turned off the light again. "Sure, she's a slick one!" Larry the Bat, his left hand free again, turned his flashlight upon the detective. "Youse can put yer flippers down now. Mabbe she staked youse ter de tip dat de bonds was here, eh?"

"Yes, blast you--both of you!" growled Meighan.

"Well, dey ain't," said Larry the Bat coolly; "but mabbe, after all, she wasn't handin' youse no steer."

Meighan, savage at his own helplessness, snarled his words.

"What do you mean?" he demanded.

"Mabbe nothin'--mabbe a whole lot." Larry the Bat dropped his voice mysteriously. "I was thinkin' of pullin' off a little show here, an' youse have de luck ter get an invite, dat's all. Mabbe I'll hand youse somethin' on a gold platter, an' mabbe I'll hand youse-- **this**!" The automatic was shoved significantly an inch closer to Meighan's face. "Youse know me! Youse know what'll happen if youse play any funny tricks! No guy gets de Gray Seal alive--I guess youse are wise ter dat, ain't youse? Now den, over youse go behind dat big chair on de other side of de table!"

Meighan, a puzzled look replacing the angry expression on his face, blinked. "What's the lay?" he queried.

"I'm expectin' company," grinned Larry the Bat. "Youse keeps yer yap closed till youse gets de cue--savvy? Dat's all! If youse play fair, mabbe youse'll get a look-in on de rake-off; if youse throws me down, the first shot I fires won't miss **youse**. Go on now, get down behind dat chair--quick!"

Hesitantly, following the flashlight's directing ray, covered by Jimmie Dale's automatic, Meighan, muttering, made his way across the room, and crouched down behind the back of a large lounging chair. Jimmie Dale leaned nonchalantly against the jamb of the door, the flashlight holding a bead upon the chair.

"Youse'll pardon me if I keeps de spot-light on youse," drawled Larry the Bat, "Some of youse dicks ain't trustworthy."

"Look here!" Meighan burst out. "This is a hell of a note! What--"

"Youse shut yer face!" Jimmie Dale's voice had grown suddenly cold and menacing--the stairs were creaking again, this time under a quick tread. "Listen! Say, youse don't have ter wait long fer de curtain, ter go up on de act. Don't youse make a sound!"

The doorknob turned. Jimmie Dale whipped his flashlight into his pocket--and in a flash, as a man entered, switched on the light, and slammed shut the door. A dapper individual, wearing tortoise-rimmed glasses, with black moustache and goatee, was staring into the muzzle of Jimmie Dale's automatic.

"Hello, Frenchy!" observed Larry the Bat suavely. "Feelin' faint?"

The man's face had gone a chalky white. He looked wildly around him, as though seeking some avenue of escape.

"*Mon Dieu*!" he whispered. "Larree ze Bat! It is ze Gray Seal! It is--"

"Aw, cut out dat parlay-voo dope!" Larry the Bat broke in curtly. "Youse don't need ter pull dat stuff wid me, Virat. Talk New York, see?"

Virat moistened his lips with the tip of his tongue.

"What do you want here?" he asked huskily.

"Oh, nothin' much," said Larry the Bat airily. "I thought mabbe youse might figure dere was some of dem bonds comin' ter me."

"Bonds! I don't know anything about any bonds," said Virat, in a low voice. "I don't know what you are talking about.'

"You don't--eh?" inquired Larry the Bat ominously. "Well den, I'll help ter put youse wise. But mabbe I'd better get yer gun first, eh?" As he had done to Meighan, he removed a revolver from Virat's pocket. "T'anks!" he said. He pushed Virat with his revolver muzzle toward the table, and forced the other into a chair. He sat down opposite Virat, and smiled unpleasantly. "Now den, come across! Youse croaked de Magpie ter-night!"

"You're dippy!" sneered Virat. "I haven't seen the Magpie in a month."

"An' dat's what youse did it wid." Larry the Bat, as though he had not heard the other's denial, reached into his pocket, and shoved a small, murderous, blood-stained blackjack, the leather-covered piece of lead pipe that he had found beneath the washstand, suddenly across the table under Virat's eyes.

With a sharp cry, staring, Virat shrank back.

"Sure! Now youse're talkin'!" approved Larry the Bat complacently. "But dat ain't all. Say, youse have got a gall! Youse thought youse'd plant me, did youse, wid dat gray seal on de Magpie's boot!" Jimmie Dale's voice was deadly cold again. "Well, what about dat?"

"What do you want?" mumbled Virat.

Jimmie Dale's smile was not inviting.

"I told youse once, didn't I? What do youse suppose I want! If I got ter fall fer it, I want some of dem bonds--dat's what I want!"

A look of relief spread over Virat's face.

"All right," he said hurriedly. "I--that's--that's fair. I--I'll get them for you." He started up from his chair, his eyes travelling instinctively toward the door.

"Youse sit down!" invited Larry the Bat coldly.

"But--but you said--I--I was going to get them," faltered Virat.

"Sure!" said Larry the Bat. "Dat's de idea! An', say, I'm in a hurry. Dey ain't over dere, Frenchy--try nearer home!"

Virat's hands trembled as he unbuttoned his vest. He reached around under the back of his vest, drew out a flat package, and laid it on the table. He began to untie the cord.

"Wait a minute!" said Larry the Bat pleasantly. "I ain't in so much of a hurry now dat I got me lamps on 'em! Youse can count 'em out after--half for youse, an' half fer me. Tell us how youse fixed de lay."

And then, for the first time, Virat laughed, though still a little nervously.

"Yes, that's square," he agreed eagerly. "I--I was afraid you were going to pinch them all. I'll tell you. It was easy. I piped the Magpie off to a chap named Kenleigh having the bonds up there in his rooms in an apartment house. I couldn't crack Kenleigh's safe myself, but it was nuts for the Magpie--see? He cracked the safe. I was with him, and I copped that near-diamond pin of his, and left it there so there wouldn't be any guessing as to who pulled off the job, and then we beat it back to his place to divide--and I beaned him. I wasn't looking into any gun then, and handing over fifty thousand--and besides, with the Magpie out of the way, I had *some* alibi." Virat laughed shortly. "That's where you come in. Everybody knew you had it in for him. All I had to do was--well, what you said I did. If you hadn't tumbled to it, and I'm damned if I can see how you did, there wasn't anything to it at all. It was open and shut that the Magpie pinched the swag, and that you croaked him and beat it with the bonds."

"Say," said Larry the Bat admiringly, "youse're some slick gazabo, youse are! But how did youse know dat guy Kenleigh had de goods?"

"That's none of your business, is it?" replied Virat, a little defiantly. "You're getting yours now."

Larry the Bat appeared to ponder the other's words, a curious smile on his lips.

"Well, mabbe it ain't," he admitted. "Let it go anyway, an' split the swag. Count 'em out!"

Virat picked up the package again, and began to untie it--and again Jimmie Dale's hand slipped into his pocket. And then, quick as the winking of an eye, as Virat's hands came together over a knot, Jimmie Dale leaned across the table, there was a click, and the steel were locked on the other's wrists.

There was a scream of fury, an oath from Virat.

"Dat's yer cue, Meighan," called Larry the Bat calmly. "Come out an' take a look at him!"

A ghastly pallor spreading over his face, staring like a demented man, as Meighan, rising from behind the lounging chair, advanced toward the table, Virat huddled back in his seat.

"Know him?" inquired Larry the Bat.

The detective bent sharply forward.

"My god!" he exclaimed. "It's--no, it can't--"

"Mabbe," murmured Larry the Bat, "youse'd know him better when he ain't dolled up." He swept the glasses from Virat's nose, and wrenched away the black moustache and goatee.

"Kenleigh!" gasped Meighan.

"Mabbe," said Larry the Bat, with a twisted grin, "dere's somethin' he may have fergotten ter wise youse up on, but he didn't mean ter hide nothin' in his confession--did youse, Frenchy? An' mabbe dere's one or two other things in de years he's been playin' Kenleigh dat he'll tell youse about, if youse ask him--nice and pleasant-like!"

Larry the Bat edged around the table, and, covering Meighan with his revolver, backed to the door.

"Well, so long, Meighan!" he said softly, from the threshold. "T'ink of me when dey pins de medal on yer breast fer dis!"

And then Jimmie Dale laid Meighan's revolver down on the floor of the room, and locked the door on the outside with a pick-lock, and went down the stairs.

CHAPTER IX
'WARE THE WOLF

Jimmie Dale's fingers, in the darkness, were deftly tying around his body the leather girdle with its finely-tempered, compact kit of burglar's tools. It was strange, this note of hers to-night--strange, even, where all the notes that she had ever written had been strange! It had been left half an hour ago at the door of the St. James Club--and he had hastened here to the Sanctuary. It was curiously strange! Three nights ago, he had seen Frenchy Virat safely in the hands of the police, and Frenchy Virat was still safely in police custody--but he, Jimmie Dale, was not yet done with Frenchy Virat, it seemed! The note had made that quite clear. There was still the Wolf; and it was the Wolf that filled this anxious, hurried word from her to-night.

The Wolf! He knew the Wolf well--as Larry the Bat in the old days he had even known the other personally as Smarlinghue of to-day he had progressed that far into the inner ring of the underworld again as to be on nodding terms with the Wolf. The man was a power in the underworld--and a devil in human guise. In a career extending back over many years, a career in which no single crime in the decalogue had been slighted, the Wolf had successfully managed to evade the clutches of the law until his name had become a synonym for craft and cunning in the Bad Lands, and the man himself the object of the vicious hero-worship of that sordid world where murder cradled and foul things lived. The police had marked the man, marked him a score of times; in their records a hundred unsolved crimes pointed to the Wolf--but they had never "got" him--always the thread of evidence that seemed to lead to that queer house near Chatham Square was broken on the way--and the Wolf, with steadily increasing prestige and authority in gangland, laughed in the faces of the police, and here and there a plain-clothes man, overzealous perhaps, *died*.

That was the Wolf--but that was not all! Jimmie Dale's face hardened into grim lines, as he lifted out from under the baseboard "Smarlinghue's" frayed and seedy coat, and put it on. Between the Wolf and the Gray Seal there was now a personal feud. Above the reek of those whisperings in the underworld, above that muttered slogan, "*death to the Gray Seal,*" that men flung at each other from the twisted corners of their mouths, the Wolf had snarled, and the underworld had listened, and the underworld was waiting now--the Wolf had pledged himself to rid the Bad Lands of the terror that had crept upon it. He had sworn, and staked his reputation on his pledge, to "get" Larry the Bat, *alias* the Gray Seal--and in the eyes of the underworld, as the underworld sighed with relief, it was already accomplished, for the Wolf had never failed.

Jimmie Dale stooped down, felt in under the baseboard again, and took out a little make-up box. The Wolf's incentive was not one of philanthropy toward his fellow denizens of crimeland, whose ranks had been thinned by those who, thanks to the Gray Seal, had gone "up the river," some of them, many of them, to that room in Sing Sing's death-house from which none ever returned alive; nor was it, to give the Wolf his due, through a personal fear that his own career might end, as those others' had, at the hands of the Gray Seal; nor, again, was it through any tardy, eleventh-hour conversion, any belated edging toward the way of grace that found expression in a desire to array himself on the side of those representing the forces of law and order. It was none of these things that actuated the Wolf--it was Frenchy Virat, *alias* one Kenleigh, who was awaiting trial in the Tombs. Frenchy Virat was the Wolf's bosom friend!

The wheezy, air-choked gas-jet spluttered into a blue flame, as Jimmie Dale lighted it. It disclosed, in shadow, the battered easel, the dirty canvases, some finished, some but tentative daubs, that banked the wall in disorder opposite the small French window, whose shade was closely drawn; it crept dimly into the far corner of the room and disclosed the cheap cot, unmade, the blanket upon it rumpled in negligent untidiness; it fell full, such as its fulness was, upon the rickety table that was littered with unwashed dishes and sticky paint tubes, and, at one end of the table, on an evening newspaper, and, beside the newspaper, the Tocsin's note and a newspaper clipping.

Jimmie Dale sat down at the table, brushed the dishes and paint tubes together into a heap, and propped up against them a cracked and streaked mirror. He opened his make-up box, and as, swiftly, with masterly touch, the grey, sickly pallor that was Smarlinghue's transformed his face, and as, from little distorting pieces of wax, there came into being the hollow cheeks, the thin, extended lips, the widened nostrils, he kept glancing at the newspaper, reading again an article that was set, on the front page, under heavy type captions--the article which was identical with the clipping, and which latter the Tocsin had enclosed with her note, lest he should not have seen the original himself.

UNIDENTIFIED BODY FOUND UNDER PIER IN NORTH RIVER
VICTIM OF FOUL PLAY
FACE IS MUTILATED BEYOND RECOGNITION

The details as set forth in the "story" were gruesomely interesting enough from a morbid point of view; but from the point of view of the police they were both meagre and unsatisfactory. It was murder unquestionably--and murder of a most brutal character. The headline had epitomised it--the face was mutilated beyond recognition. Every belonging, obviously with the design to prevent, or at least retard, identification, had been stripped from the body. One point alone appeared to be established, and that, if anything, but added to the mystery which surrounded the crime. According to medical opinion, the murder had been committed but a very short time before the body was discovered; and, since the victim had been found at three o'clock that afternoon, the body must have been thrown into the water in broad daylight.

Jimmie Dale worked on--his fingers seeming to fly with ever-increasing speed. There was no time to lose; every minute, every second, counted against him. If he could only have acted on the instant, as Jimmie Dale, when he had received the note at the club! But he had not had that leather girdle at the club--no blue-steel tools that would be needed, no mask, and he had not been armed--everything had been here in the Sanctuary. And, once here, since he had been forced to lose that much time, he had risked a little more, precious as the moments were, for the advantages, the safety, the freedom of movement, afforded by the character of Smarlinghue. However, it was still but barely eleven o'clock, and the chances were that the Wolf would hardly have deemed it late enough as yet to set to work. On the other hand--well, on the other hand, if the Wolf had proved the early bird, then, perhaps, he and the Wolf would have, in another place and time to-night, a more personal reckoning than was anticipated in the Tocsin's plan!

His eyes picked up snatches of her note, as they skimmed it swiftly again.

"... The Wolf ... old storehouse on river front ... through trap into the water ... old Webb ... Spider Webb ... ten thousand dollar Moorcliffe jewel robbery ... cash box ... safe behind panelling in bedroom directly opposite the door ... false bottom ... afraid of the Wolf ... last few days ... unfinished ... Wolf does not know ... man and wife upstairs ... old couple ... keep house for the Spider ... no suspicion that anything has happened ..." And then, at the end, a more personal, intimate touch: "Jimmie, it is not to save some one else that I have written this to-night, for that is now too late--it is to save *you*. The Wolf is dangerous and I am afraid. You know that he has sworn to trap you. He is cunning, Jimmie--do not underestimate him. That is why I have written this--if you succeed to-night ..."

Jimmie Dale's fingers were tearing the note now into infinitesimal shreds, and, with it, the newspaper clipping. The newspaper itself he crumpled up and tossed into the corner. He crossed the room, replaced the make-up box in its hiding place, put back the movable section of the base-board, turned out the light--and a minute later, Smarlinghue, unkempt, stoop-shouldered, let himself out, not by the French window through which he had entered stealthily in the evening clothes of Jimmie Dale, but unconcernedly, as was the right of any tenant, by the door that opened on the ground-floor passage of the tenement, and shuffled down the street.

The Wolf--and Spider Webb--and Larry the Bat! It was a curious trio! Smarlinghue's lips, perhaps because the wax beneath was not yet moulded comfortably into place, twitched queerly. One of them was dead--the Spider. There remained--the Wolf and Larry the Bat! No, he did not underestimate the Wolf--only a fool, and a blinded fool, would do that. The Wolf had shown his fangs in deadly enough fashion that morning--with a brutal murder, craftily planned, and hellishly executed! And yet the Wolf was quite hopelessly illogical! It was no secret in the underworld that the Wolf and Spider Webb had long worked together, and that the Spider was a close friend of the Wolf. Yet the Wolf had murdered the Spider, and at the same time had found a basis for his oath to end Larry the Bat, because Larry the Bat had been instrumental in handing over to the police a *friend* of the Wolf!

Smarlinghue slouched on along the street, but the "slouch" covered the ground at an amazing rate of speed. He had not far to go--but neither had he a moment that he dared lose. Spider Webb's old antique shop, but a few blocks away, nestled in a squalid little courtyard just west of the Bowery, and on the same side of the Bowery as the Sanctuary.

Some one, out of the shadows of the street, flung him a good-night. Smarlinghue mumbled his acknowledgment from the corner of his mouth, and hurried along.

His thoughts were still on the Wolf. He had not exhausted the sum of the Wolf's digressions from the realms of the logical! In the old days there had been an intimacy even between the Wolf and Larry the Bat. That underground passage from the shed into that queer house near Chatham Square, for instance--which was known only to the *most* intimate! But perhaps the Wolf had forgotten, or perhaps even the Wolf had never known he had been on quite such intimate terms with--Larry the Bat.

Jimmie Dale glanced behind him. There was no one in sight for the moment. He was at the corner of a lane now--and he chose the lane. It was a shorter, and a safer route. It bordered on the rear of the courtyard which was his objective, and obviated the necessity of attempting to steal down past the side of "The Yellow Eastern" unnoticed. No, he did not underestimate the Wolf, but if he had luck to-night--! He shrugged his shoulders in a sort of grim whimsicality.

His mind reverted to the Spider now--Spider Webb. Facetious, in a way, the name was! Webb--Spider Webb! And yet the man had come by it honestly, or dishonestly, enough! The old antique shop for years covered dealings that were shabbier than the shabbiest of its antiques! It was probable that more stolen had found Spider Webb's a clearing house than any other Mecca of the crooks in New York. It was probable, too, that it had known more police raids than any of its competitors--but, unlike many of its competitors, nothing but what indubitably belonged there had ever been found. But then again, the Spider was a specialist--he specialised in small articles, particularly jewelry--no one in the Bad Lands who knew his way about would ever have dreamed of going to the Spider with anything else! Nor was the Spider without justification in thus restricting his operations. The Spider had always managed to hide his questionable wares, until he was able to dispose of them and they passed again out of his possession, with an ingenuity that had baffled, enraged, and mortified the police--and commanded the enthusiastic confidence and admiration of the underworld! But this was, for the most part, past history, and of the days gone by, for the Spider now had grown old--had grown to be an old man-- for it had begun of late to be whispered that he talked more than he had been wont to talk in the days of his prime, that he was not as *safe* as he had been, and in consequence his trade of late had begun to drift away from him.

And herein lay the secret of the old man's murder at the hands of the Wolf. The Tocsin's note had not failed to lay stress on this. No one probably, through a career of half a score of years, knew more about the Wolf and the Wolf's doings than did the Spider. Rightly or wrongly, the word was out that the old man, in his garrulity, was not safe--and the Wolf was inviting no chances where the electric chair was concerned, that was all! The old man would henceforth be perfectly safe, as far as any *talking* went! It was brutal, hideous--but it was the Wolf! Also, the Wolf, tritely expressed, had proposed to kill two birds with one stone. The old man's trade was not entirely gone. Yesterday, an old-time lag, who had dealt with the Spider for many years, and who had "pulled" the Moorcliffe job--the robbery of a summer mansion a few miles up the Hudson--had "fenced" the proceeds at the antique shop. Ten thousand dollars' worth of first-water sparklers! Everybody that was anybody in gangland knew this. The Wolf had seen the psychological and profitable moment to strike--again that was all! And again it was diabolical--but again it was the Wolf!

Jimmie Dale's face was set like flint. And this was the man who had sworn that he would "get" the Gray Seal! A sort of unholy, passionate joy surged upon him. Well, they would see, he and the Wolf--and perhaps to-night! It was certain that the Wolf would act *alone*. The man's devilish cunning showed itself in having inveigled the old man to that storehouse on the river bank, rather than to have killer the Spider in the Spider's own home. It might be days perhaps before the Spider's absence--for the Spider's peculiar life had demanded mysterious absences before--was even commented upon, and the Wolf had taken pains to see that the body was not, immediately at least, identified. It was very simple--from the Wolf's standpoint! The Wolf was counting it none too easy a task evidently to find the Spider's ingenious and storied hiding place, and this would give him a night, two nights, or more, in which, undisturbed, he might prosecute his search. And, as he had committed alone, so he would continue to work alone, there were those even in gangland, and in spite of the acknowledged leadership, who would not look with friendly eyes upon the Wolf for this!

It was black here in the lane, and now, possibly a distance of a hundred yards up from the street, Jimmie Dale's fingers, feeling along the left-hand fence, came upon the latch of a small, narrow door--the courtyard's access to the lane. He passed through, and stood still-- listening--looking sharply about him. He knew the place well. It was the heart and centre, the core of its own particular and vicious section of the underworld. Ahead of him, flanking the two-story, tumble-down building that was the Spider's home, was a narrow alleyway, then a small and filthy court-yard, and, its rear upon this and fronting the street, the alleyway again at the side, the "The Yellow Lantern" that he had been careful to avoid a dance hall of the low-est type. The Spider had not unshrewdly chosen his location; nor the proprietor of "The Yellow Lantern" his--their clientele was a common one, and their interests did not clash!

From the direction of "The Yellow Lantern" came a hilarious uproar, subdued somewhat by the distance, out of which arose the strident notes of a tinny piano beating blatantly the measure of a turkey trot. There was no other sound. There were lights from the rear of the dance hall, enough, Jimmie Dale knew, to throw a murky illumination over the front windows of the antique shop; but there were no lights showing from the Spider's dwelling itself, that loomed black on the side of the alleyway at his right hand--the old couple that kept the Spider's house were doubtless long since in bed in their own particular apartments upstairs.

Jimmie Dale moved softly forward now, gained the back entrance of the Spi-der's house, and tried the door cautiously. It was locked. From one of the little pockets in the girdle under his shirt came a black silk mask, which he slipped over his face; from another of the pockets came a little steel picklock. He was pressed close against the door now, his body merged with the black shadows of the wall. A minute passed--and then the door swung open, and closed without a sound. An-other minute passed, and still another. From upstairs came the sound of stertorous breathing, nothing else, only quiet, and a silence that was heavy in itself--and then the round, white ray of Jimmie Dale's flashlight winked through the blackness. As between himself and the Wolf, he was first, at least, on the ground!

He was in the kitchen of the house. On the opposite side of the room from him were two doors, one of them, the one to the left, open--and the flashlight, playing through, disclosed a passageway leading, obviously, to the shop at the front, and continuing to the stairway. He crossed to the right-hand door noiselessly, opened it, and, with a low ejaculation of satisfaction, stepped in over the threshold. It was the room he sought--the Spider's bedroom, or, better perhaps, the Spider's den that served the man for all purposes. The Spider, it was very plain, was not fastidious! The room was dingy beyond description; the furnishings poor and poverty-stricken in appearance. It was here the Spider met his clients of a sort--and drove his bargains. There was no hint of affluence--the room was miserly.

The flashlight swept in a circle around the room. There was a bed in one corner, a table and two chairs in another, and a miserable washstand in still another. The centre of the room, save for an old carpet on the floor, was quite bare of furnishings. Jimmie Dale's survey of the appointments, however, was most cursory--they concerned him little. The flashlight's ray was even lifted above them, as it moved about. There was only one door--the door by which he had entered; and only one window--which, with a sudden frown, he mentally noted did not open on the alleyway, for the very sufficient reason that the alleyway was on the other side of the house. He stepped quickly to the window, and looked out. It was a moment before he could see; and then, with a quick nod of his head, he began, with extreme caution to loosen the window catches on the sill. There was a narrow space between the house and what was the blank brick wall of the building next to it, and this space extended to the rear, and therefore, indirectly, by circling the house at the back, led to the house and the door in the fence again.

Jimmie Dale smiled grimly, as he swung the old-fashioned windows back on either side. So far he was in luck to-night, and, with luck, in a very few minutes now be out and away from the house by the same way he had entered it--but luck sometimes was a fickle thing, and a goddess most to be trusted by those who looked after themselves!

He walked back to the doorway, and levelled his flashlight across the room directly in front of him. The ray fell upon the wooden panelling, and, holding the light steadily on the same spot, he moved forward across the floor to the opposite wall, dropped on his hands and knees, and began to examine the woodwork critically. It was beautiful work, this panelling that went all around the room, very old, but very beautiful work, and of very beautifully matched wood--it was entirely out of place with the rest of the room, or would have been, were it not that the panelling itself bore witness to the fact that it had been built in there when the house itself had been built, and bore witness, too, to the fact that in those days, long gone by, a relic perhaps even of Dutch handiwork, the house had not been unpretentious amongst its fellows of that generation.

"Behind panelling in bedroom directly opposite the door," she had written. Inch by inch, over an area a yard square, those sensitive finger tips of Jimmie Dale felt their way, lingering here over a knot in the wood, and there over a joint or crevice. Five minutes went by--and the five became ten. An exclamation of annoyance, low, guarded, escaped him. There was nothing--he could find nothing. The Spider's ingenuity had not been over-rated! Somewhere there must be the secret spring which operated the panel, but there was no sign of it; neither was there the slightest sign or indication that any portion of the panelling was even movable.

He drew back for an instant, frowning. Perhaps--and then he shook his head-- no, the Tocsin did not make mistakes of that kind. The safe was unquestionably behind the panelling in front of him. Well, there was a way--it was distasteful to him because it was crude and bungling, but he could afford no more time in a search, that he had already convinced himself was hopeless.

From the girdle came a half dozen little blue-steel tools. A jimmy found and nosed its way into the joint between two panels. There was a low, faint creak of rending wood. A wedge followed the jimmy. A faint creak again--and now one a little louder--and Jimmie Dale, half turned, listened intently--the narrow board was in his hand. There was nothing--no sound--save that interrupted, stertorous breathing from above, and the tinny jangle of the piano from the direction of "The Yellow Lantern."

And now Jimmie Dale smiled again--that curious flicker on his lips that mingled whimsicality and a deadly earnestness. The Tocsin had made no mistake. Showing through the aperture, gleaming under the flashlight's ray, was the nickel dial of a safe. He worked rapidly now. The first panel out, the remainder came much more readily--and finally the entire face of the safe was disclosed. Jimmie Dale stared at it--and pursed his lips. It was an ugly safe, extremely ugly--from a cracksman's point of view! Also, there seemed a hint of irony, a jeer almost, in the impassive wall of steel that confronted him. It was one of his own make--one that had helped, in the old days, to amass the millions that his father had left to him--and it was one of the *best*!

In an abstracted, deliberate way, his eyes pondering the safe, the blue-steel tools were replaced in the pockets of the leather girdle; and then the long, slim, tapering fingers closed upon the dial's knob and twirled it tentatively, and his head bent forward until his ear was pressed hard against the face of the safe.

It was very still now--only the breathing from above that seemed in cadence with those strange and paradoxical palpitations that are known only in a great silence--the piano for the moment had ceased its jangle. Jimmie Dale's fingers, from the dial, sought the floor, and frictioned briskly over the rough, threadbare carpet, until the nerves tingled under the delicate skin--and then they shot to the dial again.

Strained, every faculty keyed up to its highest tension, he crouched there against the safe. Again and again his fingers rubbed over the rough carpet, and again the sweat beads oozed out upon his forehead with the strain--and then there came through the stillness a long-drawn intake of his breath. The handle swung the bolt with a low metallic thud--the safe was open.

There was the inner door now. Again those slim fingers, almost raw, quivering now at the tips, rubbed along the carpet, and the lips, just showing beneath the edge of the mask, grew tight with pain. Then he leaned forward, crouched once more, his head and shoulders inside the outer door, like some strange animal burrowing for its prey. Faint, musical, like some far distant tinkle, came the twirling of the dial--and then, suddenly, he drew back sharply, his hand shot to his pocket, whipped out his automatic, and, motionless there on his knees, every muscle rigid, he listened. There was the piano again, the breathing, the weird pound and thump of the silence--nothing else. He shook his head in half angry, half tolerant self-remonstrance. He was under strain, that was all--he had thought he had heard a footstep out there in the alleyway. He laid his automatic on the floor within instant reach, and turned again to the safe--acute and sensitive as his hearing was, it would haw taken good ears indeed to have distinguished a step at that distance on the other side of the house!

But now he worked, seemingly at least, with even greater rapidity than before. Imagination had had one effect, if it had had no other--it was a spur, a reminder that at any moment there might well be a footstep, and one that was born only of the imagination! His jaws clamped. He had not counted on this--an old-fashioned iron monstrosity that was dismaying only in its appearance, perhaps--but not this! He had been here far longer now than he--

'Ah'--tense, low, that deep intake of the breath again.

The inner door swung wide; the flashlight's ray leaped, dazzling white, into the interior, and, on the lower shelf, upon a flat, narrow, black tin box--the cash-box.

In an instant, Jimmie Dale had picked it up. It was not locked, and he lifted the cover. From within there scintillated back the gleam of diamonds--a handful of pendants, brooches, ear-rings lay there disclosed, and, too, a string of pearls. Ten thousand dollars! It was a modest figure! He reached his hand inside the box--and on the instant snatched it back, and thrust the box swiftly into his pocket. The flashlight was out. The room was in darkness.

This time it was not imagination--nor, he knew now, had it been imagination before. There was a faint creak of the flooring in the kitchen, a single incautious step that he placed as having come from near the doorway of the passage--and now some one had halted on the threshold of the room itself. Jimmie Dale's brain was working with lightning speed. There had been no time to reach the window--time only to snatch up his automatic and retreat a little from the immediate vicinity of the safe. Had the other heard the slight sound--it was only the brushing of his coat against the wall! Much less had there been time to close the safe--nor would it have done any good--he could not have replaced the broken panelling! And now--*what*? The man, with a stealth that he, Jimmie Dale, except for that one incautious footfall, could not have excelled, must have entered through a window from the alleyway into the passage. It was dark, utterly dark--save that the window showed dimly like a faint transparent square set in the blackness.

He could not see, but he could *sense* the other standing there in the doorway, motionless, silent, as though listening. Perhaps a minute passed. There was something nerve-racking now in the silence, something sinister, something pregnant with menace. And then, suddenly, there came a low, scratching sound, and a match flame spurted through the darkness, and lighted up a face--a face that was thrust forward through the doorway with a sort of pent-up and malicious eagerness; a vicious face, with sharp, restive black eyes under great, hairy eyebrows; a face with a huge jaw, outflung now, that was like the jaw of a beast. It was the Wolf!

CHAPTER X
THE CHASE

I t held for the fraction of a second, that light--no more. It travelled upward past the face, as though the Wolf were holding it above his head to get his bearings; and then, with a sharp and furious oath, the match was hurled to the floor, there was a scuffling sound-- and then silence again.

Jimmie Dale's automatic was thrust a little forward in his hand, as he crouched against the wall. He could have shot the man, as the other stood in the doorway. The Wolf had offered a target that it would have been hard to miss--and it would, one day, have saved the law the same task! He was a fool, perhaps, that he had not taken what was, perhaps again, the one chance he had for his life, for he was at a decided disadvantage now, since he knew intuitively that the Wolf, scuttling back, had now craftily protected himself behind the jamb of the door, and yet at the same time still commanded the interior of the room. But he could not have fired in cold blood like that--even upon the Wolf, devil though the man was, murderer a dozen times over though he the man to be! He, Jimmie Dale, had never shot to *kill* not yet--but in a fight, cornered, if there was no other way...!

He moved a little, a bare few inches, then a few more--without a sound. In the light of the match, the Wolf must have seen the dismantled panelling and the open safe, and a masked figure crouched against the wall--and the Wolf would have marked the position of that crouched figure against the wall!

Silence--a minute of it--still another!

Again Jimmie Dale moved inch by inch--toward the window. And yet to attempt the window was to invite a shot and expose himself, for, dark as it was, his body would show plainly enough against the background of that lesser gloom of window square.

Jimmie Dale's eyes strained through the blackness across the room. He could just make out the configuration of the doorway. The Wolf was just on the other side of it, just inside the kitchen, he was sure of that. Almost a smile was flickering over Jimmie Dale's tight-pressed lips. There was a way--there was a way now, if the Wolf did not get him with a chance shot. He moved again, and reached the window, crouched low beneath the sill--and passed by the window.

And then the Wolf spoke from the doorway in a hoarse whisper, and in the whisper there was a low, taunting laugh.

"I been waitin' for you to try the window, but you're too foxy--eh? All right, my bucko--then I'll get you another way--with just one shot, see? And then--*goodnight*! And say, whoever t'hell you are, thanks for crackin' the box for me!"

The man's voice came from the *right* of the doorway--and the door opened *inward*--and he, Jimmie Dale, remembered that he had opened it *wide*. It was slow, very slow, this creeping inch by inch through the darkness. It seemed as though his breath were as stertorous as that breathing from above, and that the Wolf must hear.

And then the Wolf laughed low again.

There was a curious crackling noise, as of paper being torn--and then, quick, in the doorway, came a yellow flame, and the Wolf's hand showed from around the edge of the jamb, and, making momentary daylight of the room, a flaming piece of paper, tossed in, fell upon the floor.

There was a flash, the roar of the report--and another--as the Wolf fired! There was the sullen *spat* of a bullet upon the panelling an inch from Jimmie Dale's head--and a sharp and sudden pain, as though a hot iron had seared his leg.

And now Jimmie Dale's automatic, too, cut flashes with its vicious flame-tongues through the black. Coolly, steadily, he was firing at the doorway--to hold the Wolf there--to keep the Wolf now in the position of the Wolf's own choosing. The paper was but a dull cinder in the centre of the room; twisted too tightly, it had gone out almost immediately.

There came screams, loud, terrified, in a woman's voice from the floor above--and the hoarser tones of a man shouting. A window was flung open. Snarling blasphemous, furious oaths, the Wolf was firing at the flashes of Jimmie Dale's revolver--but each time as Jimmie Dale fired, the sound drowned in the roar of the report, he moved a good yard forward.

Came the trampling of feet from overhead now; and now, as the woman still screamed, answering shouts and yells came from the dance hall. Jimmie Dale had the foot of the bed now near the corner. He again, and instantly flung himself flat upon the floor--and, in the answering flash of the Wolf's shot, placed the exact location of the **door** itself. There was tumult enough now to deaden the slight sound he made. He crept swiftly past the bed to the wall, against which the door, wide open, was swung back, felt out with his hand, the edge of the door, and, leaping suddenly to his feet, hurled the door shut upon the Wolf. There was a scream of pain--the door as it slammed perhaps had caught the Wolf's arm or wrist--but before it was opened again Jimmie Dale was across the room, and, flinging himself through the window, dropped to the ground.

The door crashing back against the wall again, the Wolf's baffled yell of rage, and an abortive shot, told him that his ruse had been solved. He was running now, as rapidly as he could in the darkness and in the narrow space between the Spider's house and the wall of the brick building. Yells in increasing volume sounded from the direction of "The Yellow Lantern"; and now he could hear the pound of feet racing across the courtyard toward the antique shop. The woman, from the open window above, was still screaming with terror.

If he could gain the door in the fence--and the lane! But there was still the Wolf to reckon with! The Wolf had only to run through the kitchen and out by the back entrance--the shorter distance of the two. But the Wolf had already lost a few seconds so that now the race was a gamble. Could he, Jimmie Dale, get there **first**! He could not run in the other direction--that would take him into the courtyard, and the courtyard now, as evidenced by the yells and shouting, was filled with an excited crowd emptying from the dance hall.

He reached the rear end of the house, and darted across the wider space here, racing for the opening in the fence--and suddenly changed his tactics, and began to zigzag a little. A revolver flash cut the night. Came the Wolf's howl from the back stoop, and, over his shoulder, Jimmie Dale saw the other, dark-shadowed, leap forward in pursuit--and heard the Wolf fire again.

He flung himself against the fence door, and it gave with a crash. Pandemonium reigned behind him. In a blur he saw the courtyard, that was dimly lighted now by the open doors and open windows of the dance hall, swaying with shapes, and, like ghostly figures, a mob tearing toward him down the alleyway.

The Wolf's voice, punctuated with a torrent of blasphemy and vile invective, shrilled out over the tumult:

"Come on! Here he is! Out in the lane!"

"Who is it?" shrilled another voice.

"I don't know!" yelled the Wolf. "Catch him, and we'll damn soon find out!"

Jimmie Dale was running like a hare now down the lane. The Wolf leading, still firing, the crowd poured out into the lane in pursuit. Jimmie Dale zigzagged no longer, there was greater risk in that than in risking the shots--it was black enough in the lane to risk the shots; but his lead, barely twenty-five yards, was too short to risk their gaining upon him through his running from side to side.

His brain, cool in peril, worked swiftly. The Sanctuary! That was the one chance for his life! He had been no more than a masked figure huddled against the wall of the room in there. The Wolf had not recognised him. He would be safe if he could reach the Sanctuary! There were two blocks to go along the street ahead, then the next lane, and from that into the intersecting lane, the loose board in the fence that swung at a touch, the French window--and the Sanctuary. But to accomplish this he must *gain* upon his pursuers, not merely hold his own, but increase the distance between them by at least another fifteen or twenty yards; he must, in other words, be out of range of vision as he disappeared through the fence. Well, he should be able to do that! It was the trained athlete against an ill-conditioned, dissolute mob!

He swerved from the lane into the street. There was grim and hellish humour in the thought that a *wolf* should be leading the snarling, howling pack, blood mad now, at his heels! The Wolf had ceased firing--obviously because the Wolf's revolver was empty. The others, a lesser breed, and previously intent on a peaceful orgy at the dance hall, were evidently not armed.

Jimmie Dale gained five yards, another five, and another ten. He had no fear of being recognised as Smarlinghue even here, where, poorly illuminated as the street was, it was like bright sunlight compared with the darkness of the lane. There was no stooped, bent figure, no slouching gait--there was, instead, a tall, broad-shouldered man, whose face was masked, and who ran with the speed of a greyhound, and whose automatic, spitting ahead of him as he ran, invited none of the few pedestrians, or those rushing to their doorways, to block his path.

He swerved again, into a lane again, the lane he had been making for; and, as he swerved, he flung a sidelong glance down the street. Yes, his twenty-five yards were fifty now, except for the Wolf, who ran perhaps ten yards in advance of any of the others. The howls, yells, shouts and execrations welled into a louder outburst as he dashed into the lane. Ten from fifty left forty. Forty yards clear! It was a very narrow margin, even allowing for the blackness of the lane--but it was enough--it was slightly more than the distance along the intersecting lane to the rear of the Sanctuary--he would have pushed aside that loose board before the Wolf turned the corner from one lane into the other!

Forty yards! Perhaps he could make it forty-five! Forty-five would be *safer*; and--he reeled suddenly, and staggered, and, with a low cry, his hands reached upward to his temples. His head was swimming--a dizziness, a nausea was upon him--his strength seemed as it were being sapped from his limbs. What was it? He--yes--the wound in his leg! Yes--he remembered now--that burning like the searing of a hot iron. He had forgotten it in the excitement. But it could not amount to anything--or he would not have been able to have come this far. It was only a passing giddiness--he was better now--see, he was still running--he had only slowed his pace for an instant--that was all.

They swept into the lane behind him. He looked back--and his lips grew tight, and bitter hard. It was no longer forty yards--he was *not* running so fast now--and it was the Wolf, and the Wolf's pack, who were gaining.

He swerved for the third time--into the stretch of intersecting lane. The Sanctuary was just ahead, but he must reach that loose board in the fence and have disappeared before the Wolf swung around the corner behind him--or else--or else, since that led to nowhere to the French window of Smarlinghue's room, the game was as good as up if he attempted it!

He strained forward, striving to mass his strength and fling it into one supreme effort. He was close now--only another five yards to go. Yes--he was weak. His teeth set. Four yards--three! If only there were not that glimmer of light, faint as it was, seeping down the lane from the street lamp across the road from the Sanctuary! Two yards--now! No! The Wolf's yell, as the man tore around the corner of the two lanes, rang out like a knell of doom.

Drawn, white-faced, Jimmie Dale, stumbling now, lurched past that loose board he had counted upon for what was literally his life--lurched past, and stumbled on. He could not run much farther. There was one chance left--just one--that there should be no one to see him enter the *front* door of the Sanctuary, no one lounging about, no one in the tenement doorway. If that chance failed--well, then it was the end-- *the* end of Smarlinghue, the end of Jimmie Dale, the end of Larry the Bat, the end of the Gray Seal--and the Wolf would have kept his pledge to gangland. But it would be an end that gangland would long remember, and an end that the Wolf would share!

The street was just before him now. He turned into it--and there came a little cry, a moan almost, of relief. The doorway of the tenement was *clear*. He sprang for it, entered, and, suddenly silent now in his tread, reached the door of his own room, slipped through and closed it softly behind him.

And now Jimmie Dale worked with frantic speed. He could hear them racing, yelling, shouting along the lane. A match crackled in his hand, and the gas-jet spluttered into flame--the light in the room could not be seen from the lane. He ran across the room, tearing off his mask as he went, and, wrenching the cash-box from his pocket, tucked mask and cash-box behind the disordered array of dirty canvases on the floor--he dared not take the risk or the time that loosening the base board would entail. He flung his hat into a corner, and, ripping off his coat, tossed it upon the cot; then, snatching up a paint tube, he smeared a daub of paint upon the palette that lay on the table, and laid a wet brush hurriedly several times across the canvas on the easel.

From the corner of the lane and street outside came the scuffling to and fro of many feet, as though in uncertainty, in indecision, in hesitancy. A dozen voices spoke at once, high-pitched, wild, frenzied.

"Where is he?... Which way did he go?... Where--"

And then the Wolf's voice, above the rest, in a sudden, excited yell:

"What's that across there! It's him! There he is! He's kept on up the lane! He's--"

The voice was lost in a chorus of shouts, in the pound and stampede of racing feet again, of the pack in cry. The sounds receded and died in the distance. Jimmie Dale drew his hand across his forehead and brought it away damp with sweat. He staggered now to the wash-stand, and from the drawer took out a bottle of brandy, and, heedless of glass, uncorked it, and lifted it to his lips. He would never know a closer call! He had been weaker than he had thought! Thank God for the brandy! The fiery stimulant was whipping the blood in his veins into life again, and--the bottle was still held to his lips, but he was no longer drinking. His eyes were on the washstand's mirror. He heard no sound, but in the mirror he saw the door of his room open, close again, and, leaning with his back against it-- *the Wolf!*

Not a muscle of Jimmie Dale's face moved. He allowed another gulp of brandy to gurgle noisily down his throat. The cool, alert, keen brain was at work. It was certain that the Wolf had at no time that night recognised him as Smarlinghue. The Wolf, therefore, at worst, could be no more than *gambling* on the chance that the object of the chase had taken refuge here in the tenement, and, naturally enough then, was beginning his investigation with the ground floor room. And yet, why then had the Wolf, deliberately in that case, sent his pack off on a false scent? In the mirror he could see that huge jaw outthrust, the black eyes narrowed, an ugly leer on the working face--and a revolver in the Wolf's hand that held a bead on his, Jimmie Dale's, head.

It was "Smarlinghue," the wretched, nervous, drug-wrecked creature that turned around--and, as though startled at the sight of the other, almost let the bottle fall from his hand.

"So it was you--eh--Smarlinghue! Curse you!" snarled the Wolf. "Come out here, and stand in the centre of the room!"

Smarlinghue cringed. He put down the bottle with a trembling hand, and slouched forward.

"I ain't done nothing!" he whined.

"No, you ain't done a thing--except crack a box and pinch about ten thousand dollars' worth of sparklers!" The Wolf's face, if possible, was more ugly in its threat than before.

Smarlinghue, in a sort of stupefied amazement, stared around the room--as though he expected to see a gleaming heap of diamonds leap into sight somewhere before him. He shook his head helplessly.

"I don't know what you're talking about," he mumbled. "I--I heard a row outside there a little while ago. Maybe that's it."

"Yes-- *mabbe* it is!" sneered the Wolf viciously. "So you don't know anything about it--eh? You've got a hell of a good memory, haven't you! You don't know anything about the Spider's safe, or about a little fight in the Spider's room, or about jumping out of the window, and beating it for here with the gang after you--no, you don't! You never heard of it before--of course, you didn't!"

Smarlinghue began to wring his hands nervously one over the other. He shook his head helplessly again.

"It wasn't me!" He licked his lips. "Honest, it wasn't me! I--I don't know what you're talking about. I ain't been out of this room. Honest! Somebody's trying to put me in wrong. I tell you, I ain't been out of here all night. I--look!" With sudden, feverish eagerness, as though from an inspiration, he pointed to the paint brush, the palette, and the canvas on the easel. "Look! Look for yourself! You can see for yourself! I've been painting."

And then the Wolf laughed--and it was not a pleasant laugh.

"Yes, you've been painting!" he jeered. "Sure, you have! I know that! Only you've been *painting* a damned sight more than you thought you were!"

The revolver muzzle covered Jimmie Dale steadily, unswervingly; in the Wolf's face was malicious and sardonic mockery--but the Wolf's eyes were no longer on Jimmie Dale's face, they seemed curiously intent upon the floor at Jimmie Dale's feet. Mechanically Jimmie Dale followed their direction--and his eyes, too, held on the floor. For a moment neither spoke. *The game was up*! His boot top was soaked with blood, and, trickling down the side of the boot, a little crimson stream was collecting in a pool upon the floor.

"You *painted* some of that on the doorstep!" The Wolf's taunting laugh held a deadly menace. "And you painted a drop or two of it along the street as you ran. I thought when you bust away from the Spider's and that cursed gang nosed in that I was going to lose out; but I figured that I had hit you, and I was keeping my eyes skinned to see. And then you commenced to do the drip act--savvy? I was still look-ing for it when I came out of the lane--you remember, Smarlinghue, don't you?--you got your memory back, ain't you?--that I was a bit ahead of the rest of 'em? It didn't take a second to spot that on the doorstep, and there's some more of it in the hall. Damned queer, ain't it--that it led right to Smarlinghue's room!" The laugh was gone. The Wolf began to come forward across the room. The snarl was in his voice again. "You come across with those sparklers, and you come across--*quick*!"

But now Smarlinghue was like a crazed and demented creature, and he shook his fists at the Wolf.

"I won't! I won't!" he screamed. "You went there to do the same thing! I had as much right as you! And I *got* them--I *got* them! They said he had them there, they were all talking about them to-day, and I *got* them! I won! They're mine now! I won't give them to you! I won't! I tell you, I won't!"

"Won't you?" The Wolf had reached Jimmie Dale, and one of the Wolf's hands found and shook Jimmie Dale's throat, while the revolver muzzle pressed hard against Jimmie Dale's breast. "Oh, I guess you will! D'ye hear about a man being murdered to-day with his face cut up? Oh, you did--eh? Well, I happen to know that man was the Spider, and one of these days, mabbe, the police'll tumble to who it was, too. Get me? Suppose I call some of that gang back, and show 'em the *painting* you've done along the hall--eh? And then, by and by, when the bulls get wise, it'll be yours for the juice route, not just a space or two for cracking a box! Get me again?"

Smarlinghue, struggling weakly, pulled the other's hand from his throat.

"You--you were there, too, at--at the Spider's," he choked craftily. "You're--you're in it as--as bad as I am."

"Sure, I was there!" mocked the Wolf, and snatched at Jimmie Dale's throat again. "Sure, I was there--everybody saw me! The Spider was a *friend* of mine, and everybody knows that, too. I was just going there to pay a pal a little visit--see? And that's how I found you there--see? Anything wrong with that spiel? It's a cinch, aint it?" The fingers closed tighter and tighter on Jimmie Dale's throat. "And that's enough talk--give me them sparklers!" He flung Jimmie Dale savagely away. "Get 'em!"

Smarlinghue reeled backward in the direction of the disordered canvases on the floor. It was quite true! If the Wolf carried out his threat--which he most certainly would do if he did not get the diamonds for himself--Smarlinghue, and not the Wolf, would be held for the Spider's murder. Jimmie Dale stooped, fumbled amongst the canvases, and produced the cash-box. Well, the diamonds would have to go, that was all--he had no choice left to him. But he was still "Smarlinghue," still the half cowed, yet half defiant, pale-faced creature that shook with mingled rage and fear, as he turned again. He clutched the cash-box to him, as though loath to let it go; but, too, as though fascinated by the Wolf's revolver, he moved reluctantly toward the Wolf, who now stood by the table.

Smarlinghue's hands twined and twined over the box, caressing it in hideous greed and avarice; and he mumbled, and his lips worked.

"Half--give me half?" he whispered feverishly.

"I'll give you-- ***nothing***!" snarled the Wolf.

"Half--give me a quarter then?" whimpered Smarlinghue.

"***Drop it***!" The Wolf's revolver jerked forward into Jimmie Dale's face.

And then Smarlinghue screamed out in impotent rage, and, wrenching the cover of the cash-box open, flung the jewels in a glittering heap upon the table-- and, dancing in demented fashion upon his toes, like a man gone mad, he hurled the cash-box in fury from him. It went through the canvas on the easel, and clattered to the floor.

The Wolf laughed.

But Smarlinghue had retreated now, and, crouched upon the cot, was mumbling through twisted lips.

And again the Wolf laughed, and, gathering up the jewels, dropped them into his pocket, and backed to the door. He stood there an instant, his eyes narrowed on Jimmie Dale.

"I got the stuff now"--he was snarling low, viciously--"and mabbe that puts it a little more up to me. But if you ever open your mug about this, I'll do to you what I did to the Spider to-day--and if you want to know what that is, go and ask the police to let you have a look! D'ye understand?"

Came the brutal, taunting laugh again, and the door closed behind the Wolf, and his step died away along the passage, and rang an instant later on the pavement without.

It was a moment before Jimmie Dale moved--but into Smarlinghue's distorted features there came a strange smile. He reeled a little from weakness, as he walked to the door, locked it, and, returning, stooped and picked up the cash-box from the floor. In the false bottom, the Tocsin had said. From the leather girdle came a sharp-pointed tool. He pried with it for an instant inside and around the bottom edges, and loosening a sheet of metal that fitted exactly to the edges of the box, lifted out from beneath it several folded sheets of paper. He glanced at the typewritten sheets, a curious, menacing gleam creeping into the dark eyes, then thrust the papers inside his shirt; and, dropping into a chair, unlaced and kicked off his blood-soaked boot.

He was very weak; he had lost, he must have lost, a great deal of blood--but there was something to do yet--still something to do. There was still--the Wolf!

He tore the sheet on the cot into strips, and washed and dressed his wound--a flesh wound, but bad enough, he saw, just above the knee. And then, this done, he took a damp piece of cloth, went to the door again, opened it, and looked out. There was neither any one in sight, nor any sound. The passage was murky; one gas-jet alone lighted it, and that was turned down. There were little spots, dark spots on the floor--but the Wolf had told him that. He passed his hand over his head--he was a little dizzy. Then slowly, laboriously, he removed the spots from the hallway--and one from the doorstep.

Back in his room once more, he locked the door again. A sense of utter exhaustion was stealing upon him--but there was still something yet to be done. Another gulp of brandy steadied him, steadied his head. He took the papers from his pocket and read them now. Here were the details, minute, exact, with the names of those involved, names of those who would squeal quickly enough to save themselves once they were in the clutches of the law, of two of the most famous murder mysteries that New York had known; the details of two, and, unfinished, the partial details of another. It was the evidence the police had long sought. It was the death sentence upon the Wolf--for murder.

Jimmie Dale's face, very white now, was set and hard. The Spider had been too late--to save himself. Beginning to fear the Wolf, as the Tocsin had explained, he had begun to make a record of those days gone by, meaning to hold it over the Wolf's head in self-protection, deposit it somewhere where it would come to light if any attack were made upon him--only the Wolf had struck before the Spider had finished all he had meant to write, before he had told any one or had warned the Wolf that the papers were in existence. Too late to save himself--and yet, if the Wolf still paid the penalty for murder, did it matter if he were *convicted* for the taking of another life than that of Spider Webb! It was like some grim, retributive proxy! The Spider, at least, had not been too late--for that!

For a moment longer, Jimmie Dale sat there, staring at the papers in his hand.

They were unsigned, the Spider's name nowhere appeared--the Spider had been crafty enough to deal only with crimes in which he had had no personal share. There was nothing, not even handwriting, as the papers now stood, to intimate that they had emanated from the Spider; and therefore, in their disclosure, there could be no suspicion in the Wolf's mind that they bore any relation to this night's work. Nor would the Wolf, tried for another crime, ever mention this night's work. It would be the last thing the Wolf would do. The Wolf had double-crossed the underworld, and the underworld, if it found it out, would not easily forgive--and even in a death cell, clinging to the hope of commutation of sentence, the Wolf would never run the risk of his additional guilt of the Spider's murder leaking out. The role of "Smarlinghue" in the underworld was safe.

And now Jimmie Dale's lips twitched queerly. The papers were unsigned. He took from the leather girdle the thin metal box, the tweezers, and a diamond-shaped, adhesive, gray paper seal--and, holding the seal with the tweezers, he moistened it with his tongue, and pressed it down upon the lower sheet. It was signed now! Signed with a signature that the police-- *and the Wolf*--knew well!

He rose unsteadily, and, taking the empty cash-box, loosened the base-board from the wall near the door, hid the cash-box away, and felt through the pockets of his evening clothes--there was a blank envelope there, he remembered, in which he had placed some memoranda--an envelope, and the little gold pencil in his dress waistcoat pocket. He found them, and, kneeling on the floor, printing the letters, he addressed the envelope to police headquarters, folded and placed the documents inside, and sealed the envelope.

He replaced the base-board, and stood up--but his hand caught at the wall to support himself.

"To-morrow," said Jimmie Dale weakly--he was groping his way back across the room to the cot "I--I guess I'm all--all in--to-night."

CHAPTER XI
THE VOICES OF THE UNDERWORLD

Futility! And on top of futility, a week of inaction, thanks to that flesh wound in his leg. Futility seemed to haunt, yes, and torture him! Even his rehabilitation of Larry the Bat, with all its attendant risk and danger, had been futile as far as *she* was concerned. And he had counted so much on that! And that had failed, and nothing was left to him but to pursue again the one possible chance of success, the hope that somewhere in the innermost depths of the Bad Lands he might pick up the clue he sought. And so, to-night, he was listening again to the voices of the underworld--and so far he had heard nothing but ominous mutterings, proof that the sordid denizens of crimeland were more than usually disturbed. The Wolf had gone to join his *friend* Frenchy Virat in the Tombs! The twisted lips of the underworld whispered the name of the Gray Seal!

Jimmie Dale's fingers, twitching, simulating even in that little detail the drug-wrecked role of Smarlinghue that he played, clutched with a sort of hideous eagerness at the hypodermic syringe which he held in his hands. How many times, here in Foo Sen's, or in other lairs that were but the counterpart of Foo Sen's, had he lain, stretched out, a pretended victim to a vice that robbed his face of colour, that shook his miserably clad body, that clouded his eyes and stole from them the light of reason--*while he listened*! How many times--and how many times in the days to come would he do it again! Would it never be his, the secret that he sought--the clue that would divulge the identity of those who threatened the Tocsin's life; those who, like human wolves, like a hell-pack snarling for its prey, had driven her again into hiding and made of her a hunted thing!

The fingers closed convulsively over the hypodermic. Wolves! A hell-pack! A tinge of red dyed the grey-white, hollowed cheeks, as a surge of fury swept upon him. No, it was not futility; no, it was not wasted effort--this haunting of the dens of the underworld! In his soul he knew that some day he would pick up the trail of that hell-pack and those human wolves--and when that some day came it would be a day of reckoning, and the price that he would exact would not be small!

He lay back on the bunk that Foo Sen had ingratiatingly allotted him. The air was close, heavy with the sweet, sickish smell of opium, and full of low, strange sounds and noises. And these sounds, in their composite sense, emanating from un-seen sources, were as the ominous and sinister evidence of some foul and grotesque presence; analysed, they resolved themselves into the swish of hangings, the swish of slippered, shuffling feet, the stertorous breathing of a sleeper, the clink of coin as of men at play, the tinkle of glass, the murmur of voices, the restive stir of reclining bodies, whisperings.

And now he looked about him through half closed eyes. He was in a little compartment, whose doorway was a faded and stained hanging of flowered cre-tonne, and whose walls were but flimsy-boarded affairs that partitioned him off from like compartments on either side. It was very near to the pulse of the under-world. Above ground, opening on a street just off Chatham Square, Foo Sen's, to the uninitiated, was but one of the multitudinous Chinese laundries in New York; below, below even the innocent cellar of the house, a half dozen sub-cellars were merged into one, and here Foo Sen plied his trade. And Foo Sen was cosmopolitan in his wares! Here, one, hard pressed, might find refuge from the law; here a pipe and pill were at one's command; here one might hide his stolen goods, or hatch his projected crime, or gamble, or debauch at will--it was the entree only that was hard to obtain at Foo Sen's!

Jimmie Dale's lips twisted in a grim smile. The old days of Larry the Bat had supplied Smarlinghue with the means which, in the last six months, had been turned to such good account that the Smarlinghue of to-day was almost as fully in the confidence of the underworld as had been the Larry the Bat of yesterday. And yet there had been nothing! No clue! He had wormed himself again into the inner circle of crimeland; he lay here in Foo Sen's to-night, as he had once lain in one of Foo Sen's competitor's dives as Larry the Bat, months ago, on the night the place had been raided--but there was still nothing--still no clue--only the shuffle of slip-pered feet, the stertorous breathings, a subdued curse, a blasphemous laugh, a coin ringing upon a table top, the murmur of voices, whisperings!

One might hear many things here if one listened, and he **had** heard many things in his frequent visits to these hidden dens of this lower world that shunned the daylight--many things, but never the **one** thing that he risked his life to hear--many things, from these **friends** of his who, if in Smarlinghue they but suspected for an instant the presence of Larry the Bat, would literally have torn him limb from limb--many things, but never the one thing, never a word of **her**--many things, the hatching of crime, as now, for instance, those muttering voices were hatching it from the other side of the partition next to his bunk. Subconsciously he had caught a word here and there, and now, without a sound, he edged his shoulders nearer to the partition until his ear was pressed close against a crack. It did not concern **her**, but he listened now intently.

"Aw, ferget it!" a voice rasped in a hoarse undertone. "Sure, I saw it! Ain't I just told youse I saw Curley hand de dough over dis afternoon! Fifteen thousand dollars all in big new bills, five-hundred-dollar bills I t'ink dey was--dat's wot!"

"How d'youse know it was fifteen thousand?" demanded another voice.

There was a short, vicious laugh; then the voice of the first speaker again:

"'Cause I heard him say so, an' de old guy counted it, an' sealed it up in an envelope, an' gave Curley a receipt, an' tucked de green boys into de safe. Aw, say, dere's nothin' to it, I can open dat old tin box wid a toothpick!"

"Mabbe youse can, but mabbe de stuff ain't dere now--mabbe it's in de bank," demurred the second voice.

"Don't youse worry! It's dere! Where else would it be! Ain't I told youse it was near five o'clock when I went dere--an' dat's after de banks are closed, ain't it? Well, wot d'youse say?"

"I don't like pinchin' any of Curley's money." The second speaker's voice was still further lowered. "It ain't healthy ter hand Curley anything."

"Who's handin' Curley anything!" retorted the other. "It ain't got nothin' to do wid Curley. It ain't Curley's money any more. He paid it over for whatever he's blowin' himself on, an' he's got his receipt for it. It's none of his funeral after dat! How's he goin' to lose anything if we lift de cash? An' if he ain't goin' to lose nothin', wot's he goin' to care! Ferget it! Wot's de matter wid youse!"

There was a moment's apparent hesitancy; then, hoarsely:

"Youse are sure, eh, dat nobody saw youse dere?"

"Say, youse have got de chilly feet fer fair ter-night, ain't youse! Well, can it! No, dey didn't pipe me, youse can bet yer life on dat. I was goin' inter de office w'en I hears some spielin' goin' on inside, an' I opens de door a crack, an' I keeps it open like dat--savvy? An' w'en de old guy shoots de ready inter de box, an' I makes me fade-away, I didn't shut de door hard enough ter bust de glass panels, neither--see? Dat's de story, an' it's on de level. I beats it den, an' I been huntin' fer youse ever since. Now, wot d'youse say--are youse on?"

"Sure!" The second speaker's voice had lost its hesitancy now; it was gruff, as- sured, even eager. "Sure! I guess youse have pulled a winner, all right! Wot's de lay? Have youse doped it out?"

"Ask me!" responded the other, with a complacent chuckle. "Youse look after de old guy, dat's all youse have ter do. Hook up wid him, an' keep him busy at his house. Get me? De old nut has a crazy notion of goin' down ter de office in de mid- dle of de night sometimes, an' dere's no use takin' any chances. Youse can put up some hard luck story on him, throw in a weep, an' youse got his goat fer as long as youse can talk. Leave de rest ter me. Only, say, youse keep away from me fer de rest of de night--get me? Dey might smell a plant after youse bein' wid him. Youse go somewhere to an all-night joint so's youse have an alibi all de way through, an'--"

The voice ceased abruptly. In a flash the left sleeve of Jimmie Dale's ragged, threadbare coat was pushed up, leaving the forearm exposed. The hypodermic nee- dle pricked the flesh. There was no sound of any step; but the cretonne hanging wavered almost imperceptibly, as though some one, or perhaps but a current of air from the passage without, had swayed it slightly. Jimmie Dale was mumbling inco- herently to himself now; his lips, like his fingers, working in nervous twitches. A few seconds passed--a half minute. Still mumbling, Jimmie Dale, with a caress like that of a miser for his gold, was fondling the shining little instrument in his hand-- and then the hanging was suddenly thrust aside.

Jimmie Dale neither looked up, nor appeared to be conscious of any one's pres- ence--but he had already recognised the voices of the two men from the adjoining compartment, who, he was quite well aware, were staring in at him now. The small- er, with sharp, cunning, beady, black eyes, the prime mover in the scheme that had just been outlined, was a clever and dangerous "box-worker,", known as the Rat;

the other, a heavy, vicious-faced man, with eyes quite as beady and unpleasant as those of his companion, was Muggy Ladd, who made his living as a "stagehand" for those, such as the Rat, who were more gifted than himself.

"Satisfied?" inquired the Rat "He's full up to de eyes wid it now. Foo said he'd been hittin' it up hard fer de last hour." The Rat addressed Jimmie Dale. "Hello, Smarly!" he called out.

Jimmie Dale lifted his head, and blinked at the cretonne hanging.

"Lemme alone!" he complained thickly. "Go 'way, an' lemme alone!"

"Sure!" said the Rat genially. "Sure, we will! Sweet dreams, Smarly!"

The hanging fell back into place. Jimmie Dale continued to blink at it, and mumble to himself. The Rat's pleasant little plan of robbing somebody's safe of fifteen thousand dollars had nothing to do with *her*--but it involved a moral obligation on his part that he had neither the right nor the intention to ignore. And the fulfilment, or the attempt at fulfilment, of that obligation had suddenly assumed unexpected difficulties. Even while he had listened, and before the Rat was halfway through his story, he, Jimmie Dale, was conscious that he had made up his mind the Rat would rob no safe of fifteen thousand dollars that night if he could prevent it, and he had intended following the Rat from Foo Sen's. He dared not do that now. Muggy Ladd's cautiousness, that had evidently induced the Rat to inspect his, Jimmie Dale's, compartment, had made that impossible. The Rat had seen him there; and, forced to the deception in order to avert any suspicion that he had overheard the others' conversation, the Rat had seen him in the condition of one who was apparently already far gone under the influence of drug. To risk the attempt to follow the Rat now, to risk discovery by the Rat, was to risk, not only the admission that he had been playing a part, but to risk what he had fought for and staked his life for months now to establish--the role, the character of "Smarlinghue" in the underworld. Nor, for the same reason, would he dare move from the place for some little time--there was Foo Sen and the attendants.

Jimmie Dale dropped his head down on the bunk, turned heavily over, facing the partition, and flung his arm across his face. His lips had ceased their nervous working; they were drawn together, thin and hard now. It was bad enough to be forced to remain temporarily inactive, though that in itself was not so serious, for it was still early, not much more than nine o'clock, and it was only fair to presume that the Rat would make no move for some hours to come; but what was much more serious was the fact that, unable to follow the Rat, he would be obliged to solve for himself the problem of whose was the safe, and whose the fifteen thousand dollars that was the Rat's objective. The Rat had referred to "the old guy"--that meant nothing. "Curley," however, was a little better--Curley, who had paid over the money to the "old guy."

Jimmie Dale's forehead, hidden by his arm, furrowed deeply. From Muggy Ladd's initial objection to touching anything that concerned Curley, it could mean only one Curley. He, Jimmie Dale, knew this Curley by sight, and, slightly, by reputation. Curley and his partner, Haines, kept a small wholesale liquor store in one of the most populous, where all were populous, quarters of the East Side; also Curley had a pull as a ward politician, which might very readily account for Muggy Ladd's diffidence; and Curley was credited with doing a thriving business--both ways--as ward heeler and liquor purveyor. Certainly, at least, he was known always to have money; and had even been known at times to lend it freely to those in want--for a consideration. Yes, it was undoubtedly and unquestionably Curley, of Haines & Curley, familiarly known on the East Side as Reddy Curley from his flaming red hair--but to whom had Curley paid over the sum of fifteen thousand dollars?

For a moment the frown on Jimmie Dale's forehead deepened, then he nodded his head quickly. If he could find Curley, or Haines, or even Patsy Marles, the clerk who worked in the liquor store--which might possibly still be open for another hour or so yet--it should not, after all, and without even any undue inquisitiveness on the part of Smarlinghue, prove very difficult to obtain the necessary information, for, if Curley had been in a deal involving fifteen thousand dollars, he was much more likely to be boastful than reticent about it. It resolved itself then after all, into simply a matter of time.

Whisperings, a raucous laugh, a curse, the clink of coin, the rattle of dice, the scuffle of slippered feet, the low swish of the loose-garbed Chinese attendants went on interminably. Jimmie Dale began to toss uneasily from side to side of his bunk, and began to mumble audibly again. Perhaps half an hour passed, during which, from time to time, the curtain of the compartment was drawn quietly aside and the impassive face of one or other of the Chinese attendants was thrust through the opening--and then suddenly Jimmie Dale raised himself up on his elbow, and pointed a shaking finger at one of these apparitions.

"Foo Sen"--he licked his lips as he spoke--"you tell Foo Sen come here!"

The face disappeared, and a moment later another--the wizened, yellow face of a little old Chinaman--took its place.

"You wantee me, Smarly'oo?" inquired the proprietor suavely.

"Tell 'em to help me out of this." Jimmie Dale essayed vainly to rise, and fell back on the bunk. "D'ye hear, Foo Sen--tell'em! Goin' home!"

"Alee same bletter stay sleep him off," advised Foo Sen.

Jimmie Dale succeeded in sitting upright on the edge of the bunk--and snarled at the other.

"You mind your own business, Foo Sen!" he flung out gutturally. "Goin' home! Tell 'em to help me out--sleep where I like! Makes me sick here--rotten smell--rotten punk sticks!"

"You allee same fool," commented Foo Sen imperturbably, as he clapped his hands. "Mabbe you no get home; mabbe you get run in police cell sleep him off, instead. That your business, you likee that--all right!"

Foo Sen smiled placidly, and was gone.

An instant later, Jimmie Dale, his arms twined around the necks of two Chinamen, and leaning heavily upon them, and stumbling as he walked, was being conducted through a maze of dark and narrow passages that gradually trended upward to a higher level--and presently a door closed behind him, and he was in the open air.

It was dark about him, not even the glimmer of a window light showed from anywhere--but in Foo Sen's there were eyes that saw through the darkness, and his progress, alone now, was both unsteady and slow. He was in a very narrow alleyway between two houses--one of the several hidden entrances to Foo Sen's. The alley opened in one direction on a lane, in the other direction on the street. Jimmie Dale chose the direction of the lane, reached the lane, and, still stumbling and lurching, made his way along for a distance of possibly fifty yards; then, well clear of the neighbourhood of Foo Sen's, he began to quicken his pace--and twenty minutes later, frowning in disappointment, he was standing in front of Reddy Curley's liquor store, only to find that the place was already closed for the night.

CHAPTER XII
IN THE SANCTUARY

It was ten o'clock now, an hour since the Rat and Muggy Ladd had left Foo Sen's. Again Jimmie Dale told himself that it was still early, that the Rat would wait for a much later hour--but at the same time he acknowledged to himself a sense of growing and premonitory uneasiness. Certainly, in any case, he had no time to lose. He turned quickly and hurried along the block that separated him from the Bowery--he had a fair idea of the haunts usually frequented in the evening by the men he sought, and, even failing to find the men themselves, there was always the chance, and a very good one, that, where Curley was known, Curley's fifteen thousand dollar deal might be the subject of gossip which would answer his, Jimmie Dale's, purpose quite as well.

But an hour went by--and yet another. Midnight came--and midnight had brought him nothing. It seemed as though he had combed the East Side from end to end, and he had found neither Curley, nor Haines, nor Patsy Marles--nor had he heard anything--nor had such guarded questions as he had dared to ask without involving possible disastrous consequences to "Smarlinghue," should the Rat, after all, succeed and hear of his activities, had any result. And then, still maintaining his efforts with dogged determination, though conscious now that with the hour so late he might perhaps better return to the Sanctuary, change, say, into the clothes of Jimmie Dale, and, crediting the Rat with already having made a successful inroad on the safe, devote his energies to running down the Rat, and, if possible, to salvaging the plunder, he was in the act of entering again one of the dance halls he had already visited earlier in the evening, when one of the men he was searching for lurched out through the doorway. It was Patsy Marles, garrulous, drunk, exceedingly unsteady on his feet, and accompanied by three or four companions. They crowded out past Jimmie Dale, and gathered aimlessly on the pavement. Marles' voice rose in earnest insobriety for what was very probably by no means the first time.

"Betcher life! Spot cash--fifteen thousand--spot cash! Sure, I saw it! Only--hic!--got one boss now. Little ol' Reddy got the--hic!--papers from lawyer 'safternoon. Know ol' Grenville, don't you--that's him--ol' Grenville. Come on, whatsh's use standin' round here doin' nothin'!"

Jimmie Dale did not enter the dance hall--instead, scuffling hurriedly along to the next corner, he turned off the Bowery, and, choosing the darker and more dimly lighted streets and, at times, a lane or alleyway, broke a run. In the space of a little more than a second he had at last obtained the information that he had searched for vainly for over two hours. There seemed something mockingly ironical in the fact that he had been obliged to search for those two hours! What had happened in that time? Two hours! It was three hours now since the Rat had left Foo Sen's!

He shook his head with sudden impatience at himself. He would gain nothing by speculating on possibilities! He **had** the information now. The one thing to do was to act upon it. So it was old Grenville's safe! Old Grenville, the lawyer; honest old Grenville, the East Side called him, the one man, perhaps, whose word was accepted at its face value, and who was both liked and trusted everywhere in the Bad Lands--because he was honest! Jimmie Dale's lips tightened as he ran. It was more than ordinarily dirty work, then, on the Rat's part. Grenville was an old man, close to seventy, at a guess; and if any one had earned immunity from the depredations of the underworld it was this curious and lovable old character--honest Grenville. The man was not a criminal lawyer, he had made no enemies even in that way; he was more a paternal family solicitor, as it were, to the dregs of humanity that had crowded his queer and dingy office now, so report had it, for over forty years. He was credited with having amassed a little money, not a fortune, perhaps, for there were many fees never collected and never asked for amongst the needy, but enough to live comfortably on in the simple and unpretentious way in which old Grenville lived.

Yes, it was dirty work--miserable, dirty work, the work of a hound and a cur! And the Rat's logic was unassailable. From Patsy Marles' maudlin babbling it was evident that Reddy Curley had bought Haines, his partner, out; that the price was fifteen thousand dollars; and that Grenville, acting for Haines obviously, had received the purchase money from Curley, and in return had handed over what the Rat had taken to be a receipt, but what was probably in reality much more likely to have been a Bill of Sale. But in either case, it was neither Curley nor Haines who would suffer--it was old Grenville, who, if the funds were stolen and not recovered, would have to make the amount good out of his own pocket, and who, as all who knew old Grenville knew well, would unhesitatingly do so at once if it took the last cent that pocket held.

Jimmie Dale had halted before a small building on one of the cross streets near the upper end of the Bowery. There were some half dozen signs on the doorway, for the most part time worn and shabby, amongst them that of Henry Grenville, Attorney-at-Law.

There were no lights in any of the windows, but Jimmie Dale, as he tried the door, found it unlocked, and, opening it noiselessly, stepped inside. Here, a single incandescent suspended over the stair well gave a murky illumination to the surroundings. A narrow corridor, dotted with office doors, was on his left; the stairway--there was no elevator--was directly in front of him. He stood motionless for an instant, listening. There was no sound. He moved forward then, as silent as the silence around him, and began to mount the stairs. Old Grenville's office, he knew, was at the rear of the corridor on the first landing.

It was after midnight now, quite a little after midnight. Jimmie Dale's fingers, in the right-hand pocket of his tattered coat, closed over the stock of his automatic. Still no sound! Was he too late to forestall the Rat; or, by no means an unlikely possibility, was the Rat there now; or was--a low, muttered exclamation, that mingled surprise and bewilderment, came suddenly from Jimmie Dale's lips. He had reached the landing, and here, from the head of the stairs, he could see a dull yellow glow thrown out into the corridor through the glass panel of the lawyer's door.

An instant's pause, and then, chagrined, the sense of defeat upon him, he moved forward again as silently as before. He reached the door and crouched beside it. A murmur of voices came to him from within. Jimmie Dale's lips parted in grim irony. The game was up, of course, but he was occupying precisely the same coign of vantage that, according to the Rat, the Rat had occupied that afternoon, and if the Rat had been able, undiscovered, to see and hear, then he, Jimmie Dale, could do the same. The slim, tapering, sensitive fingers closed on the doorknob--a thin ray of light began to steal through between the door-edge and the jamb--and grew wider--and the voices, from a confused murmur, became distinct. And now, through the narrow crack of the slightly opened door, he could see inside; and he could see that, as he had already realised, he was too late, very much too late, in time only, as it were, for the post-mortem of the affair--even the police were already on the spot!

It was a curious scene! A rickety old railing across the middle of the musty, bare-floored room served to indicate that the space beyond was the old lawyer's "private" office. And here, inside the railing, a desk, or, rather, a great, flat, deal table, spread with a red, ink-stained cloth, was littered with books and papers; while behind the table, again, stood a huge, old-fashioned safe, its door swung wide open, its erstwhile contents scattered in disorder about the floor.

Jimmie Dale's eyes swept the interior of the room with a single, quick, comprehensive glance--and then, narrowed, travelled from one to another of the faces of the four men who were gathered around the table. He knew them all. The stocky, grizzle-haired man in the centre was a plain-clothes man from headquarters, named Barlow; at the lower end of the table Reddy Curley and Haines, his partner, faced each other, Curley drumming indifferently with his fingers on the table-top, Haines scowling and chewing his lower lip, a certain coarse brutality in both their faces that was neither pleasant nor inviting; but it was the white-haired old man, bent of form, standing at the head of the table, upon whom Jimmie Dale's eyes lingered. Old Grenville! The man's hand, as he raised it to pass it across his eyes, was shaking palpably; his face, kindly still in spite of its worn and haggard expression, was pale with anxiety and strain. Barlow was speaking:

"You say there's nothing else missing, Mr. Grenville, except the sealed envelope that contained the fifteen thousand dollars given you by Mr. Curley this afternoon?"

The old lawyer shook his head.

"I can't say," he answered. "As I told you, I often come here at night to work. To-night a client kept me very late at my house, so it was only, I should say, a quarter of an hour ago when I reached here. I telephoned you at once, and, awaiting your arrival, I did not disturb anything, so I have not examined any of the papers yet."

"I don't think it's a question of papers," observed the Headquarters man dryly.

"There was nothing else taken then," decided Grenville slowly; "for there was no other money in the safe at the time--in fact, I rarely keep any there."

"Well then," said Barlow crisply, "it's pretty near open and shut that some one was wise to that fifteen thousand being there to-night, and it wasn't just a lucky haul out of any old safe just because the safe looked easy." He turned toward Curley and Haines. "Were either of you talking with any one around the East Side to-night who would be likely to make a tip of it, or pass the tip along?"

"We weren't there at all to-night," Curley replied. "Haines and I were out in my car, and we'd just got back when you picked us up at the store on the way up here. But, at that, I guess you're right. We didn't make any secret about it, and I daresay after I'd got the business tacked away safe in my inside pocket this afternoon"--he grinned maliciously at Haines--"I may have mentioned it to one or two."

"Got it tucked away safe, have you? Own it, do you?" Haines caught him up truculently.

"Sure!" Curley had wicked, little greenish-grey eyes, and their stare was uninviting as he fixed them on his quondam partner. "If you want to grouch, go ahead and grouch! We've been pretty good friends for a pretty good number of years, but I ain't a fool. Sure, it's mine now! I didn't ask you to employ Grenville, did I? I was satisfied to take any old piece of paper with your fist on it, saying you'd sold out to me; but no, you were for having the thing done with frills on it Well, I'm still satisfied! I came here at five o'clock this afternoon, and paid the coin over to your attorney, and I got a perfectly good little Bill of Sale for it--and that lets me out. It's up to you and your Mister Attorney. Why don't you ask him what *he's* going to do about it, instead of trying to take it out on me the way you've been doing ever since Barlow told us what had happened, and--"

"Mr. Curley is perfectly right, Mr. Haines"--the old lawyer's voice was quiet, though it trembled a little. "The title to the business is now vested in Mr. Curley, and you are entitled to look to me for compensation. I"--he hesitated an instant--"I--I hope the money may be recovered, otherwise--"

"Eh?" inquired Mr. Haines sharply.

"Otherwise," the old lawyer went on with an effort, "I am afraid I shall have a great deal of difficulty in raising so large a sum."

"The hell you are!" said Mr. Haines uncharitably, and leaned forward over the table. "Don't try to come that dodge! Everybody says you're well fixed. Everybody says you've got a neat little pile salted away."

The lawyer's face was ashen, and his lips were quivering; but there was a fine dignity in the poise of the old man's head, and in the squared shoulders.

"Nevertheless, I am, unfortunately, telling you the truth, in spite of any rumours, or public belief to the contrary," he said steadily. "A few thousands, a very few, is all I have ever been able to lay aside. Those are at your disposal, Mr. Haines, and the balance I promise to procure as speedily as possible; but in plain words, if this money is not recovered, and I do not say this to invite either sympathy or leniency, but because you have questioned my word, I shall have lost everything I own."

Mr. Haines scowled.

"Well, I'm glad to know you've at least got enough!" he said roughly. "It sure will surprise a whole lot of people that fifteen thousand wipes Mr. Henry Grenville out!"

A flush dyed the old lawyer's cheeks. He made as though to speak--and, instead, turned silently away from the table, his back to the others. There was silence in the room now for a moment. Again Jimmie Dale's eyes travelled swiftly from one to another of the group--to Curley, grinning maliciously at his ex-partner again--to Haines, gnawing at his lower lip, and scowling blackly--to Barlow, obviously uncomfortable, who was uneasily tracing patterns with his forefinger on the top of the table--and back to the old lawyer, whose shoulders now, as though carrying a load too heavy for their strength, had drooped pathetically, and into whose face, in spite of a brave effort at self-control, had crept a wan and miserable despair.

"Look here!" said Barlow gruffly. "It strikes me you can settle all this some other time. It's got nothing to do with the guy that pulled this break, and I'm losing time. Headquarters is waiting for my report. You two had better beat it; Mr. Grenville won't mind, I guess--I've got your end of the story, and--"

Jimmie Dale was retreating back along the corridor--and a minute later he was in the street, and scuffling along in a downtown direction. His hands, in the pockets of his tattered coat, were clenched, and through the pallor of Smarlinghue's make-up a dull red burned his cheeks. Old Grenville--and the Rat! The smile that found lodgment on Smarlinghue's contorted lips was mirthless. The old man had taken it like the gentleman he was. He had not perhaps hidden the quiver of the lip--who would at seventy! It was not easy to begin life again at seventy! Old Grenville--and the Rat! Well, the game was not played out yet! There would be an accounting of that fifteen thousand dollars before the morning came, and, as between old Grenville and the Rat, it might not perhaps be old Grenville who paid!

Hurrying now, running through lanes and alleyways as he had come, Jimmie Dale headed for the Sanctuary. It was very simple now. The Rat, his work completed, would lay very low--asleep probably, in the *innocent* surroundings of his own room! The Rat would not be hard to find. It was necessary only that, in the little interview he proposed to have with the Rat, "Smarlinghue" should have disappeared!

He reached the tenement where, for months now, that ground floor room, opening on the small and dirty courtyard in the rear, had been his refuge, Smarlinghue's home in the underworld, glanced quickly up and down the street to assure himself that he was not observed, then, darting into the dark hallway, he crossed it silently, unlocked the Sanctuary door, stepped through, and closed and locked the door behind him. Nor, even now, did he make the slightest sound. From the top-light, high up near the ceiling and far above the little French window whose shade was drawn, there came a faint and timid streak of moonlight. It did not illuminate the room; it but lessened the degree of blackness, as it were, giving a dim and shadowy outline to objects scattered here and there about the room--and to a darker shadow amongst those other shadows, a shadow that moved swiftly and in utter silence, a shadow that was Jimmie Dale at work.

No one had seen him enter--not that there should be anything strange in the fact that Smarlinghue should enter Smarlinghue's own room, but it would not be Smarlinghue who went away! No one had seen him enter--it was vital now that he should not be heard moving around the room, and so invite the chance of some aimless caller in the person of a fellow-tenant, for it was no longer Smarlinghue who would be found there!

The ragged outer garments he had been wearing lay discarded in a heap on the floor, close to that section of the wall near the door where the base-board, ingeniously movable, would, in another moment or so, afford them safe hiding until such time as "Smarlinghue" should reappear in person again; from the nostrils, from beneath the lips, from behind the ears, the tiny, cleverly-inserted pieces of wax, distorting the features, had vanished; and now, over the cracked basin on the rickety washstand, the masterly-created pallor was washed rapidly away--and the thin, hollow-cheeked, emaciated face of Smarlinghue, the drug fiend, was gone, and in its place, clean-cut, clear-eyed, was the face of Jimmie Dale, clubman and millionaire.

He smiled a little whimsically, a little wanly, as he stole back across the room. It was a strange life, a *dangerous* life! He wondered often enough, as he was wondering now, what the end of it would be--would he find the Tocsin--or would he find death at the hands of the underworld--or judicial murder at the hands of the law for a hundred crimes attributed to the Gray Seal! Crimes! The smile grew serious and wistful, as he knelt on the floor and began to loosen the section of the baseboard in front of him. There had never been a crime committed by the Gray Seal! Yes, it was strange, bizarre, incredulous even to himself sometimes, this life of his--the strange partnership formed so long ago now with *her*, the Tocsin, who had prompted those "crimes" that righted a wrong, that brought sunlight into some life where there had been gloom before, and hope where there had been misery--and the love that had come--and then disaster again, and her disappearance--and his resumption once more of a dual life and a role in the underworld--and, yes, in spite of her own danger, those "calls to arms" to the Gray Seal again for the sake of others, while she refused, through love for him, through fear of the peril that it would bring him, help for herself.

He shook his head, as, the base-board removed now, he reached into the hollow beyond for the neatly-folded, expensively-tailored tweeds of Jimmie Dale. She was wrong in that. Could anything add to the peril in which he lived, as it was! If only in some way he might reach her, see her, talk to her, if only for a moment, he could make her see that, and understand, and--

A low, startled cry burst suddenly from his lips; he felt the blood ebb from his cheeks--and surge back again in a burning, mighty tide. It was dark, he could not see; but those wonderfully sensitive finger tips, that were ears and eyes to Jimmie Dale, were telegraphing a wild, mad, amazing message to his brain. The Tocsin had been here--here in the *Sanctuary*! She had been here--here in this room--and within the last few hours--sometime since seven o'clock that evening, when, as Jimmie Dale, he had come here to assume the role of Smarlinghue preparatory to his vigil in Foo Sen's!

His hand, thrust in through the opening to reach for his clothes, had found an envelope where it lay on the top of the folded garments--and his hand was still thrust inside--there was no need to look--the texture of the paper was hers-- *hers*--the Tocsin's! The blood was racing wildly through his veins. There was a mad joy upon him--and a sense of keen and bitter emptiness. Wild thoughts, in lightning flashes, swept his brain. She must have been here, then, many times before ... she knew the Sanctuary as well as he did ... she knew the secret hiding place behind the base-board ... she had come, of course, knowing he was absent ... she might come some day *thinking* he was absent ... yes, why not--why not ... perhaps--perhaps that was the way ... some day she might come again....

He laughed a little in a shaken way, and drew out the letter. With a mental wrench, he forced his mind into a calmer state. It was very singular that she should have placed the letter in that hiding place! It could evidence but one thing--that the contents of the letter, unlike any she had ever written before, were not of a press-ing nature, for she would know very well that it might have been many hours, days even, before he might go there for the clothes of Jimmie Dale again! What, then, did it mean? Had she decided at last to tell him all, to let him take his place beside her, share her danger, fight with her! Was that it?

He reached hurriedly into the opening again, drew out the little leather girdle, and from one of its pockets took out a flashlight. He had not dared to light the gas before; dressed, or, rather, undressed, as he was at present, and no longer Smarlin-ghue, he dared much less to light it now.

He tore the envelope open, and, still kneeling on the floor, the flashlight upon the pages, began to read:

"Dear Philanthropic Crook: You will be surprised to find this letter in such a place, won't you? Yes, you are quite right, for once, as you will already have told yourself, there is no hurry--for it is too late to hurry. Listen, then! Henry Gren-ville's safe--the old East Side lawyer, you know--"

He had read eagerly so far. He stared at the letter now, and the words only danced in an unmeaning jumble before him. It was not for herself, it was not that she had thrown the barriers down and was bidding him come to her; it was again another "call to arms" to the Gray Seal--and for another's sake. And there came to Jimmie Dale a miserable disappointment, for his hope, shattered now, had been greater than he had admitted even to himself. And then he was aware that, sub-consciously, it had seemed to him a most curious coincidence that the letter should be dealing with the robbery of Henry Grenville's safe that night. Yes, certainly, it was a most curious coincidence, when he was even then on his way--to the Rat! He shrugged his shoulders in his whimsical way. Well, for once, he had forestalled the Tocsin! There could be little here that he did not already know. He began to read again, but skimming over the words and sentences hurriedly now.

"... Curley ... liquor business ... buying out partner, Haines ... this afternoon ... fifteen thousand dollars ... large bills, one-hundred, five-hundred and thousand-dollar denominations ... sealed in envelope by Grenville ... placed by Grenville in his safe ... head of one of the most successful and desperate gangs in the country ... years under cover through position occupied ... take your time, Jimmie, and be care-ful before you act ... rest of gang is 'working' Boston and New England this week ... backyard from lane, high board fence ... in cellar ... cleverly concealed door at right of coal bin ... knot in wood seventh board from wall on level with your shoulders ... short passage beyond leading to door of den ... sound-proof room ... exit through other side ... sliding panel to room above ... opened by hanging weight inside ..."

In a stunned way now, Jimmie Dale stared for a long minute at the letter in his hand--then he read it again--and yet again. And then, the flashlight out, as he tore the letter into fragments, he stared again, for a long minute--into the blackness.

It was damnable, it was monstrous, this thing that he had read; it plumbed the dregs of human deviltry--but for once the Tocsin was at fault. Of the plot that had been hatched, of those details that she described, there could be no doubt, there was no question there, and there the Tocsin, he knew, had made no mistake; but the Tocsin, yes, and those who had hatched the crime themselves, had taken no account of the possible intervention of an outsider in the person of--the Rat! There was even a sort of grim irony in it all--that the Rat should quite unconsciously have feathered his nest at the expense of a far more elaborately arranged crime than his own, and at the expense of those who were of even a more abandoned, dangerous and unscrupulous type of criminal than himself!

Jimmie Dale's face hardened suddenly--and suddenly he stooped and pulled his clothes from their hiding place, and began to dress. For once, his inside information outreached hers. It was still--the Rat. Her letter changed nothing, save that afterwards, perhaps--well, that afterwards, perhaps, there was another, others beside the Rat, with whom an accounting would be made!

CHAPTER XIII
THE SECRET ROOM

Jimmie Dale dressed quickly now. From the pockets of the little leather girdle to the pockets of his tweeds he transferred a steel picklock, a pair of light steel handcuffs, a piece of fine but exceedingly strong cord, a black silk mask, and that small metal case, within which, between sheets of oiled paper, lay those gray-coloured, diamond-shaped, adhesive paper seals that were known in every den in the underworld, known in every police bureau of two continents, as the insignia of the Gray Seal. He slipped the flashlight into his pocket, took his automatic from the discarded garments of Smarlinghue--and, thrusting the ragged clothing into the opening, put the removable section of the base-board back into place.

And now, twin to that streak of lesser gloom that came from the top-light, another filtered into the room. The small French window opened and closed without sound--the room was empty. A shadow in the courtyard, close against the wall of the tenement, moved forward a foot, a yard--a loose board in the fence bordering the lane swung silently aside--and in a moment more, striding nonchalantly up the block, Jimmie Dale turned into the Bowery.

He had some distance to go, almost back as far as the liquor store at the lower end of the Bowery, for the Rat lived, if he, Jimmie Dale, was not mistaken, just one block this side, in a small one-story frame building on the corner of a cross street; and--it seemed incongruous, queerly out of place somehow--the Rat lived with his mother. Home ties, or home relationships, hardly seemed in harmony with the Rat! Still, in this case, it was perhaps very debatable ground as to which was the more pernicious, the old woman or the son! Ostensibly, she kept a little variety store; but her business, if report were true, was the edifying occupation of school mistress-- the children graduating under her tuition being ranked by common consent as the most accomplished pickpockets in gangland!

Jimmie Dale shrugged his shoulders, as he swung at last from the Bowery into a narrow, poorly lighted street. Well, at least, if the Rat's criminal career ended to-night, the Rat's punishment need excite no sympathy for the old woman, as far as he, Jimmie Dale, was concerned--it was a pity only that she had not been behind the bars herself long ago! Yes, this was the place--the small frame building diagonally across from the corner on which he had halted. He crossed over for a closer inspection. The front of the house was dark, the little store windows shuttered. He hesitated an instant, then walked around the corner to survey the building from the side and rear. Here, from a window that gave on the intersecting street, there showed a light. The window was low, scarcely above the level of his head, but held no promise on that score as a source of information, for the shade within was tightly drawn. Jimmie Dale scowled at it for a moment, noted its proximity to the backyard and the front of the building. The Rat, then, or the Rat's mother, was still up, and he would need to exercise more than ordinary caution--or else wait--indefinitely, perhaps.

He shook his head at that alternative, as he looked sharply up and down the street. He would gain little by waiting, and--ah! He was crouched in the doorway now, the deft fingers working swiftly with the picklock. There was a faint metallic click, barely audible above his low-breathed exclamation--and the door opened and closed behind him.

The flashlight in his hand winked once--and went out. Small, glass-topped counters were on either side of the somewhat restricted aisle in which he stood; directly in front of him, at the rear of the store, was a door, leading, obviously, to the living rooms beyond.

The old days of Larry the Bat, the rickety, creaky stairs of the old Sanctuary had trained Jimmie Dale's step to a silence that was almost uncanny. It might have been a shadow moving there across the floor of the store, a shadow flitting through that doorway beyond. There was no sound.

And now, at the end of a short, dark passage, he stopped before the door of what was, from its location, the lighted room he had seen from the street; and, slipping his mask over his face, he placed his ear against the door panel to listen. He was rewarded only by absolute silence. His lips, under the mask, twisted queerly, as, softly, cautiously, he tried the door. It gave under the steady pressure that he exerted upon it--gave without sound for the measure of a fraction of an inch--it was unlocked. And now Jimmie Dale could see into the room--and suddenly he stepped noiselessly forward, his automatic holding a bead on the crouched figure of the Rat, asleep apparently in his chair, whose head, flung forward, was buried in his crossed arms upon the table in the centre of the room.

"Good evening!" said Jimmie Dale, in a velvet voice.

There was no answer--the man neither turned his head, nor looked up.

And for a moment Jimmie Dale did not stir--only into the dark eyes shining through the mask there came a startled gleam, and through the heavy, palpitating silence the quick, sudden intake of his breath sounded clamourously loud. He saw now--the *gray* of the cheek just showing above the arm that pillowed it, the stiff, hunched, unnatural position of the body, the crimson pool on the floor by the chair leg. *The man was dead*!

Tight-lipped, the strong jaw outthrust a little, his face hard and set, Jimmie Dale moved to the Rat's side, and bent over the man. Yes, it was-- *murder*! The Rat had been stabbed in the back just below the left armpit. He glanced sharply around the room. There was no sign of struggle, except--yes--there were bruises on the man's neck, as though a hand had grasped it fiercely, and--he bent over--yes, faintly, but nevertheless distinctly enough, two blood-stained finger prints were discernible on the Rat's collar. He lifted the Rat's hands and examined them critically--it might perhaps have been the man himself clutching his own throat, as he choked and struggled for breath--no, the Rat's fingers showed not the slightest trace of blood.

And then, instinctively, Jimmie Dale reached out toward the other's pocket; but, with a hard smile, dropped his hand to his side, instead. The sealed envelope, the fifteen thousand dollars, was not there-- *it was where the Tocsin had said it was*! The Tocsin, not he, had been right! And yet, too, in a way, he had not been entirely wrong. It *was* the Rat who had stolen the sealed envelope from the safe-- or else the Rat would not now be dead!

His mind, alert and keen now, was dovetailing together the pieces of the puzzle. Those who had originally planned the crime had in some way discovered that the Rat, in the actual theft, had forestalled them. Possibly, for instance, bent on the same errand, they had seen the Rat leaving the building; then, finding the safe already looted, they had put two and two together, and had trapped the Rat here--and the Rat had paid the price! It might have been that way, but that in itself was a detail, immaterial--they *had* discovered that it was the Rat. The Rat's murder proved it. It was not enough that they should recover the envelope--there would have been no way to avoid exposure or cover their own crime except by murdering the Rat.

He looked down at the silent form sprawled over the table, and his face relaxed, softened a little. The Rat was only the Rat, it was true, and the man was a thief, an outcast, a pariah, a prey upon society; but life to the Rat, too, had been sweet, and his murder was a hideous thing--and even such as the Rat might ask justice. Justice! It had been dirty work--miserable, dirty work, he had called it when he had thought the Rat alone involved--but now, thanks to the Tocsin, he knew it for what it really was, knew it for its damnable, hellish ingenuity, and its abominable, brutal callousness! Justice! Yes--but how?

He began to move about the room, his mind for the moment diverted in an endeavour to reconstruct the scene as it must have been enacted here around him. The Rat had broken into the safe *before* eleven o'clock--that was obvious now. In fact, it was quite likely to have been much nearer ten! He had returned here and had been sitting there at the table, counting over his ill-gotten gains, perhaps, his back to the door, just as he sat now, and they had stolen in upon him. But where was the old woman? True, perhaps little, if any, noise had been made, and yet--Jimmie Dale, pausing on the threshold of the door, listened intently. One of the two rooms, whose doors he saw between this end room and the door opening into the store, must be hers, and if she were there, asleep, for instance, his ear was surely acute enough to catch, in the stillness that lay upon the house, the sound of breathing. But there was nothing. Under the mask, his brows drew together in a perplexed frown. And then suddenly he stood rigid, tense. Yes, there was a sound at last--and an ominous one! The front door leading into the store was being opened, came the scuffling of footsteps--and then a woman's voice, shrill, wailing:

"W'en I come in not twenty minutes ago dere he was--dead. My Gawd--knifed he was! An' den I runs fer youse at de station. I gotta right ter cry, ain't I! He's my son, he is--ain't he! I gotta right--"

"Keep quiet!" snapped a man's voice gruffly. "We've heard all that a dozen times now. It's a pity you didn't think more about being his mother twenty years ago! Mike, you'd better lock that front door!"

Jimmie Dale drew back, and closed the door softly. If he were caught here now! The old woman had brought the police back with her--two of them, it appeared. He smiled in a hard way. Well, he did not propose to be caught. His hand reached up to the electric light switch, there was a click, and the room was in darkness. In the fraction of a second more he was at the window. Shade and window were swiftly, silently raised, and he looked out cautiously. The street was deserted, empty; there was no one in sight. It was very simple, a drop of a few feet to the sidewalk, a dash around the corner--and that was all. They were coming now. He swung one leg over the sill--and sat there motionless, his mind balancing with lightning speed the pros against the cons of a sudden inspiration that had come to him. Justice... justice on those guilty of this wretched murder here, and guilty of many another crime almost as grave...he had asked himself how...here was a way...a daredevil, foolhardy way? ... no, the possibility of being winged by a chance shot, perhaps, but otherwise a safe way ... escape through that panel door operated by weights ... and it was not far to that den the Tocsin had described ... nor would he be running into a trap himself ... the gang was not there ... perhaps no one ... but perhaps, with luck, those he might wish would be there ... it would be a gracious little act on the part of the Gray Seal, would it not, to invite the police, this Mike and his companion, to that den--they would be deeply interested! He laughed low--they were almost at the door now. Well? The doorknob rattled. Yes, he would do it! Yes-- *now*! He stretched out suddenly, and with the toe of his boot kicked over a chair that was within reach. The crash, as the chair fell, was answered by a rush through the door, a hoarse, surprised and quick-flung oath--and, as Jimmie Dale swung out through the window and dropped to the street, the flash and roar of a revolver shot.

Like a cat on his feet, he whirled as he touched the pavement, and darted along past the backyard fence, heading for the lane; and, as he ran, over his shoulder, he saw first one and then the other of the two men, both in police uniform, drop from the window and take up the pursuit. Another shot, and another, a fusillade of them rang out. A bullet struck the pavement at his feet with a venomous *spat*. He heard the humming of another that was like the humming of an angry wasp. And he laughed again to himself--but short and grimly now. Just a few yards more--five of them--to the corner of the lane. It was the chance he had invited--three yards--two--his breath was coming in hard, short panting gasps-- *safe*! Yes! He had won now--they would not get another shot at him, at least not another that he would have any need to fear!

He swerved into the lane, still running at top speed. A high board fence, she had said--yes, there it was! And it corresponded in location with where he knew it should be--about three lots in from the street. He sprang for it, and swung lithely to the top--and hung there, as though still scrambling and struggling for his balance. The officers had not turned into the lane yet, and he had no intention of affording them any excuse for losing sight of their quarry!

Ah! There they were! A yell and a revolver shot rang out simultaneously as they caught sight of him--and Jimmie Dale dropped down to the ground on the inside of the fence. In the moonlight he could see quite distinctly. He darted across the yard, heading for the basement door of the building that loomed up in front of him.

The little steel picklock was in his hand as he reached the door. A second--two--three went by. He straightened up--and again he waited--stepping back a few feet to stand sharply outlined in the moonlight.

Again a shout in signal that he was seen, as one of the officers' heads appeared over the top of the fence--and Jimmie Dale, as though in mad haste, plunged through the door.

And now suddenly his tactics changed. He needed every second he could gain, and the police now certainly could no longer lose their way. He swung the door shut behind him, locked it to delay them, and snatched his flashlight from his pocket. He was at the top of a few ladder-like steps that led down into the cellar of the building, and halfway along the length of the cellar the ray of his flashlight swept across a huge coal bin, its sides, it seemed, built almost up to the ceiling.

Jimmie Dale was muttering to himself now, as he took the steps at a single leap, and raced toward the side of the bin that flanked the wall--"seventh board from the wall--knot on a level with shoulders"--and now he was counting rapidly--and now the round, white ray played on the seventh board. They were smashing at the cellar door now. The knot! Ah--there it was! He pressed it. Two of the boards in front of him, the width of a man's body, swung back. He left this open--a blazed trail for his pursuers, battering now at the cellar door--and stepped forward into a little opening, too short to be called a passage, and, silent now, halted before another door.

Brain and eyes and hands were working now with incredible speed. That it was a sound-proof room was not, perhaps, altogether an unmixed blessing! Was the place deserted? Was there any one within? He could hear nothing. Well, after all, did it make any ultimate difference? The room itself would condemn them!

The picklock was at work again--working silently--working swiftly. And now, in its place, his automatic was in his hand.

He crouched a little--and with a spring, flinging wide the door, was in the room. There was a smothered cry, an oath, the crash of an overturned chair, as two men, from a table heaped with little piles of crisp, new banknotes, sprang wildly to their feet: And Jimmie Dale's lips twisted in a smile not good to see. Standing there before him were Curley and Haines.

"Keep your seats, gentlemen--please!" said Jimmie Dale, with grim irony. "I shall only stay a moment. It is Mr. Curley and Mr. Haines, I believe--in their *private* office! Permit me!"--he reached out with his left hand, and closed the door. "Ah, I see there is a good serviceable bolt on it. I have your permission?"--he slipped the bolt into place. "As I said, I shall only stay a moment; but it would be unfortunate, most unfortunate, if we were by any chance interrupted--prematurely!"

Haines, ashen white, was gripping at the table edge. Curley, a deadly glitter in his wicked little eyes, moistened his lips with the tip of his tongue.

"How'd you get here, and what the hell d'you want?" he burst out fiercely.

"As to the first question, I haven't time to answer it," said Jimmie Dale evenly. "What I want is the sealed envelope stolen from Henry Grenville's safe--and I'm in a *hurry*, Mr. Curley."

"You're a fool!" said Curley, with a sneer. "It's--"

"Yes, I know," said Jimmie Dale, with ominous patience, "it's counterfeit, you miserable pair of curs! Counterfeit like the rest of that stuff there on the table! Nice place you've got here--everything, I see--press, plates, engraver's tools--nothing missing but the rest of the gang! Perhaps, though, they can be found! Now then, that envelope--quick!" Jimmie Dale's automatic swung forward significantly.

"It's in the drawer of the table," snarled Curley. "Curse you, who--"

"Thank you!" Jimmie Dale's lips were a thin line. "Now, you two, stand out there in the middle of the floor--and if either of you make a move other than you are told to make, I'll drop you as I would drop a mad dog!" He jerked the two chairs out from the table, and, still covering Curley and Haines, placed the chairs back to back. "Sit down there, stretch out your arms full length on either side, the palms of your hands against each other's!" he ordered curtly; and, as they obeyed-- Haines, cowed, all pretence at nerve gone, Curley cursing in abandon--he slipped the hand-cuffs over their wrists on one side, and, taking the piece of cord from his pocket that he had intended for the Rat's ankles, he deftly noosed their wrists on the other side with a slip knot, which he fastened securely.

He stepped over to the table.

"Counterfeiting five-hundred and thousand-dollar bills is rather out of the or-dinary run, isn't it--I see these on the table here are the regular small variety!" he observed coolly, as he pulled the drawer open. "The big ones make a quick turn-over, though, if you have the plant to turn them out, and can swing a scheme to cash them--after banking hours--and steal them back! Hello, what's this!"--the sealed envelope, torn open at one end, evidently by the Rat in his examination, but still full of the counterfeit notes, was blood-smeared, and on the upper left-hand corner there showed the distinct impression of a finger print.

There was a sudden crash against the door.

Both men, in their chairs, strained around--and now Curley, too, had lost his colour.

"My God, what's that!" he whispered.

The thin metal case was in Jimmie Dale's hand. With the tweezers, he lifted one of the little gray seals to his lips, moistened it, and, using his elbow, pressed it firmly down upon the envelope.

Came another furious thud upon the door--and another.

"What's that!" Curley's voice was a frantic scream now. "For God's sake, do you hear, what's that!"

Jimmie Dale, under a pencilled arrow mark indicating the finger print, was scrawling a few words in printed characters.

"It's the police," said Jimmie Dale calmly. "Somebody murdered the Rat to-night!" He surveyed the envelope in his hand critically. Between the arrow mark and the gray seal were the words: "Look on the Rat's collar--and these gentlemen's fingers." He laid the envelope down on the table--and, as the door suddenly splintered and sagged under a terrific blow from some heavy object, he retreated hurriedly to the farther end of the room. Here a half dozen steps led upward, and hanging from the ceiling beside them was a cord to which was attached a leaden weight. He jerked the cord quickly. A panel above him slid noiselessly back. He leaped to the top of the stairs, and paused for a moment.

"They've been looking for this place for several years, I guess," said Jimmie Dale softly. "And I guess it will change hands to-night for the last time--and without the need of any Bill of Sale from old Henry Grenville! But we were speaking of the Rat--and why the Rat was murdered. If the Rat had had a chance to spread the news that the money paid by Mr. Curley this afternoon was counterfeit, it--"

Jimmie Dale did not finish his sentence. In a bound, as the door from the cellar crashed inward, he was through the panel opening and in the room above. There was light from the open panel behind him--enough to show him that he was in a small room which was fitted up as an office--the office of Haines & Curley, wholesale liquor dealers!

In an instant he was out of the office, and running silently down the length of the store. He snatched off his mask, reached the front door, opened it, stepped out on the quiet, deserted street--and a moment later Jimmie Dale was but one of the many that still, even at that hour, drifted their way along the Bowery.

CHAPTER XIV
THE LAST CARD

Two weeks had gone by--or was it three? How long was it since he had found the Tocsin's letter in the secret hiding place of the new Sanctuary! It had seemed to him then that he had been given a new lead, a new hope; for, once he had recovered from his startled amazement at the realisation that she was as conversant with the secrets of the new Sanctuary as she had been with the old, there had come the thought of turning that very fact to his own account--that if he were unable to reach or find her by any other means, he might succeed, instead, by letting her unwittingly come to him. She had come there once to the Sanctuary when he had been absent; she was almost certain to come there again--when she *thought* he was absent! He had put his plan into execution. For days at a stretch he had remained hidden in the Sanctuary--and nothing had come of it--and then the inaction, coupled with the knowledge that the peril which faced her, even though his previous efforts to avert it had all been abortive, had made it unbearable to remain longer passive, and he had given it up, and gone out again, combing and searching through the dens and dives of the underworld.

That had been two weeks ago--or three. And the net result had been nothing!

Jimmie Dale allowed the evening newspaper to slip from his fingers. It dropped to the arm of his lounging chair, and from there to the floor. It was no use. He had been reading mechanically ever since he had returned from the club half an hour ago, and he was conscious in only the haziest sort of way of what he had been reading. The market, the general news items, the editorials, had all blended one into the other to form a meaningless jumble of words; even the leading article on the front page, that proclaimed as imminent the final and complete expose of what had come to be known as "The Private Club Ring"--an investigation that, from its inception,

he had hitherto followed closely, promising as it did to involve and link in partnership with the lowest of the underworld names that heretofore had stood high up in
the social circles of New York--seemed uninteresting and unable to hold his attention to-night.

He rose impulsively from his chair, and, walking down the length of the richly
furnished room, his tread soundless on the thick, heavy rug, drew the portieres
aside, and stood looking out of the rear window; It was dark outside, but presently
the shadows formed into concrete shapes, and, across the black space of driveway
and yard, the wall of the garage assumed a solid background against the night. He
passed his hand over his forehead heavily, and a wanness came into his face and
eyes. Once before be had stood here at this window of his den, the room that ran
the entire depth of his magnificent Riverside Drive residence, and old Jason had
stood at the front window--and they had watched, Jason and he--watched the
shadows, that were not shadows of walls and buildings, close in around the house.
That was the night before he had escaped from the trap set by the Crime Club; the
night before the old Sanctuary had burned down, and police and underworld alike
had believed the Gray Seal buried beneath the charred and fallen walls; the night
before she, the Tocsin, had come for a little while into her own, and for a little
while--into his arms.

His lips twisted in pain. A little while! Days of glad and glorious wonder! They
were gone now; and in their place was emptiness and loneliness--and a great, over-
mastering fear and terror that would clutch at times, as it clutched now, cold at his
heart.

It was not so very long ago that night, only a few months ago, but it seemed as
though the years had come and rolled away since then. She was gone again, driven
by a peril that menaced her life into hiding again--a peril that she would not let him
share--because she *loved* him.

The pain that showed on his twisted lips was voiced in a low, involuntary
cry. Because she loved him! His hands clenched hard. Where was she? Who was it
that dogged and haunted her, that was wrecking and ruining her life? God knew!
And God knew, employing every resource he possessed, he had done everything
he could to reach her. And all that he had accomplished had been the creation of a
new character in the underworld! That was all--and yet, strangely enough, in that

way there had come to him the one single gleam of relief that he had known, for out of the creation of that character had sprung again the activities of the Gray Seal, and with the resumption of those activities, since, as in the old days, those "calls to arms" of hers had come again he knew that, at least, she was so far alive and safe.

Jimmie Dale swung from the window, and began to pace rapidly up and down the room. Safe--yes! But for how long? She had outwitted those against her up to now, but for how long would--

He had halted abruptly beside the table. Some one was knocking at the door.

"Come!" he called.

And old Jason entered--and it seemed to Jimmie Dale that he must laugh out like one suddenly over-wrought and in hysteria. In the old butler's hand was a silver card tray, and on the tray was--but there was no need to look on the tray, old Jason's face, curiously mingling excitement and disquiet, the imperturbability of the butler gone for the nonce, was alone quite eloquent enough. But Jimmie Dale, master of many things, was most of all master of himself.

"Well, Jason?" His voice was quiet and contained as he spoke. He reached out and took from the tray a white, unaddressed envelope. It was from her, of course-- even Jason knew that it was another of those mysterious epistles, one of the many that had passed through the old butler's hands, that had in the last few years so completely revolutionised, as it were, his, Jimmie Dale's, mode of life. "Well, Jason?" He was toying with the envelope in his hand. "How did it come this time?"

"It was in another envelope, Master Jim, sir--addressed to me, sir," explained the old butler nervously. "A messenger boy brought it, sir. I opened the outside envelope, Master Jim, and--and I knew at once, sir, that--that it was one of those letters."

"I see." Jimmie Dale smiled a little mirthlessly. What, after all, did the "how" of it matter? It was a foregone conclusion that, as it had been a hundred times before, it would avail him nothing so far as furnishing a clue to her whereabouts was concerned! "Very well, Jason." His tones were a dismissal.

But Jason did not go; and there was something more in the act than that of a well-trained servant as the old man stooped, picked up the newspaper from the floor, and folded it neatly. He laid the paper hesitantly on the table, and began to fumble awkwardly with the silver tray.

"What is it, Jason?" prompted Jimmie Dale.

"Well, Master Jim, sir," said Jason, and the old face grew suddenly strained, "there *is* something that, begging your pardon for the liberty, sir, I would like to say. I don't know what all these strange letters are about, and it's not for me, sir, it's not my place, to ask. But once, Master Jim, you honoured me with your confidence to the extent of saying they meant life and death; and once, sir, the night this house was watched, I could see for myself that you were in some great danger. I--Master Jim, sir--I--I am an old man now, sir, but I dandled you on my knee when you were only a wee tot, sir, and--and you'll forgive me, sir, if I presume beyond my station, only--only--" His voice broke suddenly; his eyes were full of tears.

Jimmie Dale's hand went out, both of them, and were laid affectionately on the old man's shoulders.

"I put my life in your hands that night, Jason," he said simply. "Go on. What is it?"

"Yes, sir. Thank you, Master Jim, sir." Jason swallowed hard; his voice choked a little. "It isn't much, sir, I--I don't know that it's anything at all; but nights, sir, when I'm sitting up for you, Master Jim, and you don't come home, I--"

"But I've told you again and again that you are not to sit up for me, Jason," Jimmie Dale remonstrated kindly.

"Yes, I know, sir." Jason shook his head. "But I couldn't sleep, sir, anyway--thinking about it, Master Jim, sir. I--well, sir--sometimes I get terribly anxious and afraid, Master Jim, that something will happen to you, and it seems as though you were all alone in this, and I thought, sir, that perhaps if--if some one--some one you could trust, Master Jim, could do something-- *anything*, sir, it might make it all right. I--I'm an old man, Master Jim, it--it wouldn't matter about me, and--"

Jimmie Dale turned abruptly to the table. His own eyes were wet. These were not idle words that Jason used, or words spoken without a full realisation of their meaning. Jason was offering, and calling it presumption to do so, his life in place of his, Jimmie Dale's, if by so doing he could shield the master whom he loved.

"Thank you, Jason." Jimmie Dale turned again from the table. "There is nothing you can do now, but if the time ever comes--" He looked for a long minute into Jason's face; then his hands were laid again on the other's shoulders, and he swung the old man gently around. "There's the door, Jason--and God bless you!"

Jason went slowly from the room. The door closed. For the first time that he had ever held a letter of hers in his hand Jimmie Dale was for a moment heedless of it. If the time ever came! He smiled strangely. The love and affection that had come with the years of Jason's service were not all on one side. Not for anything in the world would he put a hair of that gray head in jeopardy! It was not lack of faith or trust that held him back from taking Jason into his full confidence--it was the possibility, always present, that some day the house of cards might totter, the Gray Seal be discovered to be Jimmie Dale, and in the ruin, the disaster, the debacle that must follow, the less old Jason knew, for old Jason's own sake, the better! It was the one thing that would save Jason. The charge of complicity would fall to the ground before the old man's very ingenuousness!

And then Jimmie Dale shrugged his shoulders, a sort of whimsical fatalistic philosophy upon him, and, as he tore the envelope open, he sat down in the lounging chair close to the table. Another "call to arms"! An appeal for some one else--never for herself! He shook his head. How often had he hoped that the summons, instead, would prove to be the one thing he asked and lived for--to take his place beside her, to aid *her*! Not one of these letters had he ever opened without the hope that, in spite of the intuition which told him his hope was futile, it would prove at last to be the call to him for herself! Perhaps this one--he was eagerly unfolding the pages he had taken from the envelope--perhaps this one--no!--a glance was enough--it was far remote from any personal relation to her.

"Dear Philanthropic Crook"--he leaned back in his chair, as his eyes travelled hurriedly over the opening paragraphs, a keen sense of disappointment upon him, despite the intuition that had bade him expect nothing else--and then suddenly, startled, tense, he sat upright, strained forward in his seat. He could not read fast enough. His eyes leaped over words and sentences.

"... They are playing their last card to-night ... David Archman ... it is murder, Jimmie ... letter signed J. Barca ... Sixth Avenue stationer ... Martin Moore ... Gentleman Laroque, the gangster ... Niccolo Sonnino ... end house to left of courtyard entrance ... safe in rear room ... lives alone ... tonight ..."

For a moment Jimmie Dale did not move as he finished reading the letter, save that his fingers began to tear the pages into strips, and the strips over and over again into tiny fragments--then, mechanically, he dropped the pieces into the pocket of his dinner jacket and mechanically reached for the newspaper that Jason had picked up and laid on the table. And now a dull red burned in his cheeks, and the square jaw was clamped and hard. Strange coincidence! Yes, it was strange--but perhaps it was more than mere coincidence! He had an interest, a very personal, vital interest in that article on the front page now, in this combine of those who were frankly of the dregs of the criminal world and those of a blacker breed who hid behind the veneer of respectability and station.

He read the article slowly. It was but the resume of the case that had been under investigation for the past few weeks, the sensation it had created the greater since the publicity so far given to it had but hinted darkly at the scope of the exposure to come, while as yet no names had been mentioned. "The Private Club Ring," as set forth in the paper, operated a chain of what purported to be small, select and very exclusive clubs, but which in reality were gambling traps of the most vicious description--and the field of their operations was very wide and exceedingly lucrative. Men known to have money, whether New Yorkers or from out of town, were "introduced" there by "members" whose standing and presumed respectability were beyond reproach--and they were bled white; while, to add variety to the crooked games, orgies, revels and carousals of the most depraved character likewise furnished the lever for blackmail--the "member" *ostensibly* being in as bad a hole, and in as desperate a predicament as the "guest" he had introduced!

The article told Jimmie Dale nothing new, nothing that he did not already know, save the statement that the evidence now in the possession of the authorities was practically complete, and that the arrest and disclosure of those involved might be expected at any moment.

He put down the paper, and stood up--and for the second time that night began to pace the room. If the article had told him nothing new, it at least explained that sentence in the Tocsin's letter--*they are playing their last card to-night.* They must strike now, or never--the exposure could be but a matter of a few hours off!

A face crowned with its gray hair rose before him, a kindly face, grave and strong and fine, the face of a man of sterling honesty and unimpeachable integrity--the face of David Archman, the assistant district attorney, who had both instituted and was in charge of the investigation that now threatened New York with an upheaval that promised to shake many a social structure to its foundations. Yes, they would play their last card, a vile, despicable and hellish card--but how little they knew David Archman! They would break his life; it would, indeed, as the Tocsin had said, be murder--but they would never break David Archman's unswerving loyalty to principle and duty! They had tried that--by threats of personal violence, by the offer of bribes in sums large enough to have tempted many!

His face hard, his forehead gathered in puzzled furrows, Jimmie Dale stepped to the door, and locked it; then, drawing aside the portiere that hung before the little alcove at the lower end of the room, knelt down before the squat, barrel-shaped safe, and his fingers began to play over the knobs and dials.

Yes, it was a vitally personal matter now; there was an added incentive to-night spurring the Gray Seal on to act. David Archman had been his father's closest friend; and he, Jimmie Dale, himself had always looked on David Archman, and with reason, as little less than a second father. His frown grew deeper--he did not understand. But Tocsin did *not* make mistakes. He had had evidence of that on too many occasions when he had thought otherwise to question it now--but David Archman's son in *this*! It seemed incredible! The boy, he was little more than a boy, scarcely twenty, was and always had been, perhaps, a little wild, but a thief, an associate and accomplice of the city's worst crooks and criminals was something of which he, Jimmie Dale, had never dreamed until this instant, and now, while it staggered him, it brought, too, a sense of merciless fury--a fury against those who would stab like inhuman cowards, pitilessly, at the father through the son. Their last card! The safe swung open. Their last card was--Clarie Archman, the son!

He reached into the safe, took out an automatic, and placed it in his pocket. There was no necessity to go to the Sanctuary--what he would need was here in duplicate, and it would be Jimmie Dale, not Smarlinghue, who played the role of the Gray Seal to-night. A dozen small steel picklocks in graded sizes followed the revolver, and after these a black silk mask and a pocket flashlight--the thin, metal insignia case containing the little diamond-shaped, gray-coloured paper seals, never absent from his person since the night he had lost and recovered it again, was already reposing in an inner pocket of his clothes.

His face was still hard, as he stood up and closed the safe. The way out, the way to save David Archman was plain, of course. It was even simple--if it was not too late! And the way out was another "crime" committed by the Gray Seal! Instead of Clarie Archman and J. Barca, alias Gentleman Laroque, robbing the safe of one Niccolo Sonnino, dealer in precious stones, it would be the Gray Seal--if it was not already too late to forestall the others!

If it was not too late! He looked at his watch. It was twenty minutes after eleven. Yes, there should be time; but, if not--what then? And what of that letter? His teeth clamped. Well, he would try it; and he would make every second count now! He was lifting the telephone receiver of the private house installation now, calling the garage. Benson, his chauffeur, answered him almost on the instant.

"The light touring car, Benson, please, and as quickly as possible," said Jimmie Dale pleasantly.

"Yes, sir--at once," Benson answered.

Jimmie Dale replaced the receiver on the hook, and, running now across the floor, unlocked the door, crossed the hall, and entered his dressing room. Here, he changed his dinner clothes for a dark tweed suit--the location of Niccolo Sonnino's place of business was in a neighbourhood where one in evening dress, to say the least of it, would not go unobserved--transferred the metal case and the articles he had taken from the safe to the pockets of the tweed suit, and descended the stairs.

Standing in the hallway, Jason, that model of efficiency, with an appraising glance at his master's changed attire, handed Jimmie Dale a soft hat--and opened the door.

"Benson is outside, Master Jim," said Jason; but the look in the old man's eyes was eloquent far beyond the respectful and studied quiet of his words. The old face was pale and grave with anxiety.

"It's all right, Jason--all right *this* time," Jimmie Dale smiled reassuringly.

"Thank you, sir," said Jason, in a low voice. "I hope so, sir. And, begging your pardon, Master Jim, sir, I pray God it is."

And for answer Jimmie Dale smiled again, and passed down the steps, and entered the car. But the smile was gone as he leaned back in his seat after giving Benson his directions--speed, and a corner a few blocks away from Chatham Square--he was not so sure that it was all right. It was entirely a question of time. Given the time and the opportunity--Niccolo Sonnino out of the road, for instance--given twenty minutes ahead of Clarie Archman and Gentleman Laroque, it would be simple enough. But otherwise--his lips thinned--otherwise, he did not know.

Otherwise, there was promise of strange, grim work before daylight came, work that might lead him out of necessity to the role of Smarlinghue, and as Smarlinghue--anywhere! He did not know; he knew only one thing--that, at any cost, if it lay within any power of his to prevent it, David Archman should not live a broken man.

The car speeded its way rapidly along in a downtown direction, Benson keeping, wherever possible, to the unfrequented streets. Jimmie Dale, busy with his problem, his mind sifting and turning this way and that the curious, and in some cases apparently conflicting details of the Tocsin's letter, paid little attention to his surroundings, save to note approvingly from time to time that a request to Benson to hurry was equivalent to something perilously near to a contempt of speed laws. It still seemed incredible that Clarie Archman was a thief, a safe-tapper, even if but an amateur one. The boy must have travelled a pace of late that was fast and furious. How had he ever become intimate enough with Gentleman Laroque to be associated with the other in such a crime as this? How had Laroque come to play a part in the miserable scheme of trickery that was the Private Club Ring's last card.

Jimmie Dale shook his head helplessly at the first question--and shook it again at the second. He knew Laroque--he knew him for one of the most degraded, as well as one of the most dreaded, gang leaders in crimeland. Laroque, in unvarnished language, was a devil, and, worse still, a most callous devil. Laroque stood first and all the time for Laroque. If murder would either further or safeguard Laroque's personal interests, Laroque was the sort of man who would stop only to consider, not whether the murder should be committed, but the method that might best be employed in order to implicate as little as possible one Laroque! Also, to those in the secrets of the underworld, Gentleman Laroque added to his accomplishments, or had done so before he rose to the eminence of gang leader, the profession of "box-worker"--not a very clever exponent of the art, crude perhaps in his methods, but at the same time efficacious, as a dozen breaks and looted safes in the years gone by bore ample witness.

Grimly whimsical came Jimmie Dale's smile. Gentleman Laroque would have made a very much better "confidence" man than safe-worker. The man was suave, polished when he wanted to be, educated; he possessed all the requisites, and, in abundance, the prime requisite of all--a cunning that was the cunning of a fox. This might even have explained his acquaintanceship with Clarie Archman, except for the fact that it did not explain Clarie Archman's co-operation in a premeditated robbery with any one!

Again Jimmie Dale shook his head--and there came another question, one for which no answer, even of a suggestive nature, had been supplied in the Tocsin's letter. Why had Niccolo Sonnino's safe been selected as the one especial and desirable nut to crack? He knew Niccolo Sonnino, too, in a general way, as all who resided near or had any dealings in the neighbourhood where Sonnino lived, knew the man. True, combined with a small trade in jewelry and precious stones, the former cheap and the latter of an inferior grade to fit the purses of his customers, the man was a money-lender--but in an equally small way. Loans of minor amounts, a very few dollars as a maximum, was probably the extent of Sonnino's ventures along this line. Sonnino himself was a crafty little man, but craftiness, if it did not transgress the law, was not a crime; he was undoubtedly a usurer in his petty way, and he was both feared and disliked, but beyond that no one pretended to know anything about him. Ordinarily, Sonnino's safe, then, might be expected to be rather a barren affair, hardly a lure for a Gentleman Laroque brand of crook! Why, then, Sonnino's safe to-night? What was in that letter signed "J. Barca" that Clarie Archman had received? J. Barca was Gentleman Laroque; that would have been evident in any case, even if the Tocsin had not expressly said so--but the letter! Did the letter, apart from its incriminating ingenuity, supply the answer to his question? Had Sonnino, for instance, by some lucky turn, disposed of his stock in bulk, and was thus for the moment in possession of an unusually large amount of cash; or, inversely, had Sonnino received an unusual stock of stones? Either of these theories, and equally neither one of them, might furnish the answer! Jimmie Dale shrugged his shoulders grimly. He would find the answer--in Sonnino's safe! One thing, however, one thing that might have had some bearing on Laroque's choice, one thing for which he, Jimmie Dale, was grateful to Laroque for making such a choice, was that Sonnino's place lent itself admirably to attack--from the standpoint of the attacker! A black courtyard, screened completely from the street; a house that--

Jimmie Dale looked up suddenly, and, as suddenly, leaning forward, he touched Benson's shoulder. They were just approaching a restaurant and music hall known as "The Sphinx," that was popular for the moment with the slumming parties from uptown.

"This will do. You may let me out here at The Sphinx, Benson," he said quietly; and then, as the car stopped: "I shall not be long, Benson--perhaps half an hour-- wait for me."

Benson touched his cap. Jimmie Dale ran up the steps of the restaurant, en- tered, threaded his way through several crowded rooms where the midnight rev- elry was in full swing--and passed out of the place by a convenient rear exit that gave on the adjoining cross street. The car standing in front of The Sphinx would attract no notice; and he was now on the same street as Sonnino's place, and only two short blocks away.

He started forward from the restaurant door--and paused, struggling with a refractory match in an effort to light a cigarette. A man brushed by him, making for the restaurant door, a tall, wiry-built, swarthy, sharp-featured man--and Jimmie Dale flipped the stub of his match away from him, and went on. Sonnino himself! There was luck then at the start--the coast was clear!

CHAPTER XV
CAUGHT IN THE ACT

It was one of those countless streets on the East Side each so identical with another--dark, not over clean, flanked on both sides with small shops, basement stores and tenement dwellings that crowded one upon the other in a sort of helpless confusion. Jimmie Dale moved quickly along. The whimsical smile was back on his lips. Sonnino, whose business, the money-lending end of it, would naturally have kept him late at work, was now evidently intent on a belated meal; Sonnino, therefore, could be counted upon as a factor eliminated for at feast the next half hour--and half an hour was enough, a little more than enough!

Jimmie Dale glanced back over his shoulder. There was no one in sight. A yard ahead of him, one of those relics of barbaric architecture, tunnelled as it were through the centre of a building that the space overhead might not be wasted, was the black driveway that gave entrance to the courtyard behind, where Sonnino lived alone in one of a half dozen small, tottering-from-age frame houses. Jimmie Dale drew closer to the wall, came opposite the driveway--and disappeared from the street.

It was the Gray Seal now, the professional Jimmie Dale, as silent in his movements as the shadows about him. He traversed the driveway, and emerged on the courtyard. Here, it was scarcely less dark. There was no moon, and no lights in any of the houses that made the rear of the courtyard. He could just discern the houses as looming shapes against the sky line, that was all.

He crossed the courtyard, and, reaching the line of door-stepless, poverty-stricken hovels--they appeared to be little more than that--crept stealthily along to the end house at the left, halted an instant to press his face against a black window pane, then tried the door cautiously. It was locked, of course. Again there came the whimsical smile, but it was almost hidden now by the black silk mask that he slipped quickly over his face. His finger tips, that were like a magical sixth sense to Jimmie Dale, embodying all the other five, felt tentatively over the lock, then slipped into his pocket, selected unerringly one of his picklocks, and inserted the little steel instrument in the keyhole. An instant more and the door was opening without a sound under Jimmie Dale's hand. And then, the door open, he stepped over the threshold, and, in the act of closing the door behind him, stood suddenly rigid--and where the whimsical smile had been before, his lips were now compressed into a thin, straight line.

"What's that?" came a hoarse, shaken whisper out of the blackness beyond.

"What's *what*?" demanded another voice--the whisper this time sharp and caustic. "I didn't hear anything!"

"Neither did I," admitted the first speaker. "It wasn't that--it was like a draft of air--as though the door or a window had been opened."

"Forget it!" observed the second voice contemptuously. "Cut out the jumps--we've got to get through here before Sonnino gets back. You'd make a wooden Indian nervous!"

There was silence for an instant, then a curious gnawing sound punctuated with quick, low, metallic rasps as of a ratchet at work--and upon Jimmie Dale for a moment came stunned dismay. Time, the one factor upon which he had depended, was lost to him; Clarie Archman and Gentleman Laroque were already at work in there in that room beyond. He stood motionless, his brain whirling; and then slowly, without a sound, an inch at a time, he began to close the door behind him. He could see nothing; but the door connecting the two rooms was obviously open--the distinctness with which the whispering voices had reached him was proof of that. They were working, too, without light, or he would have got a warning gleam when he had looked through the window. And now--what now? The picklock was shifted to his left hand, as he drew his automatic from his pocket. There was only one answer to the question--to play the game out to the end, whatever that end might be!

Beneath the mask his face drew into chiselled lines, as the picklock silently locked the door. There was one exit from that inner room, and only *one*--through the room in which he stood. The Tocsin had drawn an accurate word-plan of the crude, shack-like place, and now in his mind he reconstructed it here in the darkness. The doorway into a small hall that led to the stairs adjoined the doorway of that inner room where the two were now at work--and in that room were no windows, it was a sort of blind cubby-hole where Niccolo Sonnino transacted his most private business.

Jimmie Dale crept forward up the room. There was no answering creak of board or flooring, no sound save that gnawing sound, and the rasping click of the ratchet. His place of vantage was against the wall between the two doors--there, be could both command the exit from, and see into, the inner room, while the doorway into the hall provided him with a means of retreat should the necessity arise. And then, suddenly, halfway up the room, he dropped down behind what was evidently a jeweller's workbench. A whisper, obviously Laroque's this time, came once more from the inner room.

"Shoot the flash again!" And then, savagely: "Curse it, not on the *ceiling*! Can't you hold it steady! What the devil is the matter with you!"

There was no answer. A dull glimmer of light filtered through the doorway, but from the position in which he lay Jimmie Dale could distinguish nothing in the inner room itself.

"All right! That'll do!" Laroque growled presently.

The light went out. Jimmie Dale crept forward again. And now he gained the rear wall of the room, and crouched down close against it between the two doorways.

Came the sound of breathing now, heavy, as from sustained exertion, making almost an undertone of the steady *click-click-click* of the ratchet, and the sullen gnaw of the bit. The minutes passed. The flashlight went on again--and Jimmie Dale strained forward. Two dark forms, backs to him, were outlined against the face of the safe which was at the far side of the room, a nickel dial glistened in the white ray--he could make out nothing else.

Then darkness again. And again, after a time, the flashlight. Ten, fifteen, perhaps twenty minutes dragged by. Jimmie Dale might have been a shadow moving against the wall for all the sound he made as he changed his cramped position; but, just below the mask, his lips were pressed fiercely together. Would Gentleman Laroque never get through! Sonnino was not only likely to return in a very few minutes now, but was almost certain to do so. Under his breath Jimmie Dale cursed the gangster's bungling methods--and not for their crudity alone. His first impulse had been to surprise the two, hold them up at the revolver point, but the result of such an act would have been abortive, for the disfigured safe would stand a mute, incontrovertible witness to the fact that an ***attempt*** to force it had been made-- and, whether it was actual robbery or attempted robbery that was proved against the son, it in no way deflected the blow aimed at David Archman. And, besides, there was the letter! If he, Jimmie Dale, had been in time even to have prevented Gentleman Laroque from sinking a bit into the safe, the letter would have counted not at all--but now it counted to the extent that it literally meant life and death. Who had it? Not Clarie Archman--that was certain. And the Tocsin had not said-- obviously because she, too, had been in the dark in that respect. Therefore he could only wait, watch and follow every move of the game throughout the rest of the night, if necessary! It was the only course open to him; the letter, not the robbery, was paramount now.

A curious, muffled, metallic thump, mingled with a quick, low-breathed, tri- umphant oath, came suddenly from the inner room--and then Laroque's voice, ea- ger, the words clipped off as though in feverish elation:

"There she is! One nice little job--eh? Well, come on--shoot your light into her, and let's take a look at the Christmas tree!"

The flashlight's ray flooded the interior of the open safe. Laroque, on his knees, laughed suddenly, and thrust his hand inside.

"What did I tell you, eh?" he chuckled. "I got the straight tip, eh? Four thou- sand, if there's a cent!"

Laroque began to remove what were evidently packages of banknotes from the safe--but Jimmie Dale was no longer watching the scene. He had edged suddenly back into the doorway of the hall, and was listening now intently. A footstep--he could have sworn he had caught the sound of a footstep--seemed to have come from just outside the front window. But all was still again. Perhaps he had been mistaken. No! Slight as was the sound, he heard, unmistakably now, a key grate in the lock-- and then, stealthily, the front door began to open.

A bewildered look came into Jimmie Dale's face, as he retreated further back into the hallway itself now. It was probably Sonnino; but why did Sonnino come stealing into his own house like--well, like any one of the three predatory guests already there before him? And then Jimmie Dale's face cleared. Of course! From the window the glow of the flashlight in the inner room could be seen. Sonnino was forewarned, and undoubtedly--forearmed!

The front door closed softly, so softly that had Jimmie Dale, supersensitive as his hearing was, not been intent upon it, it would have escaped him. The glow from the inner room, faint as it was, threw into shadowy relief a man's form tiptoeing forward--and then a board creaked.

" *What's that*!" came in a wild whisper from Clarie Archman.

"Got 'em again!" Laroque snapped back. "You make me tired!"

"Let's get out of here! Let's get out of here--quick!" Clarie Archman's voice, not so low now, held a tone of frantic appeal.

"Nix!" said Laroque, in a vicious sneer. "Not till the job's done! D'ye think I'm going to spend half an hour cracking a safe and take a chance of missing any bets? We've got the coin all right, but there ought to be one or two of Sonnino's sparklers lying around in some of these drawers, and--"

There was a click of an electric-light switch, a cry from Clarie Archman, the inner room was ablaze with light, and--Jimmie Dale had edged forward again out of the hallway--Sonnino, revolver in hand, was standing just over the threshold facing Gentleman Laroque and the assistant district attorney's son.

Then silence--a silence of seconds that were as minutes. And then Gentleman Laroque laughed gratingly.

"Hello, Sonnino!" he said coolly. "A little late, aren't you? You've kept me stalling for the last five minutes. Know my friend--Mr. Martin Moore, alias Mr. Clarie Archman? Clarie, this is Signor Niccolo Sonnino, the proprietor of this joint."

And then to Jimmie Dale, where before his mind had groped in darkness to reconcile apparently incongruous details, in a flash there came the light. The "plant" was a little more intricate, a little more cunning, a little more hellish--that was all!

The boy, white to the lips, was swaying on his feet, grasping at the table in the centre of the room. He looked from one to the other, a miserable, dawning understanding in his eyes.

"You--you know my name?" His voice was scarcely audible.

"Sure!" said Laroque--and yawned insolently.

"So!" purred Sonnino, in excellent English. "Is it so! A thief! The son of the so-honest Mister Attorney--a thief!"

"It's a lie!" The boy's hands, clenched, were raised above his head, and then shaken almost maniacally in Gentleman Laroque's face. "It's a lie! I--I don't understand, but--but you two, you devils, are together in this!"

"Sure!" retorted Laroque, as insolently as before--and flung the other's hands away. "Sure, we are!"

"It's a lie!" said the boy again. "I was in a hole. I needed money. You told me you knew a man who would lend it to me. That's why I came here with you, and then--and then you held me here with your revolver, and began to open that safe."

"Sure!" returned Laroque, for the third time. "Sure--that's right! Well, what's the answer?"

"This!" cried the boy wildly. "I don't know what your game is, but this is my answer! Do you think I would have touched that money, or have let you--once I got out of here where I could have got help! I'm not a thief--whatever else I may be. That's my answer!"

Niccolo Sonnino's smile was oily.

"It is a little late, is it not?" he leered. "Listen, my little young friend; I will tell you a story. You work for a bank, eh? The bank does not like its young men to speculate--yes? But why should you not speculate a little, a very little, if you like--if you get the very private and good tips, eh? It is not wrong--no, certainly, it is not wrong. But at the same time the bank must not know. Very well! They shall not know--no one shall know. You are not the young Mr. Archman any more, you are--what is the name?--Martin Moore. But Martin Moore must have an address, eh? Very well! On Sixth Avenue there is a little store where one rents boxes for private mail, and where questions are never asked--is it not so, my very dear young friend?"

The boy was staring in a demented way into Sonnino's face, but he did not speak.

"Aw, hand it to him straight!" Gentleman Laroque broke in roughly. "I don't want to hang around here all night. Here, Archman, you listen to me! We piped you off on that lay about two weeks ago--and it looked good to us, and we played it for a winner, see? You got introduced to me, and found me a pretty good sort, and we got thick together--you know all about that. Also, you get introduced to some new brokers, who said they'd take good care of your margins--maybe they only ran a bucket-shop, but you didn't know it! All right! You got snarled up good and plenty. Yesterday you were wiped out, and three thousand dollars to the bad besides, and they were yelling for their money and threatening to expose you. They gave you until to-morrow morning to make good. You told me about it. I told you this morning I thought I knew a man who would lend you the coin, and"--he laughed mockingly, and jerked his hand toward the safe--"well, I led you to it, didn't I?"

"I--I don't understand," the boy mumbled helplessly.

"Don't you!" jeered Laroque. "Well, it looks big enough for a blind man to see! We've got this robbery wished on you to a fare-thee-well! A young man who speculates, who uses an assumed name, and runs a private letter box on Sixth Avenue, and has forty-eight hours in which to square up his debts or face exposure, has a hell of a chance with a jury-- *not*!"

The boy circled his lips with the tip of his tongue.

"But why--why?" he whispered. "I--I never did anything to you."

"Sure, you didn't!" Laroque's tones were brutally amiable now. "It's your father. We've an idea that maybe he won't be so keen about going ahead with that little investigation of the private clubs after we've put a certain little proposition about his son up to him."

"No, no! No--you won't!" Clarie Archman's voice rose suddenly shrill, beyond control. "You won't! You can't! You're in it yourselves"--he pointed his finger wildly at one and then the other of the two men--"you--you!"

"Think so?" drawled Laroque. "All right, you tell 'em so--tell the jury about it, tell your father, who is such a shark on evidence, about it. Sure, I'm in on it with you--but you don't know who I am. They'll have a hot time finding J. Barca, Esquire! I'm thinking of taking a little trip to Florida for my health, and my valet's got my grip all packed! Savvy? And now listen to Sonnino. Sonnino's a wonder in the witness box. Niccolo, tell the jury what you know about this unfortunate young man."

Sonnino, a wicked grin on his face, made a dramatic flourish with the hand that held the revolver.

"Well, I was asleep upstairs. I wakened. I thought I heard a noise downstairs. I listened. Then I got up, and went down the stairs quiet like a mouse. I turned on the light quick--like this"--he snapped his fingers. "Two men have broken open my safe, and they have my money, a lot of money, for I keep all my money there; I do not bank--no. They rush at me, they knock me down, they make their escape, but I recognise one of them--it is Mister the young Archman, who I have many times seen at The Sphinx Cafe--yes. Well, and then on the floor I find a letter." He grinned wickedly again. "Have you the letter that I find--Mister Barca?"

"Sure," said Gentleman Laroque--and reached into his pocket. "It was addressed to Martin Moore on Sixth Avenue, wasn't it?"

"My God!" It came in a sudden, pitiful cry from the boy, and his hand involuntarily went to his own pocket. "You--you've got that letter!"

"Do you think you're up against a piker game!" exclaimed Laroque maliciously. "Well then, forget it! You didn't have this in your pocket half an hour before it was lifted by one of the slickest poke-getters in the whole of little old New York." He was taking a letter from its envelope and opening out the sheet. "That's the kind of a crowd that's in on this, my bucko! Listen, and I'll read the letter. It looked innocent enough when you got it, in view of what I told you about knowing a man who would lend you the money. But pipe how it sounds with Sonnino's safe bored full of holes. Are you listening? 'It's all right. Niccolo Sonnino has got his safe crammed full to-night. Meet me at Bristol Bob's at eleven. J. Barca.'"

There was silence in the room. Clarie Archman had dropped into a chair, and had buried his face in his arms that were out-flung across the table.

Then Laroque spoke again:

"Do you see where you stand--Clarie? Tell your story--and it's the *story* that sounds like a neat 'plant' of your lawyer's to get you off. You only get in deeper with the jury for trying to *trick* them, see? Here's the evidence--and it's got you cold. Sonnino recognises you. The letter is identified at the Sixth Avenue place, and *you* are identified as the guy that's been travelling under the name of Martin Moore. J. Barca has flown the coop and can't be found, and--well, I guess you get it, don't you?"

"What--what do you want?" The boy did not lift his head.

"We want your father to let up, and let up damned quick," said Laroque evenly. "But we'll give *you* a chance to get out from under, and you can take it or leave it--it doesn't matter to us. Your father's got the papers and the affidavits in the

'Private Club' case in his safe at home to-night, and a lot of those affidavits he can never replace--we've seen to that! All right! You've got the combination of the safe. Go home and get that stuff and bring it here. If it's here by four o'clock--that gives you about three hours--you're out of it. If it isn't, then your father gets inside information that the gang is wise to the fact that his son pulled a break tonight, but that they can keep Sonnino's mouth shut if he throws up the sponge, and that if he doesn't call it off with the 'Private Club Ring,' if he's so blamed fond of prosecuting, hc'll get a chance to prosecute his own son--as a thief!"

The boy did not move.

"And just one last word," added Laroque sharply. "Don't make the mistake of thinking that if you refuse to get the affidavits it puts a crimp in us. It's only because we're playing white with you, and to give you a chance, that you're getting any choice at all. We didn't intend to give you one, but we don't want to be too rough on you, so if you want to get out that way, and will agree to keep on queering your father's game if he starts it over again, all right. But you want to understand that we hold just as big a club over your father's head the other way."

" *White!* Playing white! Oh, my God!" Clarie Archman had lurched up from the chair to his feet. His face, haggard and drawn, was the face of one damned.

"Good-night!" said Laroque callously. "You know the way out! You've got till four o'clock. If you're not back here then--" He shrugged his shoulders significantly. "You see, I'm not even asking you what you are going to do. We don't care. It's up to you. Either way suits us. And now--beat it!"

Jimmie Dale drew back for a second time that night into the hallway. A step, slow, faltering, unsteady, like that of a man blinded, passed out from the inner room, and passed on down the length of the front room--and the door opened and closed. Clarie Archman, with God alone knew what purpose in his heart, was gone.

From the thin metal case, by means of the tiny tweezers, Jimmie Dale took out a gray seal, laid the seal on his handkerchief, folded the handkerchief carefully, placed it in his pocket--and crept forward toward the inner door again. The two men were bending over the table, over the money on the table, dividing it. Jimmie Dale's lips were mercilessly thin; a fury, not the white, impetuous heat of passion, but a fury that was cold, deadly, implacable, possessed his soul. He crept nearer--still nearer.

"The crowd that put this up says we keep it between us for our work," said Laroque shortly. "A third for you, the rest for me. You sure you put *all* they gave you in the safe--Niccolo?" He screwed up his eyes suspiciously. "You sure you ain't trying to hold anything out on me? If you are, I'll make you--"

The words died short on his lips--his jaw sagged helplessly.

Jimmie Dale was standing in the doorway.

"Niccolo, drop that revolver!" said Jimmie Dale softly. His automatic held a bead on the two men.

The revolver clattered to the table top. Neither of the men spoke--only their faces worked in a queer, convulsive sort of way, as they gazed in startled fascination at Jimmie Dale.

"Thank you!" said Jimmie Dale politely. He stepped briskly into the room, shoved Sonnino unceremoniously to one side, shoved his revolver muzzle none too gently into Laroque's ribs, and went through the latter's clothes. "Yes," he said, "I thought quite possibly you might have one." He pocketed Laroque's revolver, and also Sonnino's from the table. "And now that letter--thank you!" He whipped the letter from Laroque's inside coat pocket and transferred it to his own, then stepped back, and smiled--but the smile was not inviting. "I've only about five minutes to spare," murmured Jimmie Dale. "I'm in a *hurry*, Niccolo. I see some wrapping paper and string over there on top of the safe. Get it!"

The man obeyed mechanically, in a stupefied sort of way, and placed several of the sheets and a quantity of string upon the table. Laroque, silent, sullen, under the spell of Jimmie Dale's automatic, watched the proceedings without a word.

"Now," said Jimmie Dale, and an icy note began to creep into the velvet tones, "you two are going to make the first charitable contribution you ever made in your lives--say, to one of the city hospitals. Make as neat and as small a parcel of that money as you can, Niccolo."

"Not by a damned sight!" Laroque roared out suddenly. "Who the blazes are you! Curse you, I--" He shrank hastily back before the ominous outthrust of Jimmie Dale's automatic.

"Wrap it up, Niccolo, and tie a string around it!" snapped Jimmie Dale.

And again, but snarling, cursing now, the man obeyed.

Jimmie Dale's hand went into his pocket, and came out with his handkerchief.

He carried the handkerchief to his mouth, moistened the adhesive side of the gray paper seal, and pressed the handkerchief down upon the top of the parcel.

"It would hardly do for any one to know where the money really came from-- would it?" observed Jimmie Dale, and smiled uninvitingly again.

The two men were leaning, straining forward, their eyes on the diamond-shaped gray seal--and into their faces there crept a sickly fear.

"The Gray Seal!" Sonnino stumbled the words.

"Put an outside wrapper around that package!" instructed Jimmie Dale coldly. He watched Sonnino perform the task with trembling fingers; and then, placing the package under his arm, Jimmie Dale backed to the door. There was a key in the lock on the inner side. He transferred it coolly to the outer side--and his voice rasped suddenly with the fury that found vent at last.

"You are a pair of hell hounds," he said between his teeth; "but you are angels compared with the gang that hired you for this. Well, the game is up! David Archman will settle with *them* when they face the investigation--and I will settle with *you*! One night, a year ago, in last January, a certain Fourth Avenue bank was looted of eighteen thousand dollars-- *do you remember, Laroque?* Ah, I see you do! The police are still looking for the man who pulled that job. What would you say, Laroque, would be the sentence handed out for that little affair to a man with, say, *your* past record?"

Laroque's lips were twitching; his face had gone gray.

"Fourteen years would be a light sentence, wouldn't it?" resumed Jimmie Dale, an even colder menace in his voice. "And you remember Stangeist, and the Mope, and Australian Ike, don't you, Laroque--you remember they went to the death house in Sing Sing--and you remember that the Gray Seal sent them there? Yes, I see you do; I see your memory is good to-night! Listen, then! I have heard it said that Gentleman Laroque, with his gangsters behind him, would stop at nothing where Gentleman Laroque's own skin was concerned. I have heard it said that where Gentleman Laroque was known he was *feared*. Very well, Laroque, it is your turn to choose. You can choose between yourself and this 'Private Club Ring' who have purchased your services in this game to-night. I fancy you can find a means of inducing Sonnino here to keep his mouth shut; and I fancy that of the two evils--holding young Archman as a club over his father, or of your employers facing their trial and conviction--you can convince the 'Private Club Ring' that the lesser, the lesser as regards *your* risk, say, is to face that trial and conviction. Do I make myself plain--Laroque? It is simply a question of not a word being said of what has happened to-night--or fourteen years in Sing Sing for you! I do not think you will find the task difficult when you add, to whatever arguments of your own you may see fit to employ, the fact that the Gray Seal, if your principals make a move, will expose them for this night's work on top of what they will already have to answer for. Well--Laroque?"

There was silence for a minute. Sonnino, cringing, the suavity, the oiliness of manner gone, a man afraid, kept his eyes on the table, and kept passing his hands one over the other. Laroque was the gambler--a twisted smile was forced to his lips.

"You win," he said hoarsely. "You can take it from me, I'll go up the river for fourteen years for no one--I'll take blasted good care of that! But you"--a rage, un-governable and elemental, found voice in a sudden torrent of blasphemous invec-tive--"you--we'll get you yet! Some day we'll get you, you cursed snitch, you--"

"Good-night!" said Jimmie Dale grimly, and, stepping swiftly back over the threshold, shut and locked the door.

He gained the street, gained his car in front of The Sphinx--and, twenty min-utes later, after a break-neck run in which Benson for the second time that night defied all speed laws, Jimmie Dale alighted from his car at a street corner well up-town, dismissed Benson for the night, retraced his way half the distance back along the block, disappeared into a lane, and presently, taking a high fence with the agil-ity of a cat in spite of, his encumbering package, dropped noiselessly down into a backyard.

It was well known ground to Jimmie Dale--as a boy he had played here in the Archman's backyard, played here with Clarie Archman. His face masked again, he moved swiftly toward the rear of the house. There was still Clarie Archman. What would the boy do? Jimmie Dale's hand, a picklock in it again, clenched fiercely. It was a hell's choice they had given the boy--to rob his father, or go down himself, and drag his father with him, in ruin and disgrace! What would the boy do? Jimmie Dale was working silently at the back door now. It opened, and he stepped inside. He was here well ahead of the other, there was no possibility, granting even the start the boy had had, that Clarie Archman could have made the trip uptown in the same time. It was more likely that the boy might even linger a long while in misery and indecision before he came home. That was why he, Jimmie Dale, had dismissed Benson and the car for the night, and--

With a mental jerk, Jimmie Dale focused his mind on his immediate surroundings. It was dark; there were no lights in any part of the house, but he needed none, not even his flashlight--he knew the house as well and as intimately as his own. He was in the rear hall now, and now he opened a door, paused cautiously as the dull yellow glow from a dying grate fire illuminated the room faintly, then stepped inside. It was the Archman library, the room where David Archman did a great deal of his work at night A desk stood at the lower end of the room; and in the corner near the portiered windows was the lawyer's safe.

Jimmie Dale closed the door, moved toward the window, drew the portieres aside, released the window catch, silently raised the window itself--it was only a drop a few feet to the yard! And then Jimmie Dale sat down at the desk.

A clock somewhere in the house struck a single note--that would be halfpast one. Time passed slowly, interminably. The clock struck again--two o'clock. And then suddenly Jimmie Dale rose from his chair, and slipped into the window recess behind the portieres. The front door closed, a step came along the hall, the library opened, closed again--and Clarie Archman, his face as the flickering firelight played upon it, like a face of death, came forward into the room.

For a moment the boy held motionless beside the desk, his eyes fixed in a sort of horrible fascination upon the safe--and then, slowly, he moved toward it, and dropped on his knees before it, and his fingers began to twirl the knob of the dial. His fingers shook, and he was a long time at his task--and then the handle turned, and the safe was unlocked, but Clarie Archman did not open the door. Instead, he drew back suddenly, and rose swaying to his feet, and covered his face with his hands.

"I can't! Oh, my God, I--I can't!" he moaned. He lowered his hands after a moment, and gazed around him unseeingly, a queer, ghastly look came into his face. "I--I guess--I guess there's only one--one way to--to beat them," he whispered. "One way to beat them, and--"

The package in Jimmie Dale's hand dropped suddenly to the floor, he wrenched the portieres aside, and, with a low, sharp cry, sprang forward. The boy had taken a revolver from his pocket, and was lifting it to his head. Jimmie Dale struck up the other's hand--but in time only to deflect the shot; too late to prevent it being fired. There was a flash in mid-air, the roar of the report went racketing through the silent house, and the revolver, spinning from the other's hands, struck against the wall across the room.

And then Jimmie Dale had the boy by the shoulders, and was shaking him violently. Clarie Archman was like one stunned, numbed, and bereft of his senses.

"It's all right--you're clear! Do you hear--try and understand--you're clear!" Jimmie Dale whispered fiercely. "Here's your letter!" He thrust it into the other's hand. "Destroy it! Those men--Sonnino--Barca--will say nothing. You don't owe anybody any money--that bucket-shop was in the game with the rest, and--" Cries, voices, were coming from above now; and Jimmie Dale, like a flash, turned from the boy, leaped for the safe, wrenched the door open, reached in with both hands, and, snatching up an armful of the contents, spilled books and papers on the floor. He was back beside the boy in an instant. "Listen! You heard some one in here as you entered the house--you came into the room--*you caught me in the act*--you fired--you missed. And now--*fight*! Fight--pull yourself together--fight. They are coming!"

He caught the boy around the waist, and the two, locked together, reeled this way and that about the room. A chair, deliberately kicked over by Jimmie Dale, crashed to the floor. The cries drew nearer. Footsteps came racing madly down the stairs--and then the door of the library burst open, and David Archman, in pajamas, dashed through the doorway, and without a second's hesitation, made for the two struggling forms--and Jimmie Dale, releasing his hold upon the boy, suddenly sent the other staggering backwards full into David Archman, checking David Archman's rush--and, turning, sprang for the window, snatched up his package, hurled himself over the sill, dropped to the ground, and, racing for the fence, climbed it, and made the lane, just as a shot, from David Archman, no doubt, was fired from the window.

A moment more, and Jimmie Dale, his mask in his pocket, had emerged from the lane, and was walking nonchalantly along to the street corner; another, and he had boarded a street car--but under Jimmie Dale's coat was a most suspicious bulge.

Conscious of this, he left the street car a few blocks farther along, when he was far enough away to be certain that he would have eluded all pursuit--and walked the rest of the distance to Riverside Drive. If he had escaped unscathed, the package of banknotes had not--it was his coat that shielded them from view, not the wrappers, for the wrappers had been torn almost entirely away in his hasty exit over the fence.

He reached his home, and mounted the steps cautiously. There was Jason to consider--Jason with his lovable pernicious habit of sitting up for his master. Jason must not see those banknotes, that was obvious, and if Jason--yes!--Jimmie Dale was peering now through the monogrammed lace that covered the plate glass doors in the vestibule--yes, Jason was still sitting up. And then Jimmie Dale smiled that strange whimsical smile of his. Jason was still sitting up--asleep in the hall chair.

Softly, without a sound, Jimmie Dale opened the front door, entered, passed the old man, and went up the stairs. In his dressing room, he hid away the package that tomorrow, or at the first opportunity, would enrich some deserving charity, and, as silently as he had come up the stairs, he descended them again, passed by the old man again, and went out to the street once more. There was just one reason why Jason, tired out and asleep, sat there--only one--because Jason, old Jason, faithful, big-hearted Jason, loved his Master Jim.

Into Jimmie Dale's eyes there came a mist. Perhaps that was why, because he could not see clearly, that he stumbled on his way up the steps again; perhaps that was why he made so much noise that it was Jason who opened the door and held out his hands for Jimmie Dale's coat and hat.

"What!" said Jimmie Dale severely. "Sitting up again, Jason? Jason, go to bed at once!"

"Yes, sir," said Jason. "Thank you, sir. Thank you, Master Jim, sir--I will."

CHAPTER XVI
ONE CHANCE IN TEN

It was three nights later. Old Jason had placed a tray with after-dinner coffee and a liqueur set on the table at Jimmie Dale's elbow--that was fully an hour ago, and both coffee and liqueur were untouched. Things were not going well. Apart entirely from all lack of success where the Tocsin was concerned, things were not going well. The fate of Frenchy Virat, the fate of the Wolf, and, added to this, the Gray Seal's intervention in the plans and purposes of one Gentleman Laroque and certain gentlemen still higher up than Laroque, had not passed unmarked or unnoticed in the underworld. And now in the underworld a strange, ominous and far-reaching disquiet reigned. It was an underworld rampant with suspicion, mad with fury, more dangerous than it had ever been before.

Jimmie Dale's hand reached abstractedly into the pocket of his dinner jacket for his cigarette case. He lighted a cigarette, leaned back once more in the big, leather-upholstered lounging chair, and his eyes, half closed, strayed introspectively around the luxuriously appointed room, his own particular den in his Riverside Drive residence. Once, a very long while ago, years ago, so long ago now that it seemed as though it must have been in some strange previous incarnation, back in those days when the Tocsin had first come into his life, and when he had known her only as the author of those mysterious letters, those "calls to arms" to the Gray Seal, she had written: "Things are a little too warm, aren't they, Jimmie? Let's let them cool for a year."

A blue thread curled lazily upward from the tip of the cigarette. Jimmie Dale's eyes fastened mechanically on the twisting, wavering spiral, followed it mechanically as it rose and spread out into filmy, undulating, fantastic shapes--and the strong, square jaw set suddenly hard. It was not so very strange that those words should have come back to him to-night! Things were "warm" now--and he could not let them "cool" for a year!

"Warm!" He smiled a little mirthlessly. The comparison was very slight! Then, at the beginning, at the outset of the Gray Seal's career, the police, it was true, had shown a certain unpleasant anxiety for a closer acquaintanceship, but that was about all. To-day, lashed on and mocked by a virulent press, goaded to madness by their own past failures to "get" the Gray Seal, to whose door they laid a hundred crimes and for whom the bars of a death cell in Sing Sing was the goal if they could but catch their prey, the police, to a man, were waging a ceaseless and relentless war against him; and to-day, joining hands with the police, the underworld in all its thousand ramifications, prompted by fear, by suspicion of one another, reached out to trap him, and to deal out to him a much more speedy, but none the less certain, fate than that prescribed by the statutes of the law!

He shook his head. It could not go on--indefinitely. The role was too hard to play; the dual life, in a sort of grim, ironical self-mockery, brought even in its own successful interpretation added dangers and perils with each succeeding day. As it had been with Larry the Bat, the more he now lived Smarlinghue the more it became difficult to slough off Smarlinghue and live as Jimmie Dale; the more Smarlinghue became trusted and accepted in the inner circles of the underworld, the more he became a figure in those sordid surroundings, and the more dangerous it became to "disappear" at will without exciting suspicion, where suspicion, as it was, was already spread into every nook and corner of the Bad Lands, where each rubbed shoulders with his fellow in the lurking dread that the other was--the Gray Seal!

The police were no mean antagonists, he made no mistake on that score; but the peril that was the graver menace of the two, and the greater to be feared, was--the underworld. And here in the underworld in the last few days, here where on every twisted, vicious lip was the whisper, "Death to the Gray Seal," there had come even another menace. He could not define it, it was intuition perhaps--but intuition had never failed him yet. It was an undercurrent of which he had gradually become conscious, the sense of some unseen, guiding power, that moved and swayed and controlled, and was present, dominant, in every den and dive in crimeland. There had been many gang leaders and heads of little coteries of crime, cunning, crafty in their way, and all of them unscrupulous, like the Wolf, for instance, who had sworn openly and boastingly through the Bad Lands, and had been believed for a season, that they would bring the Gray Seal to a last accounting--but it was more than this now. There was a craftier brain and a stronger hand at work than the Wolf's had ever been! Who was it? He shook his head. He did not know. He had gone far into the innermost circles of the underworld--and he did not know. He sensed a power there; and in a dozen different, intangible ways, still an intuition more than anything else, he had sensed this "some one," this power, creeping, fumbling, feeling its implacable way through the dark, as it were, toward *him*.

Yes, it was getting "warm"--perilously warm! And inevitably there must come an end--some day. The warning stared him in the face. But he could not stop, could not heed the warning, could not let things "cool" now for a year, and stand aside until the storm should have subsided! Where was the Tocsin? If his peril was great--what was hers!

He surged suddenly upward from his chair, his hands clenched until the knuckles stood out like ivory knobs. The Tocsin! The woman he loved--where was she? Was she safe *to-night?* Where was she? He could not stop until that question had been answered, be the consequences what they might! Warnings, the realisation of peril--he laughed shortly, in grim bitterness--counted little in the balance after all, did they not! Where was the Tocsin?

The telephone rang. Jimmie Dale stared at the instrument for a moment, as though it were some singular and uninvited intruder who had broken in without warrant upon his train of thought; and then, leaning forward over the table, he lifted the receiver from the hook.

"Yes? Hello! Yes?" inquired Jimmie Dale. "What is it?"

A man's voice, hurried, and seemingly somewhat agitated, answered him.

"I would like to speak to Mr. Dale--to Mr. Dale in person."

"This is Mr. Dale speaking," said Jimmie Dale a little brusquely. "What is it?"

"Oh, is that you, Mr. Dale?" The voice had quickened perceptibly. "I didn't recognise your voice--but then I haven't heard it for a long while, have I? This is Forrester. Are--are you very busy to-night, Mr. Dale?"

"Oh, hello, Forrester!" Jimmie Dale's voice had grown more affable. "Busy? Well, I don't know. It depends on what you mean by busy."

"An hour or two," the other suggested--the tinge of anxiety in his tones growing more pronounced. "The time to run out here in your car. I haven't any right to ask it, I know, but the truth is I--I want to talk to some one pretty badly, and I need some financial help, and--and I thought of you. I--I'm afraid there's a mess here. The bank examiners landed in suddenly late this afternoon."

"The-- *what*?" demanded Jimmie Dale sharply.

"The bank examiners--I--I can't talk over the 'phone. Only, for God's sake, come--will you? I'll be in my rooms--you know where they are, don't you--on the cottier over--"

"Yes, I know," Jimmie Dale broke in tersely; then, quietly: "All right, Forrester, I'll come."

"Thank God!" came Forrester's voice--and disconnected abruptly.

Jimmie Dale replaced the receiver on the hook, stared at the instrument again in a perplexed way; then, called the garage on the private house wire. There was no answer. He walked quickly then across the room and pushed an electric button.

"Jason," he said a moment later, as the old butler appeared on the threshold in answer to the summons, "Benson doesn't answer in the garage. I presume he is downstairs. I wish you would ask him to bring the touring car around at once. And you might have a light overcoat ready for me--Jason."

"Yes, sir," said the old man. "Yes, Master Jim, sir, at once." His eyes sought Jimmie Dale's, and dropped--but into them had come, not the questioning of familiarity, but the quick, anxious questioning inspired by the affection that had grown up between them from the days when, as the old man was so fond of saying, he had dandled his Master Jim upon his knee. "Yes, sir, Master Jim, at once, sir," Jason repeated--but he still hesitated upon the threshold.

And then Jimmie Dale shook his head whimsically--and smiled.

"No--not to-night, Jason," he said reassuringly. "It's quite all right, Jason--there's no letter to-night."

The old man's face cleared instantly.

"Yes, sir; quite so, sir. Thank you, Master Jim," he said. "Shall I tell Benson that he is to drive you, sir, or--"

"No; I'll drive myself, Jason," decided Jimmie Dale.

"Yes, sir--very good, sir"--the door closed on Jason.

Jimmie Dale turned back into the room, began to pace up and down its length, and for a moment the reverie that the telephone had interrupted was again dominant in his mind. Jason was afraid. Jason--even though he knew so little of the truth--was afraid. Well, what then? He, Jimmie Dale, was not blind himself! It had come almost to the point where his back was against the wall at last; to the point where, unless he found the Tocsin before many more days went by, it would be, as far as he was concerned--too late!

And then he shrugged his shoulders suddenly--and his forehead knitted into perplexed furrows. Forrester--and the telephone message! What did it mean? There was an ugly sound to it, that reference to the bank examiners and the need of financial assistance. And it was a little odd, too, that Forrester should have telephoned him, Jimmie Dale, unless it were accounted for by the fact that Forrester knew of no one else to whom he might apply for perhaps a large sum, of ready money. True, he knew Forrester quite well--not as an intimate friend--but only in a sort of casual, off-hand kind of a way, as it were, and he had known him for a good many years; but their acquaintanceship would not warrant the other's action unless the man were in desperate straits. Forrester had been a clerk in the city bank where his, Jimmie Dale's, father had transacted his business, and it was there he had first met Forrester. He had continued to meet Forrester there after his father had died; and then Forrester had been offered and had accepted the cashiership of a small local bank out near Bayside on Long Island. He had run into Forrester there again once or twice on motor trips--and once, held up by an accident to his car, he had dined with Forrester, and had spent an hour or two in the other's rooms. That was about all.

Jimmie Dale's frown grew deeper. He liked Forrester The man was a bachelor and of about his, Jimmie Dale's, own age, and had always appeared to be a decent, clean-lived fellow, a man who worked hard, and was apparently pushing his way, if not meteorically, at least steadily up to the top, a man who was respected and well-thought of by everybody--and yet just what did it mean? The more he thought of it, the uglier it seemed to become.

He stepped suddenly toward the telephone--and as abruptly turned away again. He remembered that Forrester did not have a telephone in his rooms, for, on the night of the break-down, he, Jimmie Dale, had wanted to telephone, and had been obliged to go outside to do so. Forrester, obviously then, had done likewise to-night. Well, he should have insisted on a fuller explanation in the first place if he had intended to make that a contingent condition; as it was, it was too late now, and he had promised to go.

The sound of a motor car on the driveway leading from the private garage in the rear reached him. Benson was bringing out the car now. Jimmie Dale, as he prepared to leave the room, glanced about him from force of habit, and his eyes held for an instant on the portieres behind which, in the little alcove, stood the squat, barrel-shaped safe. Was there anything he would need to-night--that leather girdle, for instance, with its circle of pockets containing its compact little burglar's kit? He shook his head impatiently. He had already told Jason--if in other words--that there was no "call to arms" to the Gray Seal to-night, hadn't he? It was habit again that had brought the thought, that was all! For the rest, in the last few days, since this new intuitive danger from the underworld had come to him, an automatic had always reposed in his pocket by day and under his pillow by night; and by way of defence, too, though they might appear to be curious weapons of defence if one did not stop to consider that the means of making a hurried exit through a locked door might easily make the difference between life and death, his pockets held a small, but very carefully selected collection of little steel picklocks. He smiled somewhat amusedly at himself, as he passed out of the room and descended the stairs to the hall below. The contents of the safe could hardly have added anything that would be of any service even in an emergency! His mental inventory of his pockets had been incomplete--there was still the thin, metal insignia case, and the black silk mask, both of which, like the automatic, were never now out of his immediate possession.

He slipped into his coat as Jason held it out for him, accepted the soft felt hat which Jason extended, and, with a nod to the old butler, ran down the steps, dismissed Benson, who stood waiting, and entered his car.

It was three-quarters of an hour later when Jimmie Dale drew up at the curb on the main street of the little Long Island town that was his destination.

"Pretty good run!" said Jimmie Dale to himself, as he glanced at the car's clock under its little electric bulb. "Halfpast nine."

He descended from the car, and nodded as he surveyed his surroundings. He had stopped neither in front of the bank, nor in front of Forrester's rooms--it was habit again, perhaps, the caution prompted by Forrester's statement relative to the bank examiners. If there was trouble, and the obvious deduction indicated that there was, he, Jimmie Dale, had no desire to figure in it in a public way. Again he nodded his head. Yes, he quite had his bearings now. It was the usual main street of a small town--fairly well lighted, stores and shops flanking the pavements on either side, and of perhaps a distance equivalent to some seven or eight city blocks in length. Two blocks further up, on the same side of the street as that on which he was standing, was the bank--not a very pretentious establishment, he remembered; its staff consisting of but one or two apart from Forrester, as was not unusual with small local banks, though this in no way indicated that the business done was not profitable, or, comparatively, large. Jimmie Dale started forward along the street. On the corner just ahead of him was a two-story building, the second floor of which had been divided into rooms originally designed to be used as offices, as, indeed, most of them were, but two of these Forrester had fitted up as bachelor quarters.

Jimmie Dale turned the corner, walked down the side street to the office entrance that led to the floor above, opened the door, and ran lightly up the stairs. At the head of the stairs he paused to get his bearings once more. Forrester's rooms were here directly at the head of the stairs, but he had forgotten for the moment whether they were on the right or left of the corridor; and the corridor being unlighted now and without any sign of life left him still more undecided. It seemed, though, if his recollection served him correctly, that the rooms had been on the right. He moved in that direction, found the door, and knocked; but, receiving no answer, crossed the hall again, and knocked on the door on the left-hand side. There was no answer here, either. He frowned a little impatiently, and returned once more to the right-hand door. Forrester probably was up at the bank, and had not expected him to make the run out from the city so quickly. He tried the door tentatively, found it unlocked, opened it a little way, saw that the room within was lighted--and suddenly, with a low, startled exclamation, stepped swiftly forward over the threshold, and closed the door behind him.

It was Forrester's room, this one here at the right of the corridor--his recollection had not been at fault. It was Forrester's room, and Forrester himself was there--on the floor--dead.

For a moment Jimmie Dale stood rigid and without movement, save that as his eyes swept around the apartment his face grew hard and set, his lips drooping in sharp, grim lines at the corners of his mouth.

"My God!" Jimmie Dale whispered.

There was a faint, almost imperceptible odour in the room, like the smell of peach blossom--he noticed it now for the first time, as his eyes fastened on a small, empty bottle that lay on the floor a few feet away from the dead man's outstretched arm. Jimmie Dale stepped forward abruptly now, and knelt down beside the man for a hurried; examination. It was unnecessary--he knew that even before he performed the act. Yes--the man was dead He reached out and picked up the bottle. The odour was tell-tale evidence enough. The bottle had contained prussic, or hydrocyanic acid, probably the moist deadly poison in existence, and the swiftest in its action. He replaced the bottle on the spot where he had found it, and stood up.

Again, Jimmie Dale's eyes swept his surroundings. The room in which he stood was a sort of living room or den. There was a desk over by the far wall, a couch near the door, and several comfortable lounging chairs. Forrester lay with his head against the sharp edge of one of the legs of the couch, as though he had rolled off and struck against it.

Opposite the desk, across the room, was the door leading into the second room of the little apartment. Jimmie Dale moved toward this now, and stepped across the threshold. The room itself was unlighted, but there was light enough from the connecting doorway to enable him to see fairly well. It was Forrester's bedroom, and in no way appeared to have been disturbed. He remembered it quite well. There was a door here, too, that gave on the hall. He circled around the bed and reached the door. It was locked.

Jimmie Dale returned to the living room--and stood there in a sort of grim immobility, looking down at the form on the floor. He was not callous. Death, as often as he had seen it, and in its most tragic phases, had not made him callous, and he had liked Forrester--but suicide was not a man's way out, it was the way a coward took, and if it brought pity, it was the pity that was blunted with the sterner, almost contemptuous note of disapproval. What had happened since Forrester had 'phoned, that had driven the man to this extremity? When Forrester had 'phoned he had appeared to be agitated enough, but, at least, he had seemed to have had hopes that the appeal he was then making might see him through, and, as proof of that, there had been unmistakable relief in the man's voice when he, Jimmie Dale, had agreed to the other's request. And what had been the meaning of that "financial help"? Had, for instance--for it was pitifully obvious that if the bank had been looted an *innocent* man would not commit suicide on that account--a greater measure of the depredation been uncovered than had been counted on, so much indeed that, say, the financial assistance Forrester had intended to ask for had now increased to such proportions that he had realised the futility of even a request; or, again, had it for some reason, since he had telephoned, now become impossible to restore the funds even if they were in his possession?

A sheet of note paper lying on the desk caught Jimmie Dale's eyes. He stepped forward, picked it up--and his lips drew tight together, as he read the two or three miserable lines that were scrawled upon it:

What's left is in the middle drawer of the desk. There's only one way out now--I don't see any other way. I thought that I could get--but what does that matter! God help me! I'm sorry.

FLEMING P. FORRESTER.

I'm sorry! It was a pitiful epitaph for a man's life! I'm sorry! Jimmie Dale's face softened a little--the man was dead now. "I'm sorry.... Fleming P. Forrester"--he had seen that signature on bank paper a hundred times in the old days; he had little thought ever to see it on a document such as this!

He stared at the paper for a long time, and then, from the paper, his eyes travelled over the desk, then shifted again to Forrester--and then, for the second time, he knelt beside the other on the floor. For the moment, what was referred to as "being all that was left" in the middle drawer of the desk could wait. There was another matter now. He felt hurriedly through Forrester's vest and coat pockets--and from one of the pockets drew out a folded piece of paper. It was not what he was looking for, but it was all that rewarded his search. He unfolded the paper. It was dirty and crumpled, and the few lines written upon it were badly penned and illiterate:

The ante's gone up--get me? Six thousand bucks. You come across with that to-morrow morning by ten o'clock--or I'll spill the beans. And I ain't got any more paper to write any more letters on either--savvy? This is the last.

There was no signature. Jimmie Dale read it again--and abruptly put it in his own pocket. Yes, he had liked Forrester--well enough for this anyway! The man might have a mother perhaps--it would be bad enough in any case. And those other things, the empty bottle, the sheet of note paper with its scrawled confession--what about them? He returned with a queer sort of hesitant indecision to the desk. He had no right of course to touch them unless--

He shook his head sharply, as he pulled open the middle drawer of the desk.

"Newspapers--publicity--rotten!" he muttered savagely. "One chance in ten, and--ah!"

From the back of the drawer where it had been tucked in under a mass of papers, he had extracted a little bundle of documents that were held together by an elastic band. He snapped off the band, and ran through the papers rapidly. For the most part they were bonds and stock certificates indorsed by their owners, and evidently had been held by the bank as collateral for loans.

And then suddenly Jimmie Dale straightened up, tense and alert. He had no desire, very far from any desire to be caught here, or to figure publicly in any way in the case. The street door had opened and closed again. Footsteps, those of three men, his acute, trained hearing told him, sounded on the stairs. Again there came that queer, hesitant indecision as he stood there, while his eyes travelled in swift succession from the bank's securities in his hand to the note on the desk, to the empty bottle on the floor, to the white, upturned face of the silent form huddled against the couch.

"One chance in ten," muttered Jimmie Dale through his set lips. "One chance in ten--and I guess I'll take it!"

The footsteps came nearer--they were almost at the head of the stairs now. But now Jimmie Dale was in action--swift as a flash and silent as a shadow in every movement. The bundle of securities was thrust into his pocket, the sheet of note paper followed, and, as a knock sounded on the door, he stooped, picked up the bottle from the floor, and darted into the adjoining room--and in another instant he had reached the locked door and was working at it silently and swiftly with a picklock.

CHAPTER XVII
THE DEFAULTER

At the other door the knocking still continued--and then it was opened--and there came a chorus of low, horrified, startled cries, and the quick rush of feet into the room.

The picklock went back into Jimmie Dale's pocket, and crouched, now, his hand on the knob, turning it gradually without a sound, drawing the door ajar inch by inch, he kept his eyes on the doorway connecting with the other room. He could see the three men bending over Forrester. Their voices came in confused, broken, snatches:

"... Dead!... Good God!... Are you sure?... Perhaps he's only fainted.... No, he's dead, poor devil!..."

And then one of the men, the youngest of the three, a slight-built, clean-shaven, dark-eyed man of perhaps twenty-eight or thirty, rose abruptly, and glanced sharply around the room.

"Yes, he's dead!" he said bitterly. "Any one could tell that! But he wouldn't be dead, and this would never have happened if you'd done what I wanted you to do when you first came to the bank this afternoon. I wanted you to have him arrested then, didn't I?"

One of the others--and it was obvious that the others were the two bank examiners--a man of middle age, answered soberly.

"You're upset, Dryden," he said. "You know we couldn't do that--"

"On a teller's word against the cashier's--of course not!" the young man broke in caustically. "Well, you see now, don't you?"

"We couldn't do it then without proof," amended the bank examiner quietly.

"Proof!" Dryden exclaimed. "My God--*proof!* Who tipped your people off to have you drop in there this afternoon? I did, didn't I? Do you think I'd do that without knowing what I was about! Didn't I tell you that there was nothing but the office fixtures left! Didn't I? There were only the two of us on the staff, and didn't I tell you that I had discovered that the books were cooked from cover to cover? Yes, I did! And you had to get your pencils out and start in on a thumb-rule examination, as though nothing were the matter! Well, what did you find? The securities in a mess, what there was left of them--and what was supposed to be twenty thousand dollars that came out from the city yesterday nothing but a package of blank paper!"

"You didn't know that yourself until half an hour ago when we started to check up the cash," returned the other a little sharply.

"Well, perhaps, I didn't," admitted Dryden; "but I knew about the books."

"Besides that," continued the bank examiner, "Mr. Forrester was in town this afternoon when we got to the bank and this is the first time we have seen him, so we could not very well have done anything other than we have done in any case. I mention this because you are talking wildly, and that sort of talk, if it gets out, won't do any of us any good. You don't want to blame Mr. Marner here and myself for Mr. Forrester's death, do you?"

"No--of course, I don't!" said Dryden, in a more subdued voice. "I don't mean that at all. I guess you're right--I'm excited. I--well"--he motioned jerkily toward the form on the floor--"I'm not used to walking into a room and finding *that*."

It was Marner, the other bank examiner, who broke a moment's silence.

"We none of us are," he said, and brushed his hand across his forehead. "A doctor can't do any good, of course, but I suppose we should call one at once, and notify the police, too. I--"

Jimmie Dale had slipped through the door and out into the hall. A moment more and he had descended the stairs and gained the street, still another and he had stepped nonchalantly into his car. The car started forward, passed out of the lighted zone of the town's main street--and in the darkness, headed toward New York, Jimmie Dale, his nonchalance gone now, leaned forward over the wheel, and the big sixty horse-power car leaped into its stride like a thoroughbred at the touch of the spur, and tore onward at dare-devil speed through the night.

His lips twisted in a smile that held little of humour. Back there in that room they would call a doctor, and they would call the police. And the doctor would establish the fact that Forrester had died from the effects of a dose of prussic acid; and the police would establish--what? Prussic acid was swift in its effect. If Forrester had died from that cause, how had he taken it himself, and out of what had he taken it? What the police would see would be quite a different thing from what he, Jimmie Dale, had seen when he opened the door of that room! Instead of the evidence of suicide, there was now every evidence of **murder**. The bank examiners on entering the room, started at what they saw, obsessed with the wreckage of the bank, might still for the moment have jumped to the conclusion, natural enough under the circumstances, of suicide; but the police, after ten minutes of unemotional investigation, would father a very different theory.

Jimmie Dale's jaws clamped, as his eyes narrowed on the flying thread of gray road under the dancing headlights. Well, the die was cast now! For good or bad, his response to Forrester's telephone appeal had become the vital factor in the case. For good or bad! He laughed out sharply into the night. He would see soon enough--old Kronische, the wizened, crafty, little chemist, who burrowed like a fox in its hole deep in the heart of the Bad Lands, would answer that question. Old Kronische had a record that was known to police and underworld alike--and was trusted by neither one, and feared by both. But he was clever--clever with a devilish cleverness. God alone knew what he was up to in the long hours of day and night amongst his retorts and test tubes in his abominable smelling little hole; but every one knew that from old Kronische **anything** of a chemical nature could be obtained if the price, not a small one, was forthcoming, and if old Kronische was satisfied with the credentials of his prospective client.

Yes--old Kronische! Old Kronische was the man, the one than; there was no possible hesitancy or question there--the question was how to reach old Kronische. Jimmie Dale shook his head in a quick, impatient gesture, as though in irritation because his brain would not instantly respond to his demand to formulate a plan. It seemed simple enough, old Kronische was perfectly accessible--but it was, nevertheless, far from simple. He could not go to old Kronische as Jimmie Dale, there was an ugly turn that had been taken in that room of Forrester's now. If, as Jimmie Dale, he had had reason to keep out of the affair before, it was imperative that he should do so now--or he might find himself in a very awkward situation, so awkward, in fact, that the consequences might lead anywhere, and "anywhere" to Jimmie Dale, to the Gray Seal, to Smarlinghue, might mean ruin, wreckage and disaster. Nor, much less, could he risk going to old Kronische as Smarlinghue. He could not trust old Kronische. How, if old Kronische chose to "talk," could Smarlinghue account for any connection with what had transpired in Forrester's room? How long would it be, even if Smarlinghue were no more than put under surveillance, before the discovery would be made that Smarlinghue was but a role that covered--Jimmie Dale!

And then Jimmie Dale's strained, set face relaxed a little. His brain had repented of its stubbornness, it seemed, and was at work again. There was a way, a very sure way as far as old Kronische being "talkative" was concerned, but a very dangerous way from every other point of view. Suppose he went to old Kronische--as Larry the Bat!

The car tore on through the night; towns and villages flashed by; the long, deserted stretches of road began to give way to the city's outskirts--and Jimmie Dale began to drive more cautiously. Larry the Bat! Yes, it was perfectly feasible, as far as feasibility went. The clothes that he had duplicated at such infinite trouble were still hidden there in the Sanctuary. But to be caught as Larry the Bat meant--the end. That was the one thing the underworld knew, the one thing the police knew-- that Larry the Bat was, or had been, the Gray Seal. Still, he had done it once before, and it could be done again. He could reach old Kronische's without much fear of discovery after all, he would take good care to secure the few minutes necessary to make a "getaway" from the old chemist's, and **afterwards** old Kronische could talk as much as he liked about--Larry the Bat! Yes, that was the way! Old Kronische-- -and Larry the Bat. He, Jimmie Dale, would drive, say, to Marlianne's restaurant, and telephone Jason to send Benson for the car--Marlianne's, besides being a very natural stopping place, possessed the added advantage of being quite close to the Sanctuary.

His decision made, Jimmie Dale gave his undivided attention to his car, and ten minutes later, stopping in the shabby street that harboured Marlianne's, he entered the restaurant, threaded his way through the small crowded rooms--for Marlianne's, despite its spotted linen, was crowded at all hours--to a sort of hallway at the rear of the place, and entered the telephone booth.

He called his residence, and, as he waited for the connection, glanced at his watch. He smiled grimly. He could congratulate himself for the second time that night on having made a record run. It was not yet quite half-past ten, and he must have been at least a good twenty minutes in Forrester's rooms. He rattled the hook impatiently. They were a long time in getting the connection! Halfpast ten! He could be at the Sanctuary in another few minutes, ten minutes at the outside; then, say, another twenty to rehabilitate Larry the Bat, and by eleven he--

"Yes--hello!"--he was speaking quickly into the 'phone, as Jason's voice reached him. "Jason, I am down here at Marlianne's. Tell Benson to come for the car, and--" He stopped abruptly. Jason was talking excitedly, almost incoherently at the other end.

"Master Jim, sir! Is that you, sir, Master Jim! It--it came, sir, not ten minutes after you left to-night, and--"

"Jason," said Jimmie Dale sharply, "what's the matter with you? What are you talking about? What came?"

"Why--why, sir--I beg your pardon, sir, but I've been a bit uneasy ever since, sir. It's--it's one of those letters, Master Jim, sir."

A sudden whiteness came into Jimmie Dale's face, as he stared into the mouth-piece of the telephone. A "call to arms" from the Tocsin-- *now*--to-night! What was he to do! It was not a trivial thing which that letter would contain--it never had been, and it never would be, and no matter under what circumstances it found him, he--

Jason's voice faltered over the wire:

"Are you there, sir, Master Jim?"

"Yes," said Jimmie Dale quietly. "Bring the letter with you, Jason, and come down with Benson. I will wait for you here--in the car outside Marlianne's. And hurry, Jason--take a taxi down."

"Yes, sir," said Jason, his voice trembling a little. "At once, Master Jim."

Jimmie Dale hung up the receiver, returned to the street, and seated himself in his car. How long would it take them to get here? Half an hour? Well then, for half an hour his hands were tied, and he could do nothing but wait. He glanced around him. It was curious! It was here in this very place that he had once found a letter from her in his car; it was even here that, without knowing it at the moment, he had really seen her for the first time. And now--what did it hold, this letter, this "call to arms" that he sat here waiting for, while out there in that little town a man lay dead on the floor of his room, and around whom, where there had once been the evidence of a coward's guilt, crowned with the sorriest epitaph that ever man had written, there was now the evidence of a still blacker crime--the crime of murder.

He lighted a cigarette and smoked it through. Could it be *that*--in her letter! Intuition again? Well, why not--if old Kronische should answer the question as the chances were one in ten that old Kronische might answer it! Yes--why not! It would not be strange. Intuition--because somehow the feeling that it *was* so grew stronger with each moment that passed--well, once before to-night he had said that intuition had never failed him yet!

The minutes dragged by interminably. He smoked another cigarette, and after that another. The clock under the hood showed five minutes past eleven; the minute hand crept around to eight, nine, ten minutes past the hour--and then a taxi swerved on little better than two wheels around the corner--and Jimmie Dale, springing from his seat, jumped to the pavement as the taxi drew up at the curb.

Jason, palpably agitated, and followed by Benson, descended from the taxi. Jimmie Dale dismissed the cab, and motioned Benson to the car.

"Well, Jason?" he said quickly.

"It's here, sir, Master Jim"--the old butler fumbled in an inner pocket, and produced an envelope--"I--"

"Thank you! That's all--Jason." Jimmie Dale's quick smile robbed his curt dismissal of any sting. "Benson, of course, will drive you home."

"Yes, sir." The old man went slowly to the car, and climbed in beside the chauffeur. "Good-night, sir!" Jason ventured wistfully. "Good-night, Master Jim!"

"Good-night, Jason--good-night, Benson!" Jimmie Dale answered--and, turning, started briskly along the street. Jason's "good-night" had been eloquent of the old man's anxiety. He would have liked to reassure Jason --but he had neither the time, nor, for that matter, the ability to do so. The old man would be reassured when he saw his Master Jim enter the house again--and not until then!

Jimmie Dale glanced about him up and down the street. The car had gone, and he was well away from the entrance to Marlianne's. The street itself was practically deserted. He nodded quickly, and stepped forward toward a street lamp that was close at hand. As well here as anywhere! There was nothing remarkable in the fact that a man should stand under a street lamp and read a letter--even if he were observed.

He tore the envelope open, and, standing there, leaned in apparent nonchalance against the post--but into the dark eyes had leaped a sudden flash. One word seemed to stand out from all the rest on the written page he held in his hand--"Forrester." He laughed a little in a low, grim way. His intuition had been right again then, and that meant-- *what*? If she, the Tocsin, knew, then--his mind was working subconsciously, leaping from premise to a dimly seen, half formed conclusion, while his eyes travelled rapidly over the written lines.

"Dear Philanthropic Crook:--You will have to hurry, Jimmie.... I do not know what may happen.... Forrester ... bank cashier at"--yes, he knew all that! But this--what was this? "Money lender.... Abe Suviney... bled him ... early days in city bank ... fellow clerk's defalcation.... Forrester borrowed the money to cover it and save the other.... Suviney used it as a club for blackmail.... Forrester was trapped ... could not extricate himself without inculpating his friend ... friend died ... Suviney put on the screws ... to say anything then was to have it look like a dishonourable method of covering a theft of his own ... would ruin his career ... original amount four thousand ... Forrester has been paying blackmail in the shape of exorbitant interest ever since ... Suviney finally demanded six thousand to-day to be paid at once ... this has nothing to do with the bank robbery, but would look black ... added evidence...." He read on, his mind seeming to absorb the contents of the letter faster than his eyes could decipher the words. "English Dick ... confession forged ... organisation widespread ... enormously powerful ... leadership a mystery ... rendezvous that English Dick visits is at Marlopp's ... Reddy Mull's room ... rear room ... leaves cash and securities there under loose board, right-hand corner from door ... twenty thousand cash to-night...."

Jimmie Dale was walking on down the street, his fingers picking and tearing the sheets of paper in his hand into minute fragments. There was a sort of cold, unemotional, unnatural calm upon him. It was all here, all, the Tocsin had--no, not all! She had not known of the last act in the brutal drama, for her letter had been written prior to that. She had not known that there was-- *murder*. But apart from that, to the last detail, in all its hideous, relentless craft, the whole plot was clear.

There was no need to go to old Kronische now, no need to assume the role of Larry the Bat. The question was answered--the confession *was* a forgery--the evidence, not of suicide, but of murder, that he, Jimmie Dale, had left behind him in that room, was the evidence of fact.

He walked on--rapidly now--heading over in the direction of the Bowery. There had been neither ink nor pen upon the desk where he had found the confession, nor had there been a fountain pen in Forrester's pocket when he had searched the other! He laughed out a little harshly. A strange oversight on some one's part if there had been foul play--so strange that he had hesitated to believe it possible! And so it had been--one chance in ten, for there was nothing to have prevented Forrester from having written the note elsewhere than in his own room. But if Forrester had written it, he must of necessity have written it very recently, certainly *after* he had telephoned, that is, within an hour; whereas, if it had been written by some one else and brought there, if it was forged, if it was murder and not suicide, the note must have taken long and painstaking effort to prepare beforehand. That was the question that old Kronische, the chemist, was to have answered, a question that was very much in the cunning old fox's line--did the condition of the ink show that the note had been written within the hour? It was a very simple question for old Kronische, the man would have answered it instantly, for even to him, Jimmie Dale, the writing had not looked *fresh*. But there was no need of old Kronische now! And he, Jimmie Dale, understood now, too, the reason for Forrester's appeal over the telephone. In some way Forrester, without going to the bank itself, had learned that the bank examiners had suddenly put in an appearance, had either discovered or deduced that something was wrong, and had realised that should Suviney's demand for money, or Suviney's blackmailing story become known, it would appear as damning evidence of a past record looming up to point suspicion toward him now. That was what he had meant by saying he needed financial help.

Jimmie Dale slipped suddenly into a lane, edged along the wall of the tenement that made the corner, pushed aside a loose board in the fence, passed into the little courtyard beyond, and, still hugging the shadows of the building, opened a narrow French window, and stepped through into a room. He was in the Sanctuary.

CHAPTER XVIII
ALIAS ENGLISH DICK

But Jimmie Dale lost no time in the Sanctuary. In the darkness he crossed the room, and from behind the movable section of the baseboard possessed himself of a pocket flashlight, and a small, but extremely serviceable, steel jimmy--and in a moment more was back in the lane, and from the lane again was heading still deeper into the heart of the East Side.

English Dick! A twisted smile crossed his lips. Well as he knew the underworld and its sordid citizenship, he might be forgiven for not knowing English Dick. The man's reputation had reached into every corner of the Bad Lands, it was true; but it had not been known that the man himself was on this side of the water. And that the secret had been kept spoke with grim and deadly significance for the power and cunning of the master brain to which the Tocsin had referred, for English Dick was known as the most famous forger in Europe, the best in his line, and as such, from afar, was worshipped as a demi-god by the underworld of New York.

Block after block of dark, ill-lighted streets Jimmie Dale traversed, until, perhaps fifteen minutes after he had left the Sanctuary, he swerved suddenly for the second time that night into a lane. He might not have known English Dick, but he knew Reddy Mull, and he knew Marloff's! Reddy Mull was a gangster, a gunman pure and simple, whose services were at the call of the highest bidder; and Marlopp's was a pool and billiard hall--to the uninitiated. Marlopp's, however, if one had ears well trained enough to hear, resounded to the click of ivory that was not the click of pool and billiard balls! Upstairs, if one could get upstairs, a gambling hell supplanted the billiard hall below. It was an unsavoury place, the resort of crooks, some of whom lived there--amongst them, Reddy Mull.

Jimmie Dale, close against the fence, and halfway down the lane now, paused and looked about him, straining his eyes through the blackness--then with a lithe spring he caught the top of the fence, swung himself over, and dropped to the ground on the other side. The rear of a row of low buildings now loomed up before him across a narrow yard. Window lights showed here and there from the houses on either side; and from the upper windows of the house directly in front of him faint threads of light filtered out into the darkness through the cracks of closed shutters, but the lower part of the house was in blackness.

He crept forward silently across the yard. There was a back entrance, but it led to the basement--Jimmie Dale's immediate attention was directed to the rear window, the window of one Reddy Mull's room. And here, crouched beneath it, Jimmie Dale listened. From the front of the establishment came muffled sounds from the pool and billiard hall; there was nothing else.

The window was above the level of his head, but still easily within reach. He tested it, found it locked--and the steel jimmy crept in under the sash. A moment passed, there was a faint, almost indistinguishable creak; and then Jimmie Dale, drawing himself up with the agility of a cat, had slipped through, and was standing, listening again, inside the room.

The sounds from the pool room were louder, more distinct now, even rising once into a shout of boisterous hilarity; but there was no other sound. The round, white ray of Jimmie Dale's flashlight circled the room suddenly, inquisitively--and went out. It was a bare, squalid place, dirty, filthy, disreputable. There was a bed, unmade, a table, a few chairs, a greasy, threadbare carpet on the floor--nothing else, save that his eyes had noted that the electric-light switch was on the wall beside the jamb of the door.

The flashlight winked again--and again went out. Jimmie Dale slipped his mask over his face, and moved forward toward the wall.

"Under loose board, right-hand corner from door," murmured Jimmie Dale. He was kneeling on the floor now. "Yes, here it was!" His flashlight was boring down into a little excavation beneath the piece of flooring he had removed. He stared into this for a moment, his lips twitching grimly; then, with a whimsical shrug of his shoulders, he replaced the board, and stood up. He had found the hiding place without any trouble--but he had found it *empty*. "I guess," said Jimmie Dale, with a mirthless smile, "that there's a good deal of the bank's property at large--temporarily!"

There was a chair by the wall close to the door, he had noticed. He moved over, and sat down--but, instead of his flashlight, his automatic was in his hand now. There was the chance, of course, that English Dick had already been here with that twenty thousand from the bank, and in that case, as witness the empty hiding place, Reddy Mull had already passed it on; but it was much more likely that neither one of the two had yet arrived. Which one would come first then--English Dick, or Reddy Mull? If it were Reddy Mull it would be unfortunate--for Reddy Mull. His, Jimmie Dale's, immediate business was with English Dick, and he was quite content to leave Reddy Mull to the later ministrations of the police.

Jimmie Dale's fingers tested the mechanism of his automatic in the darkness. Whose was the master brain behind all this? This crime to-night bore glaring evidence to the work of some far-flung, intricate and powerful organisation--the Tocsin was indubitably right in that. Was this the first concrete expression he had had of that undercurrent he had sensed of late as permeating the underworld, that he had sensed was reaching out as one of its objects for *him* and that--

He came suddenly without a sound to his feet, and pressed back close against the wall, his body rigid and thrown forward like one poised to spring. There was a footstep outside the door, the rasp of a key in the lock, then a faint, murky path of light as the door opened, and a man stepped forward over the threshold. The key was inserted with another rasping sound in the inner side of the lock, the door closed, the key turned and was withdrawn, thrust evidently into its possessor's pocket--and then Jimmie Dale, silently, in a lightning flash, was upon the other, his hand at the man's throat, the cold, round muzzle of his automatic against the other's face. There was a choked cry, the thud as of something dropping on the floor--and then Jimmie Dale spoke.

"Put your hands up over your head!" he breathed grimly--and, as the other obeyed, his own hand fell away from the man's throat, and in a quick, deft sweep over the other's clothing located the bulge of a revolver, and whipped it from the man's pocket. He pushed the man with his automatic's muzzle back against the wall, closer to the electric-light switch. Was it Reddy Mull--or English Dick? And then Jimmie Dale laughed low, unpleasantly, as he switched on the light. He was staring into a face that was white and colourless--the face of a man with a heavy black moustache, and whose slouch hat was jammed far down over his eyes. The process of elimination made it very simple--it was English Dick.

The man blinked, and wet his lips with his tongue, and at sight of Jimmie Dale's mask, perhaps because it suggested a community of interest, tried to force a smirk.

"What's--what's the game?" he stammered.

"This--to begin with!" said Jimmie Dale grimly--and, stooping, picked up from the floor a small black satchel, the object that English Dick had dropped on entering the room. "Go over to that table!" ordered Jimmie Dale curtly.

The man obeyed.

"Sit down!" Jimmie Dale was clipping off his words in cold menace.

Again the man obeyed.

Jimmie Dale, his back to the door as he faced the other across the table, snapped open the bag. It was full to the top with banknotes and securities. Under his mask his lips curled in a hard, forbidding smile. He took from his pocket the package of the bank's securities he had found in the drawer of Forrester's desk, and laid it in silence on the table beside the satchel; beside this again, still in silence, he placed the bottle that had contained the hydrocyanic acid, and--after an instant's pause--spread out the sheet of note paper bearing Forrester's forged signature.

The man's face, white before, had gone a livid gray.

"W-what do you want?" he whispered.

"I want you to write another confession." There was a deadly monotony in Jimmie Dale's voice, as he tapped the paper with the muzzle of his automatic. "This one is out of date."

"I don't know what you mean," faltered English Dick. "So help me, honest to God, I don't!"

"Don't you!" There was a curious drawl in Jimmie Dale's voice--and then in a flash his free hand swept across the table, jerked away the other's moustache, and pushed the slouch hat up from the man's eyes. "I mean that the game is up--***Dryden***."

There was a low cry; and the man, with working lips, shrank back in his chair.

"You cur!" The words were coming fast and hot from Jimmie Dale's lips now. "English Dick, alias Dryden, the bank teller! So, you don't know what I mean! Listen, then, and I'll tell you! Six months ago you got a position in the bank. Since then you've forged names right and left on securities, falsified the books, and stolen cash and securities. Day by day, working in with your gang, you've brought the loot here, coming in disguise of course, as you've come to-night, for it wouldn't do for 'Dryden' to be seen in this neighbourhood! And you turned the loot over to Reddy Mull--by leaving it, if he didn't happen to be around, under that loose board there in the corner."

"My God!" The man's face was ghastly. "Who--who are you?"

"To-day," went on Jimmie Dale, as though he had not heard the other, "you came to the climax of the plan you had been working on for those six months--the bank was wrecked--and what little there was left you took"--he jerked his hand toward the open satchel--"replacing it at the last moment with previously prepared dummy packages. And you took it, you cur"--Jimmie Dale's voice choked suddenly--"not only at the expense of a man's life, but of his good name and reputation. You might have known, I do not know whether you did or not, that Forrester had some private trouble with a money lender, but I do not imagine that had anything to do with your having selected Forrester's bank. Your object was to exploit a small bank where, with only one man from whom to hide your work, you could loot it thoroughly; and a forged confession clever enough to deceive any one in its handwriting and signature, and the man found dead from a dose of prussic acid, the empty bottle on the floor beside him, needed no other evidence to stamp him as the guilty man."

English Dick was struggling to his feet; his eyes, in a sort of horrible fascination, on Jimmie Dale.

Jimmie Dale, pushed him savagely back into his seat. "Yes--you cur!" he said again. "You got your first fright when you found those evidences of suicide were gone--you even lost your nerve a little in your bluff with the bank examiners--and you hurried here the moment you could get away from the preliminary police investigation that followed--I was even afraid you might get here a little sooner than you did. Shall I give you the details of this afternoon and to-night? The plant was ready. You had sent for the bank examiners. You had already prepared the forged confession, and had a small package of securities ready. Forrester had gone to New York. You turned over the confession and the package of securities to your accomplice, or accomplices, to be left in Forrester's room. I imagine that you telephoned, or sent a message, to New York to Forrester telling him that the bank examiners were in the bank, that there was something the matter, and for him to go to his rooms, and, say, meet you there before going to the bank. Your accomplice, for you established an alibi by remaining with the bank examiners, stole in after him, or even in the dark hallway stunned him with a black-jack, then forced the poison down his throat, laid him on the floor, placed the empty bottle beside him, and left the confession on the desk. The plan was very cunningly worked out. The bruise on Forrester's head was most obviously accounted for--his head had struck, of course, against the leg of the couch--he was found lying in that position! It is strange, though, isn't it, how some-times the most cunning of plans go astray in the simplest and yet the most perverse of ways? Who, under the circumstances, would have thought of it! Your accomplice had simply to place a document already prepared upon the desk. Even you did not think to warn him yourself. It did not enter his head to see if there were pen and ink there with which it might have been written, or, failing that, a fountain pen in Forrester's pocket--and there was neither the one nor the other. That's all--except the name of the man who killed Forrester." Jimmie Dale leaned forward sharply. "Who was it?"

English Dick wet his lips again.

"I--they--they'd kill me like--like a dog if I told," he mumbled.

" *They?*" The monosyllable came curt and hard.

"I don't know," said English Dick. "That's God's truth--I never knew--there's a big gang--none of us know.".

"But you know who worked with you in this." Jimmie Dale was speaking through clenched teeth. "You know who killed Forrester."

"Yes." The man's whisper was scarcely audible.

"Who?"

"Reddy--Reddy Mull."

"Yes," said Jimmie Dale in his grim monotone, "I thought so."

He reached into the satchel where a small package of securities were wrapped up in a sheet of the bank's stationery, removed the sheet of paper, and spread it out before English Dick. "Write it down!" he commanded--and the muzzle of his auto-matic jerked forward to touch the fountain pen in the other's vest pocket. "Write it--all of it--your own share--Reddy Mull's--the whole story!"

The man's lips seemed to have gone dry again, and again and again his tongue circled them.

"I can't!" he said hoarsely. "I daren't--they'd kill me. And--and if they didn't, it would send me up, and perhaps--perhaps to the chair."

"You take your chances on that"--Jimmie Dale's voice was low and even--"but you take no chances here--for there are none." The automatic in Jimmie Dale's hand edged ominously forward. "It's Forrester's exoneration--or you. Do you understand? And you make your choice-- *now* ."

For an instant the man's eyes met Jimmie Dale's, then shifted, as though drawn in spite of himself, to the muzzle of Jimmie Dale's automatic; and then his hand reached into his pocket for his pen.

From the pool room in front came an outburst of hand-clapping and applause--there was evidently a match of some kind going on. Jimmie Dale, his eyes on English Dick, as the latter began to write with a sort of feverish haste as though fear and a miserable desire to have done with it spurred him on, picked up the articles from the table, and placed them in the satchel. He waited silently then--and then English Dick pushed the paper toward him.

Jimmie Dale picked it up, and read it. It was all there, all of it--and the signature this time was not forged! He placed the paper in the satchel, and closed the satchel.

English Dick passed his hand across a forehead that beaded with perspiration.

"What are you going to do?" he asked under his breath.

"I'm going to see that this--and you--reaches the hands of the police," said Jimmie Dale tersely. "We'll leave here in a moment--by the window. There's a patrolman who passes the end of the lane once in a while, and I expect, with the aid of a piece of cord and a pocket handkerchief as a gag, that he'll find you there. My method may be a little crude, but I have reasons of my own for not walking into a police station with you. but before we go, there's still that matter of--the men higher up. They needed a clever penman for this job and one who wouldn't be recognised--and they got the best! Who brought you over from England?"

"A friend over there, one of the 'swell ones,' put it up to me," English Dick answered heavily.

"Yes--and here?" prodded Jimmie Dale. "Who got you into the bank here?"

"I don't know." English Dick shook his head. "I reported to a man called Chester. He doped out the story I was to tell, and told me to go to the bank and apply for the job, and that it was already fixed."

"I'd like to meet 'Chester,'" said Jimmie Dale grimly. "Where does he live?"

"I don't know," said English Dick again. "I tell you, I don't know! They're big-- my God, they'll get me for this, if the law doesn't! I don't know where he lives--he always came to me. The only one I know is Reddy Mull, and--"

His voice was drowned out in a louder and more prolonged burst of applause from the pool room, which mingled shouts, cries and the thunderous banging of cue butts on the floor.

"A good shot!" said Jimmie Dale, with a grim smile.

"Yes," said English Dick, "a good shot"--but into his voice had crept a new note, a note like one of malicious triumph.

Jimmie Dale's lips set suddenly hard and tight. Yes, he **heard** now--perhaps too late--what the other **saw**. The uproar that had drowned out all other sounds had subsided--*the door behind him had been unlocked and was now opening slowly*.

And then Jimmie Dale, quick as thought is quick, his fingers closed on the satchel, hurled himself around the table and to the floor. There was the roar of a report, a flash of flame, as Reddy Mull, hand thrust in through the partially open doorway, fired--a wild scream, as the shot, meant for him, Jimmie Dale, found another mark directly behind where he had been standing--and English Dick, reeling to his feet, pitched forward over the table, carrying the table with him to the floor. It had taken the time that a watch takes to tick. Came the roar of a report again, as Jimmie Dale fired in turn--at the electric-light bulb a few feet away from him on the wall. There was the tinkle of shattering glass--and darkness. Came shouts, cries, a yell from the door from Reddy Mull, a fusillade of shots from Reddy Mull's revolver, the rush of many feet from the pool room--and Jimmie Dale, in the blackness, dropped silently from the window to the ground.

He gained the street; and, five minutes later, blocks away, he entered the private stall of a Bowery saloon. Here, Jimmie Dale added another paper to the contents of the satchel. The characters printed, and badly formed, the paper looked like this:

WITH THE COMPLIMENTS OF THE

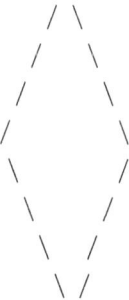

"And I guess," said Jimmie Dale grimly to himself, "that if I slip this to the police, the police will get--Reddy Mull."

CHAPTER XIX
THE BEGINNING OF THE END

How far away last night, with Forrester's murder and the sordid denouement in Reddy Mull's room, seemed! How far away even half an hour ago this very night seemed! Just half an hour ago! Then, with no thought but one of dogged perseverance to keep up his quest, with neither hint nor sign that his quest was any nearer the end than it had ever been, he had entered Bristol Bob's, here, in the role of Smarlinghue; and now, as a rift that had opened in the clouds, there had come sudden and amazing joy. It held him now in thrall. It threatened even to make him *forget* that he was for the moment Smarlinghue-- forget what, as Smarlinghue, Smarlinghue dare not forget--the role he played.

He leaned forward suddenly and caught up his whisky glass--whose contents had previously and surreptitiously been spilled into the cuspidor on the floor beside his chair. He lifted the glass to his mouth, his head thrown back as though to drain a final, lingering drop, then he thumped the glass down on the table, licked his lips- -thin and distorted by "Smarlinghue's" makeup--and wiped them with the sleeve of his threadbare coat.

A man at the next table, well known as the Pippin, young, flashily dressed, his almost effeminate features giving an added touch of viciousness, through incongruity, to his general appearance, twisted his head around and grinned with malicious derision.

Jimmie Dale's fingers searched hungrily now through first one and then another of his ragged pockets, and finally extricated a dime and a nickel. With these he tapped insistently on the table, until an attendant answered the summons and supplied him with another drink.

He sat back then for a time; now eyeing the liquor, as though greedy for its taste, yet greedy, too, to prolong the anticipation, since from his actions there was apparently no means of further replenishing the supply; now glancing around the smoke-laden room where, on the polished section of the floor in the centre, a score of laughing, shrieking couples whirled and pranced in the unrestrained throes of the underworld's latest dance; now permitting his eyes to rest with a sudden scowl on the man at the next table. He had no concern with the Pippin--nor had the Pippin any concern with him. The man, as he imbibed a number of drinks, simply seemed to find a certain: malevolent amusement in a contemptuous appraisal of his, Jimmie Dale's, person; but the other, in spite of the new, glad exhilaration Jimmie Dale was experiencing, annoyed Jimmie Dale--the blatant expanse of pink shirt cuff, for instance, in order to display the Pippin's diamond-snake links, famous from One end of the underworld to the other, was eminently typical of the man. The cuff links were undoubtedly an object of envy to the society in which the Pippin moved; they were even beautiful cuff links, it was true, oriental in design, never to be mistaken by any one who had ever seen them, and the stones with which they were set were credited generally in the underworld as being genuine, but--Jimmie Dale was hesitantly lifting his glass again in a queer, miserly sort of way. The Pippin had jerked a cigarette box from his pocket, stuck what was evidently the single cigarette it had contained between his lips; and now, tossing away the box, he pushed back his chair and stood up--but on the floor beneath the table, where it had fluttered unobserved when the cigarette box had been jerked from the pocket, lay a small folded piece of paper.

"If you hang around long enough, Smarly," gibed the Pippin, as he passed by on his way toward the door, "maybe some of the rubber-necks off the gape-wagon will take pity on you and buy you another--the slumming parties are just crazy about broken-down artists!"

"You go chase yourself!" said Smarlinghue politely, through one corner of his twisted mouth.

Jimmie Dale's eyes followed the other. The Pippin, threading his way amongst the tables, gained the door, and passed out into the street. And then Jimmie Dale's eyes reverted to the piece of paper under the adjacent table. It was not at all likely that it was of the slightest importance or significance, and yet--Jimmie Dale stretched out his foot, drew the paper toward him, and, stooping over, picked it up.

He unfolded it, and found it to contain several typewritten lines. He frowned in a puzzled way as he read them; then read them over again, and his frown deepened.

Melinoff has the goods. Go the limit if he squeals. Not later than ten-thirty to-night.

Jimmie Dale's eyes lifted and strayed around the noisy, riotous dance hall. Just what exactly did the message mean? The Pippin was a bad actor--literally, as well as metaphorically. The Pippin, if asked, would probably still have styled himself an actor; but, though still young, his career on the stage had ended several years ago rather abruptly--with a year's imprisonment! Jimmie Dale did not recall the details of the particular offence of which the Pippin had been found guilty, save that it had been for theft. It did not, however, matter very much. The Pippin of to-day as he was known to the underworld, to which strata of society he had immediately gravitated on his release from prison, was all that was of immediate interest. He had associated himself with a gang run by one Steve Barlow, commonly known as the Mole, and under this august patronage and protection had already more than one "job" of the first magnitude to his credit. The Pippin, in a word, was both an ugly and an unpleasant customer.

Jimmie Dale's eyes continued to circuit the seedy dance hall. What was it that the Pippin was to procure from Melinoff, and for which, if necessary, the Pippin was to go "the limit"? Melinoff himself was not without reproach, either! What was the game? Melinoff was an old-clothes and junk dealer, and, as a side line, at times a very profitable side line, had been known to act as a "fence" for stolen goods. He had skirted for years on the ragged edge with the police, and then, caught red-handed at last, had changed his occupation for a more useful one during a somewhat pro-longed sojourn in Sing Sing. Affairs after that had not prospered with Melinoff. His wife, honest if her husband was not, and already an old woman, had been hard put to it with the shabby shop and the meagre business she was able to transact; so hard put to it, indeed, that the wonder had been that she had managed to keep the roof over her head. She had died a few months after her husband's release. Melinoff, if he had had no other virtue, had at least loved his wife, and the Melinoff of old, then a sprightly enough man for his years, was no more, and it was a decrepit, stoop-shouldered, dirty and grey-bearded figure that shuffled now around the old-clothes shop, apathetic of "bargains," where before it had been a man whose keenness was matched only by the sort of eager craft and low cunning with which he had conducted his business.

A smile, half grim, half whimsical, flickered across Jimmie Dale's lips. There were strange lives, strange undercurrents, always, ceaselessly, at work here in the underworld, here where the grist from the human mill found its place. Melinoff, the Pippin, each of those whirling figures out there on the floor, each of those men and women whose laughter rose raucously from the tables, or whose whisperings, as heads were lowered and held close together, seemed an unsavoury, vicious thing, had known a strange and tortuous path; yet strangest, most tortuous of them all, was--his own!

His fingers, as he thrust the Pippin's note into the side pocket of his coat, touched the torn fragments of another note, tiny little particles of paper, torn over and over again into fine and minute shreds--the Tocsin's note--the note that seemed suddenly to have changed all his life. It had come as her communications had always come--without bridging the way that lay between them, without furnishing him with a clue through the method employed for their transmission that would avail him anything, or supply him with any means of reaching her. It had been thrust into his hand by a street urchin, as he had entered the door of Bristol Bob's that half an hour before. He had not even questioned the urchin--it would have been useless, futile, barren of results. A hundred previous experiences had at least taught him that! He could surmise about it, though, if he would; and, in view of the contents of the note itself, surmise, in all probability, with fair accuracy. The Tocsin had satisfied herself that he was neither at home nor at the club, and had, therefore, chosen an inconspicuous messenger to search for "Smarlinghue" through the underworld. And there would have been no risk. For the first time in all the years that her letters had been the motive force, the underlying basis of the Gray Seal's acts, it would not, as far as dangerous consequences were concerned, have mattered if the note had gone astray, or had even been read by others. He need not even have torn it up, as he had done through force of habit, for there was no "plan" to-night, no coup to carry through. The note, for the first time, was not a "call to arms;" it was what he had been longing for, always hoping for, yet never permitting himself to build too strongly upon lest he should lay up for himself a store of disappointment too bitter for endurance--it was a note of *hope*. There were just a few lines, a few sentences;

and it had contained neither form of address nor signature. To any one save himself it meant nothing, it had no significance. Snatches of it ran through his mind again:

"... It is the beginning of the end.... The way is clearing ... I am very happy to-night, and I wanted to tell you so...."

The end at last! The end of the years of peril; the end of that fear gnawing always at his heart that she might never live to come out into the sunlight again; the end of this dual life he led; the return to a normal existence where surroundings like the present, where the dens and dives of the underworld, the secret rookeries nursing their hell-hatched crimes, the taint and smell of evil, and the reek of soul-filth would be hereafter no more than a memory! To be through with it all, through with it all, and to know her love instead--because she was safe!

He stared about him, and stared with queer incredulity at his own miserable clothing. Was it true, was it reality--this figure that the underworld knew as Smar-linghue, who sat here, and with dirty fingers played with a whisky glass on the cheap, liquor-spotted table, and out of half-closed, well-simulated drug-laden eyes gazed on those dancing figures out there on the floor to whom the law from cradle-hood had been a natural enemy, and to the door of hardly one of whom but lay crimes that ranged from the paltry to the hideous!

Reality! Yes, it was real! God knew the abysmal depths of its reality. Months piled on months there had been of it! Those voices out there that rose in a jangle of ribald mirth were the same voices that, hushed in deadlier menace, had whispered that grim slogan, "Death to the Gray Seal!" through every hidden cranny in the underworld; these men and women here around him were of the same breed as those who only last night had struck down and brutally murdered Forrester, and not content with murder had plotted to rob their victim of his good name as well!

Jimmie Dale's hand clenched suddenly--his mind was off at a tangent, away for the moment from her. Well, they had failed last night in all save murder! Failed--and one of them had already paid the price, and another, in the Tombs awaiting trial, faced the certainty of the death chair in Sing Sing! But those two, Reddy Mull, and English Dick, had been little more than tools. Whose was the hidden master brain behind them, controlling this evil power that struck in the dark; that lately, though unseen, was permeating the underworld with its presence; that intuitively he had felt was reaching out, feeling its way, to grapple with and, if it could, to strangle him the Gray Seal! He had felt the menace, known that it existed, and the slogan ringing always in his ears, the Whispered "Death to the Gray Seal" had taken on a deeper significance, had brought him a more acute and imminent sense of peril than ever before; but it was only last night, for the first time, that he had equally *felt* that he had had any concrete knowledge of, or contact with this new antagonist. And last night, if there had been a challenge he had accepted it, and if there had been no challenge he had at least thrown down the gauntlet himself! If this was actually the criminal organisation that was arrayed against him, the master brain at the head of it would now have a greater incentive than ever to trap and exterminate the Gray Seal, for English Dick lay dead, and Reddy Mull was behind the bars, and twenty thousand dollars in cash that they had schemed for was in the hands of the police--thanks to the Gray Seal! Added incentive! They would move heaven and earth to reach him now! All the trickery, all the hell-born ingenuity that they possessed would be launched against him now, and--Jimmie Dale's face, that had been set and hard, relaxed suddenly. Well, granted all that! What did it matter now? They would but hunt a myth! Between them and himself now there stood the Tocsin's note. "The way is clearing.... I am very happy to-night." She would not have written that unless she were very sure. To-morrow, perhaps, and Smarlinghue, and the Gray Seal, and Larry the Bat would have passed forever out of existence, and there would be only Jimmie Dale, and *she,* and love--and a phantom left behind in the underworld against whom the underworld and this evil genius of crime might pit their wits to their hearts' content!

There was an uplift upon him, a sense of freedom so great that it seemed actually physical as well as mental. Peril, danger, the strain of the dual life until the nerves were worn raw, the constant anxiety for her safety--all were gone now. "It is the beginning of the end ... the way is clearing"--she had written that tonight. And it meant that, refusing, as she had said, to let him come into the shadows again, she had won through--alone. It brought a little, curious pang of disappointment to him that he should share now only in the reward; but the pang was swallowed up in that it brought him a deeper knowledge of her unselfish love, her splendid courage, and--he could find no other word--her wonderfulness.

Jimmie Dale's fingers stole into the side pocket of his coat to play again in a curiously caressing way with the little torn fragments of her note--and touched again the piece of paper that the Pippin had dropped. He took it out mechanically, and read it over once more. One sentence seemed suddenly to have become particularly ominous--"if he squeals go the limit." He knew nothing as to the authorship of those words, but from what he knew of the Pippin there was a certain ugliness to the word "limit" that he did not like. The "limit" with the Pippin might mean-- ***any- thing***.

He thrust the paper back into his pocket, and sat for a moment staring mus- ingly at his whisky glass. Well, why not? Before half past ten, the message said; and it was scarcely ten o'clock yet. In view of the Tocsin's note, be had intended returning to the Sanctuary, resuming his own proper character, and, either at the St. James Club, or at his home, wait for further word from her. There was, indeed, nothing else that he could do--and Melinoff's, for that matter, was on the way from Bristol Bob's to the Sanctuary. Yes, why not? If the Pippin was up to any dirty work, or even if the two of them, Melinoff and the Pippin, were in it together, and the word "squeal" implied that Melinoff was to be held strictly up to his full share of some mutual villainy should he show any inclination to waver, it might not be an altogether unfitting exit from the stage if the Gray Seal should make his final bow to the underworld by playing a role in the Pippin's little drama, whatever that drama might prove to be!

Yes, why not! He passed Melinoff's place in any event, and there was no reason why he should remain any longer here in Bristol Bob's. The second glass of whisky followed the first--into the cuspidor. Again the threadbare sleeve was drawn across the thin, distorted lips, and, pushing back his chair, Jimmie Dale rose from the table and made his way out into the street.

CHAPTER XX
THE OLD-CLOTHES SHOP

Ten minutes later, still in the heart of the East Side, Jimmie Dale reached his destination, and paused on the edge of the sidewalk, ostensibly to light a cigarette while he looked tentatively around him, before the entrance to a courtyard that ran in behind a row of cheap and shabby tenements. He shook his head, as he tossed the match away. It was still early; there were too many people about, to say nothing of the group of half-naked children playing in the gutter under the street lamp in front of the courtyard entrance, and "Smarlinghue" was far too well known a character in that section of the Bad Lands to warrant him in taking any chances. If anything was wrong in Melinoff's dingy little place behind there, if anything had transpired, or was about to transpire that would ultimately, say, invite the attention of the police, it might prove extremely awkward--for Smarlinghue--should it be remembered that he had entered there! There was a better way--a much better way, and one that was exceedingly simple. It would hardly occasion any comment, even if he were noticed, if he entered one of the *tenements*, where, with probably a dozen families living in as many rooms, one could come and go at all hours without question or hindrance.

He moved slowly along, and, out of the radius of the street lamp now and away from the children, paused again, this time before the last tenement in the row that the front of the courtyard in the rear. For the moment there were no pedestrians in the immediate neighbourhood, and Jimmie Dale, stepping through the tenement doorway, gained the narrow, unlighted hall within. He stopped here, hugged close against the wall, to listen, and, hearing or seeing nothing to disturb him, moved forward again, silently, without a sound, along the hall. There must be, he knew, a rear exit to the courtyard behind. Yes--here it was! He had halted again, this time before a door. He tried it, found it unlocked, opened it, stepped outside, and closed the door behind him.

It was dark out here in the courtyard, and objects were only faintly discernible; but there were few localities in that neighbourhood with which Jimmie Dale, either as Smarlinghue, or in the old days as Larry the Bat, was not intimately acquainted. To call it a courtyard hardly described the place. It was more an open backyard common to the row of tenements, and rather narrow and confined in space at that. It was dirty, cluttered with rubbish, and across it, facing the rear of the tenements, was a small building that many years ago had been, possibly, a stable or an outhouse belonging to some private and no doubt pretentious dwelling, which long since now, with the progress northward of the city, had been supplanted by the crowded, poverty-stricken, and anything but pretentious tenements. This outhouse had been to a certain extent remodelled, and to a certain extent made habitable, and as long as any one could remember Melinoff with his old-clothes shop had been its tenant.

Jimmie Dale began to make his way cautiously across the yard, wary of the tin cans and general rubbish which an inadvertent step might metamorphose most effectively into a decidedly undesirable advertisement of his presence. There was no light that he could see in Melinoff's at all; and he frowned now in a puzzled way. Had the Pippin been and gone; or was he, Jimmie Dale, ahead of the Pippin? The Pippin would have had ample time, of course, to get here, for he, Jimmie Dale, had probably remained in Bristol Bob's a good half hour after the Pippin had left. In that case, then, Melinoff must have gone away with the Pippin again--that would account for there being no light. But, on the other hand, if the Pippin had not yet arrived, and Melinoff *expected* the visit, it was most curious that the place was in darkness!

And then Jimmie Dale smiled a little mockingly at himself. His deductions would perhaps have been of infinitely more value if he had first waited to make sure of the premise on which they were based! As a matter of fact, there *was* a light! He had reached the front of the little place, and peering cautiously through the window could make out, across the black interior, a thread of light that came through the crack of a closed door, and from what was, evidently, another room in the rear.

Jimmie Dale's fingers closed on the heavy, cumbersome, old-fashioned door latch, pressed it down noiselessly, and exerted a little tentative pressure on the door itself. It was locked. A minute passed in absolute silence, as a little steel instrument was inserted in the lock--and then the door swung inward and was dosed again, and Jimmie Dale, rigid and motionless, stood inside.

He was listening now for some sound, the sound of voices, or the sound of movement from that lighted room. There was nothing. Jimmie Dale's lips tightened suddenly. It was very curious! There was an "upstairs" to the place, such as it was, but if Melinoff was up there alone, or with the Pippin, they were up there in the dark unless they were in the rear upstairs room; in which case they could not, in view of the ramshackle nature of the building, have made the slightest movement without making themselves heard from where he stood.

From his pocket Jimmie Dale produced a flashlight. The ray played once, as though with queer, diffident curiosity, about him, swept once more in a circuit around the room, swiftly, in an almost startled way this time--and there was darkness again. And, instead of the flashlight, Jimmie Dale's automatic was in his hand now, and he was moving quickly and silently forward toward that thread of light and the closed door leading into the rear room.

Around him everything was in disorder; not the disorder habitual to such a place where odds and ends of the heterogeneous accumulation of Melinoff's stock in trade might be expected to be deposited wherever convenience and not system dictated, but a disorder that seemed to hold within itself something of ominous promise. Old clothes, for instance, that might at least have been expected, even with the most profound carelessness and indifference, to have received better treatment, were strewn and scattered about the floor in all directions.

And now Jimmie Dale stood still again. There was a sound at last; but a sound that he could not immediately define. It came from the room beyond--like a dull, muffled thud mingling with a low, long-drawn gasp. It was repeated--and then, unmistakably, there came a moan.

In a flash now, Jimmie Dale, his automatic thrust forward, was at the door. He stooped with his eye to the keyhole; and the next instant, his face hard and tense, he flung the door open, and jumped forward into the room.

Those words of the Pippin's note seemed to be searing through his brain in letters of fire--"go the limit--go the limit." There was no need to speculate longer on their meaning; they meant-- *murder*. On the floor, a dark ugly, crimson pool beside him, lay Melinoff, the old-clothes dealer. And as Jimmie Dale sprang to the other's side, there came again that curious muffled thud--as the old man weakly lifted his head a few inches from the floor only to have it fall limply back again. The man was nearly gone--it needed no experienced eye to tell that. Melinoff's face was grayish in its pallor, and his eyes, open, seemed to have lost their lustre; but as Jimmie Dale knelt and lifted the man's shoulders and supported the other's head upon his knee, the light in the old-clothes dealer's black eyes seemed suddenly to return and to glow with a strange, passionate, eager fire, as they fixed on Jimmie Dale's face. Melinoff's lips moved. Jimmie Dale bent his head to Catch the words that were almost inaudible.

"The--the Pippin. Here"--the old man's hand struggled toward his side where a dark crimson blotch had soaked his shirt--"here--he--he stabbed me--because--because--" The voice failed and died away, and the man's head fell back on Jimmie Dale's arm.

Jimmie Dale raised the other's head gently again.

"Yes!" he said quickly, striving to rouse the other. "Yes; go on! I understand. The Pippin stabbed you. Because--what? Go on, Melinoff! Go on! I am listening."

The eyes opened once more--but the light was dying out of them, and they were filming now. And then suddenly the man forced himself forward into a sitting posture, and his voice rang wildly through the room:

"It is a lie! A lie! I played square--do you hear! Old Melinoff played square! I did not understand at first--but I did not forget. I remembered. Old Melinoff would never forget--never forget--never for--"

A tremor ran through the old man's form, the voice was stilled--it was the end.

For a moment, his lips tight and set, Jimmie Dale held the other there in his arms, as he stared at a little object on the floor where Melinoff had been lying, and that previously had been hidden beneath the other's body--an object that glittered and sparkled now as the light caught it. There had even been then, it seemed, no need for Melinoff's dying accusation--the evidence of the Pippin's guilt would have been plain enough to the first person who found old Melinoff and moved the old man's body. For himself, Jimmie Dale, the Pippin's note, since it had actuated him in coming here, would have been enough to have fixed the guilt in his mind where it belonged; but the police, for instance, would not have been so well informed! The police, however, would now have all, and more than all the evidence they required. That little thing that glittered there was one of the Pippin's notorious diamond-snake cuff links.

Jimmie Dale did not disturb it. He laid old Melinoff back on the floor, and the old man's body covered the cuff link again as it had done before. He stood up then, and looked around him. The room seemed to have been used for no one particular purpose. It was partitioned off from the shop proper, it was true; but, equally, it appeared to have been used as a sort of overflow for the shop's stock in trade. Here, as in front, clothing of all descriptions littered the floor; and also there were signs that a violent struggle had taken place. The room, which had obviously served, apart from being a store-room, as kitchen, dining room, and, in fact, for everything save a bedroom, was in a state of chaos--chairs were upset, a table stood up-ended against the wall, aid broken crockery was strewn everywhere.

At the rear of the room was another door. Jimmie Dale reached up, turned off the gas-jet, crossed to the door, found it unlocked, opened it a few inches, and looked out. It gave on the rear of the courtyard, and in the darkness he could just make out a high fence that bordered the adjoining property. It was presumably the way by which the Pippin had made his escape, since he, Jimmie Dale, had found the front door locked.

He closed the door again, relighted the gas, and, moving swiftly now, passed through into the shop and locked the front door. Then, returning to the upper end of the shop close to the connecting door, which he closed until it was just ajar, Jimmie Dale slipped a black silk mask over his face, seated himself on a box of some sort that he found at hand, and, save that his fingers mechanically tested the automatic in his hand, remained motionless, his eyes fixed on the rear door across the lighted room in which old Melinoff lay.

It was dark here and silent, except that from out across the courtyard came faintly now and then the voices of the children at play in the gutters, and except that a faint glow stole timidly out from the slightly opened door only to merge almost immediately with the surrounding blackness. The tight lips had curved downward at the corners of his mouth into a grim, merciless droop; and into the dark, steady eyes there had come a smouldering fire. It was a brutal, cowardly thing that had been done there in that room, and the Pippin had finished his work and gone--but it was not at all unlikely that the Pippin would be back!

The sharp lines at the corners of Jimmie Dale's mouth grew a little more pronounced. Nor should the Pippin be long in returning! A man could not very well lose a cuff link and be unaware of that fact for any extended length of time. And that cuff link was damning, irrefutable, incontrovertible evidence, exactly the evidence the police required to convict the guilty man! Yes, undoubtedly, the Pippin would be back--and at any moment now. Figuring that the Pippin had left Bristol Bob's half an hour before he, Jimmie Dale, had started out, and allowing, say, twenty minutes for the struggle and subsequent murder here, the Pippin could only have been gone a matter of some ten minutes. In the excitement, and probably a run through lanes and alleyways, it was quite possible that the Pippin would not have noticed his loss in that length of time; but he could not, with a loose cuff, and especially when it was usually fastened by so highly prized a link, have remained much longer than that in ignorance of his loss.

Jimmie Dale smiled grimly now in the darkness. It was almost analogous to Meighan's waiting for the return of the Magpie, except that he, Jimmie Dale, had neither the desire nor the intention of usurping the functions of the police. "Smarlinghue," for very obvious reasons, could neither appear nor bear witness in the case; he could take no chances of the discovery being made that "Smarlinghue" was but a *character* that cloaked Jimmie Dale and the Gray Seal--and, above all, he could take no chances to-night when at last he was on the threshold of the return to his old normal life again! But he had, nevertheless, no intention of permitting the Pippin to elude the law, or to escape the consequences of the act to which that mute form lying in there on the crimsoned floor bore hideous testimony. The cuff link, obviously loosened and dropped unnoticed on the floor during the struggle, would not only connect the Pippin with the crime, but would convict him of it as well; he, Jimmie Dale, therefore, did not propose to allow the Pippin to return and remove that evidence--that was all. It should not be very difficult to prevent it; nor should it even necessitate his showing himself to the Pippin. A shot, for instance, fired at the floor, as the Pippin stole in through that rear door again should be enough to send the man flying back for shelter to the recesses of the underworld. The Pippin's nerves, as he crept back to the scene of his crime, would be badly frayed and unstrung, unless he was a man lacking wholly in imagination, which the Pippin, once having been an actor, inherently could not be; and, coupled with this, prompting the Pippin to run at once for cover, would be the fact that he could not by any means be certain that the link had been lost there in the room itself, since it might equally have, been forced loose during his escape, say, for instance, while climbing the series of backyard fences that would have confronted him from the moment he left Melinoff's rear door--providing always, of course, that the Pippin, as it seemed logical and as the evidence seemed to indicate, *had* made his escape in that manner.

The minutes passed; at first quickly enough, and then they began to drag heavily. Jimmie Dale's mind was back now on old Melinoff. What had the man meant by his feverish, eager, pitiful insistence that he had not forgotten, that he had remembered, that he could never forget, and that he had not understood at first? The answer to that question would supply the motive for the Pippin's crime, and for half an hour, sitting there in the darkness, Jimmie Dale pondered the question, but the answer would not come. There were theories without number that he could formulate; but theories at best were indefinite. What had Melinoff meant by saying he had played square? Was it some previous criminal undertaking between himself and the Pippin, in which the Pippin believed himself to have been betrayed by Melinoff, while Melinoff, on the other hand, protested that--and then Jimmie Dale shrugged his shoulders impatiently. What was the use of speculation? The vital matter of the moment was the Pippin's delay in returning for that cuff link!

Another fifteen minutes passed, and still another--and then Jimmie Dale restored his mask to his pocket, rose from his seat, and made his way to the front door of the shop. He had waited there a full hour and over now, his only purpose had been to prevent the removal of the evidence of the Pippin's guilt by the Pippin, and logic told him it was useless to wait longer. It was only fair to assume that the Pippin would have discovered his loss within a reasonably short time after leaving Melinoff's; and, granting that, it was absolutely certain that the Pippin, if he were coming back at all, would have come without an instant's delay if he believed that his life hung on the recovery of his property. He had not come, and therefore, conversely, the Pippin must have weighed the chances and concluded that the risk attendant on his return to the scene of his crime was greater than the risk he ran of the cuff link having been lost in that exact spot. Nor was the Pippin's presumed reasoning entirely faulty--from the Pippin's standpoint. It was obvious that he did not know *where* he had lost the link; it was only a *chance* that he had lost it on the actual scene of the crime; and even if he had lost it there, and even if he returned, it was only a *chance* that he would be able to find it again--and against this was the very grave risk and danger of returning to Melinoff's after having once got safely away. But whatever the Pippin's reasoning might have been, the one morally certain fact remained--every minute of delay increased the risk that the cuff link would be found by some one else, and if the Pippin were coming back at all he would have been back long before this.

Jimmie Dale closed the door of the old-clothes shop behind him, crossed the yard, and using the back door of the tenement again; gained the street. Well, he was quite satisfied! The hour he had spent there mattered little. He had desired only one thing--that the evidence of the Pippin's guilt should not be disturbed. And for the rest--he smiled whimsically as he started briskly along the street--there was Carruthers, of the **Morning News-Argus,** who, if, in the old days, he had been one of the most dogged and relentless in his efforts to run the Gray Seal to earth, was at the same time, though without knowing it--Jimmie Dale's smile broadened--the Gray Seal's most intimate friend and old college pal! If the Pippin was just as surely brought to book that way, why do old Carruthers and his sheet out of a "scoop"!

Jimmie Dale made his way rapidly now over to the Bowery, and here headed in an uptown direction. Two blocks further along, however, on the corner occupied by the Crescent saloon, he turned into the cross street, and passed in through the saloon's side entrance. The Crescent saloon, as he had previously more than once had occasion to remark, was nothing if not thoughtful of the peculiar needs of its somewhat questionable class of patrons. Around the corner of the little passageway, just as it turned into a small lounging room before the barroom proper was reached, was a telephone booth whose privacy could scarcely be improved upon. He opened the door of the booth, stepped inside, and closed the door carefully and tightly behind him. The *Argus* being a morning paper, Carruthers, except on very rare occasions, was always to be found at his office until late into the night; but Jimmie Dale, having deposited his coin in the slot, was rewarded with the information that he had met with one of those "rare occasions." Carruthers was at his home on Long Island, and had not been at the office at all that day. Jimmie Dale shrugged his shoulders, as he found and gave the Long Island number. It did not matter very much; it was simply the difference in time, amounting to, say, the half hour or so that it would take Carruthers to get back to the city and act.

The 'phone was answered.

"Mr. Carruthers, if you please ... yes, personally," said Jimmie Dale pleasantly.

There was a moment's wait, then Jimmie Dale spoke again--his voice still pleasant, but changed in pitch and register to a bass that was far from Jimmie Dale's, though one that Carruthers might possibly remember!

"Mr. Carruthers? ... Good evening, Mr. Carruthers--this is the Gray Seal speaking, and I--" A receptive smile stole suddenly across Jimmie Dale's lips--Carruthers, to put it mildly, was impulsive. "The Gray Seal--yes. I can hear *you* perfectly.... What? ... No, it is not a hoax!"--Jimmie Dale's voice had sharpened perceptibly--"I called you once before, you will perhaps remember though it is a very long time ago, in reference to a certain diamond necklace and a--you will pardon the term-- gentleman by the name of Markel. ... Ah, you recognise the Gray Seal's voice now, do you! ... No, don't apologise.... I thought perhaps you might be interested in the possibility of another scoop.... Yes, quite so! ... I would suggest then that you get the police to accompany you to the back room of Melinoff's, the old-clothes dealer's shop.... Yes, I thought you might know the place. Perhaps, too, you know of a man who is commonly called the Pippin? ... No? Well, no matter. The police do! You'll find the evidence under Melinoff's body.... I beg your pardon? ... Yes--murder.... What? ... It is a cuff link, the Pippin's cuff link, that was dropped in the struggle.... What? ... No, I do not know why; I have told you all I know. There is nothing more, Mr. Carruthers--except that I should advise you to work as quickly as possible, as otherwise some one may stumble on the crime before you do. Good-night, Mr. Carruthers."

Carruthers was still talking, wildly, excitedly. Jimmie Dale calmly hung up the receiver, left the telephone booth, and went out to the street again--by the side entrance. If Carruthers made inquiry of central as to where the call had come from, the reply that it was from the Crescent saloon would in no way serve Carruthers, or any one else. No one, even in the Crescent saloon, would be able to furnish any information as to who had telephoned. It was, therefore, in a word, up to Carruthers now; the Pippin would be brought to account; and as far as he, Jimmie Dale, was concerned, his connection with the affair was at an end.

Jimmie Dale walked quickly along, turning from one street into another. Here and there, in front of various resorts, and on the corners, he passed little groups of men engaged in bated, low-toned conversation. Ordinarily this would have interested Jimmie Dale, for the groups were composed, not of ordinary citizens, but of the dregs and scum of the underworld, and it was evident that something quite out of the usual run of things had suddenly seized upon the Bad Lands as a subject for gossip. But it was already long after eleven o'clock, and to-night, with Melinoff's murder disposed of now, he was through, he hoped, with the underworld forever. He was anxious only to reach the Sanctuary without any further delay, and, thereafter, equally without further loss of time, to get to his home or to the club, where at any moment he might expect to hear from the Tocsin, and where, most important of all, she would bare no difficulty in communicating instantly with him.

He turned the corner of the street on which the Sanctuary was situated--and halted abruptly. A man coming rapidly from the other direction had grabbed his arm.

"'Ello, Smarly!" greeted the other. "Heard de news?"

Jimmie Dale, with the top of his tongue, shifted the half burnt section of the cigarette that was hanging from his upper lip to the opposite corner of his mouth, as he looked at the other. It was the Wowzer, dip and pick-pocket, the erstwhile pal of one Dago Jim, who, on a certain night, also of the very long ago, that Jimmie Dale had very good cause to remember, had killed Dago Jim in a certain infamous dive. Well, if he, Jimmie Dale, was, after all, to learn the cause of the excitement that seemed suddenly to have possessed the underworld, he could at least have asked for no better or more thoroughly posted informant than the Wowzer. And now his curiosity was aroused. For an instant the idea that it might be Melinoff's murder flashed across his mind; but he dismissed that idea at once. Murder was too trite a thing in the underworld to cause any widespread commotion!

"Hello, Wowzer!" he returned, as he shook his head. "No, I ain't heard anything."

"Youse can take it from me den," said the Wowzer, "dat dere's something doin'!

Dey got her!"

"Got who?" enquired Jimmie Dale in a puzzled way.

The Wowzer leaned forward secretively.

"Silver Mag!" he said.

It seemed to Jimmie Dale as though the clutch of an icy hand was suddenly at his heart, as though the ground beneath his feet had grown suddenly unstable and that the Wowzer's face, close to his own, was swirling around and around in swift and endless gyrations--but he was conscious, too, that he was master of himself. The muscles of his face twitched--but it was to express incredulity. His tongue carried the cigarette butt languidly back to the other corner of his mouth.

"Aw, go on!" said Jimmie Dale. "Try it on somebody else! Silver Mag croaked out the night they had that fire down there in the old tenement."

"Yes, she did--nix!" scoffed the Wowzer, with a short laugh. "De same way dat blasted snitch of a Gray Seal did--eh? Say, Smarly, I'm handin' it to youse straight. Dey caught her snoopin' around one of de en-trays into Foo Sen's half an hour ago. Say, de whole mob all de way up de line's been tipped off. I'm givin' youse de real thing. Youse must have been asleep somewhere, or youse'd have been wise before."

"Sure--I believe you!" said Jimmie Dale earnestly. "Who caught her, Wowzer?"

"De Mole," replied the Wowzer. "An' he's got her now over in his layout."

It was a moment before Jimmie Dale spoke. There seemed to be a horrible, ghastly dryness in his mouth; there seemed to well up from his soul and overwhelm him a world of mocking and sardonic irony. The Mole! The Mole was the leader of the gang with which the Pippin was allied; it was at the Mole's place that the Pippin usually lived; it was at the Mole's place that the police would first institute their search for the Pippin--and five minutes ago, through Carruthers, he had unleashed the police! The Wowzer's face seemed to be swirling around and around in front of him again. To get away--and *think*! He could have groaned, cried out aloud!

"Say, thanks, Wowzer, for piping me off!" said Jimmie Dale effusively.

"Oh, dat's all right," responded the Wowzer graciously. "Only keep it under yer hat except wid de crowd. De bulls ain't on, an' de Mole saw her first--see? Dere ain't goin' to be no buttin' in till she gets hers! An' de word's out not to do any pushin' an' crowdin' around de Mole's fer front seats, 'cause den de bulls 'd get wise--savvy? Just leave it to de Mole--get me?"

"Sure--I get you," said Jimmie Dale. "Well, so long, Wowzer--and thanks again."

"S'long, Smarly," replied the Wowzer.

CHAPTER XXI
SILVER MAG

It was not far to the Sanctuary, only halfway down the short block to the corner of the lane; but it seemed a distance interminable to Jimmie Dale. His brain was whirling in a chaotic turmoil; and the turmoil seemed barbed with a horrible fear that robbed him for the moment of his mental poise. It was as a man dazed, unconscious of the physical process by which he had arrived there, that he found himself standing in the Sanctuary, leaning like a man spent with effort against the door which, mechanically, he had closed behind him.

In hideous, baleful, jeering reiteration those words which she had written were racing through his brain. "I am very happy to-night, and I wanted to tell you so ... happy to-night ... happy to-night ... happy to-night." Happy to-night--what depth of irony! Happy to-night--and they had caught her--as the "way was clearing"---- with the end of peril, with the end of the miserable, hunted existence she had been forced to lead just in sight! Silver Mag--the Tocsin! And he--he, who, too, had been happy to-night, he, who had known that mighty uplift upon him, he, who had dreamed that the morrow might bring life and love and sunshine--he was facing now a blackness of despair that he had never known before. Unwittingly, if such danger as she was in *could* be made the greater, he had made it so. If the underworld was the implacable enemy of Silver Mag, because Silver Mag was known as the ally in the old days of Larry the Bat, and known, therefore, as the ally of the Gray Seal; so, for the same reason exactly, the police were her implacable enemy! And, whether she fell into the hands of one or the other, the end ultimately differed only in the method by which her death would be accomplished; it was murder at the hands of the Mole and his gang; it was the death chair in Sing Sing as an accomplice of the Gray Seal at the hands of the police. "Death to the Gray Seal!"----that was the slogan of the underworld. "The Gray Seal dead or alive--but the Gray Seal"--that was the fiat of the police. And both held good for Silver Mag! With the Mole alone there might have been a chance--but now, he had launched the police as well against her, had sent them to the Mole's, for that was the first place they would raid in their hunt for the Pippin.

The sweat beads started out on Jimmie Dale's forehead. She had discarded the character of "Silver Mag" that night in the tenement fire when he had discarded the character of "Larry the Bat"--and "Silver Mag" had never been seen again until to-night. But he, Jimmie Dale, *had* appeared since then as Larry the Bat--and for some reason to-night she must have found it necessary, in working out her plans to their consummation no doubt, to have assumed again the character of Silver Mag--and she had been caught! But the Mole, it was absolutely certain, if left alone, would first exhaust every means within his power of forcing from Silver Mag the information that he would naturally believe she had concerning the whereabouts of the Gray Seal, before wreaking the vengeance of the underworld upon her; but equally the Mole, if interrupted by the police, would, in a sort of barbarous rivalry, if he, Jimmie Dale, knew the underworld at all, never surrender Silver Mag--alive. It would be the old cry, hideously worded, as he had heard it that night of the long ago in the attack on the old Sanctuary--the Gray Seal and Silver Mag were their "*meat!*" Something like a moan was wrung from Jimmie Dale's lips. With the police out of it there would have been time; with the police a factor, granted even that the Mole gave her up, her death was certain.

The mind works swiftly. An eternity seemed bridged as he stood there against the door, his hands pressed to his temples--in reality scarcely a second had passed. Time! It was like a clarion call, that word, clearing his brain, lashing him into instant action. There *was* time, a small, pitifully inadequate margin, but yet a margin--the few minutes left before Carruthers would have the police hammering at the Mole's door. There was a chance, still a chance to save her life. And if he succeeded in getting her away from the Mole's--what then! It would be touch and go! What of the afterwards--a means of retreat--a temporary sanctuary? Yes, yes--he must think of everything!

He was working with mad speed now, stripping off his clothes, delving into that secret hiding place behind the movable section of the base-board near the door.

And now the gas, with its poverty-stricken, meagre, yellow flame, illuminated the place dimly--and Jimmie Dale, with his make-up box and a cracked mirror, worked against the flying minutes. There was only one way to go--as Larry the Bat. It would give the Mole and the underworld nothing to work on afterwards if Larry the Bat went to the rescue of Silver Mag; and if he won through there would then still be "Smarlinghue's" sanctuary, this place here, as a temporary refuge. The transformation to Larry the Bat stole an extra minute or two from the priceless store, but it was the only way--to risk it as Smarlinghue or Jimmie Dale, to risk recognition, would be the act of a fool, for it would render abortive the initial success, if, by any means, he could succeed even to that extent. Thank God for the circumstances that, prior to this, had led him to duplicate Larry the Bat's disreputable apparel; thank God for one chance of life--*for her*--that this afforded now.

The gas was out again, the room was in darkness. Through the little French window, and hugged close against the wall of the tenement, and through the loose Aboard in the fence that gave egress to the lane, Jimmie Dale, as Larry the Bat now, slunk along. And then, in the lane, he broke into a run. And now, an added peril came--a glimpse of Larry the Bat by any of gangland's fraternity, man or woman, and it would be the end! His position now was analogous to hers as Silver Mag before she had been caught! There would be no parley--it would be the end! But that was the chance he took, the only chance there was--for her.

But Jimmie Dale knew the East Side. By alleys and lanes, through yards and over fences, Jimmie Dale made his way along; and when forced into the open to cross a street, it was a dark, ill-lighted section that was chosen, and where for a short distance here and there he must needs keep to the street he held deep in the shadows of the buildings, crouching in doorways to avoid passers-by. It took time--he dared not calculate how long. Carruthers was not the man to let the grass grow under his feet! Carruthers would probably, before leaving home, have telephoned some Headquarters' man to meet him--the detective would have telephoned Headquarters from Melinoff's--and after that it would not take the police long to reach the Mole's!

It took time, this tortuous threading of the East Side--he did not know how long it had taken--but at last, as he swung into a long, black, and very narrow alleyway, he drew a quick breath of relief. So far, at least, he was ahead of the police. It was still and silent, there was no sound of any disturbance, and the Mole's now was only a little way ahead. He stole forward noiselessly. It was very quiet--much more quiet even than usual in that far from savoury neighbourhood. He remembered, with a grim smile of satisfaction, that the Wowzer had explained there was to be no crowding for front seats for fear of attracting the attention of the police. It had been very thoughtful of the Mole to pass that word around--very! With the underworld, prompted by curiosity and seething with hate, swarming here, the single chance he, Jimmie Dale, had of reaching her would have been swept away. He paused now, his lips set hard, crouched by the fence that separated the Mole's backyard from the alleyway. His plan was simple; but it depended for its ultimate success almost entirely on his ability to secure an instant means of disappearance for the Tocsin the moment she was outside the Mole's walls. That he could find her, that he could get her out of the house was another matter--he could only trust to his wits and nerve in that respect. But if he succeeded in that, then--he moved silently a little further up the lane, crossed to the other side and halted again, this time before the back door of a shed. In an instant his picklock was at work; in another he had opened the door a bare fraction of an inch. His lips grew tighter, as he retraced his steps to the Mole's fence. If that shed were ever needed at all, there would not be time to fumble in the dark for knob or latch--and there would be no necessity for that fumbling now! From the shed there was a very sure means of escape across a small intervening yard, and out through an areaway into the street, for the shed was one of the many entrances to Foo Sen's, a place with which he was very intimately acquainted--all this, of course, provided that, if the Tocsin were seen to enter the shed, *some one* held the pursuers back long enough to afford her time to reach the street.

Jimmie Dale shrugged his shoulders, as he opened a low gate in the fence silently and stepped through, into the yard beyond, leaving the gate open behind him. He was not a fool, blinded to what probably lay ahead! He could not hope to reach the Tocsin, much less effect her rescue, without warning the inmates of this house that loomed up before him now, without a fight with the Mole and the Mole's gangsters. It was not likely that *he* could reach the shelter of that shed, but the Tocsin could, and, once inside, throwing away her cloak and wig, "Silver Mag" would disappear, and after that there was the Sanctuary, and then her own brave wits. There came a queer twist to Jimmie Dale's lips, and then a shrug of his shoulders again. It was not likely to be the ending to the night that he had thought it might be when sitting there in Bristol Bob's only a few short hours ago!

Faint streaks of light through the interstices of a shuttered window showed just in front of him, as he stole forward across the yard. Window or back door, it mattered little to Jimmie Dale now, so that he could gain an entry into the house unobserved. It was very quiet--even ominously quiet--that impression came to him suddenly again. The quarter here was full of dives and gambling hells and resorts frequented by the worst in crimeland--but it seemed that the Mole's injunction had been obeyed to the letter! It boded little good--for her! Jimmie Dale's face, under the grime of Larry the Bat's make-up, grew white and set, as he approached the window. God in Heaven, was he already too late! The Mole, with his little tobacco shop in front as a blind, and his rooms above rented to "lodgers," thus housing the gang of Apaches that worked under his leadership, had had every opportunity, once the Tocsin was in his power in there, of doing as he would. And then another thought came flashing quick upon him. If they had gone that far, if she were dead, they must have discovered that under the cloak and the gray, straggling hair of Silver Mag--was Marie LaSalle. He forced a grip of iron upon himself, fighting mentally like a madman with himself for his self-control. The night with every passing moment seemed yawning wider and wider before him in a chasm that threatened ruin, and disaster, and the wreckage of everything that in life was worth the living, and-- *no* ,' Not yet! The luck had turned! She was there! Silver Mag was there! There! And safe so far!

The window was shoulder high. He was peering in through the blind. There was no light in the room itself, but a faint glow came in through the open doorway of a lighted room beyond--enough to enable him to make out a woman's form, the grizzled hair streaming over the threadbare cloak, as she lay on a cheap cot across the room, her face to the wall, her hands bound together behind her back.

It was Jimmie Dale working with all the art he knew; now; and those slim, sensitive, wonderful fingers were swift and silent as they had never been before. A steel jimmy loosened the shutters, and they swung apart with out a sound. He could see better now--see, at least, that she was alone in the room. He tapped softly on the window pane. It was too dark to see her face, but he saw her raise her head quickly, and then, evidently, quick to meet an emergency as she always was, rise from the cot and steal to the edge of the open door. He was working at the window now. A fever of anxiety was him--it seemed that his fingers stumbled, that they lost their cunning, that an eternity passed as she stood there apparently on guard by the door, her bound hands behind her back like some piteous appeal to him to hurry-- to hurry--and, in the name of all that life meant to both of them, to make haste.

And now cautiously, inch by inch, he was raising the window; and in another moment, in obedience to his whisper, the bound wrists were thrust within his reach, and he was severing the cords with his knife.

"Thank God!" breathed Jimmie Dale fervently. "Now jump--across the yard-- the door of Foo Sen's shed--it's open-- *quick*--"

There came a sudden crash from the front of the house, a sudden turmoil from within, a burst of shouts, a chorus of yells. The police! And now another shout, another burst of yells--from the rear--from the lane! Jimmie Dale's lips were like a thin, straight line. She was free from the house now, standing beside him here in the darkness. He reached swiftly up and closed the shutters--left open they invited immediate attention. His mind was working in lightning flashes. The police were at the front and rear, of course--they would not raid the front and leave the rear unguarded! But why the shouts out there in the lane--why had they not rushed in at once--and why now that *shot*! It was followed by another, and still another--and then a fusillade of them, as though the shots were returned.

"Quick!" he whispered again, and led the way toward the gate in the fence. The police would be pouring out of the house from the back door in a minute--the only chance was a dash for it. His mind was groping now, bewildered. What did it mean? The police who had obviously been detailed to the lane at the rear of the Mole's were fighting now--with whom--why? But the fight was working further on down the lane in the opposite direction from that shed door. "Quick!" he said again. "The shed door--on the other side--quick!"

Together they darted into the lane. From behind, the back door of the Mole's house was flung open, and there came the rush of feet. From down the lane the short, vicious tongue-flames of revolvers stabbed through the black. But in the darkness, save for those quick, myriad flashes like gigantic fireflies winking in the night, he could see nothing. They were racing, racing like mad, he and this form beside him for whose safety he prayed so wildly, so passionately in his soul now. It was only a step further--just another one--and the police, coming out of the Mole's, had not reached the gate yet. Just another step--and then a bullet, straying from the fight down there along the lane, drummed past his ear in an angry buzz--and the form beside him lurched heavily, stumbled, and pitched forward. And, with a low, broken cry, Jimmie Dale swung out a supporting arm, and pushing the shed door open with his elbow, gained the interior, and lowered his burden gently, a dead weight now, to the floor.

And then Jimmie Dale sprang to the door, and swung a heavy bolt that was there into place; then, running across the shed, he locked the other door as well. It was, perhaps, needless precaution. No one had seen them enter here, and there was little chance of the police developing any interest in the shed; while from the other side--Foo Sen's--the fact that there was a police battle in the lane would only cause the inmates of the dive to give the shed and lane the widest possible berth!

It had taken scarcely a second to lock the doors, and now he knelt beside a form that was ominously still upon the floor, and called her name over and over again.

"Marie! Marie! Marie!" he whispered frantically.

There was no answer--no movement. The strong, steady hands shook, those marvellous fingers, usually so deft and sure, faltered now as they loosened the cloak and threw the hood back over the wig of tangled, matted hair. It was not the darkness alone that would not let him see--there was a mist and a blur before his eyes. And now he loosened the heavy wig itself to give her relief--she would have no further need of that, for it would not be as Silver Mag that she left here--if she left here at all--no, no! his mind seemed breaking--she would leave here, she *must*--yes, yes, she was breathing now--she was not dead--not dead!

He wrenched his flashlight from his pocket. To find the wound and stop the flow of blood! The ray shot out--there was a cry from Jimmie Dale--and like a man distraught he reeled to his feet--and like a man distraught stared at the upturned face, ghastly white under the flashlight's glare.

It was the Pippin.

The wig of grizzled hair that he had unconsciously been holding dropped from Jimmie Dale's hand, and his hand went upward to his temple. Was he mad! Was this joy, relief, rage or fury that, surging upon him, was robbing him of his senses! The Pippin! How could it be the Pippin! The cloak with its hood, and the long, gray matted wig were very like Silver Mag's--very like Silver Mag's! The Pippin! The Pippin!--one-time actor who had murdered old Melinoff, ***the old-clothes dealer!*** No--he was not mad! Dimly, his mind groping in the darkness, he began to see.

The Pippin's eyes opened.

"Who's there?" he demanded weakly.

Jimmie Dale, without a word, leaned forward, and threw the ray of light upon his own face.

A queer smile flickered across the Pippin's lips; his voice, weak as it was, was debonair and careless.

"Well, we nearly got you, Larry--at that! You fell for it, all right. Only--only some one"--his voice weakened still farther--"must have spilled the beans--to the--police."

Jimmie Dale made no answer. His lips were thinned and tight together. It was plain enough now. It had been a plant to get *him*--to get Larry the Bat, who was known to the underworld to be the Gray Seal--to get the Gray Seal through an appeal to the Gray Seal's loyalty toward his pal, Silver Mag! A plant, devilish enough in its ingenuity--Silver Mag impersonated--the "news" of her capture spread broadcast through the underworld on the chance that it would reach the ears of Larry the Bat, and tempt Larry the Bat into the open--as it had done! He knew now why the Pippin had gone to Melinoff's--old Melinoff's stock, more than any other dealer's, would be the most likely to supply the Pippin with the garments that, if not too closely inspected, would pass muster for Silver Mag's. He knew now why the underworld, believing what it had been told, had been warned to keep away from the Mole's--he knew now that it was because he was to have no inkling that he was walking into a baited trap.

He had torn the Pippin's clothing loose, found the bullet hole in the left side, perilously near the heart, and was striving now to staunch the other's wound. The man had little call for mercy, but at least--

The Pippin pushed his hand away.

"It's no use," said the Pippin. "I'm--I'm done for. But--but I don't understand. When you came to the window, I went to the door and tipped them off that you were there, and the gang that was waiting started around into the lane so that you wouldn't get any chance to make a break that way. I--I don't understand. Where--

where did the police come from?"

"I sent them--from Melinoff's," said Jimmie Dale grimly.

The Pippin came up on his elbow.

"You!" he gasped. "You--you know what happened there--you were wise to everything all the time?"

"No," said Jimmie Dale. "I only knew you had murdered Melinoff. You left one of your cuff links there."

"Did I?" said the Pippin. He sank back on the floor again. "I didn't know it. It--it must have fallen out of my shirt when I undressed. I came away wearing women's things, and carrying my own clothes in a bundle." He laughed shortly, huskily. "That's what was the matter with Melinoff. It was the old fool's own fault! I didn't want to hurt him! He didn't understand at first when I was pawing all his stuff over, but when he saw me try the things on, and tumbled that I was--was going to play Silver Mag, he said he wouldn't stand for it. Ha, ha! Silver Mag!" The Pippin's voice had taken on a queer mumbling note, and his mind seemed to be functioning suddenly in a half-wandering way. "Some role, Silver Mag! I was the star to-night! You remember Silver Mag--how she used to go around in the old days and hand out the silver coins, never a bill, just coins, to the families whose men were doing spaces up the river in Sing Sing? She kept old Melinoff's wife going while he was in limbo--that's what he said. I didn't want to hurt the old fool, but he wouldn't keep his mouth shut. Ha, ha! Silver Mag! It was some play on the boards to-night! Clever brain, the Big Fellow's got! It wasn't any good if Silver Mag and Larry the Bat were together, but Silver Mag was seen buying a ticket and getting on a train for Chicago last night--and last night, later than that, the Gray Seal sent the Forrester stuff to the police--so they couldn't have been together this evening unless he went afterwards to Chicago, too--and he didn't do that because all the trains were watched. It was the biggest chance that ever came across of getting the Gray Seal in a trap. Some stage setting--some play--clever brain that--"

The voice trailed off. Outside there was quiet now, save for the crunch of an occasional footstep. The police who, as Jimmie Dale understood quite clearly now, had run into the Mole's gang as the two converged at the rear of the Mole's house, had evidently now got the better of the gangsters. And that convergence, too, explained why the Pippin had accompanied him so meekly toward the shed--the Pippin's one aim and object at that moment had been to avoid the police! He leaned suddenly forward over the man--the Pippin was going fast now. There was one thing yet, a thing that was vital, paramount, above all others.

"Pippin," he said quietly, "you're going out. Who put up this plant? It wasn't the Mole, he's not big enough, he's only a tool like yourself. Who was it?"

"No--not the Mole," murmured the Pippin. "He--he isn't big enough. Clever brain--clever brain--clever--"

"Who was it? Answer me, Pippin!"

"Yes," said the Pippin, and the queer smile came again, "I--I'll tell you. It--it was some one"--Jimmie Dale could scarcely hear the words--"some one--who will--get you yet!"

The smile was still on the Pippin's lips--but the man was dead. Jimmie Dale stood up again, and then Jimmie Dale, too, smiled; but it was a grim smile, hard and ominous. In his mind he had answered his own question.

It was that unseen hand of last night--only to-night the challenge had been *direct*. Well, he would pick up the gauntlet again--and at the same time, perhaps, add a little "atmosphere" to Carruthers' scoop! From his pocket came the thin, metal insignia case; and, lifting it with the tiny tweezers, moistening the adhesive side with his tongue, Jimmie Dale stooped down and fastened a gray seal on the floor by the Pippin's side.

And then Jimmie Dale crept out of the shed toward Foo Sen's, and crept into the dark areaway, and, as he had come, by alleyways and lanes, and through yards, and by ill-lighted, unfrequented streets, returned again to the Sanctuary--alone.

CHAPTER XXII
THE TOCSIN'S STORY

It was a whimsical movement, a whimsical trick of Jimmie Dale's--that outward thrust of his hand that he might study it in a curiously impersonal, yet mercilessly critical way. He laughed a little harshly, as he allowed his hand to drop again to the arm of his chair. No, there was no tremor there--mentally he might be near the breaking point, his nerves raw and on edge; but physically, outwardly, he gave no sign of the strain that, cumulative in its anxiety, had increased hourly, it seemed, in the three days that had passed since the night he had so narrowly escaped the trap laid by that unknown master criminal, whose cunning, power and malignant genius was dominating and making itself felt in every den and dive of the underworld, and for whom the Pippin and the Mole that night had been but blind tools, pawns moved at the will of this unseen, evil strategist upon a chessboard of inhuman deviltry.

An evening newspaper lay open on the table. Jimmie Dale's eyes fixed for an instant on a glaring headline, then travelled slowly around the little room--one of the St. James' Club's private writing rooms--and came back to the paper again. The failure of that night, the Pippin's death, the stir and publicity, the stimulus given to police activity, had, it seemed, in no way acted as a deterrent upon the sinister ingenuity which, he made no doubt, was likewise the author of the mysterious crime that to-night was upon every tongue in the city--the murder of one of New York's most prominent bankers under almost incredible circumstances, and the coincident disappearance of a number of documents which were vaguely hinted at as being of international importance and of priceless worth. The crime had been committed in broad daylight, in mid-afternoon, in the banker's private office, and within call of the entire staff of the bank. No one had been seen either to enter or leave the office during an interval of some fifteen to twenty minutes, previous to which time it had been established by one of the staff that the banker was engaged in his usual occupation at his desk, and at the expiration of which he had been discovered by the cashier lying dead upon the floor, his skull fractured by a blow that had evidently been dealt him from behind, the desk in disorder as though it had been hurriedly searched, and the papers, known to have been in the banker's possession at that time, gone.

Jimmie Dale brushed his hand across his eyes in a dazed way. No, of course, he did not know, he could not actually know that it was the same guiding evil genius at work here that had murdered both Forrester and old Melinoff, but something beyond actual proof, a sense of intuition, made of it a certainty in his own mind, at least, which left no room for argument. There had been viciously clever work here, as daring and crafty as it was remorseless in its brutality, and--he laughed suddenly, harshly as before, and, rising abruptly from his chair, stepped to the window, pushed aside the portieres, and stood staring down on Fifth Avenue, whose great, wide, lighted thoroughfare seemed a curiously and incongruously lonely spot now in its evening quiet and emptiness.

Suppose it was so! Granted that his intuition was in no way astray! What did it matter? It was a thing extraneous, of no personal significance to him! It was even strange that it had succeeded in intruding itself upon his thoughts at all, when mind and soul in these last few days had fought and groped and stumbled against the sickness of a fear that, growing upon him, had blotted out all other things from his consciousness. The Tocsin! Where was she? What had happened? Had she----no, he dared not let himself believe what a brutal logic told him now he should believe. He would not! He could not! And yet since that night when her note had come, the note that had been so full of a glad spontaneity, so full of *victory*--"It is the beginning of the end ... The way is clearing ... I am very happy tonight, and I wanted to tell you so"--since that night there had been no word from her.

No, that was not literally true. There **had** been word from her; but, rather than having brought hope and reassurance to him, it had only increased his fear and anxiety. That night, after a return to the Sanctuary, where, in lieu of the character of Larry the Bat, he had resumed his own personality again, be had hurried to his home to await the expected word from her that would tell him her success, which her note had indicated was to be looked for at any moment, had been achieved. The night, however, had brought forth nothing; but in the morning, amongst the mail which old Jason, his butler, had handed him, had been a letter from her. It had been written evidently in leisure, and evidently prior to the hurried little note that happiness, a surge of joy, a gladness and a hope whose share she could not hold back from him, had undoubtedly prompted her to write; it had been born out of impulse, that note, an impulse due, apparently, to a sudden turn in the brave fight she was waging which seemed to place the final victory almost within her grasp. The letter was not at all like that; it struck a far sterner note--the possibility of defeat--not in despair, not in a tone of failing courage, but as one who, weighing the chances, was not blind to an opponent's strength, but who, even in one's own defeat, still sought to snatch final victory even after death.

Jimmie Dale turned from the window, sat down again in his chair, and drew the letter from his pocket--and, sitting there, the strong jaws clamped and locked, his face drawn in rigid lines, the dark, steady eyes cold and hard, read it again, as he had read it many times before since Jason had handed it to him that morning several days ago:

"Dear Philanthropic Crook: I wonder if I am writing those words for the last time? I believe I am. I do not mean I am in such danger that I will never have the opportunity again; but, rather, that I will never have the *need* to do so. But to-night should tell. It is very near the end--one way or the other--and I believe it is *my* way. Oh, Jimmie, I pray God it is, and that tomorrow--but I did not start this letter to you to talk of *that*.

"Long ago--do you remember, Jimmie?--I wrote you that I would not, could not bring you into the shadows again for me, and that I must fight this out alone. It must be that way, Jimmie; there is no other way, and what I am about to say must not lead you to think that I am hesitating now, or have changed my mind. It is only this--that the game is not won until the last card is played, and, while I am almost certain that I see the way now, there *is* still that last card to play. Do not let us mince matters, Jimmie. If I fail, you know what it means. But, in the bigger way, Jimmie, I can only count for but very little in the balance. There is the afterwards that is of far more moment--that justice, swift and sure, should put an end to the depredations and the menace to society that exists to-day in the person of one of the cleverest and most conscienceless fiends that ever plotted crime. Nor, in case you should have to take up the work where I leave off, would you be even then obliged to come into those shadows again. It is very strange, Jimmie. It is almost like some grim, terribly grim, ironical joke. Everything, all the power, all the resources that this man possesses have been used against me in the last few months, because he knows that unless he accomplishes my death he must remain in hiding just as he has forced me into hiding; and yet at the same time--and this he does not know, because he does not know that he is known to you, and that you, as Jimmie Dale, a man whose position and prominence would carry conviction with every word you might say, are in a position to testify against him--with my death he automatically accomplishes his own destruction. And so you see, Jimmie, in one sense at least, I cannot fail! No, I do not mean to speak lightly--I--I have as much as you, Jimmie--to live for.

"Listen, then! We knew, you and I, that while both my supposed uncle and the head of the Crime Club were killed that night of the old Sanctuary fire, and that the greater number, almost all in fact, of the members of the band were caught by the police, that a few of them still evaded the trap and escaped. But we believed these were so few in number and were so thoroughly disorganised that nothing more was to be feared from them. And this in a very great measure is true; but it is not alto-gether true. No, I am not going to tell you that the Crime Club rose from its ashes and is in operation again; but one of the men who escaped that night, one of the Club's leaders, possessed evidently of the secret as to where the Club's surplus funds were hidden, is the man who, through a lavish use of those funds, is operating now through the underworld, who is responsible for Forrester's murder, and is the man who through all these months has sought to reach me. I referred to him as 'one of the leaders'--I believe him now to have been the most dangerous of them all. You know him as--Clarke. Do you remember, Jimmie? He was the man who so cleverly impersonated Travers as the chauffeur, after they had killed Travers. He was the man who was at the house that night when Travers first learned that my father and my uncle had been murdered, and that the same fate was in store for me. I told you that from where he sat in the room that night I could not see his face, that Travers told me who he was--but, apart from not being able to recognise him on that par-ticular occasion, I knew him well, for he had been a frequent visitor to the house even prior to my father's death, and subsequently in company with Travers as one who appeared to have struck up an intimacy with my supposed uncle.

"The day after the Crime Club was raided by the police, you will remember that Clarke not being amongst those caught, I gave the authorities what particulars I could in reference to the man. But nothing came of it. A description and the name of 'Clarke' was little enough to work on. The man had disappeared. Time passed, and I supposed, as no doubt you, as well, supposed, that Clarke had made good his escape, that he was probably well content with such good fortune, and that nothing more, if he could help it, would ever be heard of him. Jimmie, I was wrong. Within a month a series of narrow escapes from accidents, any one of which might easily have accomplished my death, seemed to follow me persistently. I will not take the time now to enumerate them all--they were so commonplace, so liable to happen to any one, such for instance as escaping by a hair's-breadth from being run down by a speeding car swerving, around the corner as I started to cross the street, or again by an iron tackle falling from a scaffolding where work was in progress on the building in which, pending the remodelling of my own house, as you know, I had taken an apartment, that at first I attached no ulterior significance to them. But finally, as they persisted, I became convinced that they were deliberate and premeditated attempts upon my life. I said nothing to you, as I did not wish to alarm you. And then one night Clarke showed himself.

"Do you remember the colourless liquid, the poison instantaneous in its action and defying detection by autopsy, which was so favourite a method of murder with the Crime Club? I had expected to be out for the evening, and had given the maids permission to go out together. It was about halfpast eight when I left the apartment. I had only gone a few blocks when I returned for something I had forgotten. I was in my bedroom when I heard the hall door open stealthily. I switched off the bedroom light instantly, and slipped into the clothes closet, leaving the door just ajar. I knew, of course, that if it were another attack directed against me, it was one that was prearranged and that was being made on the presumption that I was out and that the apartment was empty. There was silence for a moment or two, then a step crossed the threshold of the bedroom, and the light went on. It was Clarke. There was a little night table beside the bed on which my maid, before she had gone out, had placed as usual a carafe of ice water and a small tray of biscuits. Clarke was evidently very well acquainted with this fact. He stepped at once to the table, took a vial from his pocket, poured the contents into the carafe--and the next instant the room was in darkness again, and Clarke was gone. I acted as quickly as I could. I dared not move or give any sign of my presence until he was out of the apartment, for I would have accomplished nothing except my death. But the minute the outer door closed I picked up the telephone to communicate with the vestibule. It was a ground-floor apartment, as you know. The one chance was to have the hall porter intercept Clarke in the vestibule. As a matter of fact, the telephone was not answered for fully a minute or so--too late, of course! Clarke had vanished. The boy at the telephone desk said he had been busy with another call. That is all, Jimmie. I saw clearly that night that there was only one thing left for me to do if I hoped to save my life, and that was to fight Clarke with his own weapons. And so I wrote you; and you know now why Marie LaSalle 'left the city for an extended trip,' as her bankers informed you, and why during all these months I have 'disappeared.'

"I come now to the last thing I have to say--the reason for writing this letter. My death was essential to Clarke, because he believed that I was the ***only*** one who could positively identify him ***as*** 'Clarke,' and that, therefore, as long as I lived he could not resume his own identity and personal freedom of action for fear that I might, even if only through inadvertence, recognise him. He could take no chances. But I believe I have beaten Clarke. I have discovered that 'Clarke' is in reality Peter Marre, the shyster lawyer, better known among his clientele as Wizard Marre. But Marre, too, has disappeared--you understand, Jimmie? And now, hidden, under cover, never showing himself personally, 'Clarke' is working, not only to reach me, but to further all his other schemes, through some agency without appearing himself either as Marre or as 'Clarke.' I believe it is only a matter of a few hours now before I shall either have got to the bottom of who and what this agency is, or else--again do not let us mince matters, Jimmie--'Clarke' will have been too much for me. And in that latter case is found the whole object of this letter. Once I am removed from his path, and believing that no one else could, or would, link 'Clarke' and Peter Marre together, he will naturally resume the freedom of his former life, and Peter Marre will appear again in his old-time surroundings, a Peter Marre unhampered by fear of discovery, and therefore a Peter Marre a hundredfold more dangerous than ever before. And so, Jimmie, if that should happen, you have simply to get this information into the hands of the police without appearing yourself, say, through the agency of the Gray Sealand I shall not have brought you into the shadows again."

The letter was signed simply--"Marie." But there was a postscript:

"You will hear from me the moment that I can tell you I am free at last."

Jimmie Dale sat staring at the postscript. He made no movement; and there was no sound in the room, save that the sheets of paper crackled slightly in his hand. He was afraid to-night, afraid as he had never been in his life before; and the fear that was gnawing at his heart was mirrored in a gray, rigid face, and in the misery that had crept into the dark, half-closed eyes. It was three days ago since he had received that letter, and the awaited, promised word had not come--three days, and the letter stated that it would be but a matter of a few hours before the decision that meant life or death was reached. And the hurried little note, so obviously written subsequent to the letter, though it had been received prior to it, but bore out in its very optimism the fact that the final card was then almost in the very act of being played. And since then--there had been nothing.

He put little faith in the Pippin's belief that she had gone to Chicago. He found no relief in that possibility at all. That they had seen her buy a ticket and board a train--yes. That for her own ends she had let them see her do that--yes. But whether she had ever gone or not was quite a different matter! Her letter would certainly indicate that she had not. But even if she had! She could have communicated with him from Chicago just as easily as she could have communicated with him from any place here in New York!

Jimmie Dale's hand lifted and pressed hard against his temple, as though to still the dull, constant throbbing that brought to his mental agony the added torment of physical pain. For these three days now he had fought with mind and body and soul against the one conclusion that was tenable--the conclusion which to-night, robbing him of every hope in life, bringing a grief and anguish greater than he could bear, cold logic was finally forcing him to accept. She would have known the torment of anxiety in which he lived, and if her plans had only been delayed or checked, if it had been no more than that, she would surely have communicated with him and allayed his fears.

A low sound, a moan of bitter pain, came from Jimmie Dale's lips. Logic had won at last, and was triumphant in the blackest hour that had ever come into his life. The one glimmer of hope to which, as time went on and one by one other hopes had vanished, he had still clung tenaciously, had surrendered, too, and gone down before the face of that brutal logic that weighed neither human agony nor suffering in its remorseless conclusions. Clarke, it was true, had not yet resumed his former life as Peter Marre--but he, Jimmie Dale, was forced to admit now that that meant little or nothing. A thousand and one reasons might account for Clarke postponing his re-entry into his old life--that the man had allowed three days to pass proved nothing.

Marre! Peter Marre! Wizard Marre! A smile that held no mirth hovered for an instant over Jimmie Dale's lips. Yes, he knew Marre, Marre of the underworld, well! The man was brilliant, clever--and possessed of a devil's soul! Also Marre, as certainly no other man had ever held it, held the confidence of crimeland--and crimeland had supplied the tricky lawyer with his clientele. And so Marre was "Clarke," one of the leaders of the old Crime Club! Jimmie Dale's smile disappeared, and his lips drew straight and tight together. It was quite easily understood now. The returns in a financial sense from such a clientele, large even as they perhaps might be, were meagre and pitiful in comparison with the huge sums which, in one way and another, the Crime Club would have acquired; but the returns in another sense had been vast and of incalculable value, not only to Clarke, but to the Crime Club as well. Clarke's power in the underworld as Marre had reached the height where the underworld itself eulogised that power by bestowing on the man the "moniker" of Wizard, investing him, as it were, with a title and a peerage in that inglorious realm. And this power, supplying a foreknowledge of events through intimacy with those whispered secrets in the innermost circles of the citizenry of crimeland, must have been of immeasurable worth. And now Clarke, hidden away somewhere, acting, it appeared, through some unknown agency and go-between, was utilising that power with deadly cunning and effect--not only against the Tocsin, but against society at large, as witness the murder of Forrester of a few days ago, and presumably the murder of Jathan Lane, the banker, not longer ago than this afternoon.

Jimmie Dale shook his head suddenly. Acting through some *unknown* agency? The Tocsin had not said that. Indeed, if she had been as near to the final move in this battle of wits which she had been playing for months, as her letter indicated, she must have known by now who and what and where that agency was. And he could see plainly enough why she had kept her own counsel in that respect. It was through her great, unselfish love for him that she had intentionally refrained from giving him any clue that would enable him to find his way into the danger zone which she reserved for herself alone. Yes, he understood that--but it only made what he feared now the harder to bear. She had been right, of course, in her conclusion as to what he would have done had she given him the opportunity! It was the one thing he had been fighting for, struggling for, battling for all these months, that clue--and she had told him only that "Clarke" was behind it all, and that "Clarke" was Peter Marre. And it had served him little! As though the earth had opened and swallowed the man and his alias up, there was neither trace nor sign of Peter Marre.

He knew that well! He had not been idle since that letter came! He had instantly seized upon what he had hoped would prove the clue that he could follow to the heart of the web--and the clue had led him nowhere. Marre, like the Tocsin, was somewhere "on a trip." Marre's office was not closed. A year ago Marre had taken in with him as partner a young lawyer by the name of Cleaver, who lacked only, through experience, the same degree of dishonest finesse and cunning possessed by Marre himself--a defect which Marre had doubtless counted on speedily rectifying under his own unholy tutelage! Cleaver was carrying on the business. To all inquiries Cleaver's replies had been the same--Mr. Marre, through overwork, had been obliged to take a rest; he did not know where Mr. Marre was other than that Mr. Marre was making an extended tour through the Orient, nor did he know when Mr. Marre might be expected to return; Mr. Marre, purposely, in order that he might escape all thought and care of business, and to preclude the possibility of anything of that nature reaching him, had refrained from giving the office any specific address. But he, Jimmie Dale, had not been content with inquiries alone in those last few days--though the result here again had been nothing. He was satisfied only that, in so far as the main issue was concerned, Cleaver was not in Marre's confidence, and that Cleaver not only did not know Marre's exact whereabouts, but believed, as he had said, that Marre was travelling somewhere in the Orient.

Jimmie Dale drew his hand heavily again across his forehead. It seemed as though the very act of sitting here was a traitorous act to her, that even in this

momentary inaction he had cause for bitter self-reproach and even for contempt-
-and yet he could see no way now to take. In the last three days, as Smarlinghue,
as Jimmie Dale, yes, even as Larry the Bat again, working with feverish intensity,
with almost sleepless continuity, he had exhausted every means and effort within
his power of running Marre, *alias* Clarke, to earth. There seemed nothing now left
to do but to wait until Marre should resume his own identity; nothing left but the
promise of a vengeance that--again Jimmie Dale laughed harshly, and, as the laugh
died away, a smile took its place on the thinned lips that was not good to see. Yes,
she was right in that; he knew Marre--he knew Marre, with his thin, cruel face, his
black, sleepy eyes; his suave, ingratiating manner that hid under its veneer a devil's
treachery! Nor, well as he knew the man, was it strange that he had not known
Clarke as Peter Marre, for he had seen Clarke only once--that night in the long ago,
in Spider Jack's when the man, with consummate art, a master of disguise, had impersonated Travers, the dead chauffeur, and had succeeded in fooling even Spider
Jack himself. But he, Jimmie Dale, knew *now*. Yes, she had been right--a whiteness
came and gathered on his lips--in that sense she could not fail, Marre at least would
pay! But perhaps not quite as she suggested, perhaps not quite by the simple act of
a denunciation to the police, perhaps not quite in so simple a way as that, for, after
all--his hand clenched over the sheets of her letter--though it would be easy enough
to establish Marre's alias now that the alias was known, there might be another way
in which Marre would answer, a more *intimate* way, a more personal way! Not
murder--the skin was ivory white across his knuckles--not murder, but--

Jimmie Dale was quietly folding the sheets of paper in his hand. Some one was
knocking at the door.

"Come in!" said Jimmie Dale--and slipped the letter back into his pocket, as the
door opened.

It was one of the club's attendants.

"I beg pardon, Mr. Dale, sir," said the man; "but there is a 'phone call for you."
He glanced toward the telephone on the table. "I was not sure just where you were,
sir. Shall I ask them to connect you here?"

"Thank you!" said Jimmie pleasantly. "Very good, Masters. No--I'll attend to it
myself."

The man withdrew, and closed the door again. Jimmie Dale rose from his chair, and, stepping to the table, picked up the instrument.

"There is a call for me, I believe," he said. "This is Mr. Dale."

There was a moment's silence, then Jimmie Dale spoke again.

"Yes--hello!" he said. "Yes, this is Mr. Dale. What--"

The room seemed suddenly to swirl about him--the hand so steady a few moments ago was trembling palpably now as it held the instrument. ***Her voice***? No--he was mad! It was his brain, overwrought, strained, not to the breaking point, but beyond, that had broken at last, and was mocking at him now in some cruel phantasy. Her voice? No, it could not be, for she--for she was--

"Jimmie! Jimmie!"--the voice came hurriedly again, almost frantically this time. "Jimmie--are you there?"

"You!" His lips were dry, he moistened them with his tongue. "You!" he whispered hoarsely. "You, Marie--and I thought--I thought that you were--"

"Jimmie," she broke in, a quick, wistful catch in her voice, "I cannot stay here a moment--you understand, don't you? There is not an instant to lose--on the floor by the Sanctuary window--a note--will you hurry, Jimmie--good-bye."

She was gone. Mechanically he replaced the receiver on the hook. She was gone--but it **was** her voice he had heard--hers--and she was alive. The play of emotion upon him robbed him for the moment of coherent thought, and came and swept over him in a mighty surge and engulfed him; and now in the sudden revulsion from despair and the bitterest of agony his mind was dazed and numbed. It seemed as though he were obeying some subconscious power, as he turned and left the room; as though some influence outside of, and extraneous to, himself gave him a spurious self-mastery, a self-command, a mask of nonchalance, as he walked calmly through the club lobby and out to the street.

Benson, his chauffeur, held the door of his car open for him.

"Where to, sir?" Benson asked.

"The Palace--Bowery," Jimmie Dale answered. "And hurry, Benson!"

CHAPTER XXIII
HUNCHBACK JOE

Jimmy Dale flung himself back on the seat of the big touring car. It was an address, the Palace Saloon on the Bowery, that he had often given Benson before--the nearest point to which Benson, trusted as Benson was, had ever been permitted to approach the Sanctuary itself. The night air, the sweep of the wind was grateful, as the machine sped forward. He did not reason, he could not reason--his mind was in turmoil still. Only two things were clear, distinct, rising dominant out of that turmoil--that he had heard her voice, her voice that he had never thought to hear again; and that there was need, a desperate need for haste now, because he must reach the Sanctuary without an instant's loss of time.

And then gradually his brain began to clear, to adjust itself, to function normally; and when finally the car drew up at a corner on the Bowery, it was a Jimmie Dale, keen, self-possessed and alert, who sprang briskly to the pavement.

"Will you need me any further, sir?" Benson asked.

Jimmie Dale was lighting a cigarette deliberately--it was the same question that he was pondering in his own mind, but the answer was dependent upon the contents of that note which was waiting for him in the Sanctuary.

"I am not quite sure, Benson," he replied. "In any case, you had better wait here for twenty, minutes. If I am not back in that time, you may go home. Don't wait any longer."

"Very good, sir," Benson answered.

It was only a short distance to the Sanctuary--down the cross street, a turn into another only to emerge again on one that paralleled the first, and then Jimmie Dale, walking slowly now, was sauntering along an ill-lighted thoroughfare flanked on either side with a miscellany of small shops and tenements of the cheaper class.

There were but few pedestrians in sight; but, as he neared the tenement that made the corner of the lane ahead, Jimmie Dale's pace became still more leisurely. A man and a woman were strolling up the street toward him. They passed. Jimmie Dale, at the corner of the lane now, glanced behind him. The two were self-absorbed. And then, like a shadow merging with the darkness of the lane, Jimmie Dale had disappeared.

In an instant, he had gained the loose board in the high fence; and in another, pressing close to the rear wall of the tenement, he had reached the little French window that gave on the dingy courtyard. There was an almost inaudible sound, a faint metallic *snip*, as, kneeling, his fingers loosened the hidden catch beneath the sill--and the window on well-oiled hinges swung silently inward, and closed as silently again behind Jimmie Dale as he entered.

The top-light, high up near the ceiling, threw a misty ray of moonlight along the greasy, threadbare carpet, and threw into relief a folded piece of dark-coloured paper at Jimmie Dale's feet. He stooped and picked it up--and then moving close to the window again, his fingers, in the darkness, felt over the dilapidated roller shade to assure himself that the rents were securely pinned together against the possibility of prying eyes. He stepped quickly then across the room, tested the door lock; and then the single gas-jet, air-choked, hissing spitefully, illuminated the room with a wavering meagre yellow flame.

Under the light, Jimmie Dale unfolded the paper, his face hardening suddenly. It was not like any note she had ever written him before--there was no white envelope here, no paper of fine and delicate texture, no ink-written message carefully penned; instead, evidence enough of her desperate haste, the desperate circumstances probably under which she had written it, the message was on a torn piece of brown wrapping paper, and the words, in pencil, were scrawled in hurried, broken sentences. And standing there, fighting for a grip upon himself, Jimmie Dale read the message----almost illegible! in places--and then, as though a strange incredulity, a strange inability to grasp and understand its import fully, were prompting him, he read it again, murmuring snatches of it aloud.

"... I did not mean to bring you into the shadows... but there is another life, not mine, at stake ... I have no right to do anything else ... if I intervened, or gave warning, the evidence that will convict Clarke's agent, and will convict Clarke through the agent, is lost... that is why, in spite of all, I am writing this ... do you understand? ... for three nights he disappeared, and somehow, I do not yet know how, evaded me in the daytime ... no trace, just as I believed I had the man through whom Clarke is working trapped ... dared not take the chance of giving up watch for an instant ... did not know about this afternoon until an hour ago ... too late ... Jathan Lane's murder at the bank ... Klanner, the janitor of the bank ... very fair hair, scar on left cheek bone ... worked at night ... under passage from private office ... blackjack with which murder was done, document and money in Klanner's room ... unmarried ... lives in rear room, first floor of tenement at ... you must get the evidence ... unto Caesar!.. ship chandler's store, junk shop ... Larens, Joe Larens, the hunchback ... Clarke's agent ... another murder to cover up their tracks ... must get Clarke through Hunchback Joe ... will squeal if he sees no way of escape ... Klanner's room at once ... Klanner with Kid Greer will be at Baldy Jack's at ten o'clock ... will stop at nothing ... innocent bystander ... document of international importance, ... gold and details ... Federal authorities, not the police ... will see that Secret Service men get tip where to raid at midnight ... under the sail cloth in left corner ..."

Jimmie Dale was tearing the paper into little shreds. His brain, eagerly now, was leaping from premise to conclusion, fitting the strange, complex parts of her story, seemingly so utterly at variance one with another, into a single, concrete whole. Yes, he understood why, in spite of herself, she had been forced to bring him within those shadows at the last--to save another's life, which she could not do alone without forfeiting the opportunity of securing the evidence that would condemn those actually guilty, and reach, through the lesser lights, the man higher up--Marre, alias Clarke. Yes, he understood, too, that this was the end--if all went well! A grim smile came and flickered across Jimmie Dale's lips. She believed that Hunchback Joe, if caught and trapped, would squeal to the police. The grim smile deepened. Hunchback Joe might, or might not, squeal to the police-- ***but in any case Hunchback Joe would tell his story***! He, Jimmie Dale, would see to that-- whatever the cost, whatever the consequences, if he had to choke and wring it from the man's lips. It was a surer way than trusting to the police--it was the only sure way of reaching the end. The cost! The risk! What did it matter? What was cost, or risk! Her life was in the balance!

He glanced quickly around him. Would it be as Smarlinghue to-night? He shook his head. No, if it were really the end, if he won through to-night, this would be the last time he would ever stand here in the Sanctuary, and to leave the clothes of Jimmie Dale here, even in so secure a hiding place as behind that movable section of the base-board, would impose upon him the *necessity* of returning--was but to hamper himself, and, indeed, as likely as not, if hard pressed, to court disaster.

His glance, strangely whimsical, strangely wistful now, travelled again over the room. If it was the end to-night, this was his good-by to Smarlinghue, to Larry the Bat--and the Gray Seal. This was his exit from the sordid stage of the underworld--forever. Yes, in time, suspicious of Smarlinghue's continued absence, they would investigate and search the Sanctuary here; they might even discover that hiding place in the wall--but what did it matter? They would find only the trappings of a *character* that had passed out of existence; and out of that fact the police and the underworld would be privileged to make what capital they could! No, it would not be as Smarlinghue that he would work to-night--he was well enough as he was. He had not worn evening clothes since that letter came, for the nights had been spent in constant toil, and the dark suit of tweeds he wore now was not conspicuous. Nor need he even have recourse to that hiding place again--what he required was already in his pockets--for days now, in whatever role he had played, he had been prepared for any emergency.

Jimmie Dale looked at his watch--it was ten minutes after nine--and, reaching up, turned out the light. A minute more and the French window was silently opened and closed again, and Jimmie Dale was once more on the street. Here, walking quickly, but keeping to the less frequented streets, he headed deeper into the East Side. He would have no need of Benson, and Benson without further ado at the expiration of the allotted twenty minutes would obey orders literally and go home. No, he would have no further need of Benson and the car--Jimmie Dale smiled curiously, his mind absorbed now in the immediate problem that confronted him--they worked on a carefully prepared and methodical schedule, these minions of Clarke or Marre, allowing ample time in each successive step in their plans that there might be neither confusion nor mistake in what they did. Well, what was ample time for them, was ample time for him! It was not far from the tenement where the Tocsin had said Klanner lived to Baldy Jack's--and Klanner was not due at Baldy Jack's until ten o'clock.

Under the slouch hat, pulled far down over his eyes, Jimmie Dale's brows knit-ted into a frown. It was true then, and his intuition had not been at fault! It was Clarke who had planned the murder and robbery at the bank that afternoon--and Hunchback Joe, Clarke's familiar, and his accomplices who had carried it out. Yes, it had been clever enough--but difficult enough too! Yet of two alternatives they had chosen the easiest. The document, containing the secret international arrangements for gold shipments into the United States, embracing European commitments, and including transportation details, was always, except when in the banker's personal possession, carefully locked away in the bank's vaults. In the daytime then, it was impossible for a stranger to reach those vaults; and at night time to attempt to force the strongest vaults in the City of New York, with their intricate electric-alarm system, was a task from which even Clarke might shrink!

The Tocsin had made it very clear. The document, or documents, never left the bank's premises; it never left the bank's vaults except when in the possession of the bank's president in the latter's private office. Clarke had therefore chosen the line of least resistance--the bank president's office! And that accounted, he, Jimmie Dale, understood now, for the sudden failure of the Tocsin's plans three nights ago, since it accounted evidently for the sudden disappearance of Hunchback Joe, which had checkmated her on that night and on subsequent nights--for it had taken those three nights to perfect their plans in the bank, and the work there had evidently been done under the personal supervision of Hunchback Joe.

The plan's cleverness and cunning lay in its devilish simplicity--it required only long, painstaking and laborious preparation. There were, according to the newspapers, two entrances to the banker's private office; the customers' entrance from the main rotunda of the bank, and a rear entrance leading in behind the cages to the working quarters of the staff, which was separated from the general offices by a short, narrow, enclosed passage with a second door at the extreme end. The president's office, as befitted his position, was richly furnished, and the passage, being in reality but an adjunct to the office itself, had not been overlooked--it was carpeted with a long Persian rug. That portion of the basement directly beneath the president's office and the passage had been partitioned off into a storeroom for old files and books, and was consequently rarely visited. For the rest, the method was fairly obvious. The storeroom was ceiled in with wood, which, when carefully cut away, could be replaced during the daytime, and so hide all traces of what was going on should any one enter the place. It required, then, simply a certain number of nights' work--and it had taken three. An opening had been cut through the flooring into the passage, and the surface flooring of the passage over the aperture refitted into place, so that, covered by the rug, there was no indication that anything was wrong.

The minor details the Tocsin had passed over--but to supply them required but little effort of the imagination. The president customarily devoted a certain amount of time each afternoon to the matter in question, and immediately on his return from lunch always took the papers from the vault and carried them to his private office. It became, then, simply necessary that the man, or men, hiding in the basement should know when the president was *alone*; but this would hardly be a very difficult matter, for, with nothing but the upper skin of the flooring left, one had only to post himself in the opening and he could hear as well, almost, as though he were in the private office itself. The entrance could then be effected in the security of the little passage; the rear door of the passage would be silently locked against interruption; the door leading into the president's office, where the president sat with his back to the door, would be silently opened--then a quick leap, soundless on the heavy carpet--the blow of a blackjack--the limp body caught and lowered to the floor--the documents secured--the escape.

The escape! Jimmie Dale had turned suddenly into a pitch-black areaway, and, cautiously now, was making his way to the rear of a three-story tenement of the poorer class. The escape had naturally been accomplished in exactly the same way--the rear door unlocked again to obviate any immediate attention being paid to the passage--the murderer lowering himself through the aperture, and, as he replaced the flooring, manipulating the rug so that it would drop innocently back into place--and the exit from the basement would of course already have been provided for. Jimmie Dale's face was hard. The newspapers, going to press almost at the moment the murder was discovered, though giving a general description of the bank's premises, had had no opportunity to furnish details of the ensuing police investigation; but that the police would eventually discover the hole in the flooring was obvious; that they would also discover it without much delay was equally obvious-- ***and it had been intended that they should***. Clarke's object, acting through Hunchback

Joe, had been to provide only for the *immediate* escape--and after that, with callous deviltry, he proposed to utilise this very means of escape to cover up the tracks of the tools who were doing his work, and, backed with another murder, to put the crime upon another's shoulders!

Jimmie Dale had halted now to survey his surroundings, and, his eyes grown accustomed to the darkness, he could make out a door opening on the small yard in which he stood, and to the right of the door an unlighted and closed window. That was Klanner's window. He did not know Klanner, the bank's janitor--except that he knew him as an *innocent* man, as the proposed victim of as foul and black and pitiless a conspiracy as had ever been hatched in a human brain! Nor did he know Hunchback Joe--save by reputation. The man was a comparative newcomer in the underworld. He had bought out a small ship-chandler's business, a rickety, out-at-the-heels place on an equally rickety old wharf on the East River; and it was generally understood that he was a "fence" of a sort, making a speciality of, and catering to, a certain extensive and vicious class of thieves, the wharf rats, who infested the city's shipping--his ostensible business of a ship-chandler enabling him to handle and dispose of that class of stolen property with comparative immunity.

Jimmie Dale was crouching at the door, a little steel picklock in his fingers. It was fairly evident now that the underworld in general had but an extremely superficial acquaintance with Hunchback Joe; that Hunchback Joe's minor depredations against the law were but a cloak to--the mental soliloquy ended abruptly. Jimmie Dale drew suddenly back from the door, and, retreating along the wall of the building, crouched down in the darkness beneath the window. *What was that*? It came again----a step, stealthy, cautious, from the areaway--and now another step--there were two men there.

The picklock was back in his pocket, and, in its place, his fingers closed around the stock of his automatic. A shadow showed around the corner of the building, a queer, twisted, misshapen shadow--it was followed by another. Jimmie Dale drew in his breath softly. Hunchback Joe! He had rather expected that the man would already have come and gone, that this initial act of the brutal drama staged for the night's work would already have been performed. Well, it did not matter! There was still time--time to wait while Hunchback Joe did his work here, time in turn to do his own and still reach Baldy Jack's before ten o'clock.

From somewhere in the distance came the roar and rattle of an elevated train; from a neighbouring tenement came the strains of a wheezy phonograph. The figures were at the rear door of the tenement now. A minute passed; the door opened, closed, the two figures had disappeared--and then, in a flash, Jimmie Dale had straightened up, and a steel jimmy was working with deft, silent speed at the window sash. He had the time it would take Hunchback Joe to reach and open Klanner's door from the hall inside--no more. And if he could watch Hunchback Joe at work it would simplify to a very large extent his own task when Hunchback Joe was through; there would be no necessity for a *search*, and--ah! The window gave. He raised it noiselessly, reached inside and pulled down the roller shade to within an inch of the sill, and pulled the window down again to a little below the level of the shade. The opening left was unnoticeable--but he could now both see and hear.

There came a faint sound from within--the creak of a slowly opening door, a step across the floor, then the flare of a match, and the light in the room went on.

Jimmie Dale was drawn back now against the wall at one corner of the window, his eyes on a level with the sill. He had made no mistake about that misshapen, twisted shadow--it was Hunchback Joe. Jimmie Dale's eyes travelled to the hunchback's companion--and narrowed as he recognised the other. The man was well enough known in the underworld, a hanger-on for the most part, a confirmed hop-fighter, though when not under the influence of the drug he was counted one of the cleverest second-story workers and lock-pickers in the Bad Lands--Hoppy Meggs, they called him. Again Jimmie Dale's eyes shifted--to Hunchback Joe once more. Like some abnormal and repulsive toad the man looked. His shoulders were thrust upward until they seemed to merge with the head itself, the body was crooked and bent forward, due to the ugly deformity of the man's back, while the face was carried at an upward tilt, as though tardily to rectify the curvature of the spine, and out of the sinister, bearded face, the beard tawny and ill-kempt, little black eyes from under protruding brows blinked ceaselessly.

A sudden fury, an anger hot and passionate seized upon Jimmie Dale; and there came an impulse almost overpowering to play another role, a deadlier, grimmer role than that of spectator! A toad, he had called the man. He was wrong--the man was a devil in human guise. He crushed back the impulse, a cold smile on his lips. He could afford to wait! It was not time yet. There was still the game to play out.

He would have an opportunity to give full sway to impulse before the night was out, *before* the Tocsin should have set the Secret Service men upon the other's trail--before midnight came.

Hunchback Joe was speaking now.

"Go on, Hoppy; get busy!" he ordered sharply, jerking his hand toward a, trunk that stood at the foot of the cheap iron bedstead. "Get that opened. Hurry up! And see that you don't leave any scratches on it, or--you understand!" He leaned forward, leering with sudden savagery at his companion.

Hoppy Meggs moved forward, dropped on his knees in front of the trunk, examined the lock for an instant--and grunted in contempt.

"Aw, it's a cinch! Say, I could do it wid a hairpin!" he grinned--and a moment later threw back the lid.

Hunchback Joe drew a short, ugly blackjack, a packet of papers, and a large roll of bills from his pocket, and tossed the articles into the trunk.

"Lock it again!" he instructed tersely.

Hoppy Meggs hesitated--he was staring into the trunk.

"Say, youse don't mean dat--do youse?" he demanded heavily. "Not dem papers dat--"

Hunchback Joe's smile was not pleasant.

"Lock the trunk!" he said curtly. And then, as Hoppy Meggs closed down the lid: "I didn't bring you here to offer any advice; but as I don't want you to labour under the impression that, not having any brains of your own, there aren't, therefore, any brains at all to stand between you and the police, I'll tell you. If they recover the original document, besides fixing the crime on Klanner, they'll figure they've got it back before any harm has been done, and before it has been passed on to whoever had paid down the little cash advance to Klanner for the job in the shape of that roll there--eh? And figuring that way they won't change any of the plans or details as they stand now in those papers--eh? And meanwhile a *copy* is just as good to the man who is coughing up to you and me and the rest of us for this, isn't it?"

"My Gawd!" said Hoppy Meggs in fervent admiration, as he locked the trunk.

"Yes," said Hunchback Joe--and the snarl was back in his voice. "And now you see to it that you've got the rest of what *you've* got to do straight. It won't pay you to make any mistakes! Let the Mole's crowd start something before you pull the lights--it's got to look like a drunken row where the bystander, with nobody but himself to blame for being in such a place as that, **accidentally** gets his! And you tip the Kid off again to leave Klanner by his lonesome at the table before the trouble starts, or he'll get in bad himself. The Kid can pull a fake play to make up with some moll across the room. Klanner's no friend of his, he never saw the man before--you understand?--just ran into him outside the dance hall, if any questions are asked. But I don't want any questions, and there won't be any if he plays his hand right. Tell him I said his job's over once he has Klanner inside--and to stand from under. Get me?"

"Sure!" said Hoppy Meggs.

"Well, we'll beat it, then," snapped Hunchback Joe.

The room was in darkness again. Jimmie Dale crouched further back along the wall. The rear door opened, two shadows emerged, passed around the corner of the tenement--and disappeared.

The minutes passed, five of them, and then Jimmie Dale, too, was making his way softly along the areaway to the street--but in Jimmie Dale's pockets were the short leaden blackjack, ugly for the stain on its leathern covering, the packet of papers, and the roll of banknotes that had been in Klanner's trunk. He gained the street, paused under the nearest street lamp to consult his watch, and swung briskly along again. It was a matter of only two blocks to Baldy Jack's, one of the most infamous dance halls in the Bad Lands, but it was already ten minutes to ten.

And now a curious metamorphosis came to Jimmie Dale's appearance. The neat, well-fitting Fifth Avenue tweeds did not fit quite so perfectly--the coat bunched a little at the shoulders, the trousers were drawn a little higher until they lost their "set." His hat was pulled still farther over his eyes, but at a more rakish angle, and his tie, tucked into his shirt bosom just below the collar, exposed blatantly a diamond shirt stud. But on Jimmie Dale's lips there was an ominous smile not wholly in keeping with the somewhat jaunty swagger he had assumed, and the lines at the corners of his mouth were drawn down hard and sharp. It was miserable work, the work of a hound and cur! Who, better than the **janitor** of the bank, would have had the opportunity to carry on that work there! And so they had selected Klanner as their victim. But Klanner, if allowed to talk, might be able to defend himself--therefore Klanner would not be allowed to talk. There was only one way to prevent that effectively--by killing Klanner. But, again, Klanner's death must not appear in any way to be consequent to the murder at the bank--therefore it was to bear every evidence of having been purely inadvert, and, in a way, an accident. Yes, it was crafty enough, hideous enough to be fully worthy even of the fiendish brain that had planned it! Kid Greer, having probably struck up an acquaintance with Klanner during the past few days, had inveigled Klanner to-night into Baldy Jack's, ostensibly, no doubt, for an innocent and casual glass of beer, and in a general row and melee in the dance hall--not an uncommon occurrence in a place like Baldy Jack's--Klanner would be shot and killed. The rest was obvious. The man's effects would naturally be examined, and the evidence of his "guilt" found in his trunk. It was an open and shut game against a dead man! Even his previous good record would smash on the rock of a presumed double life. The fact that Klanner had voluntarily been in a place like Baldy Jack's was damning in itself!

Jimmie Dale, approaching the garishly lighted exterior of the dance hall now, lit a cigarette. The plan, if successful, placed the guilt without question or cavil upon Klanner, but that was not all--strong as that motive might be, Clarke had had still another in view, and one that perhaps took precedence over the first. Hunchback Joe had defined it clearly enough. The documents would have been valueless to Clarke, either to sell, or to put to any use himself, if the plans and arrangements they contained were subsequently altered or changed. But it was obvious that a man in Klanner's station could have no *personal* interest in them; it was obvious, as evidenced by the money, that he was working for some one else, and therefore the documents appearing in his trunk would logically appear to have been recovered *before* he had been able to hand them over to his principal, and *before* any vital harm had been done that would necessitate any change in the details they contained.

Jimmie Dale pushed the door of the dance hall open, and stepped nonchalantly inside. It was the usual scene, there was the usual hilarious uproar, the usual close, almost fetid atmosphere that mingled the odours of stale beer and tobacco. Baldy Jack's was always popular, and the place, even for that early hour, was already doing a thriving business. Jimmie Dale's eyes, from a dozen couples swirling in the throes of the bunny-hug on the polished section of the floor in the centre of the hall, strayed over the little tables that were ranged three and four deep around the walls. At the upper end of the room a man, fair-haired and neatly dressed, though his clothes were evidently not those of one in over-affluent circumstances, sat alone at one of the tables. It might, or might not, be Klanner. Jimmie Dale strolled forward up the hall, and, as though deliberating over his selection of a seat, paused by the table. The man looked up. There was a long, jagged scar on the other's right cheek bone. It was Klanner. Jimmie Dale pulled out a chair at a vacant table directly behind the other, and sat down. A waiter, in beer-spotted apron and balancing a dripping tray, came for his order.

"Suds!" said Jimmie Dale laconically.

Again Jimmie Dale's eyes made a circuit of the place, failed to identify the person of one Kid Greer, and, giving up the attempt, rested speculatively instead on Klanner's back. Yes, he could quite fully understand why the Tocsin could not have warned Klanner to beware, for instance, of Kid Greer. Such a warning, apart from keeping Hunchback Joe from planting the evidence, would even have defeated its own end--for, even to save Klanner, the game had to be played out as Hunchback Joe had planned it. They meant to "get" Klanner, and if not here at Baldy Jack's, then somewhere else. She *knew* what they meant to do here--she *might not* know when, or how, or where they would make the attempt if they had been forced to change their plans.

Jimmie Dale tossed a coin on the table, as the waiter set down a glass of beer in front of him--and then, over the top of the glass, Jimmie Dale resumed his scrutiny of the hall. Directly behind him was a back entrance that opened on a lane at the rear of the building; and between himself and the entrance was only one table, which was unoccupied. Jimmie Dale, playing with his match box, as he lighted another cigarette, dropped the box, stooped to pick it up--and drew his chair unostentatiously nearer to Klanner.

It was ten o'clock now, time that--yes, the game was on-- *now!* A man, that he recognised as one of the Mole's gunmen, had dropped into a seat a couple of tables away from Klanner, where there was a clear space between the two men. There was a sudden jostling among the dancers on the floor--then an oath, rising high above the riot of talk and laughter--a swirl of figures--a medley of shouts and women's screams, drowning out the squeak of the musicians' violins and the thump of the tinny piano.

Jimmie Dale's jaws locked hard together. There was a struggling, Furious mob at the lower end of the hall--but his eyes now never left the gunman two tables away. Klanner, in dazed amazement, had half risen from his seat, as though uncertain what to do. The screams, shouts, oaths and yells grew louder--came the roar of a revolver shot--another--pandemonium was reigning now. It seemed an hour, a great period of time since the first shout had rung through the hall--it had been but a matter of seconds. Jimmie Dale was crouched a little forward in his chair now, tense, motionless. What was holding Hoppy Meggs! This was Hoppy Meggs' cue, wasn't it?--those shots there, aimed at the floor, had only been to create the panic--there was to be *another* shot that--

The hall was in sudden darkness. With a spring, quick on the instant, Jimmie Dale was upon Klanner's back, hurling the man to the floor. The tongue-flame of a revolver split the black over his head; there was the deafening roar of a revolver shot almost in his ears that blotted out for an instant all other sounds--and then came the shouts and cries again in an access of terror and now the rush of feet--a blind stampede in the darkness for the exits. Another shot from the gunman, as though to make his work doubly sure, followed the first--but now some of the fear-stricken crowd had come between them, plunging, falling, tripping over tables and chairs, seeking the rear exit.

"Quick!" Jimmie Dale breathed in Klanner's ear. He was half lifting, half dragging the man along. "Quick--get your feet, man!"

There was a surging mob around them now, pushing, fighting madly to reach the door; and, as Klanner regained his feet, they were both swept forward, and, lunging through the door, were precipitated out into the lane. And here, wary of a riot call that had probably already been rung in by the patrolman on the beat, the crowd was taking to its heels and dispersing in both directions along the lane.

"Quick!" said Jimmie Dale again--and, with his hand on Klanner's arm, broke into a run.

Those running in the same direction turned off from the lane at the first cross street; but Jimmie Dale held to the lane, and it was three blocks away from Baldy Jack's before he stopped.

Klanner was panting from his exertions.

"My God--what's it mean!" he gasped. "I--I thought I saw a revolver in that man's hand, the fellow next to me, just as the lights went out."

"You probably did," said Jimmie Dale grimly.

"Well----what's it mean?" repeated Klanner heavily.

It was a moment before Jimmie Dale answered. For the man's own sake, the less that Klanner knew the better, probably--and yet the man must be kept out of harm's way for the rest of the night. Having failed at Baldy Jack's, it was certain, since Clarke's whole plan hinged on Klanner's death, that they would try again. After to-night--if all went well--it did not matter, for Klanner then would be no longer a factor to Clarke or Hunchback Joe!

"It means," said Jimmie Dale gravely, "that there's been some sort of a gangster's fight pulled off, and that probably there's been dirty work--murder--in there. The police will go the limit to round up everybody they can find who was in Baldy Jack's. There's only one thing to do--keep your mouth shut and lie low to-night. You can't take any chances of getting into this--you look like a man who's got a decent job he doesn't want to lose, and you don't look like a man who is entitled to be saddled with a reputation for hanging around that sort of place. Do you live near here?"

"Yes," said Klanner, a little dully.

"Well then," said Jimmie Dale quietly, "get out of this neighbourhood for the night. Don't risk recognition while the chase is hot. Go uptown somewhere to any hotel you like, and *stay* there in your room. You can go to work just as well from there in the morning. Got any money?"

"Yes," said Klanner slowly. "Yes, I got some money--and I guess you're right. Say, who are you anyway? You seem to have a line on this sort of thing, and I guess I owe you a whole skin. If you hadn't--"

"I'm a man in a hurry," said Jimmie Dale whimsically--and then the grim note crept back into his voice. "I am giving you a straight tip. Take it--and take that street car that's coming along there." He held out his hand.

"Sure!" said Klanner. "And I--"

"Good-night," said Jimmie Dale, and started abruptly across the street, entering the lane on the other side again--but here, in the shadows, he paused for a moment, watching until Klanner boarded the uptown car.

CHAPTER XXIV
AT FIVE MINUTES OF TWELVE

Twenty minutes later, well along the East River front, in an unsavoury and deserted neighbourhood, Jimmie Dale was crouched before the door of a small building that seemed built half on the shore edge, and half on an old and run-down pier that extended out into the water. The building itself was little more than a storage shed, and originally had probably laid claims to nothing more pretentious--to-day it served as warehouse and office for Hunchback Joe's "business," and, above, for Hunchback Joe's living quarters. Jimmie Dale glanced around him sharply--not for the first time. There were no other buildings in his immediate vicinity, and such as could be seen loomed up only as black, shadowy, distant shapes--warehouses and small factories, for the most part, and empty and deserted now at night. It was intensely black--only a twinkling light here and there from a passing craft on the river, and the glow from thousands of street lamps that, like some strange aerial illumination, hovered over the opposite shore. The shed itself, windowless at least in front, was as silent, as deserted, and as black as all around it.

Jimmie Dale's hand stole into his pocket, produced a black silk mask, adjusted the mask over his face--and then the deft, slim fingers were at work with a little steel instrument on the door lock. A moment more, and the door swung silently inward, slowly, inch by inch. He listened intently. There was no sound. He stepped inside, and silently closed and locked the door behind If Hunchback Joe had not returned yet, it was necessary that Hunchback Joe should find the door as he had left it--locked! Again Jimmie Dale listened--and then the ray of his flashlight circled the place. A miscellany of ship's junk was piled without any attempt at order all over the place; a board partition with two small windows, one on each side of the door, ran from side to side of the shed about a third of the way up its length; and in the sides of the shed itself were also two small, narrow windows--too small and too narrow, Jimmie Dale noted grimly, for the passage of a man's body.

He moved forward cautiously, though he was almost certain that he was ahead of Hunchback Joe. He, Jimmie Dale, had come without an instant's loss of time from Baldy Jack's, and it was more than an even chance that Hunchback Joe would have remained somewhere in the neighbourhood until the affair was over. It would take some little time--not until after the police had restored order--to discover that the attempt upon Klanner had been abortive, that Klanner's body was *not* lying there dead on the floor. But after that--Jimmie Dale opened the door of the partition stealthily, slipped through, and, as his flashlight swept around again, nodded his head sharply--yes, he had thought so!--there was a means of communication here--a telephone. Well then, after that, Hunchback Joe would set every crook and tool over whom he had any control at work to find Klanner. But that meant different men at work in many different directions, and there must therefore be some central spot where Hunchback Joe could be instantly reached and reports made to him should Klanner be found--and what better place, what more likely place than here in the security of his own lair! Yes, Hunchback Joe, since he, Jimmie Dale, was now satisfied that the other had not yet returned, would be back here, and, in all probability, long before midnight. Midnight! Why had the Tocsin set midnight, waited for midnight as the hour for the Secret Service raid? Did she have a hidden purpose in that? Was it possible she knew that some one beside Hunchback Joe would also be here at that hour--that Clarke might be here, too! Well, why not! There might well be need for a conference between Clarke and his unholy chief of staff! There might--Jimmie Dale frowned savagely. His mind was running riot! He had not come here to speculate on possibilities; for, whatever might happen, there was definite and instant work to do.

The white ray of the flashlight played steadily now around him. The place evidently served as the office; it was partitioned off again in exactly the same manner from the rear of the shed, making an oblong enclosure the width of the shed one way, and a good fifteen feet the other. It was electric-lighted, and contained a battered table in lieu of desk, upon which stood the telephone; there were several chairs, and a safe, whose scratched, marred, and apparently ramshackle exterior did not disguise from Jimmie Dale the fact that it was of the finest and most modern make.

A rough, wooden stairway led above. Jimmie Dale mounted this, found that it gave on a crudely furnished, attic-like bedroom, and then descending again, he opened the rear door of the partition, and flashed his light around the back of the shed. There were a few packing cases here--that was all. The shed was evidently built out to the extreme end of the pier, judging from its depth; and there had been side doors, but these were boarded up and bore evidence of having been long out of use--and there were no windows.

Jimmie Dale returned now to the front of the shed.

"Under the sail-cloth in left corner," she had written. Yes, here it was! He stooped down, a twisted smile on his lips, and, taking from his pocket the packet of papers and the blackjack, tucked them under several folds of the cloth. "Unto Caesar!" she had said. Well, he had rendered back to "Caesar" the things that were "Caesar's." He straightened up. The Secret Service men would know where to look--she would have seen to that! "Unto Caesar!" The smile died away, and an angry red tinged Jimmie Dale's cheeks--he was picturing again that scene in Klanner's room, the bestial deviltry of that deformed and hideous creature who, to cover up his own guilt, was railroading an innocent man to death. "Unto Caesar!"--yes, there was grim justice here--but that was not enough! Justice might and **would** have its turn, but before then there was another sort of justice, too!

He went back into the office, and sat down in a chair beside the table where he could command the door. He laid his flashlight, the ray on, upon the table, took from his pocket the metal insignia case, lifted out a seal, dropped it by means of the tweezers on his handkerchief, folded the handkerchief carefully, and replaced the insignia case and handkerchief in his pocket; then, switching off the flashlight, he restored that, too, to his pocket.

It was dark now again--and silent. There was no sound, save the gentle lap of water against the pier, and the distant, muffled murmur of traffic from one of the great bridges that spanned the river. Jimmie Dale's automatic was in his hand. There was one man who stood between the woman whom he loved and her happiness, one man, who had driven her from her home and by every foul art and craft had sought to take her life, one man, one man only--Marre, alias Clarke. And once

Clarke were run to earth, she was free forever--no one else had any incentive in hounding her to her death.

Well, there was one man who knew where Marre was--Hunchback Joe. And, come what might, Hunchback Joe would tell him, Jimmie Dale, to-night where Marre was! He was not so sure as the Tocsin that Hunchback Joe would talk to the police; he was sure that Hunchback Joe would talk-- *to the Gray Seal*. That was all. That was what he was waiting for here now in the darkness before the police came--for Hunchback Joe.

Time passed--a half hour--an hour. It was getting perilously close to the time when the Secret Service men would be pounding at the door out there, and the margin of time left for that grim interview with Hunchback Joe was narrowing rapidly; but there was a strange, calm, cold patience possessing Jimmie Dale--the man would come, and come in time--he knew that, knew it as he knew that he sat there and lived and breathed.

The silence was oppressive, heavy; it seemed to palpitate in rhythm with the lap of the water against the pier. The minutes dragged by, another five of them-- and then suddenly Jimmie Dale sat rigidly forward in his chair. The front door had not been unlocked or opened, but there was the sound of a footstep now--from the rear section of the shed, where there had appeared to be no entrance! The footstep came nearer--the door of the partition opened--there was the click of the electric-light switch--the light came on--and then a low, savage, startled oath came from the doorway.

Jimmie Dale did not move--his automatic was covering the misshapen, toad-like figure of Hunchback Joe, as the other stood just inside the room. For a moment neither spoke--then Hunchback Joe laughed suddenly in cool contempt.

"What's the game?" he demanded. "You don't need any mask on here--I deal with your kind every day. What do you want?"

Jimmie Dale rose to his feet.

"This--to begin with!" he said--and, crossing the room, felt through the other's pockets, and possessed himself of the man's revolver. "Now go over there, and sit down at that table!"

Hunchback Joe laughed contemptuously again, as he obeyed; but there was a hint of deadly menace in his voice as he spoke.

"Go to it--while you can!" he snarled. "You've got the drop on me. Well, what do you want?"

Jimmie Dale followed, and faced the other across the table. Hunchback Joe's eyes, with that curious, unpleasant trick of which the man seemed possessed, were blinking ceaselessly.

"I want to give this back to you," said Jimmie Dale quietly--and flung the roll of bills that he had taken from Klanner's trunk down upon the table.

Hunchback Joe's eyes ceased to blink.

"Why, thanks!" grinned Hunchback Joe. "You're a queer sort of a night marauder, you are! Sure this is for me, and that you aren't making a mistake?"

"Quite sure," said Jimmie Dale, still quietly. "It's yours. It's the money you planted in Klanner's trunk a couple of hours ago."

"I never heard of Klanner," said Hunchback Joe.

"It's simply the evidence that that isn't all I found in the trunk," said Jimmie Dale. "There was a packet of papers, and the blood-stained blackjack with which Jathan Lane was murdered in the bank this afternoon."

"My God, the man's mad!" muttered Hunchback Joe under his breath. "I'm up against a maniac!"

Jimmie Dale had taken his handkerchief from his pocket, and, carrying it to his mouth, had moistened the adhesive side of the little seal. His voice rasped, as his hand went down upon the table.

"You blot on God's earth!" he said hoarsely. "That's enough of that! The buttons are off the foils to-night, Hunchback Joe!"

For the second time, Hunchback Joe's eyes had ceased to blink. He was staring at the gray seal on the table top in front of him, and now in spite of his effort to maintain nonchalance, a whiteness had come into his face.

"You!" he shrank back a little in his chair. "The Gray Seal!"

Jimmie Dale's lips were thin and drawn tight together. He made no answer.

It was Hunchback Joe who broke the silence.

"What's your price?" he asked thickly. "I suppose you've got those--those other things, or at least you know where they are."

"Yes," said Jimmie Dale grimly, "I know where they are."

"Well"--Hunchback Joe hesitated, fumbling for his words--"we're both tarred with the same brush, only you're worse than I am. I've got to pay your price, of course. Make it reasonable. I haven't got all the money in the world. Tell me where those things are, and name your figures."

"My figure"--Jimmie Dale was clipping off his words--"is a little information. A trade, Hunchback Joe--mine for yours. I want to know where Peter Marre, alias Clarke, is?"

Hunchback Joe drew back from the table with a jerk. The whiteness in his face had changed to an unhealthy, leaden gray. He shook his head.

"I don't know," he said. "That's straight--I've heard of Marre, of course, everybody has, he's a lawyer; but I never heard of Clarke, and that's--"

"A lie!" Jimmie Dale cut in, an ugly calm in his voice "You--"

But Jimmie Dale, too, was interrupted. The telephone on the table was ringing. His automatic covering Hunchback Joe, he pulled the instrument toward him, and lifted the receiver from the hook.

"Hello!" he said gruffly. "What's wanted?"

A voice responded in feverish excitement:

"Say, dat youse, Joe? Dis is Hoppy Meggs. Say, de fly cops has got tipped off; dey're on de way down to yer place now. Youse want to beat it on de jump!"

"Wait a minute!" said Jimmie Dale. He passed the instrument over to Hunchback Joe. "It's for you," he said, with a queer smile.

Hunchback Joe put the receiver to his ear--and a moment later, without a word in reply, returned it to the hook. But he had risen from his seat, and, swaying on his feet, was gripping at the table edge for support.

"I could have told you that," said Jimmie Dale evenly; "but you've got it now from a source that you won't question. I told you the buttons were off the foils tonight, but you don't seem to realise it yet. Three nights ago you laid a trap for me-- ***and the Pippin died***. Do you understand what I mean now by naked foils? You've one chance for life--and that's to answer my question. But I'll play fair with you, and tell you that I'm going to see that the police get you even if you do answer. Those documents and that blackjack are here in this place, and the Secret Service men know where to find them." Jimmie Dale's watch was in his hand. "It's five minutes to twelve. They'll be here at midnight. I've got to make my getaway before they come. I need two minutes for that, including locking you in so that ***you*** can't get away. That leaves you three minutes to make up your mind. If you answer, you can have whatever chance your lawyers can get you; if you refuse, you and I settle our score before I leave. It's three minutes against a possible commutation of sentence to life imprisonment. ***Where is Marre?***"

The misshapen, shrunken thing was rocking on its feet. There was no answer.

"There are two minutes left," said Jimmie Dale in a monotone.

The man's eyes, coal black, hunted, the pupils gone, swept the room. His lips were working; his hands, clenching and unclenching, clawed at the table.

" ***One!***" said Jimmie Dale.

There was a scream of ungovernable fury, the crash of the toppling table, and, reaching out with both hands for Jimmie Dale's weapon, Hunchback Joe hurled himself forward--but quick as the other was, Jimmie Dale was quicker, and with his left hand, palm open, pushed full into the man's face, he flung the other back.

And then there came a cry--a cry in a woman's voice;

" ***Marre!***"

It was the Tocsin's voice from the rear doorway of the office. It was her voice; Jimmie Dale could never mistake it even in its startled cry--but he did not look. His eyes were on the man who was standing on the other side of the overturned table, whose beard where he, Jimmie Dale, had grasped the other's face had been wrenched away, and whose shrunken figure seemed to tower up now in height, and whose deformity was a padded coat, awry now because of the erect and upright posture in which the man stood. It was Clarke, the master of disguise, who once had impersonated Travers, the chauffeur; it was Marre--Wizard Marre.

There was a ghastly smile on the man's face.

"Marre," he said. "Yes--Marre. But you never knew it, did you, Miss LaSalle--until now! Well, now is time enough for you, and far too soon for me!" He flung out his hand in a queer, impotent gesture, as he threw back his shoulders. "But I would like to be thought a good loser. I congratulate you, Miss LaSalle!" Again his hand was raised in gesture--and with lightning swiftness, before Jimmie Dale could intervene, swept to his vest pocket and was carried to his mouth. "And so I drink to your success, and--"

A glass vial rolled away upon the floor--and Jimmie Dale, with a bound, had caught the swaying figure in his arms. There was a tremor through the man's form--

then inertness. He lowered the other to the ground. Wizard Marre was dead. It was the colourless liquid of the old Crime Club, instantaneous in its action that--

Jimmie Dale swept his hand over his masked face, and pulled the mask away, and looked up. She, the Tocsin; yes, it was the Tocsin; yes, it was Marie--only the beautiful face was deadly pale--it was the Tocsin who was standing over him, shaking him frantically by the shoulder.

"Jimmie! Quick! Quick!" she cried. "The Secret Service men! Don't you hear them? Quick! This way!"

There was a crash, a pound upon the street door. She had caught his hand, and was pulling him forward now out into the rear of the shed. There was a light from the office doorway--enough to see. One of the packing cases was tipped over, and, on hinges, made a trap door. A short ladder led downward to where, a few feet below, two boats were moored.

"I came this way. I followed him," she said. "Quick--Jimmie!"

It took an instant, no more, to swing her through the opening, but as he lowered her down and her hair brushed his cheek, there came a quick half sob to Jimmie Dale's lips.

"Mark!" he whispered. "Marie--at last!"

Came the rip and tear and rend of wood, the thud of a falling door from the front of the shed, the rush of feet--but Jimmie Dale was in the boat now, and the packing case above was swung back into place.

"Right ahead, Jimmie!" she breathed. "The planks at the end of the pier swing aside--yes, there--no, a little to the right--yes!"

The boat shot out into the river--farther out--and the pier and shed merged into the shadows of the shore line and were lost. And then Jimmie Dale let the oars swing loose. She was crouched in the bottom of the boat close beside him. He bent his head until his lips touched her hair, and lower still until his lips touched hers. And a long time passed. And the boat drifted on. And he drew her closer into his arms, and held her there. She was safe now, safe for always--and the road of fear lay behind. And into the night there seemed to come a great quiet, and a great joy, and a great thankfulness, and a wondrous peace.

And the boat drifted on.

And neither spoke--for they were going *home*.

The Codes Of Hammurabi And Moses
W. W. Davies

QTY

The discovery of the Hammurabi Code is one of the greatest achievements of archaeology, and is of paramount interest, not only to the student of the Bible, but also to all those interested in ancient history...

Religion   **ISBN:** *1-59462-338-4*   **Pages:132**
MSRP $12.95

The Theory of Moral Sentiments
Adam Smith

QTY

This work from 1749. contains original theories of conscience amd moral judgment and it is the foundation for systemof morals.

Philosophy   **ISBN:** *1-59462-777-0*   **Pages:536**
MSRP $19.95

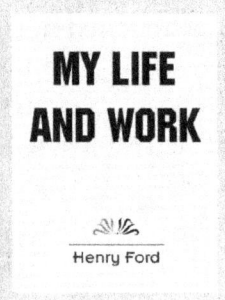

Jessica's First Prayer
Hesba Stretton

QTY

In a screened and secluded corner of one of the many railway-bridges which span the streets of London there could be seen a few years ago, from five o'clock every morning until half past eight, a tidily set-out coffee-stall, consisting of a trestle and board, upon which stood two large tin cans, with a small fire of charcoal burning under each so as to keep the coffee boiling during the early hours of the morning when the work-people were thronging into the city on their way to their daily toil...

Childrens   **ISBN:** *1-59462-373-2*   **Pages:84**
MSRP $9.95

My Life and Work
Henry Ford

QTY

Henry Ford revolutionized the world with his implementation of mass production for the Model T automobile. Gain valuable business insight into his life and work with his own auto-biography... "We have only started on our development of our country we have not as yet, with all our talk of wonderful progress, done more than scratch the surface. The progress has been wonderful enough but..."

Biographies/   **ISBN:** *1-59462-198-5*   **Pages:300**
MSRP $21.95

The Art of Cross-Examination
Francis Wellman

QTY

I presume it is the experience of every author, after his first book is published upon an important subject, to be almost overwhelmed with a wealth of ideas and illustrations which could readily have been included in his book, and which to his own mind, at least, seem to make a second edition inevitable. Such certainly was the case with me; and when the first edition had reached its sixth impression in five months, I rejoiced to learn that it seemed to my publishers that the book had met with a sufficiently favorable reception to justify a second and considerably enlarged edition. ...

Reference   **ISBN: *1-59462-647-2***

Pages:412
MSRP $19.95

On the Duty of Civil Disobedience
Henry David Thoreau

QTY

Thoreau wrote his famous essay, On the Duty of Civil Disobedience, as a protest against an unjust but popular war and the immoral but popular institution of slave-owning. He did more than write—he declined to pay his taxes, and was hauled off to gaol in consequence. Who can say how much this refusal of his hastened the end of the war and of slavery ?

Law   **ISBN: *1-59462-747-9***

Pages:48
MSRP $7.45

Dream Psychology Psychoanalysis for Beginners
Sigmund Freud

QTY

Sigmund Freud, born Sigismund Schlomo Freud (May 6, 1856 - September 23, 1939), was a Jewish-Austrian neurologist and psychiatrist who co-founded the psychoanalytic school of psychology. Freud is best known for his theories of the unconscious mind, especially involving the mechanism of repression; his redefinition of sexual desire as mobile and directed towards a wide variety of objects; and his therapeutic techniques, especially his understanding of transference in the therapeutic relationship and the presumed value of dreams as sources of insight into unconscious desires.

Psychology   **ISBN: *1-59462-905-6***

Pages:196
MSRP $15.45

The Miracle of Right Thought
Orison Swett Marden

QTY

Believe with all of your heart that you will do what you were made to do. When the mind has once formed the habit of holding cheerful, happy, prosperous pictures, it will not be easy to form the opposite habit. It does not matter how improbable or how far away this realization may see, or how dark the prospects may be, if we visualize them as best we can, as vividly as possible, hold tenaciously to them and vigorously struggle to attain them, they will gradually become actualized, realized in the life. But a desire, a longing without endeavor, a yearning abandoned or held indifferently will vanish without realization.

Pages:360

Self Help   **ISBN: *1-59462-644-8***

MSRP $25.45

QTY

The Rosicrucian Cosmo-Conception Mystic Christianity *by Max Heindel*   ISBN: *1-59462-188-8*   **$38.95**
The Rosicrucian Cosmo-conception is not dogmatic, neither does it appeal to any other authority than the reason of the student. It is: not controversial, but is: sent forth in the, hope that it may help to clear...   New Age/Religion Pages 646

Abandonment To Divine Providence *by Jean-Pierre de Caussade*   ISBN: *1-59462-228-0*   **$25.95**
"The Rev. Jean Pierre de Caussade was one of the most remarkable spiritual writers of the Society of Jesus in France in the 18th Century. His death took place at Toulouse in 1751. His works have gone through many editions and have been republished...   Inspirational/Religion Pages 400

Mental Chemistry *by Charles Haanel*   ISBN: *1-59462-192-6*   **$23.95**
Mental Chemistry allows the change of material conditions by combining and appropriately utilizing the power of the mind. Much like applied chemistry creates something new and unique out of careful combinations of chemicals the mastery of mental chemistry...   New Age Pages 354

The Letters of Robert Browning and Elizabeth Barret Barrett 1845-1846 vol II   ISBN: *1-59462-193-4*   **$35.95**
by Robert Browning and Elizabeth Barrett   Biographies Pages 596

Gleanings In Genesis (volume I) *by Arthur W. Pink*   ISBN: *1-59462-130-6*   **$27.45**
Appropriately has Genesis been termed "the seed plot of the Bible" for in it we have, in germ form, almost all of the great doctrines which are afterwards fully developed in the books of Scripture which follow...   Religion/Inspirational Pages 420

The Master Key *by L. W. de Laurence*   ISBN: *1-59462-001-6*   **$30.95**
In no branch of human knowledge has there been a more lively increase of the spirit of research during the past few years than in the study of Psychology, Concentration and Mental Discipline. The requests for authentic lessons in Thought Control, Mental Discipline and...   New Age/Business Pages 422

The Lesser Key Of Solomon Goetia *by L. W. de Laurence*   ISBN: *1-59462-092-X*   **$9.95**
This translation of the first book of the "Lerneqton" which is now for the first time made accessible to students of Talismanic Magic was done, after careful collation and edition, from numerous Ancient Manuscripts in Hebrew, Latin, and French...   New Age/Occult Pages 92

Rubaiyat Of Omar Khayyam *by Edward Fitzgerald*   ISBN:*1-59462-332-5*   **$13.95**
Edward Fitzgerald, whom the world has already learned, in spite of his own efforts to remain within the shadow of anonymity, to look upon as one of the rarest poets of the century, was born at Bredfield, in Suffolk, on the 31st of March, 1809. He was the third son of John Purcell...   Music Pages 172

Ancient Law *by Henry Maine*   ISBN: *1-59462-128-4*   **$29.95**
The chief object of the following pages is to indicate some of the earliest ideas of mankind, as they are reflected in Ancient Law, and to point out the relation of those ideas to modern thought.   Religion/History Pages 452

Far-Away Stories *by William J. Locke*   ISBN: *1-59462-129-2*   **$19.45**
"Good wine needs no bush, but a collection of mixed vintages does. And this book is just such a collection. Some of the stories I do not want to remain buried for ever in the museum files of dead magazine-numbers an author's not unpardonable vanity..."   Fiction Pages 272

Life of David Crockett *by David Crockett*   ISBN: *1-59462-250-7*   **$27.45**
"Colonel David Crockett was one of the most remarkable men of the times in which he lived. Born in humble life, but gifted with a strong will, an indomitable courage, and unremitting perseverance...   Biographies/New Age Pages 424

Lip-Reading *by Edward Nitchie*   ISBN: *1-59462-206-X*   **$25.95**
Edward B. Nitchie, founder of the New York School for the Hard of Hearing, now the Nitchie School of Lip-Reading, Inc, wrote "LIP-READING Principles and Practice". The development and perfecting of this meritorious work on lip-reading was an undertaking...   How-to Pages 400

A Handbook of Suggestive Therapeutics, Applied Hypnotism, Psychic Science   ISBN: *1-59462-214-0*   **$24.95**
by Henry Munro   Health/New Age/Health/Self-help Pages 376

A Doll's House: and Two Other Plays *by Henrik Ibsen*   ISBN: *1-59462-112-8*   **$19.95**
Henrik Ibsen created this classic when in revolutionary 1848 Rome. Introducing some striking concepts in playwriting for the realist genre, this play has been studied the world over.   Fiction/Classics/Plays 308

The Light of Asia *by sir Edwin Arnold*   ISBN: *1-59462-204-3*   **$13.95**
In this poetic masterpiece, Edwin Arnold describes the life and teachings of Buddha. The man who was to become known as Buddha to the world was born as Prince Gautama of India but he rejected the worldly riches and abandoned the reigns of power when...   Religion/History/Biographies Pages 170

The Complete Works of Guy de Maupassant *by Guy de Maupassant*   ISBN: *1-59462-157-8*   **$16.95**
"For days and days, nights and nights, I had dreamed of that first kiss which was to consecrate our engagement, and I knew not on what spot I should put my lips..."   Fiction/Classics Pages 240

The Art of Cross-Examination *by Francis L. Wellman*   ISBN: *1-59462-309-0*   **$26.95**
Written by a renowned trial lawyer, Wellman imparts his experience and uses case studies to explain how to use psychology to extract desired information through questioning.   How-to/Science/Reference Pages 408

Answered or Unanswered? *by Louisa Vaughan*   ISBN: *1-59462-248-5*   **$10.95**
Miracles of Faith in China   Religion Pages 112

The Edinburgh Lectures on Mental Science (1909) *by Thomas*   ISBN: *1-59462-008-3*   **$11.95**
This book contains the substance of a course of lectures recently given by the writer in the Queen Street Hail, Edinburgh. Its purpose is to indicate the Natural Principles governing the relation between Mental Action and Material Conditions...   New Age/Psychology Pages 148

Ayesha *by H. Rider Haggard*   ISBN: *1-59462-301-5*   **$24.95**
Verily and indeed it is the unexpected that happens! Probably if there was one person upon the earth from whom the Editor of this, and of a certain previous history, did not expect to hear again...   Classics Pages 380

Ayala's Angel *by Anthony Trollope*   ISBN: *1-59462-352-X*   **$29.95**
The two girls were both pretty, but Lucy who was twenty-one who supposed to be simple and comparatively unattractive, whereas Ayala was credited, as her Bombwhat romantic name might show, with poetic charm and a taste for romance. Ayala when her father died was nineteen...   Fiction Pages 484

The American Commonwealth *by James Bryce*   ISBN: *1-59462-286-8*   **$34.45**
An interpretation of American democratic political theory. It examines political mechanics and society from the perspective of Scotsman James Bryce   Politics Pages 572

Stories of the Pilgrims *by Margaret P. Pumphrey*   ISBN: *1-59462-116-0*   **$17.95**
This book explores pilgrims religious oppression in England as well as their escape to Holland and eventual crossing to America on the Mayflower, and their early days in New England...   History Pages 268

QTY

The Fasting Cure *by Sinclair Upton*   ISBN: *1-59462-222-1*   **$13.95**
*In the Cosmopolitan Magazine for May, 1910, and in the Contemporary Review (London) for April, 1910, I published an article dealing with my experi-
ences in fasting. I have written a great many magazine articles, but never one which attracted so much attention... New Age/Self Help/Health Pages 164*

Hebrew Astrology *by Sepharial*   ISBN: *1-59462-308-2*   **$13.45**
*In these days of advanced thinking it is a matter of common observation that we have left many of the old landmarks behind and that we are now pressing
forward to greater heights and to a wider horizon than that which represented the mind-content of our progenitors...   Astrology Pages 144*

Thought Vibration or The Law of Attraction in the Thought World   ISBN: *1-59462-127-6*   **$12.95**

by William Walker Atkinson   *Psychology/Religion Pages 144*

Optimism *by Helen Keller*   ISBN: *1-59462-108-X*   **$15.95**
*Helen Keller was blind, deaf, and mute since 19 months old, yet famously learned how to overcome these handicaps, communicate with the world, and
spread her lectures promoting optimism. An inspiring read for everyone...   Biographies/Inspirational Pages 84*

Sara Crewe *by Frances Burnett*   ISBN: *1-59462-360-0*   **$9.45**
*In the first place, Miss Minchin lived in London. Her home was a large, dull, tall one, in a large, dull square, where all the houses were alike, and all the
sparrows were alike, and where all the door-knockers made the same heavy sound...   Childrens/Classic Pages 88*

The Autobiography of Benjamin Franklin *by Benjamin Franklin*   ISBN: *1-59462-135-7*   **$24.95**
*The Autobiography of Benjamin Franklin has probably been more extensively read than any other American historical work, and no other book of its kind
has had such ups and downs of fortune. Franklin lived for many years in England, where he was agent...   Biographies/History Pages 332*

Name	
Email	
Telephone	
Address	
City, State ZIP	

☐ **Credit Card**   ☐ **Check / Money Order**

Credit Card Number	
Expiration Date	
Signature	

*Please Mail to: Book Jungle
                        PO Box 2226
                        Champaign, IL 61825*
or Fax to: 630-214-0564

ORDERING INFORMATION

web: *www.bookjungle.com*
email: *sales@bookjungle.com*
fax: *630-214-0564*
mail: *Book Jungle PO Box 2226 Champaign, IL 61825*
or PayPal *to sales@bookjungle.com*

Please contact us for bulk discounts

DIRECT-ORDER TERMS

**20% Discount if You Order
Two or More Books**
Free Domestic Shipping!
Accepted: Master Card, Visa,
Discover, American Express

www.ingramcontent.com/pod-product-compliance
Lightning Source LLC
Chambersburg PA
CBHW080726020726

47503CB00010B/2806